THE RACE
TALES IN FLIGHT

Patrick Ryoichi Nagatani

IN COLLABORATION WITH MARIE ACOSTA, KRISTIN BARENDSEN,
FELISSIA CAPPELLETI, CHRISTINE CHIN, RANDI GANULIN, FEROZA JUSSAWALLA,
NANCY MATSUMOTO, DOLORES RICHARDONE, ANDRE RUESCH,
ULRIKE RYLANCE, JULIE SHIGEKUNI

Published by Albuquerque Museum and SF Design, llc / Fresco Books

Albuquerque Museum
Albuquerque, NM
www.albuquerquemuseum.org

SF Design, llc / Fresco Books
Albuquerque, NM
www.frescobooks.com

All photographs ©2017 Patrick Nagatani
Cover illustration: Patrick Nagatani
Front and back cover cloud images: Scott Rankin
Editor: Michele M. Penhall
Book design: Nancy Stem, Fresco Books
Map design and production: Randi Ganulin
Composed in Adobe Garamond Pro

Partial funding for this publication has been generously provided
by The FUNd at the Albuquerque Museum Foundation and by
Dr. Kenneth Nakamura.

Library of Congress Control Number: 2017945954
ISBN 978-1-934491-60-7

This is a work of fiction and combines aspects of research, history,
and imagination. The names, characters, locations, and events are
used fictitiously. Any resemblance to actual events or persons, either
living or dead, is entirely coincidental.

All efforts have been made to trace copyright owners whose works are
quoted herein. Although many individuals have contributed to this
volume, any and all errors and omissions are unintentional.

To my four pilot friends whom I
have been honored to know:

Robert Heinecken (1931–2006)
Navy fighter pilot and Marine Corp officer 1954–1957

Colonel Donald Langwell (1935–2010)
U.S. Air Force pilot in Vietnam

Anne Noggle (1922–2005)
American aviator who flew in World War II with the
Women Airforce Service Pilots (WASP) 1943–1944,
and in the Korean War in 1953

Scott Rankin
My great friend from graduate school, professor of video
at Illinois State University and a serious private pilot

CONTENTS

6   ACKNOWLEDGMENTS

9   PROLOGUE

37   TRAINING

40   CHRISTINE BANFIELD—Silver 1

54   AYAME KOBAHASHI—Champagne 2

66   HAMIDAH GYAMTSO—Orange 3

80   RAYA SOL DEL MUNDO—Copper 4

94   JANET TOMIKO MOCHIZUKI—Peach 5

112   LEAH KATZENBERG—White 6

132   RADKA ZELENKOVA—Burgundy 7

154   RUTH COLEMAN—Black 8

166   TING XU CHAN—Blue 9

188   FIROOZEH IRANI—Turquoise 10

200   LUDMILLA LITVYCK—Red 11

214   CLAUDIA SCHUMANN—Green 12

230   NANIBAH JACKSON—Yellow 13

242   PICCOLA UCCELLO—Chartreuse 14

262   ARIANNE MAYA PARKER—Ochre 15

280   EPILOGUE

290   CODA

291   CONTRIBUTORS

ACKNOWLEDGMENTS

There are many individuals to acknowledge for helping me with *The Race: Tales in Flight*. I thank the nine primary writers with whom I collaborated to develop the personas and write each story in a unique voice: Marie Acosta, Kristin Barendsen, Felissia Cappelletti, Christine Chin, Randi Ganulin, Feroza Jussawalla, Nancy Matsumoto, Andre Ruesch, and Ulrike Rylance. They were all wonderful to work with. Other writers who contributed important sections include Laurie Liss, Dolores Richardone, Julie Shigekuni, and Joseph Traugott. In addition, Felissia, Nancy, and Dolores advised on the project from the very beginning. I also thank Barbara Grothus who shared with me her insight and investigations on the 33rd Parallel phenomena. Early support and information came from Jasmine Alinder, Kirsten Buick, Ruthie Macha Petty, David Wilde, and Carla Williams.

Special thanks to Randi Ganulin for her design and production of *The Race* map. Randi also collaborated with me to make the Spitfire floatplane images. The cloud images were selected from hundreds of photographs made by my friend and pilot, Scott Rankin. Scott also provided the Spitfire data that helped determine petrol capability, current instrumentation, and pilot environmental needs. Christopher Kaltenbach made the Tokyo Bay image for me.

Being primarily a visual storyteller, I conceived of this novel over eight years ago and consulted many books to help focus my writing. The most important of these works includes Annie Dillard's *The Writing Life,* Anne Lamott's *Bird by Bird—Some Instructions on Writing and Life*, Terry Tempest Williams's *When Women Were Birds—Fifty-Four Variations on Voice*, Natalie Goldberg's *Writing Down the Bones—Freeing the Writer Within,* and *The True Secret of Writing—Connecting Life with Language*, and more recently, Alice Mattison's *The Kite and the String—How to Write With Spontaneity and Control—and Live to Tell the Tale.*

Leslie Marmon Silko's magical prose in *Storyteller* became the inspiration for the witch's story in the prologue.

Other individuals who have offered generous support include Julie Shigekuni who helped to organize the final manuscript, and my acupuncturist, Kazuhiko Watase D.O.M., who allowed me to use him as a character throughout the book. I thank him for his compassion and expertise both in real life and in the stories.

I also wish to thank Ray Graham for his continued support, his generosity, and friendship during the many years that I have lived in Albuquerque.

After three years of receiving chemotherapy for my Stage 4 metastatic colorectal cancer, I have to thank my oncology group for their support and for keeping me alive: Dr. Malcolm Purdy, oncology nurse Debbie Winklejohn, and registered nurses Jessica, Deanna, Regina, and Susan. Thank you to the rest of the staff, Charity, Jan, Janie, Martin, Diedra, and Roxanne. From my extended chemotherapy treatments I developed "chemo brain" and that has encouraged dreams and deep connections with my right brain. My emotions became heightened, which enhanced my capacity for compassion and for writing. And at the Mayo Clinic, I want to thank Dr. Grace Knuttinen, interventional radiologist, for her professional skills and her compassion.

I thank Cathy Wright, Director, Albuquerque Museum, and I am eternally grateful to Andrew Connors and the staff at the Albuquerque Museum for their steadfast support. Also, Debra Romero, former Executive Director, Emily Blaugrund Fox, Executive Director of the Albuquerque Museum Foundation, and to The FUNd at the Albuquerque Museum Foundation for financial assistance for this project.

Many thanks also to Kay Fowler and Nancy Stem of Fresco Books, publishers, designers and consummate collaborators, who helped make this book possible, and my great friend and supporter Michele Penhall, editor of the final manuscript.

I sincerely thank my long time friend, Dr. Kenneth Nakamura, for his belief in this project and his financial support to realize this book.

I thank my family for their continued support and love: my son Methuen and his wife Hannah, my brothers Nick and Scott, and the rest of the Nagatani clan. I thank the Bodwell clan, especially Grandma Bodwell, Jeanean, and her partner John. In addition I thank the Langwell women, Sharon, and wonderful sister in law Sarah, for their support. Most importantly, I thank my wife and best friend Leigh Anne Langwell and my old doggie Annie, who sat patiently next to me as I wrote *The Race: Tales in Flight* for five years and who is now a loving memory.

Finally, this book is most likely my last creative endeavor, as my cancer will eventually take me to be with my mom and dad and Annie. While I am still alive, I want to thank all my supportive friends, former students, and colleagues for their heartfelt calls and messages during these past four years. Thank you for being in my life.

PROLOGUE

The eternal feminine draws us on.
Johann Wolfgang von Goethe, *Faust*

The Laguna people of New Mexico always begin
 their stories with "humma-hah"which means "long ago."
Leslie Marmon Silko, *Storyteller*

We are gathered to celebrate finishing The Race. Keiko Kobahashi sits elegantly at the head of the table with the fourteen female pilots who have just completed the journey. She is dressed in a smart Issey Miyake black suit. The rest of us are dressed in our national outfits, and we are surrounded by floor-to-ceiling views of the Golden Gate Bridge. The lobster and crab dishes are superb. It is overcast outside and raining lightly, typical of San Francisco Bay at this time of year. We have become an international sisterhood and the joyful mood that permeates the room is tempered only by compassion and sadness for the lone pilot, Arianne Parker, flying *Ochre 15,* who did not make it through to the end of the race.

Ruth Coleman, pilot of Spitfire floatplane *Black 8*, winner with the best time, rises from her chair and politely calls our attention by clinking her water glass with a spoon. As we bring our focus to her, she begins in a quiet, resolute voice to recite a poem by John Magee:

> *Oh! I have slipped the surly bonds of Earth*
> *And danced the skies on laughter-silvered wings;*
> *Sunward I've climbed, and joined the tumbling mirth*
> *Of sun-split clouds, and done a hundred things*
> *You have not dreamed of, wheeled and soared and swung*
> *High in the sunlit silence. Hov'ring there,*
> *I've chased the shouting wind along, and flung*

My eager craft through footless halls of air....
Up, up the long, delirious, burning blue
I've topped the wind-swept heights with easy grace.
Where never lark, or even eagle flew—
And, while with silent, lifting mind I've trod
The high untrespassed sanctity of space,
Put out my hand, and touched the face of God.

This poem has become a mantra for pilots. It is often repeated at memorials as a tribute to pilots of all generations. Hearing it, we recall the sky as only pilots can, as we relive our recently completed trans-Pacific journeys. For us, the sky is the source of light, moisture, and energy. It illuminates and reflects the sea. Both three-dimensional and two-dimensional, it is a place with many places in it. Thin yet deep, near yet far—always the same, yet always new. One can lose one's self in it, and it penetrates our very beings. As fellow pilots, we sit here aware that we are privileged to have lived momentarily among the clouds and now we savor our newly acquired understanding of each other's unique concerns and histories.

In early August 1945, in one of the last top-secret Allied operations of World War II, thirty-six aircraft were shipped from England to the British Royal Air Force headquarters in Burma. The carefully crated aircraft were Supermarine Spitfires. Adapted from the famous Schneider racing seaplanes, they were single-seated low-wing monoplanes with simple yet sturdy tail units. The Spitfires had elliptical petal-shaped wings with graceful and well-curved bottoms. Some 20,000 of them were built during the war years, and this faithful warplane and its brave pilots were credited with saving Britain from German invasion in the prolonged Battle of Britain.

Also in August 1945, two atomic bombs nicknamed *Fat Man* and *Little Boy* were dropped on civilian populations in Hiroshima and Nagasaki by the United States. More than 180,000 people were killed, creating a legacy of nuclear radiation and health issues that continued for many decades. World War II had ended, but the age of nuclear weapons had begun.

That same month and year, Keiko Kobahashi, mother of Ayame Kobahashi, was born in Kyoto, Japan.

By December 1945, World War II was over. The Japanese were no longer a threat, and the British influence in Burma was waning. Royal Air Force Colonel Gertrude Humphreys received orders from Lord Louis Mountbatten, 1st Earl Mountbatten of Burma, to dispense with the thirty-six Spitfire aircraft sitting unused in their crates, as it was too expensive to ship them back to England. Colonel Humphrey's father, Christmas "Toby" Humphreys, was the founder of the well-known Buddhist Society of London, the largest Buddhist organization outside of Asia. A devout Buddhist herself, she ordered the crates to be buried rather than destroyed in an area of Burma rich with ancient Buddhist stupas from the era of the Pagan Kingdom. The Spitfires were ceremoniously buried next to one of the largest stupas, known as the Temple of the Clouds. This temple, built in 1064 by King Anawratha to honor Buddha and the Celestial Bodhisattva, is still a meaningful pilgrimage site for Buddhists today.

Many years later and 5,478 miles away in a lively, smoke-filled neighborhood pub in England, a remark from a group of weathered war veterans sparks the interest of an elderly British woman, who frequents the pub for what is often one too many pints. On this night, her still sharp ears overhear the men recalling the burial of scores of newly minted Mark XIV Spitfires in Burma. "Perfectly good planes they were, too," remarks the drunkest of the three. The woman is Mary Cundall. A young widow and farmer from Lincolnshire, England, Cundall lost her husband, a Spitfire pilot, in World War II. She followed his unit's heart-stopping experiences through the devoted letters she and her husband exchanged. She listened intently to the constant news of their beloved England and of the war pouring out from the BBC on the wireless. The warm, polished wooden box and glowing dial was somehow comforting. Without realizing it, she had become an aviation enthusiast. In the years following her husband's death, her dream had been to restore the Spitfires, in his memory, and to see them fly once more.

That one chance remark was all it took for Mary Cundall, who believed she was due for some good luck, to board a plane to Myanmar (formally known as Burma) with a large portion of her life's savings. She had done research on RAF Colonel Gertrude Humphrey, the officer in charge of the Spitfire burial. So upon landing in Mandalay, she knew that the Pagan region was the best place to start her search, given its proximity to the old British headquarters. Still, it was an arduous task in scorching temperatures, drenching humidity, and uncertainty about the exact location.

Wilted and fatigued, she stopped at a local tavern for her customary pint. Mopping her forehead with a handkerchief, she looked around. The walls of the interior were mostly bare, save for a couple of family photographs haphazardly tacked up behind the bar. Suddenly, in spite of the heat, she froze in place, struck as if by the force of an invisible head slap. There, behind the bar, was a yellowed photograph of men dragging timber through a barely-scraped-out jungle road. But the broad logs tethered to elephants weren't what caught her eye. There, behind the elephants, behind the piles of logs, she could see two aircraft. She wiped her eyes and looked again. There was her dream, her obsession, a shining pair of World War II Supermarine Spitfires.

In her excitement, she addressed the bartender, a young man who spoke nearly perfect English. He called out in Burmese, and from the back room came a bent, elderly man. "This is my grandfather," the young man explained. The elderly man spoke, and to Mary's continued astonishment, the translation was exactly what she wanted to hear. "I believe you may be searching for something." said the old man. "Something I once saw as a boy, and thought was unusual even then."

The two men led her to a tree-ringed spot among the stupa sites barely two miles away. En route, the grandfather told her the story from his boyhood of hauling timber through the jungle with his father. The crates they built for the aircraft were unlike anything he had ever built, either before or since. It was near the biggest of the stupas that the old man thought the planes had been buried. Barely able to contain herself, Cundall's treasure hunt was underway.

After several subsequent trips to Myanmar over the next few years, Cundall gained the trust of government officials and signed a contract with the authorities to find and excavate the site. Her project reached a significant turning point when sanctions blocking the movement of military materials in and out of Myanmar were lifted.

In January 2013, work by scientists and archaeologists to find the thirty-six Spitfires had begun. Funding for the search was entirely on Cundall's shoulders. She selected the team that went to Myanmar led by British archeologist, Ruta Brickman. On advice from her closest friends, Cundall seriously contemplated finding a funding partner, as the search costs proved to be personally unsustainable.

Keiko Kobahashi, President and CEO of the Mitsubishi Corporation, herself an aviation enthusiast, heard from her longtime friend and well-known Japanese archae-ologist, Ryoichi, about Cundall's attempts to find the buried Spitfires. Kobahashi sent Ryoichi to Myanmar with hopes of evaluating the situation. Ryoichi had garnered some celebrity status years before by discovering luxury cars buried at sacred sites on every continent around the globe. Reportedly, he used maps that did not originate from our planet that were given to him by American Indian shamans. As a result of his group's thirty archaeological finds, Ryoichi rewrote the paradigms of archaeology and changed the way we look at geological, spiritual, and recognized time. Several of Kobahashi's colleagues suspected that Keiko and Ryoichi were more than friends, but that is a story for another time.

The Japanese group had very little chance of gaining on Cundall and Brickman's already established exploratory lead, and Keiko's innate moral stance also told her that the Spitfires, being of British origin, rightfully belonged to them. With Ryoichi's help and cell phone, Kobahashi contacted Cundall and offered to help fund the project with her own money, not corporate money. Mary Cundall now had financial backing and could fully realize her dream. Kobahashi saw the irony of the fact that a mere sixty-five years earlier the Japanese and the British had been at war in Burma and now these two former adversaries were working there together.

Ryoichi traveled around Myanmar, finally locating Ruta Brickman. This was a match made in hell. Brickman felt fundamentally threatened by Ryoichi's presence. Being something of a control freak, she resented the feeling of not being totally in charge. Her background as a scientist demanded that she follow everything by the book, while Ryoichi, along with his proclaimed otherworldly guidance, was more a by-the-seat-of-his-pants kind of archaeologist. But he did have good enough sense to back off of any aspect of leadership and let Brickman make the decisions. And Brickman couldn't help but be enthralled with the high tech equipment that Ryoichi had brought. Despite this uneasy relationship, the search continued.

In order to locate the specific Spitfire burial site, Ryoichi and Brickman had several tools on hand. First, they had eyewitness reports painstakingly gathered over fifteen years by Cundall, the most important information coming from the serendipitous meeting with the old Burmese man in the bar on Cundall's first trip to Burma. For equipment, they could use either ground penetrating radar equipment or electromagnetic detection devices, all provided courtesy of Kobahashi and her Mitsubishi connections. Near the beautiful stupa known as the Temple of the Clouds, the archaeology team carefully removed and examined one layer of soil at a time. Special Nikon camera equipment was inserted through a carefully drilled borehole to capture footage of the crates. What turned up in that footage was incredible. All thirty-six of the Spitfires were found in nearly pristine condition, their packaging intact. A secret deal with the Myanmar president to take sixty percent of the profits was negotiated. That pact, along with certain democratic reforms taken by the formerly repressive military regime, set the crated Spitfires free, and twenty-one of them were shipped back to England. With Ryoichi's help and Mary Cundall's funds, Kobahashi was able to privately purchase fifteen of the small planes and have them shipped to Japan. At great personal expense for Kobahashi, the vintage Spitfires were taken to Mitsubishi Aircraft Corporation headquarters for their transformation from dated warplanes to state-of-the-art floatplanes, capable of taking off and landing on water.

The history of Mitsubishi parallels the story of modern Japan. During World War II, Mitsubishi manufactured the A6M "Zero" aircraft. It was the primary Japanese naval fighter and was used by Imperial Japanese navy pilots throughout the war. Scores of Zero aircraft attacked Pearl Harbor in December of 1940, and they flew against British Spitfires in Burma. In the waning days of the war, the Zeros were used in Kamikaze attacks.

Today, Mitsubishi controls one of Japan's largest banks. The Mitsubishi heavy industries division includes Mitsubishi Motors, the Nikon Corporation (specializing in optics and imaging), Mitsubishi Chemical (the largest Japan-based chemical company), and Mitsubishi Atomic Industry (one of the nuclear power companies involved in the Fukushima nuclear catastrophe).

Christine Banfield, from Folland Aircraft in Great Britain, provided much of the expertise for the conversion of the vintage Spitfires. Keiko and Christine had first encountered one another as teenagers searching for pen pals in *Teen Magazine*. They had both been devoted fans of the young British actress, Hayley Mills, and adored her film, *The Parent Trap*. Once Keiko found Christine in the town of Croydon, England, they remained pen pals for many years before eventually losing track of one another. Interestingly, in another synchronistic moment in this story, Kobahashi reconnected with Banfield on Facebook. To this day, Keiko still sings "Let's Get Together" from the movie, often in her private moments, mostly in the shower. Later, Christine became godmother to Ayame, Keiko's daughter.

Christine Banfield's father was an aerospace engineer for the Folland Aircraft Company. Renamed British Aerospace, the company designed floatplanes from 1937 to 1963. Following in her father's footsteps, Christine studied aeronautical engineering, concentrating on floatplane design from a contemporary perspective. As an accomplished pilot of floatplanes and Spitfire aircraft, it gave her a satisfying sense of having come full circle by reconnecting with Keiko and traveling to Tokyo to work on the Spitfire conversions with Mitsubishi backing.

The floatplane designer had two fundamental problems not facing her land-based aircraft. First, Banfield must provide for buoyancy on the water by supporting an otherwise conventional structure on floats. The floats must be watertight and have a center of buoyancy related directly to their center of gravity, so that the aircraft "sits" in the correct attitude, and is at equilibrium when at rest. Second, floats that are ideal aerodynamically are not necessarily ideal hydrodynamically. This can be illustrated by drawing a comparison with the performance of a wing shape when traveling through the air. When air flows over the convex upper surface of a wing, suction is created which helps to lift the wing upwards. Conversely, if the floats were given a perfectly streamlined curve on its undersurface, the same principle would create a downward suction that would hold it down on the water. This is fine for a boat, but because the suction's power increases with forward speed, a floatplane so designed would be unable to take off. To overcome this, the undersurface must have a "step," behind which air can penetrate to interrupt the water flow. As speed increases, a cushion of air forms between the step and the stern, helping to separate the floats from the water until the wings have generated enough lift for the aircraft to take off.

Ms. Banfield also informed the Mitsubishi conversion crew that this was not the only hurdle to overcome. The propeller must be kept clear of interference from spray or rough water, and center of gravity calculations were complicated by the additional factors of lateral and longitudinal stability and displacement. The Spitfire floatplanes

underwent a complete marine-undercarriage conversion of the existing aircraft landing gear.

No longer needed, the newly transformed planes were fortunately relieved of the weight of heavy armaments. The floatplanes were all factory-issued silver in color and tested in and around Tokyo Harbor before being painted different colors and given identification numbers for the pilots during the long flight across the Pacific Ocean.

Through intensive applications and interviews, Keiko Kobahashi chose fifteen international women pilots from across the globe for The Race. Her corporate and organizational abilities along with her strong emotional intelligence enabled her to instinctively read people well. Keiko became the poster woman for the publication titled *The Athena Doctrine: How Women Will Rule the Future*. The four attributes contributing to her rise as CEO of Mitsubishi were candor, vulnerability, empathy, and connectedness. Her job as a leader was not to be a dictator but a facilitator. In that role, she listened to many voices. With her openness and candor she had the ability to lift people up so that everyone's voice could be heard. Ultimately the decision-making process at the giant corporation was improved so that the best ideas were brought to bear. Keiko learned from failure. Vulnerability became an effective leadership trait rooted in pragmatism. She devoted herself to studying the human condition. Her empathy signified innovation and sensitivity to others, which was a huge catalyst for creativity. She believed in collaboration and consensus building, both so valuable in a social economy and structure. With her flexibility and collaborative ideas she fostered connectedness in working together throughout all aspects of one's life.

Much of the initial idea for the race and the pilot training came from these philosophical traits. These skills allowed Keiko to slowly climb the corporate ladder to the top, and helped her to professionally and compassionately select the women pilots for the race who ranged in diversity and beliefs. Keiko clearly chose the pilots to represent international injustices and personal conflicts, particularly those involving women. The choice of using women pilots exclusively most likely came from the legacy of Amelia Earhart, whose career Kobahashi had meticulously studied throughout her life.

In June, after being chosen from the hundreds of applicants, we received a congratulatory letter personally signed by Keiko, which also informed us of the training requirements in Japan.

Some of us were reluctant to enter this race because of the lurid past and questionable assets of Mitsubishi today. During World War II, Mitsubishi used forced labor, which included Allied Prisoners of War, as well as Chinese and Korean citizens. One of us had a grandmother who suffered a cruel death in a Japanese labor camp. In the post-war period, lawsuits and demands for compensation were presented against the Mitsubishi Corporation, in particular by Chinese slave laborers. Adding to its questionable past reputation, Mitsubishi was also involved in the Opium trade in China in the late 1800s, before the Boxer Rebellion.

We all felt more comfortable with the fact that it was Keiko's personal money that was financing the race and our preparations. Even though most of us knew that her personal wealth came from the corporate monolith known as Mitsubishi, it was evident to all of us that she wanted to do this for more personal reasons. Nevertheless, some of us were cautious about being around wealth and power and we hoped that we would learn a lot more about Keiko through this forthcoming adventure.

Over a sumptuous dinner hosted by Keiko, we were all finally gathered together and had a chance to introduce ourselves. The evening actually began in a clumsy manner when we were met by a slew of social media reporters. We escaped their calls for comments by quickly entering the bamboo garden that served as a tall impenetrable wall around the restaurant that Keiko had reserved for our exclusive use. Anyone on the web who had the slightest interest in history, women, aeronautics and an international air race was abuzz about The Race. But how did they find out about our first gathering? Keiko had sworn us to secrecy about the specifics of time and place. She was the only other one who knew.

Keiko was raised with a strong Buddhist and Shinto religious background. The fact that the buried Spitfires were next to the Buddhist Temple of the Clouds in Pagan was in no small way the determining factor for her in purchasing the aircraft for this race. Shinto, the religious basis of Japan's imperial tradition, still adopts the shaman's world perspective and interacts with the spirit realm according to shamanic procedures. Most importantly, it connects its belief system to the sky and to the Sun Goddess, Amaterasu-omikami. In the eighth century A.D., the *Kojiki*, (Records of Ancient Matters) was written. According to the *Kojiki*, the sky is the primary stage of Creation. Everything begins in heaven, and the *Kojiki's* recitation begins by naming the first gods spontaneously born "in the Plain of High Heaven."

Finally, Keiko designed this race for her daughter, Ayame, from whom she had been physically and emotionally distant for years, but now hoped to form a closer relationship. Born to single mother Keiko at age seventeen, Ayame views her mother as a complicated woman, someone she wants to love but doesn't trust. In part, because she spent her childhood with her maternal grandparent, Ayame didn't have daily contact with her mother, whom she heard of mostly through stories of Keiko becoming increasingly successful and worldly. Ayame spent her high school years on an isolated farm and then lived with Keiko's friend, Christine Banfield, in England while attending college there. Ayame was surprised to learn of The Race. It is the first real contact she has had with her mother. As Keiko describes the plans to her, Ayame becomes interested. She cannot resist her mother's persuasive pull, and she believes that she can win The Race, and also wonders if perhaps her mother has staged the event for her. Ayame believes Keiko has re-established contact with her in the hope that Ayame can be an asset to Mitsubishi and eventually succeed as her heir.

Keiko made a few welcoming remarks, then each of us told a brief story about our lives and our love of flying. We started our required introductions. The order was by the color and number of our aircraft, which determined our ultimate position in the staggered start of the race. Christine Banfield started the introductions. "Hello, I am Christine Banfield. I am the same age as Keiko and certainly not the oldest pilot here." After having designed the newly built Spitfire floatplanes, Banfield petitioned to fly in the race. We were all pleased that she volunteered to be ineligible to win the two million dollar prize money, but could earn the $250,000 promised for finishing the race. Banfield was one of the more accomplished pilots and after all, it was "her" aircraft so she would have an unfair advantage. "I will be flying the *Silver 1* floatplane and in essence I will do the final testing of my design and cockpit construction. Of course, you will all have had experience in the aircraft during training and know how wonderfully it performs."

We all got along well with Christine. Her quiet but knowledgeable demeanor was good for the international group. Medium in height, about 5'7" and a bit plump, with short dirty blond hair, her looks were by no means as striking as pilots Zelenkova and Katzenberg. But as an aircraft designer, engineer and flyer, she was one of the best. We had begun to trust her and the aircraft we would be training in.

Ayame Kobahashi, the second speaker, stands in the wings alone, calmly reflecting on the circumstances that brought her to this moment in her life. After most of their lifetimes spent apart, she and her mother have reunited, a miracle in itself brought about by their monumental efforts to mend decades of separation and complicated feelings. As she stands quietly, a warm wave of relief and pride reassures her. She and her mother are embarking on a new phase of their lives and together they will make a positive move forward for the women of the world and Mother Earth. She hears her name announced and she steps out into the bright lights, smiles and in an authoritative but lively tone, begins.

"Most of you already know that I am Keiko's daughter and I that will be flying *Champagne 2*. It is important that you know that I will have no unfair advantage in this competition. I am a competing pilot in this race the same as all of you.

"I was educated to believe that the essence of a person is carried in her genes. Why else would I develop a passion for aviation, only to find a complementary interest in my mother after so many decades? But there is something more in each person than the genetic materials passed into life from birth. In pursuing my desire to fly, what I really longed for was the ability to contemplate my life unfettered by the concerns that bind me to the earth and its circumstances, to feel unhinged from time. And indeed, I felt free of both in the air, along with something more difficult to describe. I wished to have an analytic distance in order to penetrate the subject matter I sought to understand. Flight proved the perfect venue for this self-examination.

"In this race, my strongest competitors are the ones who will bank their wings on the sky as a natural extension of their bodies. These women will ride wind chambers like gamblers on a lucky streak, pacing their way intuitively through the plane's hesitations. These are the women who challenge me and are most likely to prevail.

"Until recently, I believed that my mother had her hopes pinned on me to win her race as a victory for her and Mitsubishi. But I know better now. Good luck to you all and may the wind be at your backs!"

We were sure that there never had been a Tibetan woman pilot before. How Hamidah Gyamtso became a pilot and will fly *Orange 3* floatplane aroused our curiosity. Hamidah is very short and dark skinned. Typical short hair tied in a bun and she spoke to us in remarkably perfect English. "I was born an orphan. I don't know who my parents were, but I was born in Tibet and raised by local Tibetan Buddhist nuns. In 1959, we asked the Tibetan monk, Khenpo Tsultrim Gyamtso, for protection from the invading communists. He led us to safety in neighboring Bhutan. I took his last name at that time. In 1977, he brought us to America, where he began teaching about the path of wisdom and compassion. I was ordained a Buddhist nun a few years later and I learned to speak English as well."

We were still puzzled over how this Tibetan nun became a pilot. The outspoken Firoozeh, obviously interested in the name Hamidah, spoke for us. "Yours seems like a long and complex story that we will ultimately learn more about, but for now, how did you become a pilot?"

Hamidah smiled and continued, "I fell in love." Most of us smiled with her. "My husband was a novice monk from Normal, Illinois, in the United States. His family's cultural background is Middle Eastern. We 'disrobed' and left the Buddhist monastic life and moved to the south of France. He made a better pilot than he would have a Buddhist monk. However, I continued to teach him Buddhist philosophy and he brought me to the clouds. I have been a licensed pilot for twenty years now. Our enlightenment takes place in the sky." With this remark hanging in the air, Hamidah sat, smiling stoically. After a pause, an obviously very nervous Raya Sol del Mundo started her story.

Raya claims to be born somewhere in the Southwest, USA. She is tall in stature and very lanky. "My parents are Mexican and Native American. There is a rumor in my town that I'm the product of a love affair that broke my mother's heart, but resulted in me! I don't believe any of those *chismes*. My mother is so traditional. She would never have had a wild fling like they say. Not in a million years! Still my sisters and brothers are all shorter than I, have curly hair and stubby fingers. I, on the other hand, have long straight blue-black hair, long fingers and blue eyes. I'm a genetic freak maybe, but I'm not another father's daughter.

"My arms are always too long for the sleeves on my coats and blouses, so my flight jacket was custom made to avoid that out-of-place look, especially since I'm very fashion conscious, a mindset that none of my family appreciates. They think I've been influenced by the movies and my favorite actress, Dolores del Rio.

"I use dark red lipstick to highlight my features and add dramatic flair. I'm actually very shy in spite of the drama and emotion of my inner life. I always feel physically awkward and I can't seem to walk with any grace. My gait is hurried and my long fingers often wave in front of me when I talk. I'm less self-critical of my voice—while it's deep, it's not harsh to the ear."

Talkative and transparently introspective Raya continued, "My first plane ride, a short trip from Albuquerque to Los Angeles, was heaven. I received a scholarship from UCLA and my parents went with me to tour the school. I only decided to go because I knew I'd have to fly there and back at least twice a year. And UCLA was near the Los Angeles International Airport. You might remember that before 9/11, even if you didn't have a plane ticket, you could go to the boarding area and watch the planes take off and land. I would hang out at the airport and pretend I was flying off to Argentina. I had recurring dreams of flying on a daily basis. I saw my body free of any physical bonds. I could soar in the sky and touch the clouds. I wanted to break free of gravity and metaphorically break free of ties to location. I dreamed of soaring above my *mundo*.

"It was at the airport, while living my fantasy life that I met Javier Ortega Galicia. He was a professor at the UCLA School of Theater, Film, and Television. He thought I was a model, but only because I was not in motion when he saw me gazing out the airport window. Once he saw me walk, any thought of my striding down a runway disappeared. He was, however, convinced that I should be in movies, his movies, of course. He taught me how to fly, a decision he came to regret. Once I stepped into my first cockpit, no one, not even Javier, could tie me down." Raya sat down.

Several women around our dinner table nodded in agreement with Raya's last comment. The idea of any of us being tied to the ground was ironic and we were all eager to get into the air in our beautiful floatplanes. Raya would be flying in *Copper 4*.

Even at this point in the presentations, we all felt that we were engaged with a very interesting group of dynamic women pilots, all willing to share so much with each other, even at this first group dinner meeting.

Next up was Janet Tomiko Mochizuki, a Japanese American born in Los Angeles, California. Like so many others of us, she was born in the month of August. Tomi, as she is called, is 5'4" with a wiry, athletic build with shiny, helmet-like hair and straight bangs. Although quiet and introspective, her eyes are friendly and alert, and she can be made to laugh easily. She got straight to the point.

"My twin loves are flying and ancient Japanese poetry and prose," she told us. "I grew up idolizing Peter Pan and Antoine de Saint-Exupéry, and scanning the skies for passing aircraft over San Francisco Bay with my maternal grandfather, a former Imperial Navy flying ace for Japan during World War II. Stranded in the Marshall Islands after the Americans invaded, he was presumed killed in action. In reality, however, he survived, was placed in a prison camp on Oʻahu, and somehow managed to make his way to San Francisco. It was he who first took me to the Oakland flight-training center where I eventually earned my flight certificate.

"My mother, too, inherited the love of flight," Tomi continued, "but she was a victim of her times, and was sadly never permitted by my grandfather to learn how to fly. I feel lucky that by the time I came of age, he had no such outdated qualms. Yet I also feel sad and somehow guilty. As joyful as flying is for me, it is a sore spot between my mother and me.

"I have been flying for many years now, but in small rented airplanes. This will be my greatest challenge so far and I am eagerly looking forward to training. I will be flying *Peach 5*."

We all realized that the next two pilots were in a strong position to win the race. Especially the experienced Leah Katzenberg, the Israeli. Born in Bern, Switzerland, Leah is 5'8" with green-gray eyes and an ugly bullet scar on her abdomen that she is never going to talk about. She looks like a dancer who never danced.

"I was the apple of my father's eye, a tomboy through and through, and to this day I own very few dresses." she tells us. She is wearing a cocktail dress for this festive occasion and took a bow in traditional Japanese fashion. She does this with so much sincerity that we are confused whether she is making a joke about wearing a dress or whether she is showing respect to her hostess and the group. The collective response mostly consists of uncertain smiles.

Leah disclosed her considerable time spent flying fighter jets and how a woman in Israel could achieve such a thing. "Because of my dad's involvement in the coordination of the theft of the Mirage plans in Switzerland and our subsequent exodus from the country of my birth, I wanted to give meaning to the family's uprooting and sacrifice by becoming a pilot. My path to the cockpit of fighter jets seemed almost preordained. My father was an aeronautical engineer and had a close friendship with a colonel in the IDF, and the air force wanted more female pilots. I passed my theoretical entry exam into the academy with ease.

"For me, the actual flying was initially more of a challenge than I expected and although I exceeded all the benchmarks required to be a part of this elite team, I never felt that I was as good as some of the natural aces. This international contest is my closest opportunity to take part in a kind of Olympics of flying. It is for my country, my deceased parents and myself…, and most importantly, it is away from the context of conflict…. I asked to fly the *White 6* floatplane."

We were already starting to work things out among us, especially Radka Zelenková, the Czech pilot, and the Russian pilot, Ludmilla Litvyck. Over a bottle of high-grade *sake*, the two Slavs rehashed the Soviet occupation of Czechoslovakia. They spoke English because although Radka knows Russian, she refuses to speak it. "I'm not proud of my country's imperialism." Ludmilla said in her own defense. "And I despise totalitarianism in all its forms."

"Then you must also despise Putin," Radka said.

"Putin is not a dictator."

"He would like to be."

"Well, he is terrible on human rights, I will give you this." Ludmilla said.

"He is the most anti-gay of any Russian leader since Stalin."

"Which means that he's hiding something in his own closet." Radka said.

The two laughed and clinked their glasses together.

The long historical political differences between our two countries was something each of us had to address so we could come to an understanding. This was the perfect setting to start working together, especially with abundant Japanese Kirin beer and high quality sake to warm our spirits.

Radka Zelenková is a handsome woman, tall and solidly built, with short, spiky blonde hair. She's in her mid-fifties but seems ten years younger. In her charismatic style, she told us a bit about her background.

"My grandfather escaped Nazi-occupied Czechoslovakia in 1940 and joined the British Royal Air Force. He was in line to fly a Spitfire in the Battle of Britain, but he was shot down in France a few weeks before. I joined The Race as a way to honor his memory.

"When I was growing up, a family of falcons lived in the window box of our flat in Prague. I used to watch them for hours. I longed to fly like them, and to become a pilot like my grandfather. Under Communism this was not possible, but after the Velvet Revolution, everything opened up.

"I joined the Czech Air Force and became part of a small team that supported peacekeeping efforts around Southeastern Europe and Central Asia. I served my first tour in Kosovo as a pilot of rescue helicopters. In Afghanistan and Iraq, I flew the Swedish JAS 39 Gripen fighter plane with NATO forces in a few offensives. But I'm honestly not sure if our efforts in these recent conflicts have done anything more than keep America and Europe addicted to oil and plundering the world for it. Today, I lead a squadron of Gripens when called to do so. I must say I prefer the medical evacuation missions to the combat ones. Actually, I am considering retiring from the military and flying for Czech Air."

In her charming Czech accent, Radka finished with, "I like that this race is a women's event. I want to celebrate how far we've come as women. Twenty years ago my small country hosted the Women's European Flying Championships. That is where I met my partner, Lenka. I will be flying *Burgundy 7*, which happens to be my favorite color and number."

With too much *sake* already consumed by the group and the interesting revelations already shared, we were getting quite loud and talkative. The different dialects filled the room with chatter. As Ruth Coleman stood the noise slowly quieted. We all sensed the graveness of the next speaker. Perhaps it was not graveness but importance. By the time Ruth spoke, the room was silent and respectful.

Ruth is the last of the three pilots whose names begin with 'R.' Raya, Radka, and Ruth are all problematic for spoken Japanese. Japanese people don't linguistically pronounce 'r' or 'th.' So with Ruth it is especially difficult to say. Nevertheless, with strong articulation Ruth quietly began her introduction. The tallest pilot and possibly the most physically well built, Ruth began with a short synopsis of her life that led to flying.

"I have come a long way from my poor sharecropper family upbringing in Texas. During that time I learned about my aunt Bessie who went to France and became the first Afro-American woman pilot in America. Aunt Bessie and the sky have always been in my spirit. Trying to raise a family with endless hard work and in poverty, both my parents died early. So I was raised by my grandmother in Los Angeles, California, and went to Dorsey High School where I excelled in basketball at the point guard position. I kept my studies up and stayed out of trouble and led my women's basketball team to the city championship. This earned me a sport scholarship to the U.S. Air Force Academy where I played for the League Championship two years in a row and I fulfilled my dream of flying. My dream wasn't to be in the military, but I decided to become the first Black American woman to fly in combat. I flew in the first Gulf War and had two tours of duty before I resigned from the military. After a few years working for Habitat for Humanity, I ultimately found my way to this adventure and to this gathering tonight. I fly because I feel free, even if only temporarily. I fly because I am a woman, because I am black, and because as a black woman I feel that no place—including space—should be denied me. Those are the lessons I learned. Those are the freedoms that I keep."

Ruth set the tone for the next seven women pilots. We felt an immense shift in our attitudes. We felt the importance and pride of participating with one another. We had respect for each woman who had found her way to be a pilot and we felt the awe and the immensity of the sky and clouds. It was only fitting that Ruth would be flying in floatplane *Black 8*.

Flying in the *Blue 9* is Ting Xu Chan. She is wearing a sporty racer-back cocktail dress for the occasion, and as she makes her way to the podium, her blue-black Mongolian birthmark is boldly displayed on the back of her bare right shoulder. She wears it proudly as a sign of her birth.

Ting Xu was born in a yurt under the big sky of the plains of Inner Mongolia and weaned on yak milk. She has honey-brown skin and her hair is dark brown that turns red when she spends time in the sun. Her most striking feature are her grey-blue eyes, which she inherited from her maternal great-great grandmother and which can be traced back through her maternal line to the Bourchikoun tribe of which Genghis Khan was the most famous member.

With the group equally silent and respectful as they were with Coleman, Ting Xu speaks in perfect English and gazes into the eyes of the group, "The Mongols believe that the spirit of the 'Monkh Khokh Tengger,' the eternal blue heaven, is among the objects everywhere in the universe. When I was twelve, the Chinese government relocated my family. When I was taken from the yurts and herds of my youth to a small cement apartment in Hohhot, the capitol of Inner Mongolia, I felt that the sky had been taken away from me. Since then I have searched for a way to find the spirit of the heavens again.

"It was not until I was the farthest I had ever been from my homeland that I rediscovered the sky of my childhood. My first trip was in a small plane in the American West. Floating over the stark flat earth in an endless blue sky was like eternal heaven. I knew then that I had to learn to fly to keep 'Monkh Khokh Tengger' awake in my soul. When I returned to China after graduating from college, I immediately applied to become a pilot. They strongly preferred men, but with the fantastic eyesight I inherited as part of my legacy from Genghis Khan, I was hard to refuse.

"Even though I sought 'Monkh Khokh Tengger' in the sky, I have come to know that she is part of everything and every one of us, as long as we are in harmony with the universe. I wish for you all to find a piece of the eternal blue on your journey."

Without politely waiting for Ting Xu to be seated, Firoozeh Irani trotted quickly to the microphone and started, "Salaam aleikum, Mazdani meher, I am Firoozeh Irani, named after the stones of my birth, turquoise from Iran, by the good graces of Ahura Mazda, saved and transported to worlds across the vast Pacific, to join your race and fly the *Turquoise 10*. I have come from the Caspian, all the way across this other side of the world. After training, I will be ready to fly from Tokyo to start the race with all of you."

Firoozeh, born in Isfahan, Iran, the ancient city of the angels and stone carvings, is pure Caucasian (as opposed to how we understand Caucasian), light skinned of Persian ancestry. Her hair is long in a reddish brown braid, her height about 5'3". She is slender and her eyes are greenish blue, Kashmiri blue. Her voice is lyrical yet angry. Firoozeh continued, "When I was growing up I saw many smart Air Force officers who would circle the Empress Farhadiba. I would think often, what fun to be smartly dressed in all that blue and gold and to be bowing and scraping and be admired. Yes, that is what I had thought. But in those days as I was only a teenager, I realized that the only way to wear one of those uniforms was possibly to marry an Air Force officer. So, instead I befriended Air Force officers and managed to get my flying credentials with friends in the Shah's military.

"But now I think women had more freedom back then because today Iran has changed so much. It has put us behind veils and shrouds. Genetically we are not women who can be covered up under the *purdah* or *burqa*. As daughters of Zarathustra, Pouruchista, and Pantea Arteshbod, the great commanders of Persian armies, we have always had women fighters and pilots, but now Islam has brought submission to women.

"You know what our great poet Omar Khayyam said:

"'Tis all a Chequer-board of Nights and Days
Where Destiny with Men for Pieces plays:

Hither and thither move, and mates, and slays,
And one by one back in the Closet lays."

Other than understanding Firoozeh's social and political ideology, we were not sure of her flying abilities, but felt that Keiko must know what she is doing in choosing Firoozeh for this race.

There was no doubt about flying abilities when it came to Ludmilla Litvyck, the Russian pilot, flying in *Red 11*. Other than her flying abilities, we knew very little of her. As a modern Russian woman she had been allowed more of the European trappings of womanhood, to whatever extent a childhood in the Urals was allowed. She was able to choose a career that was neither masculine nor feminine, and was given the ability to extend her education beyond her social standing. Ludmilla quietly shared with us, "I have learned growing up in the Urals, as a descendant of the inter-marriage of Cossacks and Russian Jews, that breathing freely and deeply in the long months of winter would do nothing but freeze my lungs and cause a sure and painful death.

"My career choice, first to fly and then to design aircraft, was laughable before the fall of Communism, but my so-called brilliant ascent coincided with the fall of the system and the short-lived but well-loved rise of democracy in my country. I kept my flying skills sharp because I believed that Russia was a glass house and democracy a fiction that would fall when the powers that be decided that the freedom experiment was over. I knew that flying was the skill that could transport me both figuratively and literally from these shards and lift me to safety."

Quietly and with amazingly good English, Ludmilla finished her heart felt introduction, "With a heavy heart, I am leaving behind my love and my lover to join The Race. I care not about winning. There is no one to go home to and no system to ensure or even celebrate a victory of any sort. I have taken this challenge as an invitation to escape what was cold in my heart and to breathe some warm air into my lungs. I am going to fly just to fly."

We were curious to find out exactly what Ludmilla meant by these tantalizing bits of information, but decided to let the introductions continue.

Claudia Schumann is of medium height. She used to be of slender build but has started filling out over the last decade or so. She wears her hair in a pixie cut, dyed auburn red. Her freckles make her look younger, especially when she smiles. Her body, however, is unmistakably that of a woman who devoted years of her life to bearing and raising children. She wears an interesting necklace that looks like an old coin.

"My name is Claudia Schumann and I will be flying *Green 12* and as you can probably hear from my accent, I am German. I was born in the sleepy little town of Weimar in East Germany with no real hope of ever flying anywhere in my lifetime. Some of you might recall that during the Cold War, East Germans were not free to travel. Even travelling to another communist country wasn't easy and required lots of red tape and travel permits were handed out in the most arbitrary manner by despotic government officials. Most people in East Germany, including my own parents, resigned themselves to that and spent their vacations puttering around in their tiny allotment gardens or travelling the country in a 'Trabant,' the little East German car made from cardboard."

Claudia focused on some point at the far end of the room, almost as if lost in her memories. "Not me though. I was fiercely hoping to board a plane one day and to get up into the sky and out of that small world that suffocated me. In 1979, a family from East Germany escaped to the West in a homemade hot air balloon and they became my heroes. You can say I wanted to be able to fly in order to escape from my life."

She smiled a sad little smile. "Well, I eventually did learn to fly, otherwise I wouldn't be standing here in front of you right now, but it was not until the Wall came down. However, I haven't flown a plane in quite some time for," she seemed to struggle for words and her voice tensed a bit, "personal reasons which I will spare you. Anyway, I am looking forward to the training, the race, the plane and the feeling of being my own master once again." Claudia looked around at all of us, raising her glass. "And I guess it is never too early in this adventure to offer a toast to my fellow sisters in racing. May the best pilot win. Prost!"

Speaking softly and simply, Nanibah Jackson, a Navajo/Laguna American Indian, introduced herself. Born in Albuquerque, New Mexico, U.S.A. Nanibah is short and muscular, about 5' 3" with long dark black hair, piercing eyes, and dark skin like most Navajo women. She almost looks Japanese.

"My father took up photography and would go off for days exploring and making pictures around the rez with his grandfather's 35mm Leica camera. Later, when he bought a Japanese-made Nikon camera, he would joke about having a camera made by the same subsidiary company that manufactured the wartime Zero airplane. My father was a decorated Navajo code-talker in the U.S. Marines Corps in the Pacific Theater of World War II. Whew, how much more ironic stuff can there be? He would be cracking up over this race and my sister pilots. He always reminded me to get an education and a job or interest that let me be free to wander and explore as he did. He did not want me bound to the earth, but rather to dwell in the clouds that he so often photographed.

"He used to buy me model airplanes to build. Very much alone on the rez, and with 'coke bottle' glasses to correct eyes that were crossed from a cradle accident, I was always the weird one in my elementary school. I had few friends and found that making model airplanes was a way to spend time and dream. I was always interested in flight and airplanes. The first good model that I built at that time was an ME 109, a World War II German Luftwaffe warplane. I did pretend take-offs in it and imagined flying the plane as I held it in my hand and walked to secret landing strips that I had built outside of dwellings on the Laguna Pueblo. It was during those times that I found tranquility and joy in being alone and with my thoughts of being a pilot.

"My chance for real flying came when a good friend from the Bureau of Indian Affairs took me to the small Double Eagle airport outside of Albuquerque and paid for my flying lessons. My family was suspicious at first of the generosity of this white man. But he truly was a friend and not a fiend wanting to take advantage of a young Indian girl. Some things do work out nicely in life. Now I have been flying for almost thirteen years. I think I am one of the youngest pilots in this group of diverse and international women. I look forward to flying in the aircraft that fought the 109's during the war. Mine will be *Yellow 13*."

The youngest pilot, the Italian Piccola Uccello, born in San Benedetto del Tronto, Ascoli Piceno, will fly the *Chartreuse 14* floatplane. Piccola is short with dark hair and blunt features. She appears tired because of the dark circles under her eyes and her ruddy complexion. She is the only woman at the table not wearing a dress or skirt but does not look out of place because of that. The reason she seems out of place is because of her youth. Her young features give her an air of innocence, yet without the charm of beauty. As she speaks, her eyes are wide, not in naïveté but in fierce sincerity.

"*Ciao. Buonasera*. My name is Piccola Uccello. In English, I am Little Bird. I was born for flight. I've been flying since childhood. Just as Radka and Tomi were inspired by grandfathers who were pilots, it was my *Nonno* Uccello who took me out on his CANT Z.509 when I was little, and taught me to fly. I owe a lot to him. I would never have known the joy of flying if it had been up to my parents. They only accept what I do because I don't give them a choice.

"And while I truly love air travel and have always had a predilection for, and fascination with flight, piloting is not my ultimate goal. *Nonno*, who knew me better than anyone, used to say, '*La testa tra le nuvole, cuore nelle stelle.*' Head in the clouds, heart in the stars. My passion is for astronomy and astrophysics. Someday I'm going to be an astronaut. For the past four years, I've plotted my education with the sole intent of working for the *Agenzia Spaziale Italiana*. Winning this race will force them to reconsider my application.

"I'm very grateful to have this opportunity to race among such established and capable pilots. This is a special experience for me. *Nonno* would be proud. And Keiko," she said, turning to address the hostess, "I really love my Spitfire. I call her Olio d'Oliva because of the color and the slick way she moves. *Arigato*."

Arianne Maya Parker, flying *Ochre 15*, was the last to speak. Speaking shyly and very softly she spilled out the sparse details of her life as quickly as she could. "I was born in Hartford, Connecticut. My family moved from Connecticut to Spokane, Washington, when I was seven years old." Of medium height and medium build, and like an unusual botanical specimen, Arianne is difficult to classify. At first glance, her spare, graceful *mien* and pronounced cheekbones might lead one to believe she is perhaps Slavic. Her almond-shaped eyes are hazel, her lips full, her nose curved and a bit too large. Her thick eyebrows sit squarely above her eyes, straight and serious. Though she is olive-skinned, her cheeks and shoulders are lightly freckled. Her ears, though small and perfectly shaped, stick out from her head. Her deep brown hair is worn up for any activity requiring concentration and focus. She lets it down in public only at those times when she senses she can let loose and be herself—occasions that tend to be few and far between.

"Despite sincerely loving both of my immigrant parents, I grew up feeling I was their opposite." She cleared her throat nervously and continued. "They and my brother were practical, logical and confident, while I was uncertain and extremely self-critical. It was perhaps due to my lack of confidence that my mother felt it would be good for me to get out of the summertime heat and dryness of Spokane and spend time with my uncle Art, and his wife, on the other side of the Cascades, in western Washington, near Seattle.

"Uncle Art was an experienced pilot, having flown in the Korean War before I was born," she said, her soft-spoken voice occasionally cracking. "On my first trip up in Uncle Art's single-engine Cessna, I was transfixed. Flying high above the coastline, I could see the evergreen forests, lakes and peaks of the wet earth under brilliant summer sunshine. At times, as the little plane tilted and turned over the landscape, the sun, glinting down on the many waterways, sparkled and blinded me. It filled me with a bright certainty I had never felt before. It was crystalline, clear, and perfect. I felt as though I could hear the voice of the sun call out to me, a certain hum, like music, and the tinkling of bells. Once there, I never wanted to leave. But come down to earth I did. And, eventually I came out of those summer flights in my uncle's plane with a pilot's license and a longing to fly whenever I could.

"But my studies took over every fall, winter and spring. I made good enough grades to get into the University of Washington, and then went on to grad school. When the normally gray Puget Sound skies became clear and blue in the summer, I flew and my imagination could soar. It is in the air that I gather the ideas for my story writing. I bring them back down to earth with me to craft and tend to them, growing them from the tendrils of ideas found while alone high in the sky." Arianne hesitated briefly. "I still find it hard to believe that I have been included in this powerful group of women."

We all noticed Keiko smiling and nodding with obvious approval through the introductions. We felt we were as ready as we would ever be to begin our training schedule. Over six thousand nautical miles away from Japan and in another time, an elder storyteller sits with her family in a small hogan on the Laguna reservation in New Mexico. It is nearly midnight, and the moon is full.

Humma-hah. In the beginning the witch people ruled, and the world of magic existed in parallel space to the ordinary world. All was complete, and might have gone on that way except for what was about to happen. Witches were gathering from all directions. They came across the big oceans, over mountains, and from every continent. They knew nothing of cultural divisions or boundaries or politics or wars. They were young and old. Their skins were brown and black and yellow and white, and of course, red. Their hair was kinky and straight and dark and blond, and mostly long. Their eyes were large and slanted. They came to talk about their beliefs, to perform their magic, and to pay tribute to their goddesses as they had always done.

The goddesses were creators, lawmakers, prophets, healers, hunters, battle leaders, and truth-givers. Mothers of the Earth, Queens of the Universe, and Queens of the Heavens, all were venerated. From the Northwest Eskimos came Sedna who ruled over the sea animals. She used ugliness as protection, and anyone who dared look at her would be struck dead. For the ancient Aztecs there was Chalchiuhtlicue, the goddess of all the water on earth, and Coatlicue, the goddess of the earth who gave birth to the moon and stars. Xochiquetzal, goddess of flowers, dance, and love, was always surrounded by birds and butterflies. Kuan Yin, from China, the yellow witch's goddess, represented wisdom and purity and compassion. From ancient Greece came Gaea, the goddess of the earth, and Eos, the goddess of dawn who emerged every day from the ocean and rose into the sky. Hathor, from ancient Egypt, was the goddess of love and mirth who protected children and pregnant women. She embodied the sky. And Nut represented the heavens, and helped put the world in order. She existed before all else had been created. The Hawaiian goddess, Hi'iaka, was a fierce warrior and yet a kind and calm friend of humanity. Her gifts for the people included the healing arts, the creative arts, and the art of storytelling. Goddesses from the ancient Celtic lands were Danu, the earth mother, and Caillech, the wise woman who ruled the seasons and the weather and could move mountains. With the white witches came Frevia, the goddess of love and fertility who enjoyed music and song, and Frigg, the goddess of the sky and motherhood. She knew the fate of each person.

The witches talked for a very long time, mostly at night under the moon, and around the big campfire. Finally there was only one witch who had not shown off her magic. The red witch, who had observed and listened throughout, had hardly been noticed amidst the loud demonstrations. Only after the others had exhausted themselves did the red witch take her place by the fire. With an imperious glance about her, she pounded her gnarled staff on the ground three times and began to speak.

"The world of magic is fading from the universe. Soon you will wake up and it will be gone. Men will take over your caves and dwellings. These men will have moved away from the sun. They will have moved away from the moon. They will have moved away from the earth. They will have moved away from the animals and plants. They will replace you and your goddesses with their own gods and religions. Witches will be burned and stoned and cast away. The male God and his Son, and The Prophet, and the Buddha will all preach peace and harmony, but men will turn this around for their own purposes and become greedy and violent. They will live in fear. They will fear each other and they will fear themselves. And they will fear you. And they will kill the things they fear. They will create weapons, and fighting will be commonplace. They will even fight for entertainment. First stones for killing will come, and then metal, then powder that explodes. Then tainted water they will call 'chemicals.' Then gasses, then a thing called radiation, and even light that can cut and kill.

These men will kill animals and alter plants to grow for their own sustenance. They will create disease, and they will look away even as others are dying and starving. The land will be destroyed for greed and power. The world will be divided by boundaries, which large tribes of warrior men will kill to maintain. They will fear and kill each other, turning their backs to the very peace, harmony, and love that their own gods have preached. They will even convince women to be warriors for this, and to raise their children in fear and hatred and violence.

In an attempt to recreate the magic they have destroyed, men will create objects that mimic their own reality but serve only to numb the mind. People will carry these objects everywhere they go. They will stop wanting to be with one another and will instead talk only into light screens on these boxes. They will look at big light screen boxes for most of their time alive instead of being with the sunlight. They will build large structures that destroy the air and make waste that destroys all living things. The earth will turn against them for their greed and self-centeredness. They will find out what it is like to live without even the idea of magic and they will suffer accordingly. And they will have done all this for what they refer to as manhood and the good of mankind."

The witches all gasped. Some were weeping. The red witch's words pierced their hearts like daggers falling from the sky. Distraught, they told the red witch to take back this horrible and impossible story that they did not want to hear. The red witch replied, "I speak the truth. Eliminate the impossible, and what remains, however improbable, is the truth. This story I have told you is already set in motion. The days of witches and magic are ending."

The children in the hogan began to cry, but the elder woman soothed them. "Do not cry. Women still nurture and raise families with compassion and caring, while most men look for control and power, which often results in violence, in order to achieve their ends for whatever 'honorable' reason. All this has come to be. I am trapped in yesterdays, but you are not. Respect and elevate women and find men that have learned to nurture and care and live with compassion and respect. Learn to live completely in the moment. The past will vanish even as the future loses meaning.

Projected flight path across the Pacific Ocean from Tokyo Bay to San Francisco with three refueling sites indicated—Mitsubishi Ship in the North Pacific Ocean near the 33rd Parallel; Honolulu, Hawai'i on the island of O'ahu; and Mitsubishi Ship in the Pacific Ocean near the Great Pacific Garbage Patch.

G

ISLANDS

T   H

F   I   C

GREAT PACIFIC GARBAGE PATCHES   SAN FRANCISCO
                                 8143.5 KM   10072 KM
                          REFUELLING STOP 2   CLOUD NINE

N

                    HONOLULU
                      6215 KM
HAWAIIAN ISLANDS

N

165 W   155 W   145 W   135 W   125 W

TRAINING

In August our training began in Tokyo. Christine Banfield, along with two women pilot instructors who had been trained in vintage warplanes, came from the airbase in Manston, Kent, England, to initially guide us. The RAF (Royal Air Force) Manston station had borne the brunt of early German *Luftwaffe* air attacks in the long hot summer of 1940. Today, the Memorial Museum Building houses information, memorabilia, and Spitfire aircraft and is a mecca for veteran pilots who train to fly restored Spitfires. One of our trainers, a floatplane specialist, was sensitive and compassionate to all of us regardless of age and language difficulties. Our instructors' expertise proved invaluable in our readjustments as pilots to the many anachronisms of flying a contemporary retrofitted floatplane. Most of us had to adapt to the enhanced speed of the aircraft. All of us had to learn to understand the torque produced by the bigger contemporary Spitfire propellers, which rotate to the right, and therefore push the aircraft to the left. We were also schooled in rudder adjustment through stick and rudder coordination and some of us had to learn to take off from choppy waters. High altitude flying required us to adapt to using oxygen and in order to increase our speed and decrease fuel consumption, we all studied tailwinds along our route at various altitudes over the Pacific Ocean.

With the help of GPS and state-of-the-art communication systems, we learned how to navigate from the dock at Haneda Airport in Tokyo Bay to the Mitsubishi refueling ships and destinations of Oʻahu, Hawaiʻi (3,385.4 nautical miles) and then to our final destination, the Golden Gate Bridge in San Francisco (2,080 nautical miles).

We drilled arduously for three weeks before we felt qualified to fly and land on water. Some of us felt more comfortable than others in the contemporary urban culture of Tokyo. All of us enjoyed the wonderful accommodations at the luxury hotel Himemiya. For a few, the language barrier was difficult. Ayame Kobahashi was a bonding force as she spoke several languages and served as an interpreter for all of us. Those that needed interpreters were provided with one, but it was Ayame who brought us all together in understanding and friendship.

There were moments during training when we felt a life-change, both physically and psychologically. Most of us grew physically dependent on Dr. Kazuhiko Watase and his acupuncture treatments. Kaz was especially important for Nanibah, who needed help with the side effects of her chemotherapy. Kaz gave us Japanese-style acupuncture to rebuild positive energy flow but also to release negative energy.

Dr. Watase, himself a Buddhist, had assisted victims of natural disasters throughout many parts of the world including Japan's Tohoku Region after the earthquake and nuclear disaster, the United States' Midwest after devastating tornados, and in Kathmandu following the recent massive earthquake. We regarded Kaz as a great healer and were delighted he would be onboard the refueling ships to provide us with acupuncture during our air journey.

Not all the interaction between pilots went smoothly. Especially troublesome was the Iranian pilot Firoozeh Irani. She was quiet and seemingly angry most of the time. She seemed to be especially hateful toward the Chinese pilot Ting Xu Chan. We could never figure out why she picked Ting Xu to dislike. Otherwise, the pilots seemed to get along wonderfully and shared secrets, background stories, and philosophical ideas and of course, piloting skills. Interesting relationships happened as well, especially with the pilots who had particular partner gender preferences. Foremost was Radka Zelenkova, the accomplished, attractive, and outspoken lesbian Czech pilot. Dealing with her youthful sexual desires and family religious issues, the talented and youngest pilot, Italian Piccola Uccello, had a definite interest in Radka. They were seen several times engaged in deep, thoughtful conversation, yet something seemed to develop in the later days of training between Radka and Leah Katzenberg, the veteran Israeli pilot.

Many of the women had their own issues to deal with, but it was nice when they shared these inner conflicts or thoughts. It helped to establish trust and in a few cases friendship. Hamidah Gyamtso, the first female Tibetan pilot in history, offered her faith, teaching, and compassion to many of the other women. The American Indian pilot, Nanibah Jackson, shared ideological cultural religious beliefs and knowledge with Hamidah. Many of the other pilots benefited from the gatherings where both Nanibah and Hamidah led the discussions. Ayame bonded with Janet Mochizuki, the Japanese American pilot, and spent many free moments with her discussing American history, especially the World War II Japanese American Concentration Camps in the 1940s America. Ayame had not been aware of this American incarceration.

Our most memorable gathering was when a group of us met to discuss spiritual traditions, often centered on Buddhism and the spiritual universe. Ayame and Hamidah posed questions to our group of Ting Xu, Nanibah, Janet, Firoozeh, Christine, Radka, and even Arianne, who seemed open-minded to questions of the spirit despite her diffidence. On the last evening of our gathering, Hamidah explained one aspect of Buddhism that several in the group were also thinking about, "The practice of *dharma* is learning how to live, and it is both a joyful and challenging path," she explained.

"It asks that you open your mind to take a fresh look at your views and opinions and to accept nothing on faith alone. As you practice, you will be encouraged to investigate your most cherished convictions, even those you may have about the dharma itself. Happily, this can be a never ending journey of self-discovery into every aspect of your life."

As the evening and lively discussion continued, Ting Xu posed the question, "Do the actions of humans, when making decisions, radically change the manner in which the world proceeds?"

Without hesitation, Nanibah said, "The passage of time relates to chaos theory and the potential of parallel worlds able to fulfill the possibilities of human choice that can, therefore, provide insight into the various decisions that can change the way the world proceeds."

Hamidah immediately connected with this and mentioned ideas found in Buddhism. Of course, this led us to a discussion of reincarnation and the modern notion that we are allowed to choose the circumstances of our next lives. Nanibah then volunteered her own thoughts on this topic from her perspective as an American Indian. "Indians have long had their own ideas on reincarnation. The various experiences that my people describe in their stories strongly suggest the existence of another life much better than the present one, and give credence to the idea of a happy hunting ground, a world dominated by spiritual energies and concerns."

From off in one corner, almost completely forgotten, a quiet voice spoke up. We sat up slightly in our chairs on hearing her words, our curiosity piqued by the evenness of her tone. "Parallel worlds do exist," said Arianne, "and we women will be the ones who rediscover the magic necessary for bringing peace and harmony back into the world."

Other than the trip to see the Fukushima nuclear disaster site guided by Ryoichi, there were no days off in our training, but many evenings after dinner, meaningful discussions and interactions took place. Two meetings seem to stand out. After our trip to the Fukushima site, it became evident that many of us were very concerned with nuclear power, the most dangerous energy source on earth. Our evening meetings with Ryoichi were fruitful in terms of developing both solutions and an activist stand which all of us could embrace and promote in the future.

That was how six weeks of training in Tokyo went. We had bonded through our shared goals and training and, more importantly, we had come to an understanding that we did not represent governments or countries, but a sisterhood based on gender and purpose. Christine Banfield in *Silver 1* was ready to begin the staggered start in three days.

CHRISTINE BANFIELD

SILVER 1

"Haneda ground control, this is *Silver 1* requesting clearance for water takeoff, destination 172E and 33N." As I ascend into the air, the floatplane maneuvers admirably. So admirably, in fact, that I am feeling perturbed about the three pilots in training who had had to make big leaps in their piloting skills to handle this astounding airplane, mastering water takeoffs and landings. But I am happy that my goddaughter, or perhaps I should call her my adopted daughter, Ayame Kobahashi, will be flying in *Champagne 2* right behind me. I can safely monitor her flight. I should have blessed my *Silver 1* with sage as the Mexican pilot, del Sol Mundo, did. I did paste the printed words of Amelia Earhart, given to us by Keiko, on my dash, "To worry is to add another hazard." Keiko knows that I am a raging English worry wort.

My thoughts return, with pride, to my Spitfire. I provided all the controls necessary in the Spitfire floatplanes. I had the technicians at Mitsubishi outfit each of the fifteen floatplanes with a four-bladed propeller, an Aero-Vee tropical filter, and extra ventral and dorsal fins. A special heating system has been installed for high altitude flying and to handle potential icing problems when flying through clouds. This was necessary for the reworked Spitfire's maximum altitude of 43,000 feet. To fly above the clouds, and for the pilots to work with winds aloft and high altitude tailwinds, de-icing is a necessity. Our cockpits were fitted with a specially designed oxygen supply system and the 2,120 horsepower Rolls-Royce Griffon 85 engine enables the floatplane to fly at a maximum speed of 454 mph at 26,000 feet. The rate of climb for the new floatplane is 4,100 feet per minute and most importantly, with a ninety-gallon drop tank and internal fuel compartment, the range of the small plane is 2,060 miles maximum.

The most critical technological improvement in the cockpit is the new Garmin instrumentation. It provides all the pilots with enhanced situational awareness, safety, and reduced pilot workload. Along with the primary flight display and a multifunctional display, it features sophisticated graphics modeling to create a 3-D topographic landscape, a 'virtual reality' perspective view of ground and water features, obstacles and optional traffic. The Garmin's screen offers a much improved visual of primary flight data, especially at night or in marginal weather conditions. Fortunately, none of the pilots have had problems with the new GPS technology that will direct them to the first Mitsubishi refueling ship halfway to Oʻahu.

Yes, me ol' dad would have been so proud of me for adapting these historical British war machines. It was wonderful to have had an unlimited budget to transform these aircraft from RAF military aircraft to floatplanes now capable of flying at a higher altitude and for greater distances. As I plan on taking my leave from all this business soon, this will be my last effort in aeronautical engineering design, I hope. I do, however, look forward to being with Ryoichi, Keiko, and Ayame in San Francisco and beyond.

Dad was a quiet and brilliant man. He rarely spoke, but when he did, I listened with all my might, for what he said was spot on and significant in ways that I would only fully realize later. I think he always had everything planned, even his death. Happily married for sixty-seven years, my parents lived a frugal life in the same house in Croydon for all that time. My childhood seemed unremarkable, but Dad was beside himself with pride when I went into aeronautical engineering after high school.

Although I never learned how, after graduation he went above and beyond to help me secure my first position, which was with Folland Aircraft. Several years later, through his usual self-sacrificing ways, Dad made every effort to help me obtain my pilot's license, and now I have been flying for over forty years!

As the hours in flight pass, I relive caring for my dying parents. Mum and Dad both lived to be in their nineties—God bless them. Mum began showing signs of memory loss and was subsequently diagnosed with Alzheimer's disease. Together with my two dear, younger brothers, Nick and Scottie, we escalated our parental care at that time. Scottie went so far as to have his piano moved into Mum and Dad's house, so while we planned and prepared most of their meals, he played Mum's favorite songs.

Many moons and abandoned dreams ago, Mum had given up any thoughts of a career on the stage. She had done so with the intention of becoming a wife first, then a mother. Mum adored music and "The Theatre," the real theatre, not what would later come to pass as such. And every once and a while, during her last years and out of the blue, the sound of my mother's voice suddenly reciting Shakespeare's sonnets she had not read in over sixty years, thrilled me....

As her short-term memory faded, she frequently brought up very accurate memories from long ago, including her recollections as a young girl of something she had eaten at a particular party with her friends or of a red taffeta dress she had worn. It was bitter-sweet to curl up by her side and hear as she recounted the same memory over and over as if it had happened yesterday, even as the events of her life were disappearing.

On Mother's Day, Mum suddenly stopped eating. She lay in her bed and never got up again. She withered away and we never knew what was wrong. The boys and I would gather around Scottie as he played his piano. He played for her in such an emotional and spiritual way. It was painful to see our mother lying there, just skin and bones, only waking at the sounds of music when she would smile and move her frail arms. After seven weeks, she passed away with a bit of a smile on her face, hearing music as my brother played.

My father was also dying, his body being overtaken and so he let us take care of him as best as we could. He had bladder cancer, huge liver cysts along with a compromised immune system, and needed monthly blood transfusions. My brothers and I realized he was seeing doctors just to stay alive for his beloved wife. A week before Mum passed, my dad tripped in the lavatory, strained his back and had to be hospitalized. He was never able to walk again. But worst of all, he couldn't be with Mum in her last hour which hurt him tremendously. We broke the news to him and together we all grieved. After we brought Dad home from the hospital, he only got up one more time, and that was to attend our mother's memorial service in a wheelchair.

After returning home to his sick bed, he began to draw us near for long-neglected heart-to-hearts. Though Dad was once a hale and hearty eater, now he was restricted to porridge and hot tea, nothing like the bangers and mash he used to attack with zeal. We were each taking turns tending to and comforting him. Those sessions were vigils of compassion and love. But soon he stopped eating altogether. By then he couldn't bloody well be bothered with eating or living. His last meal was the boiled dinner I prepared for him. Even now, I tear up when I remember him saying to me, "Christine, that was one hell of a meal. Your mum would have been proud of you, Lassie."

Like every proud old Englishman, Dad insisted on dying on his own terms. And so he did. He stopped talking one day before the last afternoon we had with him. Standing devotedly by his side, we watched over him, dribbling water into his lips as he faded away. As my brother and I dripped water from a straw into his open mouth, my father shed a tear. I will never forget that. While the summer breeze, which was filled with the scent of Scottish heather and English roses, drifted in from the garden, a garden he worked on his entire life, we chatted. Then he passed. My brothers and I were blessed with two wonderful human beings for parents. And this we will always count as an amazing blessing.

I have shut out so many of these thoughts by working hard and now, even by coming to Tokyo to work with Keiko on this race. A year after my parents passed, I was blessed with taking in Ayame, Keiko's only child, who had just graduated with honors from high school in Japan. Raising her was a gift. Besides going on to a prestigious college to study plant science, I encouraged her to get involved with flight training. Keiko will always love me for taking in Ayame and for teaching her to fly.

Now that I am in the clouds, alone and in control, my thoughts return to the beauty and pain of those last days. The cessation of my parents' lives reinforced my fear of death and mortality. My brothers and I feel like orphans now. Dear Keiko has spoken with me about Buddhist philosophy and the idea of impermanence and has helped me in some ways to deal with death. I also benefited from talking with Hamidah and Nanibah during training. Their spiritual beliefs are so uplifting.

Although an abundance of cloud cover surrounds me, the navigation system indicates the Mitsubishi refueling ship dead ahead. Dropping altitude, I hope I will spot the ship and land this beautiful airplane. Although time has seemingly passed so quickly, for me, much of it has been in the meditative trance that pilots often experience.

My landing was perfect, and with the training the other pilots received, they will have no problem unless the ocean gets rough. Good that Keiko is using Mitsubishi ships and not military vessels as originally planned. Our refueling is taken care of in an efficient manner. To ensure fairness, each plane will be held for exactly an hour. The digital display on one of the skiffs starts the countdown and will automatically release the clamp on the pontoon legs in an hour, unless an irreparable safety issue is discovered during the routine maintenance checks that are performed during the refueling and the disposal of the plane's on-board waste. Every imaginable replacement part for the reborn Spitfires is on board, along with a top-notch crew of engineers, including some who helped me rebuild the planes in the first place. Solid and liquid rations are replenished in accordance with the renewed weight allowances for the other pilots, along with fuel.

Best of all, we all get to leave the cockpit, take a quick shower and change into fresh flight gear. After five hours of flight time, the steaming hot water feels like heaven on my back, and the subsequent twenty-minute acupuncture session with Dr. Watase is both healing and invigorating. I was spoiled by the variety and flavors of the Japanese food we had in Tokyo, because the food on this refueling ship reminds me of bland, old English food.

Already time to get going. I clamber off of the skiff and into the cockpit and start the engine. I hear the reassuring purr of the RR Griffon after being told that everything on the plane is in perfect working order. I thank the flight crew and lower and lock my window. I can see on the countdown that the clamp won't release for another 3.37 minutes, so I take my time buckling up my five-point harness and adjusting the lumbar support of my seat.

So many things have changed for me. Ayame has graduated, and has visited and worked with the Konohana Family, an agriculture-based community in Japan. After her flight, she will stay in Japan or San Francisco with her mother, I believe. I definitely will move from my flat in Croydon, probably to a quiet suburb of Tokyo, or maybe to a mountain in Hawai'i with my beloved, or perhaps I will stay in San Francisco with him, Keiko, and Ayame. The time invested in preparing for this race and the flight certainly has confirmed my retirement. For all too long I have done the predictable. I have worked as an engineer with precision and have attempted to create a semblance of security. I shrank from the unknown and chased after the familiar in my constant effort to work and be secure. I have rejected change. It is perhaps my British upbringing, but certainly it had to do with my family and vocational choice. My only adventure was helping Ayame and flying together with her.

During these past few hours, technology has dominated my mind, not supportive or kind thoughts, but rather critical ones. In England today, as I walk in downtown Croydon, all the young people seem to be constantly on their cell phones. There is no dialogue between people other than text messages and e-mails. Convenient yes, but there's no real social interaction. At least it appears like this to me. We go home and are glued to our technology, computer screens, and satellite television. Social interaction and adventure are relegated to cleverly constructed theme parks, where we receive controlled thrills while pretending we are in exotic places. All are man-made experiences, even the environment is predictable. With manicured campsites with picnic tables and electrical hookups and trails neatly paved with signage to tell us what we are experiencing, living with, and relating to the land spiritually is non-existent. Yes, and I fear, I am also responsible for a lot of this.

Being with this group of brilliant women and my intimate talks with Keiko have made me realize that life is uncertain. I want to experience the remainder of my life in all its fullness and with clarity. I want to enjoy the limitless realm of possibility. I want to understand the idea of "uncertainty" which we discussed in our late night spiritual discussions and I hope to embrace the "wave of crystallization" that took place within me.

One hundred ninety-eight miles more to reach the half way mark—O'ahu, Hawai'i, and the United States of America. All my thinking and desires are relatively paradoxical. With uncertainty comes fear and depression. Now, as I approach O'ahu, I have to be certain. Certain about the coordinates and the technological skills that I need to land this floatplane and certain about how much time I have at Pearl and what needs to be done. Control is of the essence. I have and am good at control. That's the paradox. Uncertainty can also evoke a sense of wonder and curiosity and freedom. What I must now achieve is a balance or surrender flying as well. I am certain of one thing— Ryoichi will be waiting for me.

I will only be on Oʻahu for an hour after landing. I'll get refueled there, but will skip all the other perks, and meet Ryoichi. It has been years since I have truly fallen in love this intensely, and never in my life have I been so sexually fulfilled. Both of us never knew this would happen, even though our friendship was immediate and enduring during the Tokyo training when Keiko had introduced me to Ryoichi. I already knew of Ryoichi's archaeological work and his role in finding the Spitfires in Burma. Keiko had also confided in me about their professional friendship and brief intimate relationship with Ryoichi several years ago. We all had had a little too much *sake* that evening, but even so, I thoroughly enjoyed hearing about his luxury car excavations and his alien space theories regarding the space-time continuum from his thirteen-year adventure as well as his continued commitment to the Earth. He said that rather than the archaeological past, his interest is in the future of our planet, now under the threat of nuclear technology. We all said good night, but Ryoichi and I went into the dark night, and perhaps into the future. In his room, he privately shared his pictures and journals and documentation on his legendary project as well as his activist stance on nuclear power. Listening to his low, sultry voice was seductive. It flowed over me like a set of waves until, and almost without my realizing it, his arms were around me. His warm lips were on mine. This was no ordinary man. In just the second it took to lay back on his bed, an intense kinetic energy that I had not felt before flowed through me. But it wasn't to be our night. Something blocked our way, something we both felt needed to be freed up.

The following night he took me to dinner. I was comfortable with Ryoichi and was feeling as if I was in a surreal and slow motion dream. We had a private room with white rice paper walls, thick tatami mats and dark silk pillows to sit on. The hand-carved chopsticks, or *ohashi*, were stunning in my hand. Saying the word softly to myself felt like a sensual whisper. After commenting on their beauty, he later bought me a pair made of Japanese yew wood. The shrimp they brought us were still alive and we boiled them in a broth and ate them with rice and a delicious dark, milky sauce. That evening we drank only the thickest green tea I have ever had. No *sake*, although I was feeling intoxicated by just being with him. After dinner we walked along the pier and checked on three of the floatplanes that were docked for training in the morning. Ryoichi walked me to my hotel room and we kissed. It was a kiss like I had never experienced in my entire life. His touch burned me and I wanted him to touch me and take me, but he was agitated, said good night and left.

The next morning he explained to me his resistance to having a relationship with a dear friend of Keiko's, owing to their past history. I told him I felt the same way. We wanted to be together so we had to tell her. That afternoon, after flight training, we took Keiko to lunch and explained to her our feelings for each other. Dear Keiko was magnificent as always. She smiled, gave us her blessings and expressed her happiness that two of her dearest friends had found each other. The following days and nights had no Heaven or Earth. No time or space. Only Ryoichi. Only me.

Now on approach to Oʻahu where Ryoichi and I will have a few minutes together, it is hard to keep my mind on my landing. As he has been following my progress from land, I already feel him by my side. I marvel at how our relationship became so formidable in only three weeks. He has fulfilled me spiritually, intellectually, and physically, in ways I never realized were possible for me. This must be what love in its purest form feels like. As a veil of clouds envelopes my ol' *Silver 1,* my thoughts are propelled back to the first night we made love.

I was uncharacteristically nervous. It was that nervousness that made it so memorable that it stands out in my mind even today. Nervousness turned to excitement, then passion, as his lips left mine and kissed my neck. I could smell incense in his long black hair as it covered my face. My heart was pounding. I felt his lips at my breasts, his hands over my stomach and hips, then his fingers gently moving between my legs. At my age, I thought there would be no more surprises. But clearly there are. I was shocked at how excited Ryoichi made me before he pushed himself deep inside me. He brought me to climax, and then another, before finally climaxing with me. Unbelievably, it has been like that ever since. And this, from the proper English schoolgirl, the aeronautical engineer, now remembering and giggling with girlish delight!

The precious time spent with Ryoichi on Oʻahu was too short. I asked Ryoichi to stay and wait for Ayame who was flying in next and to give a report to Keiko and me on her condition, flying time and landing on Oʻahu safely. Leaving my love on land, I am back in my plane and The Race. I will be the first to fly over the Great Pacific garbage patch half-way to the final destination of the Golden Gate Bridge. The garbage patch is located within the North Pacific Gyre, one of the five oceanic gyres. The Great Pacific garbage patch is also described as the Pacific trash vortex and is roughly between 140W latitude and 38N longitude and extends over an indeterminate area, depending on the degree of plastic concentration. I will fly low to see what is simmering beneath the unnatural discoloration in once pristine waters. There are areas where the garbage has collected to such an extent that small toxic islands are being formed, and they are growing. The patch is mostly characterized by exceptionally high concentrations of pelagic plastics, chemical sludge and other debris that has been trapped by the currents. It is one of the greatest ecological disasters of this planet because it is man-made.

The plastic particulates are a major ecological concern and very disturbing, the Great Pacific garbage patch containing among the highest known levels of particulates on earth. The plastic flotsam photo-degrades, unlike organic debris, which biodegrades. The plastic disintegrates into ever-smaller pieces, down to the molecular level, yet polymers remain small enough to be ingested by aquatic organisms and eventually enter our food chain. Besides killing fish and ocean mammals, marine birds like the Black-footed Albatross have been especially hard hit. The digestive systems of nearly all one million Laysan Albatrosses that inhabit Midway Islands, have been found to contain these polymers. Over half of their chicks die from plastic ingested in utero from their contaminated parents. This shame is ours.

As I slowly circle low over the garbage patches, I realize that I might not have the best flight time now to win this race. When I entered the race, however, it was agreed that I would not be competing to win, so all is fine with me. I believe that there are no coincidences, only synchronicity. The enormous tragedy of the birds and aquatic wildlife lost to the garbage patches continues to haunt me as I press on to the next refueling ship only an hour away.

Something barmy is happening to me, something I can't blame on the altitude. Will the scene I have just witnessed over the ocean become part of my future with Ryoichi? I have been thinking about how we will be comfortable wherever we are, but now I am also thinking that we will become involved with issues concerning the oceans and wildlife as well as the continued threat of nuclear technology. Perhaps some of the women in this race will also be reinvigorated and engage in restoring the environment in the world we all share. During training we connected with Nanibah about the nuclear waste from uranium mines on her reservation as well as the history of nuclear weapons development in New Mexico. This race has proven that we all have something to learn and to benefit from in knowing each other's diverse backgrounds and lives. I now feel that this could truly happen and I believe that this has been Keiko's master plan from the beginning.

The weather has turned bloody rotten. I pray that the others flying behind me will be able to handle the threatening skies. I will radio back to Oʻahu control to warn the other pilots about the coming storm.

Just before we all touched down in Hawaiʻi, Keiko had made a stunning announcement. In addition to awarding each pilot two hundred fifty thousand American dollars for finishing, she promised that each pilot can keep her Spitfire floatplane. For me, it was enough of a gift that Keiko accepted my petition to join the race, even though I have had to multitask to develop and design the newly outfitted Spitfires along with continuing to look after Ayame. I knew from the onset that this adventure would change my life in ways I had not anticipated, just as Ryoichi did, and continues to do. Nonetheless, it has broadsided me beyond my ken. I am my true self now. And in that spirit I will be giving my beloved *Silver 1* to Keiko as a grand keepsake of The Race. I radioed this message to her and she has accepted my gift.

Upon landing for the next refueling, I had to refocus immediately as the bloody choppy ocean created problems. It was difficult to land and cozy up to the Mitsubishi refueling ship, but I was able to get away again without a mishap. I hope the other pilots make it down safely. Kaz flew in again to give us acupuncture at this last refueling stage. I must admit that I am exhausted both physically and, psychologically. There is so much to think about in the sanctuary of my dear floatplane. Before leaving, Kaz gave me flying directions for my descent to San Francisco. This was relayed from Keiko and seems very odd, but I will give it a try. The directions are for me to descend to 7,890 feet and go through the uppermost cloud, which is known as Cloud Nine. If I remember right, Cloud Nine is one of ten types of clouds described in the 1896 edition of the *International Cloud Atlas* and given the name Cumulonimbus. But that is science. What we infer from "Cloud Nine" today is being in euphoric exaltation, blissfully happy. So I will fly through this cloud that Keiko has identified and maybe absorb some of that happiness. Crazy Kaz and Keiko. I love them both.

Now I am in the last leg of this amazing adventure. And wouldn't you know it, more dark threatening clouds force me to divert from my path to avoid turbulence. Constantly looking for openings, this difficult weather conjures up my dark conversations with Ryoichi about what he calls "Nuclear Insanity." In training, some of the other pilots and I had night meetings with Ryoichi. While touring the Fukushima disaster area, we met with Ryoichi's activist friend, Sueko Suzuki. The most poignant moment came when she shared her research and take on nuclear power. I recorded her lecture that day. "The history of nuclear power is not only a tale of science and engineering, but also a study in hubris and denial. Nuclear advocates believed they had built a power source they could control, one that would prove immune to the ravages of age, human error, or natural calamity. When the technology began to fail and assumptions about the power of nature exceeded 'design parameters,' the evidence was diminished, dismissed, or ignored."

With the disquieting Fukushima power plants in the background, we continued to soak everything in as Suzuki continued, "Fukushima forces the world's nuclear nations to confront some unpleasant issues. What happens in the aftermath of a nuclear disaster? Can government provide an adequate response? Will industry be held accountable for the damage to lives and property? The Fukushima disaster provided a textbook example of what can happen when a nuclear accident occurs in a heavily populated country. Faced with a disaster Tokyo was not able to fully manage, the government came close to collapse. Japan now faces a daunting challenge." I kept thinking that the whole world faces a daunting challenge—survival on all levels and saving our planet.

I remember seeing the BBC news announcement on August 6, 2011, made by the prime minister of Japan. I had been thinking how ironic it was that he was talking about nuclear power on that day, the sixty-sixth anniversary of President Harry Truman's nuclear attack on Hiroshima. Prime Minister Yoshihiko said, "We will deeply reflect over the myth that nuclear energy is safe…to secure safety, we'll implement fundamental measures while also decreasing the degree of dependence on nuclear power generation, to aim for a society that does not rely on nuclear power."

During one of our evening discussions led by Ryoichi and Sueko Suzuki, we all contributed to a platform addressing these challenges and the future. The discussion was one of the most rewarding moments in my sheltered techno-engineering life. The aspect of how community, in this case a community of diverse, intelligent, and compassionate women, becomes the unifying force that will allow us to move forward on all issues, including a nuclear free environment and saving the Earth. A more realistic view of our energy future and the lifestyles it will support requires complex analysis. Traditional energy planning has been based on the assumption that population growth will continue and that humans have the right to make greater demands on the world's resources. But, we live on a finite planet where continued growth is not ecologically sustainable. Switching energy sources from nuclear power and "going green" seemed to be only part of the solution. Our task was to define the problems and to come up with solutions that we might be able to work on after The Race.

One controversial solution we came up with was the necessity to control population growth. But more importantly was the philosophical re-framing within our culture that happiness as a goal is not dependent on the ever-growing consumption of goods. Much of the sickness of the "developed world" stems from excess, too many miles driven, too many calories, too many ostentatious living spaces, and too much throwaway stuff. We need to learn to live within our means by doing without extravagance. Living better with less, and more in tune with each other and our shared planet. Long-term survival in the twenty-first century depends not on consumption, but on social solidarity, cooperation, sharing, resourcefulness, knowledge, and health. It seems that the future belongs to those whose basic needs and well-being can be sustained locally, in low-impact, self-supporting communities. Reliance, on the wealthy one-percent and the government, will only sustain their wealth and their sense of power, not our existence.

It was interesting that Keiko attended the gatherings and listened intently. It seemed as if this corporate leader, and certainly a member of the one-percent, was in agreement and looking for alternative ways in the future. We all knew that the notions proposed are idealistic and that many supporters of the status quo, with their closed eyes and minds, would label these ideas as socialist. Perhaps so, but nevertheless we all agreed that the old forms of economy promoted massive inequities in the distribution of wealth and power. We all believe that the world now needs a sustainable and compassionate economy that will usher in a new era of stewardship and sharing.

My mind is racing. I want to work with Keiko and the other women to create a way to help turn these ideas into reality, not only in our countries, but throughout the world. It is to be our responsibility to save "mankind" and mother Earth and it must start soon. I look forward to finishing this flight and meeting again with the other pilots. I only hope that some of them are of the same mindset.

The weather is clearing up as I approach San Francisco. I am about to fly through Cloud Nine. The only curious thing seems to be the multitude of different kinds of birds, primarily albatross, that I am encountering as I gently drop my altitude. My biggest worry is that I will hit a bird, or worse yet, one will get caught up in my props and stall me. It is queer that these birds are this far out from any shoreline and I am feeling a bit uneasy about this.

I am aware that love has opened me up to transfiguring moments as well. But most striking to me is the fact that it all began with the interaction among my courageous fellow pilots during training and with my beloved Ryoichi. Within this space in the sky, I have let my past demons go and embraced a spectacular vision of environmental survival, love, and compassion. I am, for the better, a changed Christine and a blissfully happy Christine as I move through Cloud Nine. Thank you, Keiko and thank you also for the honor of being your Ayame's godmother.

Ayame never knew her father. It was something that her mother never revealed to her. Keiko might not have known as well. The younger Keiko had many suitors in her early corporate environment. There was a time when she did sleep her way up the competitive corporate ladder in order to move forward in a male-dominated culture. When Ayame was born, Keiko, with great pain, placed Ayame with her grandmother Yoshi in a farming community outside of Hiroshima. Yoshi's husband, Atsushi, had lost his life in World War II while on leave in Hiroshima. Atsushi was a pilot in a newly formed *kamakaze* squadron. It was ironic that his life was to be that of a short-lived suicide pilot who never fulfilled that destiny. Instead, it was the atom bomb dropped on Hiroshima that Sunday in 1945 that took his life while he was boarding a train to visit Yoshi at the family farm. Years later, Keiko found out that she had been adopted into the Kobahashi family during those turbulent post-war years when the notion of family had become shattered and more complex. Ayame's upbringing was unique because women in an isolated farming community of strong Buddhists had essentially raised her. Grandmother Yoshi recognized early on that Ayame had a keen mind. In her grade school, she was often the head of her class and a community leader. Ayame loved working on the land and her studies at the agriculture charter high school in Saijo focused on the biological sciences.

When Ayame graduated from high school, she expressed a desire to pursue a career in agriculture and environmental science. By this time, the strong and competitive

Keiko had become the CEO of Mitsubishi and she continued to support Ayame financially as she had always done. What was lacking was a lifetime of being a true mother to Ayame.

Keiko called me and asked me to take care of Ayame while she attended Newcastle University, a bit northeast of Croydon. This was a wonderful time for both Ayame and me. Ayame would come stay with me most weekends and on her breaks from studies. It was at this time that I took her to Folland Aircraft and she took to flying immediately, showing her usual ability to accomplish anything she desired.

Ayame studied Agronomy at Newcastle and graduated in a short two years with her BA. Agronomy is the science of crop production and soil management leading to improvements in crop yield and quality. She studied agricultural topics such as biology, soil science, nutrition, and management. Not satisfied with all that she wanted to learn and to be one of the top scientists in her field, Ayame was accepted into Oxford University for doctoral studies. It was here that she seriously and professionally established herself in the agricultural and environmental sciences. The best part of that time was that Oxford was driving distance from Croydon and Ayame got to live full time with me as she continued her education. We also had a lot more time to develop her piloting skills.

When Ayame graduated with her Ph.D., she was quite surprised when Keiko came to the graduation ceremony. Actually, I think she was happy to have both her mother and godmother there for her. This was the initial bonding contact for Ayame with Keiko and they both had a lot to work out together. Ayame, now an accomplished pilot and educated agriculturalist, went back to Japan to work and deepen her understanding of the ancient ways of community involvement and working the earth at the Village of Bodhisattvas, with the Konohana Family.

And just like that, overlaying my last thoughts, the Golden Gate Bridge looms ahead. The sun has come forth to illuminate the bridge and San Francisco in a magical way. I am tired, but living life in this brilliant moment. I will be the first to fly under the Golden Gate Bridge and land in the bay. I look forward to seeing my dear friends come in as well. I have cleared landing instructions and I am turning off my radio and putting on a CD to blast my way into the landing. I am playing my favorite British band, Supertramp. I bloody love "Dreamer" and am blasting it away. Here we go!

AYAME KOBAHASHI

CHAMPAGNE 2

Arigatō Gozaimasu, Lord Buddha for allowing me to follow my godmother's float-plane in my mother's race. *Okashī* that I thank Lord Buddha when it should be the Bodhisattva Kuan Yin or Kannon, but in reality my destiny has been guided all along by my mother.

Answers are what I was searching for and what brought me to The Race. Brought here, in fact, by the only person who can give them to me, Mother, Keiko Kobahashi, creator of The Race, mighty executive, overachiever, keeper of secrets, and the source of my pain. Having given this much thought, it turns out that this is her story and journey as much as it is mine, for we are mother and daughter and that can never, no matter how much I try, be undone.

Of course, my mother had her hopes pinned on me, but she refused to see, nor could she see, what her own life experience prevented her from knowing. I am Japanese because I am her daughter. Because I never knew my father and because my mother did not raise me, I am alone, and that is how I have lived my life. My mother could not imagine what it was like to greet myself in the mirror each morning, not recognizing the person who stared back. Nor was she likely aware that this is my plight. How could she know, caught up for so many years in endeavors that did not involve me? Innocence is a thing of the past. The future is uncertain. But that does not prevent us from moving forward. Inertia transports us into a future, even if that future is an illusion, and we must accept it as such.

So why did I undertake this race? Why pit myself against women who are more skilled as pilots, and who have a more natural grace and affinity for the air, than I? I would not be seated in this race were it not for my mother. I am not ashamed to admit it, nor do I wish to complain. The opportunities provided me by my mother were numerous, and before taking my place in the pilot's seat, I must acknowledge them. I received an education from one of the finest schools the world has to offer, I am blessed with good health, and have had the enormous privilege of a life unencumbered by the economic hardships that plague so much of the world's population, and I have a strong biological constitution, thanks to a fortuitous combination of genes. I am grateful beyond words and thank her with all my heart for these gifts, but they have come at a cost.

It was in training that many of the emotional questions I sought were answered, while in deep conversations with my mother, something we had never had before. One evening my mother explained to me, "Ayame, sometime a few years ago, I started meeting with Ryoichi-san and Kazuhiko-san. I had long forgotten the philosophy of Buddhism and the pathways to a life of compassion. They both helped me find what should be important in life. I shed my rapacious need for success and money and became enlightened in the Shinto's way of 'The Plain Of The High Heaven.' Embarrassed by my old mindset and wanting to make amends, I began to concentrate on building a plan to bring women into the world's forefront with focus on the Mother Earth, and to teach the people of the planet Earth about 'The Plain Of The High Heaven.' In my somewhat enlightened state, I realized that I had made a disastrous, maybe irreparable, mistake. For the first time I felt shame about what I had done, giving up my child for my own selfish aspirations. I felt a strong, dull pain in my stomach that has lasted until now. Could I make things right with my only child, a child I emotionally abandoned? It is apparent to me that I was nothing without you, Ayame, my only child, my daughter. At long last, clarity has come to me. I need to heal the wounds with you, so that maybe you and I might lead the way in working with other women and pilots to develop a community on the island of Kaua'i, where I have purchased a great deal of land. We would develop organic farming and teach our methods to the world. We would help others move away from corporate dependence and establish sustainable communities with independent power sources, food, and medicine. It will start with The Race."

My mother had never spoken to me like this. I respected her for her frankness and I even cried. This was a start for sure. Years can't be erased, but it seems that we both are trying to heal.

Now the grueling training is over. The Race administrators' efforts have been acknowledged, the participants praised with toasts and cheers, the spectators with their flags and binoculars are primed for a good show. The take-offs have been timed with *Champagne 2*, my Spitfire floatplane, flying second in a start position that can be regarded neither as optimal nor unfortunate. My mother has sworn on her honor and her considerable reputation that I would not be afforded any advantage in the race. As I make my last minute preparations for flight, I wonder if the weather gods might have been bribed. The feeling is just right, *kimochi ga ii*, the rising sun half-hidden behind a bank of clouds. I will not be blinded by glare bouncing off the water, nor hampered by wind. Instead, I will be ushered eastward over the Pacific by a current of air that normally travels inland from the Sea of Japan. Who can say why, on this morning, the jet stream has veered off its course? The sea breeze wafts in as I inspect the flight panel controls, and I am reminded of a kelp-based soup my grandmother used to prepare for my breakfast. I can see her pursed lips blowing steam over the bowl's rim, her bony fingers lifting a spoon to my mouth to sample the flavoring. I can taste the heat from my own breath, and feel the aroma dredged up from the sea floor in my lungs, the salt air on this early fall morning rich with the fragrance of memory.

I have had a life of full-fledged independence made possible by a bank account that was replenished on a monthly basis. Those were the loneliest years of my life. Mother gave me every advantage, denying me nothing but her own presence. One of those advantages allowed me to find a remedy for my sadness. Thanks to my god-mother Christine, I found the sky in my search to fill that black hole of physical and emotional emptiness, a place so vast my sadness could not even begin to fill it. I learned to fly at Christine's Folland Aircraft Company in a simple prop plane. At the moment of liftoff, my depression fell away with the ground. I would have ridden on the wings had they let me. I was a natural. I was alive. I spent all my extra time in the sky and became an accomplished pilot. Christine had me read about early pioneers of aviation and their thrill of flying. They were not amateurs at flying, they were intensely professional, and intensely serious about the craft of flying, and about their own role in history. I read all the books by these exciting writers and was extremely moved by their stories. Especially motivating was the writing of Anne Morrow Lindbergh. *We* was about her husband Charles A. Lindbergh Jr., his Paris flight, and his early life. I also especially enjoyed *North to the Orient* about the unprecedented survey flight the Lindberghs made in 1931 in a small seaplane from New York to China by the great circle route over northern Canada and Alaska, touching down in eastern Siberia and Japan. I also read Antoine de Saint-Exupéry who wrote so poetically and magically about flying in *Wind, Sand and Stars*. Beryl Markham, born in England, raised in Kenya from age four, was the first woman to fly the Atlantic from east to west in 1936, and her book, *West with the Night*, for me, was full of aviation spirit and poetic "remembrance." These wonderful tales inspired me. Although these aviators turned authors have different nationalities and different capabilities, they were unified in their love of flying the unspoiled, distant corners of the Earth, and by their affection for their fellow pilots. "The dignity of the craft is that it creates a fellowship," said Saint-Exupéry.

Although good results may hinge on the right combination of skill, preparation, and luck, the scent of victory is present this morning for only a few of my competitors. Christine, already in the air, has won the race even before her plane ascends. Having designed and engineered the floatplanes and tested each one individually, she holds secret knowledge that the rest of us are not privy to, even in flight. She flew out in the first position. All this is her right, as she and my mother Keiko, the true orchestrator and mistress of The Race, have enjoyed a friendship for nearly as long as I have been alive. Christine, raucous and carefree, my mother, shrewd and not given to laughter, the two as different as two women can be, are nonetheless as drawn to each other as I am to each of them. Christine, however, will not cross the finish line first. She will hold back the way the host is expected to *enryo* for the benefit of her guests.

As a young woman, I still believe in my uniqueness. I even fantasize about changing my name so that I would bear no trace of my mother. I resented her because although she had provided for me, she denied me her presence. I was raised by my grandmother and later after high school, by Christine. Those who should have been closest to me were no better than strangers, supportive to some extent, yet excluding me from their lives. I am grateful that in training we have begun to address some of these tensions.

Having successfully taken off and now alone in the sky, I have settled into a reflective state. Last year, I visited Christine in England. One day as I walked along the row of purple crocuses that line a walkway at my old university, Oxford, I spied Paul Beaupré, a friend with whom I'd lost contact after college. I smiled at him as he approached along the walkway, and then tapped his shoulder as he passed.

"Excuse me?" he said, seeming slightly affronted, about to turn away.

"It's Ayame," I said, causing him to look again.

But even then he hesitated. "I didn't recognize you," he said.

"Really?" He looked older, but the curl of his lip, higher on the right, curving into a prominent arch on his cheek, made him unmistakably Paul. As we parted, my lip began to tremble, and I raised a hand to hide it. Had my looks really changed so drastically? There is the face you are born with, the one you wear through innocence into adulthood. Then, there is the face you earn. These faces had been forecast to me. But who was this stranger?

That same afternoon, an invitation arrived, delivered by messenger in care of Christine, "for Ayame." To make sure that her effort would not go unnoticed, my mother had it printed on heavy, white card stock, written and embossed in purple. I was reading the details when I noticed that Christine, who seemed to be aware of what it was, nevertheless asked me.

"Is it something good?" she asked, "A wedding?"

I looked over at her, puzzled. Had the invitation arrived with instructions for the carrier to message back a response? "A race," I told her, having not yet adequately digested any of the details.

"You should go," she shrugged, which made me smile. With me, my godmother always seemed impetuous and fun loving.

"You don't even know what type of race it is, or whether I've been asked to attend as a participant or spectator!"

"That's true," she shrugged again. "May I see?"

I was happy to deposit the invitation into Christine's outstretched hand. I might have forgotten about it had she not mentioned it later that same day because I was buried beneath paperwork, which involved many recent projects with the Konohana Family Farm in Japan. "I think you should join," she said, her flight bag dangling from her shoulder, as she readied herself to leave for a day of flying.

I can tell when Christine has something on her mind. She gets that pensive look for which the only cure is to listen. Ignore it and her distraction mounts until she's useless to me. "Go ahead," I smiled, pushing back my chair, readying myself for one of her circular jags.

"When the harvest season is done at the Japanese farm, you'll have a break between projects," she said simply. "We trained you to be a superb pilot. You should do it."

My first thought was that my mother had asked Christine to convince me. But it was true. The timing was right, and while it might have otherwise amounted to nothing more than a passing fancy, I did have a penchant for aeronautics and flying, along with agriculture.

So the opening was there. In the gap between what was and what could be, stood my mother, from whom I'd been estranged for half my life, calling me back into the fold.

I can see now that identity is a great inhibitor. In hindsight, the years in which I sought to define myself were limiting, rather than enlightening, by that search. My mother was cruel to have abandoned me, but here is another version to that story. A young woman of twenty-two is captivated by a man ten years her senior who recognizes her by the sharpness of her gaze. They drink together. Upon leaving the bar, they have to prop each other up, they are laughing so hard. I am born less than a year later, a token of that passing fancy. The woman, who has never taken responsibility lightly, loves her baby, but tells only a few about her. I am her secret, kept apart from the world, given every advantage, but raised without a history. Can you imagine, Mother, what it is like to live outside of history?

Reflecting on the sequence of events that has brought me here, to this moment aloft in the sky, I think again of something my pilot friend Hamidah said, "What is history other than the story we create to see the connection between things?" During training, Hamidah was one of the pilots with whom I bonded. She shared her philosophical and spiritual knowledge with those of us who held similar beliefs. This was a blessing.

Here in the sky, I am happier and more carefree than I've ever been. It is a paradox, isn't it? When one's life is imperiled, when one moves forth under the greatest constraints, and when there is so much at stake, then one feels most free. Who knows whether my mother and I will reach our destination, and if so, which of us will finish first, but I am ready. In some strange way I believe I have waited my whole life to speak.

The water landing and refueling went perfectly. I didn't get to see any of the other floatplanes, but my acupuncture with Dr. Watase was helpful. He was very quiet with me and I sensed he knew that my troubled thoughts were about my mother. I had felt this way in my interaction with him even after my mother and I talked things out during training. He must know that I am trying to put this past to rest. One thing he said to me still resonates in my mind, "Live in the moment, Ayame."

It's hard to live in the moment on this flight. There is much to ponder during the second quarter of this journey. What I left behind is still present in my thoughts and the journey is fresh enough so that nothing can be taken for granted. The refueling went smoothly enough, and the team made very good time. According to the DME, I am now closer to O'ahu than I am to Tokyo, but I fear I have slipped off course. I am troubled by the thickness of the clouds and the ocean I can smell but can not see. There is a nautical term for a condition brought on by constant motion and a lack of visual reference points. The instrument panel is vanishing, causing me to rely on my senses, but my perception is failing me as well. I am most concerned with what we learned in training from Claudia Schumann, the German pilot. Something called the Ganzfeld Effect, which is German for perceptual deprivation. In the 1930s, research by psychologist Wolfgang Metzger established that when pilots gazed into a feature-less field of vision, they consistently hallucinated and their electroencephalograms changed. During the Ganzfeld Effect, the brain amplifies its neural noise so that it can locate lost visual clues. This neural noise is recognized in the visual cortex, and results in hallucinations and altered states of consciousness. Even though I may lose flight time, I am going to turn on my autopilot now to guide me to O'ahu, just in case.

Now I'm sure I am in some kind of dream. I am invisible here in a barracks structure. It seems to be somewhere in Utah. Of course! It is Topaz, the Japanese American relocation camp that my fellow pilot, Janet talked about in our many discussions on American history and her family's experience in the Japanese American Concentration Camps in America. Looking out the one window in the room, the sky is a deep purple and we seem to be surrounded by fog. In fact, as the room seems to sway, I swear we are floating on a cloud. The walls around me are covered with several different American flags from historical time periods. The worn wooden floors smell. I know I am hallucinating because across the room against the back wall are eight men. There are five white men of different ages, wearing expensive suits, who seem to be floating on American money, stacks of hundred dollar bills. Even more amazing to me, floating on a red carpet is the Dalai Lama, who is flanked by Jesus and Mohammed. Suspended on large eagles in the room are seven young children speaking in adult voices: an American Indian child, a young Black American boy, a Middle Eastern little girl, two Asian American children, one Japanese and the other Vietnamese, an American, and a Mexican American girl. All of them seem angry and are speaking in different dialects, yet I understand them. They are talking about American history.

Lucky for me I am awakened by a loud voice over my headset. "*Champagne 2*, pull back! You are approaching too fast and too high!" I slow down and descend. The autopilot can direct the floatplane from the refueling ship to Oʻahu, but it can't land the aircraft accurately. I gaze at the clock and can't believe that I was in a dream state for over three hours! But I don't feel rested. I need to analyze what I just went through. There is so much on my mind, but first I will land, refuel, get some acupuncture and eat. I think I need mental therapy as well.

The acupuncture by Dr. Watase's daughter helps me to relax and rejuvenate. Habib does purple ray Chromotherapy on my upper chakra brain area that I hope helps my mental state. At this point, I will do whatever might help. I need to get back in the air and then I can think about what I just went through on my flight to Oʻahu.

I am focused enough to fly out of Oʻahu on time and successfully. Now, at 20,000 feet and with fairly good weather, my mind goes back to the hallucination.

More importantly, it is what the children were talking about—aspects of American history—that was not good. Much of this I either had known or had learned from Janet and Nanibah during our training. The Japanese American youngster spoke first. "The last four wars that America fought were against Asian nations. Racism against Asian people is institutionalized through the media and governmental policies. Institutional racism dehumanizes people of color and justifies white supremacy and racist atrocities. An example of this is the American belief in Manifest Destiny, which resulted in the takeover of the Hawaiian Islands. Other examples are the Japanese American concentration camps during World War II, the Chinatown massacres, and the atomic bombs dropped on Hiroshima and Nagasaki."

The Vietnamese American child added to that, "The Vietnamese people had been fighting for liberation against colonialist and imperialist nations for over two hundred years. Before American involvement, my tiny nation had resisted and defeated China, Japan, and France. Vietnam has rich natural resources of tungsten and tin and is a potential source for cheap labor, and valued commodities for imperialist nations like the U.S. And let's not forget about atrocities like the My Lai massacre. The people of my homeland do not see the American people as being their enemy, but they do hold the U.S. Government accountable for the war of aggression."

The Mexican American girl had her turn. "Talk about cheap labor, Mexicans were welcomed for a while because of their cheap labor. But now we are seen as a threat to American society. There is continuous talk about building walls on the Mexican American border and sending generations of immigrants back to México. America was once considered the "land of the free" and was founded by immigrants, certainly all white immigrants and not people of color. At least many of the Mexicans are Christians."

This was an opening for the Middle Eastern girl. "Because we are mostly Muslims and follow the Koran rather than the Bible, we are all looked at as terrorists by Americans today. We can't even immigrate freely to America. The war on Iraq by America was an imperialistic move for oil under the false pretense that Iraq had weapons of mass destruction. America helped create the unrest and violence that is in the Middle East today, although I do understand that for centuries in the Middle East, some kind of turmoil has always created a state of unrest."

"We Native Americans, or more correctly American Indians, are also treated as immigrants, which is a laugh. We are indigenous to this land. American history is about the subjugation of our Nations and culture. We were sent to boarding schools to become Christians. Today one might look at the reservations as places of incarceration. The Trail of Tears and the Wounded Knee Massacre are permanent stains on American history. Today, the rate of suicide is increasing in Indian country particularly among Native women. For years, Indian country has suffered the highest suicide rates among all racial or ethnic groups in America. Poverty, violence, and alcoholism are only a few of the constant contributing factors that drive so many Native people to despair. Generations of abuse in the form of racism, loss of indigenous languages, and the devaluing of ancient traditions, culture, and spirituality have had a devastating impact on American Indian dignity and self-worth. Tribes have signed away rights to large amounts of land and access to natural resources in exchange for promised health care, education, and other needed services. But the U.S. government broke those promises long ago and continues to shatter them today."

I sat there learning more about American history than I had ever known. I realized that this was just American history. World history seemed to be just as atrocious. And it all seemed to be based on politics, nationalism, money, and distorted religious beliefs.

Finally, the Black American youngster angrily spoke up. "America was built on slavery. One hundred years later, a great Civil War was fought over slavery. Yes, we were freed from being classified as property and became American citizens, but only on paper. Racism continues to this day in America. Black lives do matter. Police violence against Blacks must end. It seems that only Black Americans involved in money-making sports are recognized, and even then, it is for the entertainment of the American public, which still roots for the white athlete."

The quiet white boy was the last to speak in this angry series of monologues. "I can't excuse the whites in America for all that has happened. But we should not blame individuals in our history for all these atrocities. The Vietnamese don't blame the American people for war. Blame and shame should be placed on ruling governments and politicians. Granted, throughout history they have been mostly old white men, but times are changing, it seems. I am most ashamed of the gun-toting bigots from many races in this country who deal with everything through violence. America has to face it, we are a violent culture and it only seems to be getting worse. And politicians who want to make America 'better and stronger' are so misguided. It seems that the entire world should work to become better and more compassionate."

As I gazed across the room, the five suits floating on top of the money had vanished, and right before my eyes, Jesus, Mohammed, and the Dalai Lama were transforming into a huge standing dove. This bird, symbolic of peace, spoke to the floating children. "History on this planet is filled with atrocities, incarceration, bigotry, and racism. Try to understand and learn that this is true not only in America but throughout the planet. We should learn from mistakes in history and work for a future of peace and justice and freedom for all. We should live in the moment and appreciate the beauty and compassion of others who try to preserve life rather than destroy life. The future should not be about what is good for a particular country or religion or government or group of people, but for all the people of the planet. Man's inhumanity to man must end."

We all sat transfixed, as more enlightened ideas came forth from this beautiful dove. Time passed and I soon realized that fellow pilot and friend, Janet Mochizuki, was standing next to me. The walls of the room and the figures in it had dissolved and turned to dust. Janet and I were left walking on clouds. It was then that I was snapped back from the dream by a voice urging me, "*Champagne 2*, pull back!"

I'm not sure from which hidden pocket of my brain this dream or hallucination has emerged. Right now, it feels like I have found a place within myself that has been sealed off for many years, or perhaps until now, I failed to notice these broad issues because my thoughts have been so dominated by my mother. My interaction with the other pilots and this hallucinatory dream have awakened me to move from self-pity toward a broader understanding of other individuals, the meaning of this race, and how I might contribute with my sister pilots to a better future.

My mother organized events that helped me bond and learn from the other women pilots during training. To my surprise, I have loved this assignment and now I really want to fit into my mother's grand plan.

Better get back to flying and refueling! Almost in a meditative state, my water landing at the last refueling ship is seamless. I still might be dreaming. Christine's floatplane is long gone, but I am somewhat on schedule. Wonderful that Dr. Watase has made it from the first refueling ship to be here again. The acupuncture seems not only to relax and refresh my body, but it also opens up my mind even more. Kaz seems to comprehend my new state of mind and the existence of my dream world. He is all smiles as I go through the acupuncture treatment. I love him, Christine, and most of the other pilots. And, I love my mother. Kaz tells me about passing through Cloud Nine on my last leg of the race to San Francisco. Somehow I think my grand plan has awakened me! As my beautiful floatplane lifts from the water and once again enters the sky, I can be at peace with myself and think about my coming involvement in the grand plan. With my expertise in agricultural science and my latest experience with Japanese organic farming, and specifically with the Konohana Family, Village of Bodhisattvas, I believe I can be of help.

The Konohana Family is an agriculture-based community where about 100 un-related people, members and guests, live as one big family. I was given the opportunity to be a guest and learn and participate at the Family's grounds near the foot of Mt. Fuji. All members of Konohana Family make full use of their talents in daily life, each playing a specific role. They have become a model for environmentally friendly living, achieving food self-sufficiency through sustainable, organic agriculture, a mutually supportive common economy, and harmonious social relations. At the foundation of the Konohana Family is a strong spirituality that informs the daily lives of its members and guests. This, I came to realize, is the most significant thing for all humans living on the planet. Many people think that we just stand on the ground and live by our own will, but what must be considered is that this ground is the miraculous planet Earth. It exists, moving at the speed of thirty kilometers per second, it plays an important role among other the planets, and has an even broader role in the structure of the universe. In the same way, all of our lives are part of a great, independent system beyond our thoughts and understanding. Unless we are aware of this fact, we will not be able to become our true selves. But we also exist because of our inner will. We are given life and roles through the universal will that surrounds us, and this is the same as our inner will. We will not be able to know who we are without such a viewpoint. Life is given to us so that we can know ourselves, and to know ourselves is to know the structure of this world.

This twenty-first century is the era during which humans will realize this. We all must have as our life's purpose to become a good model for this new era and to manifest the divine will on Earth, in the hope that all people will become aware of the divinity within ourselves and contribute to the larger network of goodwill, love, and harmony that encompasses the Earth.

I learned this with the Konohana Family. Perhaps it is a dream or fantasy, but I feel it is part of my mother's grand plan and that I am destined to contribute to it with her.

As for me, my life is encapsulated in this flight. Having experienced the beginning and middle, I now face the journey's end. I trained hard, took well to flying, and tried to prepare myself for drama. It is so quiet at this altitude. There is only the hum of the engine. The ground and sky have changed places. The scent of late summer is gone and the brightness of the day is replaced with thickening of clouds. Cloud Nine looms ahead. I am hurtling through space and time, prepared to meet the end of this journey when a song beams through the cockpit. Over the intercom comes, *Fantasy*, from Earth, Wind and Fire. I smile as if my mother, Kaz and Christine are mind readers.

…Take a ride in the sky, on our ship Fantasii
All your dreams will come true, right away…
…Our voices will ring forever, as one…
…All your dreams will come true, miles away…
…We then, will expand love together, as one…
…It's your day, shining day, all your dreams come true…

I send a message back that I have named my floatplane "Fantasii."

I had never cried before, but during training with my mother, I cried for the first time. And now I am crying again. It feels good because I know these tears are tears of joy and part of the awakening and expression of my inner emotional being.

The grey day has turned quickly to night. My breathing is shallow. I blink to assure myself that my eyes are not shut against the haze. My fingers grasp for the gear stick as I fly into Cloud Nine. A race is about winning. Maybe Mother never needed me to win this race, but to set my life on a clear, new course. I know now what will be and I wholeheartedly embrace it. I will work side-by-side with my mother in her stewardship to heal planet Earth and to find an ecologically perfect life plan for all its inhabitants, entrusted to women to lead the way. Our time to take the helm is now. It is clear to me that life is about enlightenment, caring, and love. I see a ball of white light hovering over me, and the cabin fills with this bright white light.

Thank you, Mother. Thank you for everything. Here I come.

HAMIDAH GYAMTSO

ORANGE 3

Om Mani Padme Hum, I pull the straps of my five-point harness over my shoulders and across my hips while settling into the seat, and then engage the clasps. The parachute on my back becomes quite uncomfortable as the harness pulls me tightly into the seat, but it is a necessity. Between the floatplane *Orange 3* and me, the harness creates an inseparable bond. I smile as I wonder how an ex-Buddhist nun from Tibet got to be in this floatplane and in The Race. I am so grateful for the flight training and guidance from Christine here in Tokyo. Most of us are completely challenged by flying the Spitfire floatplanes. Now I continue with my compassion mantra, *Om Mani Padme Hum*.

With meditative control and always embracing uncertainty, I flip on the electrical system while awaiting word to start the engine. I am relieved when all the instruments jump to life. The altitude indicator, fuel level, oil temperature, radar, and a modern Garman global positioning system, plus more than a dozen other gauges and indicators, all function well. The up and down movements of the ailerons on both wings are visible from my open cockpit, but the motions of the stabilizer and rudder can't be seen. All seem to be working correctly. Now I am strapped into the cockpit with both my little Kuan Yin statue, glued to the instrument panel, and my prayer *chakra mala* made with 108 beads, including seven chakra energy stones. Mine is red quartz, specific for the root chakra, *Om Mani Padme Hum*.

The mechanic checks my seat belt and then slides the canopy forward locking me in the cockpit. Closing the canopy is not an easy task for the mechanic who stands on the damp, slippery wing while the craft sways side to side in the waves of Tokyo Bay. My floatplane responds to the waves as if it is a fishing bobber waiting for a sturgeon to snag the bait on a hook. My excitement instantly causes me to forget the mechanic's name and I yell out "*Namaste*" as he carefully walks out on the wing and then jumps down onto the dock. It will be a long day for them, with twelve more pilots taking off after me in the next nine hours or so, *Om Mani Padme Hum*.

When it is time, I press the starter switch, and hear the clunk as the starter's solenoid engages the monster engine. The propeller begins to cycle slowly and methodically while the Rolls Royce engine pops each time the pairs of exhaust valves open, expelling a blue mist of compressed oil and air from the six exhaust stacks. Electricity flows through the spark plugs and my Spitfire springs to life, belching plumes of blue-gray smoke while burning the oil that has accumulated in the cylinders, *Om Mani Padme Hum.*

I sit up and look to my left checking the port wing tip to be sure that the vibrations from the engine and propeller are not causing it to hit the dock. The Mitsubishi workers unfasten the heavy lines from the bollards on the dock and pull the rope bumpers from between the dock and the racer's pontoons. Half a dozen workers hold the craft to the dock by hand, waiting for the engine to smooth out.

The engine warms for several minutes and the modern instruments seem to be working well as the floatplane rocks on the waves. The adjustable-pitch, four-bladed propeller catches the light as choppy waves spray the underbelly and wings with a salty mist. Once the lines holding it to the floating dock are loosened the full fuel tanks and huge pontoons create an unstable center of gravity, and the wing tips come perilously close to hitting either the water or the dock.

Despite all of the modernization, this is still a surprisingly difficult aircraft to fly. The floats create an aerodynamically unbalanced racer while the wings obscure the view of the water on takeoffs and landings. The newly-added pontoons act like pendulums that can compromise the effectiveness of the ailerons at the ends of the wings. Over-correcting with the controls could allow the pontoons to create an oscillation, rocking the racer from side to side.

Om Mani Padme Hum, notification on my scratchy head set acknowledges that my start is approaching. Christine in *Silver 1* and Ayame in *Champagne 2* are already on their way. Forty-five minutes have elapsed and it is now my turn. I slowly push the throttle forward and the deafening engine roar increases in volume. Predictably, the floatplane begins veering to the left as she moves forward, but my gentle application of the right rudder corrects the problem as the nose of the racer bobs up and down through the light choppy water. After more than 400 feet, my speed has increased to the point that the pontoons begin cutting through the shallow waves and the ride is smoother. Every so often. however, the pontoons hit a larger wave and the vibration travels through the struts into the fuselage and concentrates in my seat.

With all of the weight of the extra fuel and the drag of the pontoons cutting through the water, it takes twice as long a run to achieve flight speed as it would for an original Spitfire rolling down a runway on properly inflated tires. At flight speed *Orange 3* bounces along the waves with short periods of flight until she finally breaks free. At three hundred feet of altitude, I begin pushing the stick to the right causing the ailerons to initiate a shallow right turn. After what seems like only a few moments, I reach 3,500 feet, flying due east for about two minutes, then I throttle back a bit to prevent wasting fuel. My tank holds 85 gallons of fuel, which is good for 434 nautical miles at 20,000 feet running at a cruising speed of 324 miles an hour. My advanced satellite radio keeps me within earshot of whatever is happening. My mind finally begins to settle down when I reach my cruising altitude of 20,000 feet and I double check my compass setting, throttle, oil temperature, fuel, altitude, and GPS location.

With The Race underway and the refueling ship my next goal, my heart rate calms, I embrace the moment and, except for the engine noise, the silence, *Om Mani Padme Hum*. Silence leads me to myself. Silence in a society that worships noise is like the moon exposing the night. Within this silence, I focus and I listen. I see and I hear. The unexpected emerges. The Roman goddess of silence, *Angerona*, held her finger up to her mouth in a gesture requesting quiet. Her gesture of silence suggests inner concentration or meditation. I am with her now, *Om Mani Padme Hum*.

As an orphan, raised by Buddhist nuns in Tibet and Bhutan, I never had a real name until I became a young woman and took our teacher's name, Gyamtso, as my last name. I knew nothing but this life of living in caves and in a monastery and subordinating myself to monks. My life turned around sixteen years later, when I accompanied our teacher, Khenpo Tsultrim Gyamtso Rinpoche, to the United States of America. I learned English and faced uncertainty in this new, amazing place. It took a few more years to become a Buddhist nun in the Kagyu tradition. My ordination was beautiful. At the temple, all the novices chanted, and when it was my turn to be ordained, the senior monk whispered in my ear, "It's about time you accomplished this!" I took being a nun seriously and continued my studies with Gyamtso Rinpoche. He had helped bring Buddhism to the west and taught the path of wisdom and compassion. His teachings and spiritual experiences were often communicated through experiential songs. I still love this music and singing it to this day. Although that was the first part of my life, and it is now almost forgotten, I remember it in this concentrated silence.

Embracing uncertainty has allowed me to be in this *Orange 3* Spitfire floatplane, flying over the Pacific Ocean with my "sisters." My upbringing always influences me. In Buddhism, it is true that when you forget the self and see with unclouded eyes, there is neither male nor female to be found. But the path to my practice was difficult. Perhaps Buddhism's past rejection of women practitioners began with the Buddha.

The story that sticks with me is that Buddha allowed women to listen to the *dharma*, yet he was adamant in his rejection in allowing women to practice. I learned that it struck him as far too radical and troublesome, a contaminant that would ruin the purity of a monk's practice. His aunt, Mahāpajāpatī Gotamī, was determined to practice, but she was not allowed. Finally, he allowed her ordination because of the persistent interventions and sacrifices of one of his devoted female disciples, Ananda, who spoke on Gotami's behalf. The formation of an order of nuns happened only after she and her *sangha* sisters endured a 150-mile walk in bare feet and abided by a set of rules that enforced female subordination. That was long ago and in another time, but some of these issues continue today.

In early Buddhist teachings, the female body was thought to be impure. Outflows of tears, milk, and menstrual blood were thought to defile the body in the same way that impure mental thoughts defiled the mind. This has changed somewhat, but the strong monastic traditions of Buddhism make women, sex, and carnal love awkward and touchy subjects to discuss outside of the bounds of "loving kindness."

Other religions also have misogynistic views of women. In Catholicism, Saint Jerome said that women are a "pathway to hell," and Saint Augustine viewed women as an intellectually inferior moral threat to men. This view of women was consistent through the Middle Ages, when Thomas Aquinas wrote in *Summa Theologica* that women are "misbegotten males."

Thank goodness for scholars like Joseph Campbell, who enlightened me with his ideas on the transformation and endurance of the archetypal symbolic powers of the feminine divine. Campbell embraces the feminine, despite the past two thousand years of patriarchal and monotheistic religious traditions that have attempted to exclude women. I love what Campbell says in *Goddesses: Mysteries of the Feminine Divine:*

> *On the simplest level, then, the Goddess is the Earth. On the next, archaic, level she is the surrounding sky. On the philosophical level, she is Maya, the forms of sensibility, the limitations of the senses that enclose us so that all of our thinking takes place within Her bounds—she is IT. The Goddess is the ultimate boundary of conscousness in the world of time and space.*

And then there is the Dalai Lama, one of the world's great spiritual leaders, who has talked about how human values have deteriorated and the need to respect others. He emphasizes in the "New Reality" of human compassion that females should take a more active role. I know my fellow pilots in The Race would agree with this. Perhaps that is why we were chosen to participate in this adventure.

Today, in this cockpit amidst the clouds, I believe liberation means seeing through the self into an essential nature. So open and unbounded, even the word "love" disappears into it. Women and children are entirely welcome there. I studied Buddhist women whose lives were forgotten, like Miaozong, Jingchen, Kim Ilyop, Euyeong Song, and Kakuzan. At that time, the second part of my life began. I am sure that living with uncertainty and opening myself up to others contributed to my falling in love with a wonderful man, a novice monk at our monastery. We studied together for quite some time and I was always curious as to how a Middle Eastern man from a Muslim background turned to Buddhism. This is uncommon, but of course Habib is not a common person. He is compassionate, well-educated with a degree in religious studies and Eastern medicine, a man of the world and a pilot!

After a few years at the monastery, Habib and I "disrobed" and married. He encouraged me to keep my name, Gyamtso, and I honored him and his family by taking "Hamidah" as my first name. Hamidah is a name that occurs in the basic Muslim prayers and depending on who you ask, it means either "close to God," "grateful," or "beloved." I tend to think of those things as being the same. Gratitude is an equalizing force that allows for peace and calm to be present.

We moved to the south of France and bought a small cottage. I did not relinquish my Buddhist beliefs and searched for common ground as a layperson. In the past, it seemed that to live as a bodhisattva of compassion felt self-centered even in the Mahayana tradition, and especially in the monastic environment. Now, rather than work towards my personal enlightenment, I realize that compassion is about giving to others. As an orphan, it was natural for me to find work in a nearby orphanage, and to help children with their education, upbringing, and self-esteem. I have done this for over twenty years. I also worked at an animal shelter. These loving animals were orphans of a different kind, but also sentient beings with needs. It was at the shelter that I adopted Annie, who has brought me joy and companionship every day. She passed all the service dog tests and is an official therapy dog. She now accompanies me to the orphanage where she is greeted by many happy, smiling faces.

During the first leg of this adventure, it has been good to think about where I am in my life. As I approach the Mitsubishi refueling ship, I look forward to hot *sencha* and a bit of acupuncture from Dr. Watase. The first thing, though, is to land this floatplane safely, powering down now, *Om Mani Padme Hum*.

I am back at 20,000 ft. and catching a tailwind to Oʻahu. Alone in this airplane, and after six weeks of training in Japan, I miss my husband and Annie terribly. Habib will meet me briefly on Oʻahu and give me a Chromotherapy treatment. Some of the other pilots might also want a short Chromotherapy session along with the acupuncture from Dr. Watase's daughter, Sachi. Again, the silence in this tiny cockpit is like meditating in a cave. I am switching to autopilot and hope to stay on course and meditate for the next hour in this beautiful landscape of clouds.

Although we were discouraged from using autopilot, it has worked wonders for me this time. I think I am even ahead of my flight schedule to Oʻahu. My mind is clear and in the present, although I continue to think of Habib. Curiously, among the fifteen pilots, only three of us are married. I have been blessed with Habib. He opened two of the three doors during this second part of my life in France. Ah, besides the loving sex life we share, Habib taught me how to fly and brought me to the clouds and heavens. My enlightenment took place in the sky and I have been a licensed pilot for over twenty years. After reading about this race at a regional airport, it was Habib who encouraged me to enter. Why Keiko chose me, I am not sure. Maybe it was my unique background or the conversations on Buddhism and spirituality that I could offer to the other pilots.

Today my spirituality is centered on a distinctly western approach to the Buddha's teachings, influenced by two individuals in particular. Seven years ago I was honored to meet Thich Nhat Hanh at a retreat at Plum Village in France. I neither wanted nor needed a teacher to follow again, but he did not demand this. I embraced his ideas about discovering the magic of the present moment. And, my philosophical needs were met when I encountered Stephen Batchelor and his wife, Martine. I call it synchronistic uncertainty. They lived close to our cottage and it was in a teashop where we first met.

Batchelor left Britain when he was eighteen and was first ordained as a Tibetan monk, and later as a Korean Zen monk. Although he adopted his teachers' languages, philosophies, and customs, he eventually found himself ill suited to monastic life. He disrobed and returned first to England and then to the South of France, where he settled down with Martine, a former Korean Zen nun.

I love talking with Martine—we are both disrobed nuns. We have remarkable husbands who nurture, respect, and love us. Stephen and Martine believe that centuries of myth and dogma have become a hindrance in Buddhism. They have tried to strip away some of the lore surrounding Siddhartha Gautama and to arrive at a more historically grounded portrait of the Buddha as a human being. And they have looked beyond the doctrine that developed around the Pali Canon, especially those portions concerning the rules governing monks and nuns.

My beliefs today follow this new vision of the dharma. Following their interpretations of the teachings makes sense to me as a worldview and a form of spiritual practice, and it speaks to my current condition. First is the principle of dependent origination, or as Stephen calls it, "conditioned arising." As he explained it to me, "Conditioned arising is really hard to see because people are blinded by the contingency of their existence and attachment to their *place*. One's place is that to which one is most strongly bound. It is the foundation on which the entire edifice of one's identity is built. It is formed through identification with a physical location and social position, by one's religious and political beliefs, and through that instinctive conviction of being a solitary ego." In conversations at the teahouse he continued to help me understand. "One's place is where one stands, and whence one takes a stand against everything that seems to challenge what is 'mine.' This stance encompasses everything that lies on this side of the line that separates 'you' from 'me.'

Delight in this notion creates a sense of being fixed and secure in the midst of an existence that is anything but fixed and secure. Losing this idea would mean that everything one cherishes would be overwhelmed by chaos, meaninglessness, or madness."

In relinquishing this "space," as I understand it, one must arrive at a special "ground." This ground is quite unlike the solid ground of a place. It is the contingent, transient, ambiguous, unpredictable, fascinating, and terrifying space called "life." As Batchelor emphasized to me, "To live on this shifting ground, one first needs to stop obsessing about what has happened before and what might happen later. One needs to be more vitally conscious of what is happening now. This is not to deny the reality of past and future. It is about embarking on a new relationship with the impermanence and temporality of life. Instead of hankering after the past and speculating about the future, one sees the present as the fruit of what has been and the germ of what will be." Batchelor put into words for me what I believe and embrace today as my philosophy of life.

The second is the practice of mindful awareness, much of what Thich Nhat Hanh talks about. I try to focus upon the totality of what is happening in our moment-to-moment experience. The third is the complex but important process of the Four Noble Truths and the Eightfold Path, which is appropriate vision, thought, speech, action, livelihood, effort, mindfulness, and concentration. And the fourth is the principle of self-reliance. The Buddha wanted his students to become autonomous in their understanding of the dharma, and not to generate dependencies on his memory or on some authority figure within the monastic community.

One aspect of the practice of the dharma that I will always embrace is learning how to live a joyful and challenging life. The practice asks that I look at my views and opinions, and to accept nothing on faith alone. As I practice, I hope to investigate my most cherished convictions, even those I may have about the dharma itself. Happily, this can be a never-ending journey of self-discovery into every aspect of my life, *Om Mani Padme Hum!*

Habib continues to embrace the philosophy of secular Buddhism as I do. The practice of compassion is most important to us. His family came to the United States from Egypt before 9/11 and before the stigma of being Middle Eastern existed. Habib could not find his way to embrace Muslim beliefs and he found too many problems with Christianity. It was synchronistic for me that he pursued Buddhism, which allowed us to ultimately meet. Habib's family had been part of the *Zabbaleen* in Egypt. The *Zabbaleen* worked together in communities in big cities to collect and recycle garbage before the corporations took over and made it a less effective economy. Both of our private concerns these days have been about healing, healing the land and healing the body. After Oʻahu, Habib hopes that I can fly over the Great Pacific Garbage patch and observe what we have read regarding this ecological disaster.

I will explain to Habib that I will have to decrease my flight speed to fly that low. Two other things will probably prevent me from seeing the garbage patch. First, Banfield has already warned us all that the weather report is touch-and-go all the way to San Francisco, although some of the pilots in later flights may be fortunate enough to by-pass the bad weather. Second, I seem to be making good time with no hitches so there may be a chance to win the prize money, and that money would go a long way in helping us establish our proposed facility in France, which will include a Chromo-therapy healing center.

Om Mani Padme Hum, O'ahu ground control is coming over my headset. Time seems to be passing so quickly on this flight probably due to my long meditation sessions. I had better be more aware of my surroundings with that touch-and-go weather coming up. The voice from air traffic control on O'ahu guides me in.

My O'ahu experience was wonderful. I had a perfect water-landing site that was arranged by Mitsubishi and the time spent receiving acupuncture and Chromotherapy was invigorating. And, of course, dear Habib, rubbing my back as he applied ten minutes of green relaxing ray and ten minutes of the yellow ray over my torso. Even the udon noodles were a wonderful surprise. It was difficult to get back into the float-plane and leave this invigorating and compassionate environment.

When I return home, I want to pursue with Habib our next serious interest. During his studies, Habib came across a family from India that has a laboratory in Malaga, New Jersey. The head of the family, Dinshah P. Ghadiali, was the originator of Spectro-Chrome healing. Mr. Ghadiali passed away in 1966 but his son, Darius Dinshah Ghadiali, continues the healing system today with the Dinshah Health Society. The foreword in their manifesto, *Let There be Light,* is dedicated, "to those who seek an enlightened path in the art of healing." Naturally, Habib is interested in this method of healing the body with only colored lights—no incisions or drug techniques that typically define Western medicine.

Before embarking on our own Chromotherapy facility in France, Habib and I will research the foremost authorities and practitioners of this healing method. Published material goes as far back as 1878 with Edwin D. Babbitt's book *Principles of Light and Color*. Babbitt was a curious combination of scientist, physician, mystic, and artist. It was interesting to Habib and me that the introduction to this book was written by America's most renowned authority on color, Faber Birren. Other interesting information has come from Mary Anderson's *Colour Healing: Chromotherapy and How it Works*. But today, the most informed guide to practicing Chromotherapy is the Ghadiali text, *Spectro-Chrome Metry Encyclopedia*. I love Dinshah's poetic presentation, which is what moved me to want to learn more and apply Chromotherapy to help others.

The Sick And Suffering Mankind,
Awaiting Anxiously But Helplessly
Since The Dawn of Civilization,
For The Ray of Light
That Would Lead Them
To Therapeutical Emancipation,
From the Thraldom Of
Pills, Potions, Poisons, Pellets,
Plasters, Pumps and Poniards,
I Devotionally Present This
Spectro-Chrome Metry Encyclopedia,
The Guiding Star Of the East.

To share this information with Ayame, Tomi, Ting Xu, Firoozeh, Nanibah, and Arianne in the evenings during training was very meaningful to us all. Nanibah, with her ongoing cancer battle, has embraced Chromotherapy for herself and plans to introduce it to her people as well. Ting Xu already had some knowledge of Chromotherapy as Chinese scientists at the Beijing Institute of Scientific Study have been investigating the healing power of colored light rays for the past ten years. What I had not considered until now is the fact that my birthplace, Tibet, is no longer Tibet, but an annex of China, and because of that, I believed I am supposed to dislike all Chinese. This, however, was not the case with my Chinese compatriot Ting Xu. On the contrary, we became good friends. Partly perhaps because she is of Mongol descent, and the Tibetans and Mongols go way back in history, both sharing Buddhism and interacting with one another for the most part peacefully, and probably also for national survival. I am sure Ting Xu was relieved with our friendship, having been at odds with Firoozeh, who targeted Ting Xu during training because of personal issues. I hope Firoozeh has come to terms with her unsubstantiated anger. Anger is so stressful and damaging to human existence and has no place in The Race.

My journey with Habib, and our embrace of Buddhism and Chromotherapy comforts me now in the sanctuary of the cockpit. Here, alone, I imagine and consider the desires for magic in my life. Anger cannot exist here. With my 108-beaded Mala I will continue to recite *Om Mani Padme Hum*. And, of course, keep my eyes out for the last refueling ship.

I look forward to my acupuncture session with Dr. Watase. I might even see Ayame leaving and maybe Raya arriving to refuel as I will be, refueled and nourished, and heading out on the last leg of The Race.

The Spitfire floatplane is a very difficult aircraft to land, especially on the water. Even with the refurbished instrumentation and powerful engine and props, flying and landing this aircraft is a challenge. I have been quite pleased with myself for mastering my *Orange 3* so well. I was praised throughout training and it was difficult to suppress my ego and my happiness, although my happiness is something that I have earned.

Having landed at the refueling ship on this leg leaves me with one more takeoff and landing. The Golden Gate Bridge and San Francisco beckon. Dr. Kaz is full of surprises. During acupuncture, he told me that Keiko asked him to supply me with the coordinates for flying through what is called Cloud Nine as I lower my altitude in the approach to San Francisco. I hope I am able to continue acupuncture with him after this adventure is over and as Habib and I determine our path for the future. It will certainly involve working with Keiko and the other women.

Ayame in *Champagne 2* has refueled and departed long ago. I suppose flying on autopilot might have increased my flight time. Such is life. The meditation and thinking in the sanctuary of the cockpit throughout this adventure has been the most amazing experience of my life. Now, I have been cleared to depart and Raya Sol del Mundo in *Copper 4* is on approach. I bet that she will find the information on Cloud Nine funny, as I have observed that her head is often in the clouds, another reason to like that feisty woman! It was crazy how in training all of us dark-skinned ladies bonded together. Raya the Mexican, Ruth the Afro American… oops… the Black American in *Black 8,* and Nanibah the Native American… oops again… the American Indian in *Yellow 13*, and me! Ah… power to the dark ones! *Om Mani Padme Hum.*

In the air for this last leg… *Om Mani Padme Hum. Om Mani Padme Hum. Om Mani Padme Hum.* I remember the translation of *Om Mani Padme Hum* is roughly "Praise to the Jewel in the Lotus." I know that it is the mantra of compassion. The first known description of this mantra appears in the Karandavyuha Sutra of Mahayana Buddhism. Each of the six syllables represents one of the six realms of existence. Repeating it creates moments of peace and joy. It was nice to share this with the other pilots at our sporadic night training meetings. I especially hoped to learn more about young Piccola Uccello, a devout Catholic. While Piccola is very tied to her family, especially her mother, I don't even know who my mother and father were. I thought I had overcome that sadness, yet the love and support that several of the pilots shared with me about their families brought tears of joy to them, but a sting of pain for me. Arianna also shared that as she grew older, and with a supportive husband and two children, she expressed the profound joy of motherhood and family. It seems to me that this is the essence of the goddess, both nurturing loved ones and caring for the planet. Is this why they call it Mother Nature? Now I miss my husband and my dog Annie so much more. They are my family.

I worry about Annie these days. She is fifteen years old and for a medium-sized dog, a mix of Chow Chow and Golden Retriever, she is in pretty good shape. Her hips and rear leg muscles are starting to deteriorate and we have her on Rimadyl for inflammation and Tramadol for pain. She also receives acupuncture every two weeks that she seems to love. I hope Dr. Kaz will continue to treat her if synchronicity works in our favor. Annie also has a wheat allergy, which took us through some trying moments to figure out. For the last ten years she's had a pretty good diet and lots of love, which she gives back to us in so many wonderful ways. Annie walks with us without a leash because she is so mellow and well mannered. We only use a leash around other dogs and people who might be afraid of dogs. Like so many soulful animals with which we share the Earth, Annie has a remarkable vocabulary, and she stares at me when she wants to communicate. I call her our Buddha dog because she displays so much compassion and understanding. These days we use a ramp that she walks up when getting into the car or her bed at night. I take her on many short walks for her muscles. Habib has given her Chromotherapy as well. I also complement the acupuncture with daily physical therapy. Our veterinarian has told us this is the best we can do for Annie at this point in her life. She is our doggie daughter and I will need to go through therapy when she passes. I must continue to think of impermanence and live in every moment with her and Habib, *Om Mani Padme Hum.*

Autopilot and meditation have helped once again. I feel so comfortable in this cockpit, even with the challenging weather that is now upon me. I take back control of my floatplane once more and it actually is fun for me to dart around heavy cloud formations, although I am looking forward to flying through the heavenly sounding Cloud Nine that Kaz told me about.

Well, according to the state-of-the-art technology on this remarkable floatplane, I should start to descend. I think that the weather will also start to clear up for a nice entry into San Francisco, *Om Mani Padme Hum.*

Now at 7,890 feet and heading into Cloud Nine. I do feel the happiness effect, but I am a happy person to begin with, so all this is reinforced happiness. Hah, I smile at this line of thinking and what I feel at the moment. This Cloud Nine will be good for the other pilots to experience, *Om Mani Padme Hum.*

I have descended to 1,800 feet and the Golden Gate Bridge is visible ahead. I have come to terms with so many things and have so much to look forward to. At this moment, I am smiling with a sense of accomplishment and relief. My favorite story of Martine's is running in my head. A young monk arrives at a monastery. He is assigned to help the other monks copy the old canons and laws of the church by hand. He notices, however, that all the monks are copying from copies, not from the original manuscript. The new monk goes to the old abbot to question this, pointing out that if someone made even a small error in the first copy, it would never be picked up! In fact, that error would be continued in all of the subsequent copies. The head monk says, "We have been copying from the copies for centuries, but you make a good point, my son." He goes into the dark caves under the monastery where the original manuscripts are held inside a locked vault that hasn't been opened for hundreds of years. Hours go by and nobody sees the old abbot. So, the young monk gets worried and goes down to look for him. He sees him banging his head against the wall and wailing. "We missed the 'R'! We missed the 'R'! We missed the bloody 'R'!" His forehead is all bloody and bruised and he is crying uncontrollably. The young monk asks the Old Abbot, "What's wrong, father?" With a choking voice, the old abbot replies, "The word was CELEBRATE!"

Now the Golden Gate Bridge is before me and it is time to water-land my *Orange 3*. I did the celibate… now to celebrate! It's never too late to be in the moment, *Om Mani Padme Hum!* Namaste!

RAYA SOL DEL MUNDO

COPPER 4

When I was born, I was afflicted with a behavior that had no cure. If anyone but my mother picked me up, I would wail and throw up. I often threw up even when my mother held me, but I didn't wail. If I was hungry or wet, my cry was different. But if anyone, and many tried, besides my mother, picked me up, I'd scream and my vomit went everywhere.

At first they thought I was a colicky baby and my mother's *comadres* gave her one home remedy after another. Nothing worked. My poor mother even stopped breast-feeding me for a time, thinking it might be her milk, but when that didn't seem to have any positive results, she put me back on "the boob." She often tells the story, only among women, that her breasts were like Marilyn Monroe's. "*Asi!* Like this," she'd say and put her spread hands out about six inches in front of her breasts. "*Hay Dios mio!*" Everyone would laugh. "*Y tu esposo?* And your husband, did he ask for cookies?" More laughter! I had no idea what they thought was so funny until my best friend got pregnant in high school and was sent away after her breasts leaked in algebra class. Some jerk sitting behind me asked for cookies. That wasn't so funny.

My wailing stopped when I hit two. It was replaced by a silence and a look in my eyes that scared my family even more than my vomiting. I'd cry, someone would pick me up, and I'd suddenly stop crying and my eyes would stare as though I was looking at infinity. My mother saw it immediately, but went into denial because she was so happy that someone else could finally pick me up and I wouldn't wail and vomit. My *abuela* noticed too, but she was silent and only talked about those years to me when I was older.

As I got older, the same stare would be on my face when I was on the swings, or when I jumped rope for too long, or when I tried to climb trees. It was clear to my *abuela* that I had a problem with gravity.

That's why my passion for flying was a complete surprise to everyone. But, by the time I became a pilot, I understood my passion and the consequences. When I found out about The Race, I desperately wanted in.

When I was chosen, I didn't ask for a big supply of vomit bags. You know the kind. Every commercial flight has one tucked in the pocket in front of you with the *SkyMall* magazine offering overpriced gnomes for your front lawn. Those gnomes give me the creeps! Especially the new dog skeleton gnomes!

I secretly brought my own stash of bags. No one knew and I wasn't about to say, "By the way, if anyone needs vomit bags, I've got plenty!" As it turned out, I needed every single one of those bags during our six weeks of training.

Copper 4 was a challenge to fly. For those six weeks, my cockpit became my second home. *La Virgen de Guadalupe* took her place in the center of the control panel and my bags were secretly stashed right under my *Virgensita*. I cleansed the cockpit and body of the plane after every flight with sage from my newly adopted *comadre*, Nanibah, the American Indian pilot. We became fast friends when she asked if I might lend her my sage to cleanse her plane and we agreed to visit each other after The Race. It never occurred to either of us that one of us might not complete the flight. Personally, I thought Firoozeh, a questionable pilot, might not finish training. It was her negative attitude that seemed to hold her back. Yet her energy level was remarkable! Maybe some of her magical spiritual beliefs carried her through training. I told Nanibah that I had asked *La Virgensita* to look after Firoozeh in flight and she joined me in a short prayer to *Nuestra Señora de los Cielos*.

We became *comadres* during training even though we'd not baptized each other's children, the traditional path for becoming extended family in my community. Sometimes, when you have a strong bond with another woman, it's easy to use the affectionate "*comadre*" instead of her name. By the end of the training, I had three new *comadres*.

Training was arduous. I couldn't have finished if it hadn't been for Nanibah, Hamidah, and Ruth. We called ourselves the "dark skinned sisters." We'd crack jokes and carry on within our little "inner circle." Keiko wanted us all to bond and we did, but it was only natural that among some of us there was a closer affinity. For Nanibah, Hamidah, Ruth, and me, it was our self-defined "otherness" that we'd lived with all our lives as women of color. I had not been conscious of being an "other" during my childhood. Other kids would say things like, "You're not like other Mexicans," or "You're so lucky to have a natural tan." For a nanosecond I'd feel a barely perceptible twinge, an inner voice saying, "Red flag, not right, check it out!" But I'd ignore or suppress the feeling. I wanted to fit in so I agreed or just laughed when everyone else laughed. Now I can see that I was just beginning to sense how different I was. As a kid, it scared me and I hoped it would go away. Thankfully, I got over myself and hit full stride with a *Je ne sais quoi* approach to identity politics, feminism, and my "gift." While trying to stay empathetic, I distanced my feelings of self-consciousness and caring about what other people thought of me. That feeling was liberating.

I shared that "I don't care what you think of me" attitude with my "dark-skinned sisters." I will never forget them. I will always honor them. And I will grieve and miss them even after my physical form turns to ashes and is cast into wind.

During training I was immediately drawn to Ruth, one of the most experienced pilots of the group. A wise mentor used to say, "Surround yourself with people who know more than you, not people who know less, even though your ego may suffer." I followed that advice. With Ruth, it really paid off! I soaked up her knowledge. She didn't mind that I was constantly asking her, "Ruth, what should I do if I encounter this problem?" or "What advice can you give me about that problem?" Or sometimes, I'd make something up just to see her furrow her brow, trying to think of a response, and then look at me like "You must be kidding!" And, of course I was. But kidding aside, I was prepared and ready to go when told to board my plane and prepare to take off because I had had six weeks to watch, listen, and observe Ruth.

I was waved onto the sea dock at dusk. Several of my fellow pilots had preceded me. As I sat in the cockpit, I felt happy, knowing I'd be surrounded by the night sky. Night flying is far superior to daytime flying as far as I'm concerned. There's more mystery, magic, and possibilities for letting my mind go where it might encounter new visions that were untouched in previous adventures. This night was exceptional. A few light clouds would travel with me, otherwise the stars were brilliant in the Japanese sky.

As I waited my turn, two short-tailed albatrosses flew past my cockpit. I saw them clearly in the last rays of the sun and I wondered briefly why this young pair (they were the grey color of young albatrosses) was testing their wings so late in the day.

"Go ahead *Copper 4*. You are clear. Smooth flying with minor precipitation ahead."

I turned the key and thought about Hamidah. Even though older than the rest of us, she practically bounded into her cockpit. She missed her husband and her beloved dog, Annie. I hoped I'd see her in Honolulu but thought it unlikely, especially since both Habib and Annie would be there to greet her. I felt a pang of jealousy that she had someone waiting for her and I did not. But self-pity is not allowed in my life and my feelings of jealousy were mixed up with self-pity, so I mentally threw them out of the cockpit, which made me feel better. I hadn't been able to let go of my feelings so easily when it came to Keiko. My political activism has engrained in me a deep sense of skepticism. Even as I turned on the ignition of my lovely floatplane, I had lingering doubts about her motives.

Still, I felt guilty and embarrassed at my inherent sense of mistrust of her. I'd never met anyone who so willingly gave millions for a race without some self-interest. I wanted to believe in Keiko. I really did. Yet the question I couldn't answer, and that remained in the back of my mind for months prior to our first dinner, was why. What was Keiko's real motivation? No one does anything without a motive first provoked by self-interest. Was I honest about my motives? I couldn't claim total innocence this time. In the past, I was always "behind the eight ball" as they say. So often I realized after the fact that, while I was giving my all for *La Causa,* others were far ahead of me and using the same experiences for their PhDs and landing cushy jobs, speaking engagements, or book contracts. Me, I'd just pour my heart and soul into a major effort only to see others take the credit. What a burn!

Was Keiko seeking the same notoriety? At some point I came to terms with the fact that Keiko had money. She called the shots. What was I to gain? $250,000 was nothing to sneeze at after the recession took almost everything I'd squirreled away in property. "Property never loses value," said my smart financial advisor. Ha! The joke was on me and the millions of others who bought into the notion of permanence in a world increasingly divided by rich and poor, the have and have-nots, those who work for a paycheck and those who watch their portfolios get fatter while doing absolutely nothing in exchange.

Okay, the money certainly would help. I'd just spent five years and reams of paper to get a home loan modification, but it seemed that no one was giving home loan modifications! I didn't want to lose the one property I had left, my home. My father insisted I buy property. "*Mija,* buy a *casa*. Don't be like us, paying rent all our lives to buy someone else their piece of the American Dream. Buy a house!"

I had a tumultuous relationship with my father. I so wanted to please him. I wanted to prove that even though I was a girl, I would make him as proud of me as if I'd been a boy. Before I was born, my father and mother had names picked out for their first-born. My father, certain that I was a boy, wanted to name me Ray. My mother, certain I was a girl, wanted to call me Soledad because she felt so alone during her pregnancy. They called me *La Niña* for a month. My father finally decided that my name needed to please them both. So he named me Raya Sol.

His last name is Mundo. Raya Sol del Mundo means "Sun Ray of the World." My father had expectations. My mother was just glad to have her "light of the world." I would have been satisfied with just plain Luz. My father's expectations were a burden. I don't know whether my mother used birth control, but somehow she never got pregnant again after I was born. I felt guilty knowing that my infancy was so hard on my mother and I blamed myself that I never had siblings. On the other hand, I had my mother all to myself. I had all her stories, her lullabies and her full attention. Being an only child had some advantages, at least for as long as your mother will talk to you.

At an early age, my mother would tell me stories about México. She would tell me about the mountain volcano *Popocatétpetl* that rose above her town in Puebla. She would tell me the story of how *Popo* and *Iztaccíhuatl*, the mountains nearby, came to form an outline of two ill-fated lovers. Their mountain tops are usually seen in between the wafting clouds that surround them. She told me about the arrival of the Mother of México, who floated down to earth and emerged out of the clouds to tell Juan Diego to build a church where a temple once stood. She told me about *Quetzalcoatl*, the feathered serpent, and about the eagle devouring the serpent on a cactus in the Lake of Texcoco. Once I told my mother that I "saw" her stories from above. She was so startled that she called my *abuela* and spoke in Spanish so quickly that I could only understand a few of the words. "*Lo tiene! Que hacemos?*" My *abuela* rushed over. She didn't live far away and coaxed me into telling her what I saw. She told my mother. "*No te preocupes*. It won't hurt her. Send her to me next time." But the next time my *abuela* wasn't there. She had died of an aneurism months earlier and my mother stopped talking out of grief. My father would talk for my mother. Her silence became the new normal in our house.

My father had few stories. Later, I understood why. Eventually I realized that his stories and his refusal to visit the California missions was because his stories were buried there during the holocaust that killed his tribe and his heritage.

Flying became an obsession in my adolescence. As a fourteen-year-old female, my body began to change. Childhood curiosity turned to an inexplicable yearning for everything, including things I knew nothing about. Sex, love, euphoria, and disappointment. I wanted to stay in my childhood freedom where I could lie for hours and gaze at the clouds making shapes in the sky. I used my imagination to excel in school, especially in history and creative writing classes. "Good essay. Vivid first-person narratives. Keep up the good research for historical accuracy," etc. Those comments started in middle school and continued through college.

By the time I was seventeen, I had become self-conscious and was eager to please. I worried about how others saw me. I became restricted. Social norms dictated what good behavior was for a young lady. Still, I had recurring dreams of flying. I saw my body free of any physical bonds. I could soar in the sky and touch the clouds of my childhood. I wanted metaphorically to break free of gravity and literally break free of ties to any location. I wanted to soar above my "*mundo*," my world.

Later I realized that those dreams were prescient.

I found my chance at twenty-three. Or, he found me, Javier Ortega Galicia. Ten years older than my twenty-three, after leaving behind his very wealthy family and job (if you call following his older brother around the shop floor a job), Javier Ortega Galicia literally bumped into me at a Blockbuster in Los Angeles. Meeting Javier was destiny. He taught me how to fly, not knowing to what lengths I would take my new-found freedom. He was so smitten and to this day I don't know why, especially since, like most normal people, he hated the smell of vomit. The first time he took me up in his Cessna, he was empathetic. "Don't be embarrassed, Babe. I don't mind. It happens. It'll go away once you're more experienced." I wasn't surprised. I always knew I was different and not just because I had a "permanent tan," as my friends in high school used to say. As a kid, my being different scared me. I wanted "it" to go away when I found myself in another life and another time. Disconcerting is too tame a word for the feeling that would come over me each time I found myself somewhere else in another time. But I grew used to the experience and found pleasure in my observational post. I learned to scope out bathroom locations just in case. But Javier never got used to the blank stare let alone the putrid smell I left in his planes. Yes, he had more than one plane.

I never got used to his wealth. Call me crazy but except for the luxury of flying his planes, I never got used to his oblivion to the world we inherited. A world that despite the cultural revolution, the anti-war movement, the Chicano Civil Rights movement, and the ideals of the progressive movement, was a mess. The rich were richer and the poor, poorer. I saw people literally give their lives for justice. Even though he couldn't have had those experiences, there were other people, just as well off financially, who empathized and took action.

I didn't mention this experience of time and place movement to Javier or anyone—except Nanibah. It was an intentional omission in my application to The Race. Rather than be excluded in the select group of pilots, this elite corps, I skipped over the question "Any physical or mental concerns?" I did not want to be disqualified and I knew that keeping this one secret was important to my flight and to that of my fellow pilots. I "saw" my flight earlier in the year. I knew I'd be chosen, but only if I kept this one secret. Back then Javier thought I was delusional and I thought he was out of touch. It ended with Javier, yet I couldn't help but thank him as I peered into the night sky and felt my *Copper 4's* power and speed.

Good to be out of my past and in reality and in real time. Good to establish radio communication and to be guided to the first Mitsubishi refueling ship. Good to see the ship now and water-land *Copper 4* with no problems. I am told that comrade Hamidah in *Orange 3* is way ahead of schedule and doing well and has long left the refueling ship. I am just happy that I landed well and did not throw up. Now to fill my stomach and have Kaz refresh me with his acupuncture.

The sound of my plane was a consistent murmur that I'd hoped would put me in a meditative state. But for some reason, I began to feel distracted and edgy. I checked the controls. All was well, but one gauge seemed stuck on 00001968. I knew from previous experiences what was coming next, but why on this flight? Why was I going back to Tlatelolco? Then I threw up.

In 1967, a little known international treaty was signed at Tlatelolco. The Treaty of Tlatelolco, or the Treaty for the Prohibition of Nuclear Weapons in Latin America and the Caribbean, was drafted on February 14, 1967. Under the treaty, the parties agreed to prohibit and prevent the "testing, use, manufacture, production, or acquisition by any means whatsoever of any nuclear weapons" including "receipt, storage, installation, deployment, and any form of possession of any nuclear weapons." There are two additional protocols to the treaty. Protocol I binds those overseas countries with territories in the region (the United States, the United Kingdom, France, and the Netherlands) to the terms of the treaty. Protocol II requires the world's declared nuclear weapons states to refrain from undermining in any way the nuclear-free status of the region. It was signed by the U.S.A. the U.K., France, China, and Russia.

The treaty also provides for a comprehensive control and verification mechanism, overseen by the Agency for the Prohibition of Nuclear Weapons in Latin America and the Caribbean (OPANAL), based in México City. The nations of Latin America and the Caribbean drafted this treaty to keep their region free of nuclear weapons. The Treaty of Tlatelolco was the first time in history that such a nuclear weapon ban was put in place over such a vast, populated area. It was ratified by thirty-three countries throughout Latin America, Central America, and México. All parties agreed to not make or house nuclear weapons in an area including large portions of the Pacific and Atlantic oceans.

However, it is the event that took place at Tlatelolco on October 2, 1968, that still resonates with the Mexican people and supporters of other pro-democracy movements around the world. Very few know about the Treaty of Tlatelolco and those who do find it ironic that an agreement among nations, assuring a nuclear weapon-free zone, was signed in the very place where months later, a massacre would occur. The details of those events in 1968 are only just becoming clear with many questions still not answered. In 2008, the CIA revealed its knowledge of the Mexican government's plan, but whether there was U.S. involvement beyond sending arms and maintaining direct communication is unknown. Much of what was revealed in the disclosed documents of the Freedom of Information Act was, of course, blacked out.

It is now my first "visit" on October 2, 1968, in México City, Tlatelolco, Plaza de las Tres Culturas. There are hundreds of people in the large plaza with housing complexes and many-storied high office buildings surrounding the space.

"Sientese! Sit down!" I'm told.

Twice in the last twenty years, I've gone from the cockpit of my plane to the streets of México City, both times on October 2, 1968, both times in Tlatelolco. It makes no sense, but I can't reverse the action. I'm not able to change anything that happens. The first time I found myself observing the events of October 2, I returned and found that the treaty of 1967 existed. I assumed my own blood ties to ancient cultures, or perhaps our even older beliefs in the power of nature to intervene when the balance of our natural environment is threatened, took me to Tlatelolco so I could later discover the Treaty. It might be because my parents both have long ties to old cultures.

When I first found myself in Tlatelolco, I was on a short trip from Austin to San Francisco. It was spring and I was returning from dropping off rescue dogs, mutts really, to a farm outside of Austin. I was leaving at dusk to make the several hours' flight back to the Bay Area. I looked at my controls and one gauge seemed stuck at 0001968. In an instant I was on the ground with people running and muffled screams. I looked around and called to them but they seemed not to know I was there. I realized then that I'd been transported to… where? I wasn't sure, and when? I had even less of a clue. There was panic and I heard gunshots and the rat-a-tat-tat of semi-automatic weapons. People began to fall around me. Farmacia Tlatelolco. Abarottes Tlatelolco. Tortellia Tlatelolco. I read the names of the storefronts located on the first floor of the multi-storied building. I recognized the languages—Nahuatl and Spanish.

It seemed like a long stay that first visit to Tlatelolco, but it was actually only a brief encounter with history. I was back in my pilot's seat with hours to go before landing. It was that quick, but not so quick that I dismissed it as a fluke. I landed and immediately went straight to the library at UCLA to look up anything having to do with México, Tlatelolco, 1968. That is where I found my first piece of this history— the Treaty. I became intrigued with the contrast between a peaceful nuclear-free zone and the violence I'd witnessed. In 1967 there was a little known effort to curb the growth of nuclear weapons in the Southern Hemisphere, followed by the ensuing carnage months later at the hands of a violent, anti-democratic government. Tlatelolco was just the tip of what was to come to young idealistic students, intellectuals, artists, and anyone who sought social and political justice in Latin America.

Tlatelolco is a Nathuatl word meaning "in the little hill of land." Pre-Conquest ruins were found there, along with a church called Templo de Santiago, a former convent church built on top of the Spanish ruins from the 17th century. A large housing project, office buildings, and government offices were built on this site in the 1960s and surround the ruins and the church. The area now has a second identity as Plaza de las Tres Culturas or Plaza of Three Cultures.

In the UCLA library, I discovered that in April 1967, the external political face of many of the signatory countries to the Treaty of Tlatelolco was quite different from the internal authoritarian politics most of these countries engaged in at home. In México, August,1968, a disagreement between two student populations in México turned physical, leading to an unimaginable intervention by government forces. The army invaded the campus, an act that shocked many because of the historically acknowledged autonomy and neutrality of institutions of higher learning from government presence.

My second "visit" to Tlatelolco was a jolt. Once I realized I was in a voyeur state, I calmed down and watched. Gunfire was ringing all around. Young men and women were falling and not getting up. And then as suddenly as I had arrived, I was back. I needed to know more. I researched further.

From August to October 1968, in México City, hundreds of thousands organized, peacefully marched, and held meetings demanding true democracy, the release of political prisoners and an open government in México. On October 2nd, with the Olympic Games fast approaching, the Mexican government planned and carried out a two-hour attack on students, housewives, college professors and simple, ordinary people who had gathered in the square of Tlatelolco to hear the speakers on the third-story balcony of one of the buildings. The assembly had been peaceful. For months prior to this gathering on October 2nd, the spontaneity of gatherings and the earnest efforts of the students captivated hundreds of ordinary people. The students created "brigades" consisting of four to five people. They would hop on buses, with the driver's approval, to hand out leaflets and they stood on México City's busy intersections engaging in person-to-person political discourse.

It is this student massacre that resonates to this day in modern México. For me, it's my past consciousness awaking to a new world that until the 1950s was hidden or perhaps denied in our oh-so-wonderful lives in sunny California. What did we know or what did we care about war in far away places?

This time, my third visit, the hum of my engine is replaced by chanting voices. I find myself with people sitting on the outcropping of walls or on the ground. Many held hand-painted banners. The voices are those of mostly students but also of some men in suits and women with shopping bundles and a few children. I'm on edge. It's not only because of my gift for moving in and out of time and space that has brought me back to Tlatelolco, but because of some presence that I've picked up. The atmosphere is mixed with fear and apprehension.

I've been engulfed in the time and space of the México City massacre before. This time is different. When this happened before, I was like a phantom. People were unaware of my presence as they marched into the plaza and the space began to fill up with thousands of chanting demonstrators.

But this time, I am physically present and well aware that I am in danger. I find the speakers standing on one of the balconies of the housing project, megaphones in hand, leading chants and calling in the marchers.

"*Raya Sol! Agachate! Escondate! CORRE!*"

"*Raya Sol!* Tuck! Hide! RUN!!!"

Who knew my name? Was I visible this time, or was that my own voice I heard among the others running and hiding to flee those identified by their white gloves? We understood too late who they were. My breathing is cutting my throat. I feel I'm about to fall.

It's my plane! I am descending. I'm back in the cockpit. I'm alone somewhere over the Pacific, far away from Tlatelolco. I'm not so sure now that keeping my secret from Keiko was such a wise idea, but it's too late to turn back.

"Raya Sol. Raya Sol. Your decent into Honolulu is erratic. Raya Sol?" It was Keiko's voice. She never personally spoke to us while in flight unless absolutely necessary and Keiko was supposed to be flying to San Francisco.

"Keiko?"

"Yes. I'm here. Level out, Raya Sol. You need to level out and receive landing orders. Is that clear?"

It was only then that I noticed how low my Spitfire had descended.

"Raya Sol? Did you receive my last message? You must level out and land immediately. Your fellow pilots are behind you. Your successful landing is imperative." That was a jolt. Keiko must be having doubts. I know she's aware of other dimensions that some of us travel in from time to time. Arianne had spoken about the existence of parallel worlds during our training. She had also spoken about magic, but I kept silent. My experiences with other dimensions were not of a spiritual nature. They were experiences with ordinary people who had had enough, *"Basta!"* I hope Keiko hasn't lost what little confidence she had in me.

Copper and I leveled out. A successful landing on Oʻahu confirmed my assumptions about Hamidah. She'd landed before me and was off with Habib and Annie. I saw her briefly when she left her acupuncture session, walking past me with a quick hug and kiss on her way to spend precious moments with her family. She had just enough time to say that Ruth was doing fine, there was no surprise there, but that she hadn't heard about Nanibah. After a refueling by the expert technicians and what seemed like too short a session with Kaz, and his needles were never more needed, I climbed back into the cockpit for the third and longest leg of our journey.

As I prepared for takeoff, my thoughts went back to Nanibah. We grew very close during training. I learned about her cancer and she knows about my "gift." Nanibah wasn't surprised when I told her that I experience travel to different dimensions. She told me my talent, she called it a "talent," was from my father and my mother since my families carry Indian DNA on both sides. She'd met members of her tribe who had had similar experiences especially during ceremonies. She seemed a bit distant when I asked about her peoples' ceremonies. Our tribe had none. They didn't survive the centuries of indigenous eradication.

That's when she told me about the healing ceremonies performed by the medicine men on her reservation. Using the abbreviation of reservation, "rez," she told me, "I will return to the rez after The Race for more traditional healing ceremonies. I will also continue to receive chemo and other Western medicine treatments." And then halfheartedly, "Better living with chemistry." We both laughed!

I thought about taking off from Oʻahu for Nanibah's reservation and meeting her there. I wanted to spend more time with her knowing it was finite. I needed to hear more about her personal guiding philosophy that seemed somehow like "secular spiritualism" if that term even exists. Maybe after The Race.

Copper and I soared. The sky is filled with Cumulus clouds. I'm nearing cruising altitude, 19,680 feet. Glancing down I see the bluest, clearest Pacific Ocean cut by sludge of darkest brown muck. Its trail went as far as the horizon on the east. It makes me terribly sad. My thoughts wander and the name "Point Huron" bounces around my head. Point Huron… aren't we landing at Point Richmond? Yes, of course. I will make it.

Fifty plus years ago, a group of idealistic students gathered at Point Huron to write a manifesto calling for democracy, open government and an end to the Vietnam War. The result was the Point Huron Statement. Later a group of *Chicanos* gathered in Denver to write the Plan *Espiritual de Aztlan*. The Black Panther Party Platform and Program was written in 1966. The American Indian Movement traveled to Washington in 1972 on the Trail of Broken Treaties Caravan with their Twenty-Point Position Paper. Millions marched, chanted, prayed, and signed petitions for what was then essentially known then as "self-determination."

We spoke for the billions of the voiceless. This time, could our group of pilots speak for Tonantzin, Mother Earth? Or should we be more humble and listen to her? She is speaking. She is protesting. She is calling attention to injustice. We have droughts, crazy snow in Georgia, bristling heat in England, and glaciers melting, breaking apart and falling into the ocean.

I start thinking of my friend, Nora. I lived in México at the time and Nora helped me understand that handouts didn't ever create a revolution. Since then I have understood that social justice is not a commodity. History is replete with efforts, some successful, most not, at making the world a better place. The true price paid was not in green bills, but in red blood given by young and old, men and women, intellectuals, and farmers. Yet we are now facing a real threat that Keiko and her seemingly endless resources can help stop. Imagine if the others, the other "1%" (capital IF here) relinquished their millions, no their billions, to clean our oceans, keep the snowy mountains cold, and worked to create a world where the phrase "extinct species" is itself an outdated distinction.

Nora is dead, killed by a soldier in the service of Augusto Pinochet. She is one of thousands killed in Santiago after the military coup on September 11, 1973, leaving Chile's elected President, Salvador Allende, dead and their national poet, Pablo Neruda in self-imposed exile and deep mourning. Nora was a fighter. She believed so deeply in justice and social change that her whole persona exuded unwavering confidence in the belief that a people united will never be defeated.

Time has passed so fast. As I descend for one last refueling, I "see" Keiko standing on the cliff overlooking the San Francisco Bay from the Marin Headlands. She carries herself with that same self-assured confidence. I was mistaken about Keiko. I see Nora standing beside her. They wait. Nora waits for justice. Keiko waits for us all to make it back safely after ironing out our difficulties.

Copper is ready to depart. Her tanks are full. Food was good and acupuncture wonderful, Dr. Kaz is so very nice to me. He hints at flying through what he calls Cloud Nine. I am ready.

As I soar into the sky one last time I know that I will stay on course. No more travels. They have served their purpose. My attention is now totally focused on my cockpit gauges and the hum of *Copper's* engines. I won't need any airsickness bags for this leg of the flight.

I think of my *abuela* and wonder what words she may have spoken to me about this "gift" I have. She didn't seem to fear for me. I like to think she knew that I would be different, but that my difference would be a good thing if I could work though the fear and the loneliness.

The last thousand miles seem to fly by. I can see the smallest hint of the Pacific Coast. I'm going to finish! The land is closer and I look at my gauges to check on fuel, speed, and descent. From the left window I'm surprised to see a flock of mature, short-tailed albatrosses flying east. It is rare to see the short-tailed kind, which have only within the last few years begun showing up on the Farallon Islands. I briefly wonder why they are heading east and not northwest toward home. The thought is fleeting as *Copper* heads straight for Cloud Nine.

Emerging out of the cloud, I am euphoric. I think I feel the wheels hit the ground but something is wrong. *Copper* is weaving against all my efforts to control her. The landing strip is moving, making my landing nearly impossible. In the horizon I see sudden bursts of smoke and what appears to be lightning, but the bursts of electricity are coming from the ground not the sky. I imagine hearing the voice from the control tower calmly directing my next actions.

"*Copper 4*… Earthquake… Ascend immediately… Now!" The last order is urgent.

I accelerate speed and lift off the runway. Looking back I see smoke rising from the Marina. The mountains are moving. The ocean retreats. Fires are moving quickly through the Central Valley. I see steam rising from the Diablo Canyon Nuclear Power

Plant, the San Onofre Nuclear Generating Station, the Rancho Seco Nuclear Generating Station, and from leaks in dry casks stored at the Humboldt Bay Nuclear Power Plant. Farms are gone. Carcasses of dead animals remain on the miles and miles of uninhabitable, once beautiful, California forests.

Keiko's voice brings me back from the trance. All my "visions" have been of the past. I am hoping this was not a foreboding vision of the future.

"Raya Sol!" Keiko is standing in a small sailboat near *Copper's* wing. In her arms she's holding a spectacular lei of Hawaiian plumerias. Her voice and the fragrance of hundreds of flowers startle me. My tears make it difficult to see her.

"Your water landing wasn't perfect, but you'll have time to fix that. Let's go. You are the fourth pilot to successfully finish and we have eleven more to wait for. Your friend Hamidah waits for you on the dock. Let's go clean up and wait for the others. I'm looking forward to talking with you all about the next adventure."

"I'm anxious for Nanibah to arrive," I say not completely recognizing my own voice. "She'll land in a few hours, won't she?"

Keiko looks at me for a moment before replying. "Nanibah's journey may take longer. She will join us as soon as she can. This *lei* is from her."

That's when I noticed the note attached to the string of flowers...

Dearest Raya Sol,
Plumerias are the flowers of new beginnings.
Press the petals of one blossom between the pages of your favorite book of poetry.
It will make an imprint like a photograph.
Frame it and think of me always.
See you soon.
Love, your sister,
Nanibah

JANET TOMIKO MOCHIZUKI

PEACH 5

It is exactly 6:55 a.m., and I am ready. Strapped snugly into *Peach 5's* cockpit, I murmur a quick prayer to the *Amaterasu o-mikami* amulet that I've hung from a knob on the control panel for clear vision, stamina, and good fortune. The previous four take-offs from Haneda have gone smoothly and the sun goddess has blessed us with a spectacular 5:30 a.m. sunrise that has drenched the seas with a shining, iridescent glow. This truly is the land of the rising sun, where on this radiant morning I feel an ancient connection to its mountains, fields and sea, a deep riptide of ancestral memory tugging at my heart.

As I am cleared for takeoff, I think of the pilots who have come before me, including my grandfather, who spent time on this very site as a flight instructor teaching young Imperial Navy recruits during World War II, my fellow women pilots in The Race, and my aviator idols, Amelia Earhart, Thea Rasche, Beryl Markham, and Ruth Nichols. Also, the Japanese pilots who sacrificed their lives for their Emperor-god. With them, though not truly among them, is my mother, who felt the pull of the sky, but never achieved her dream of becoming a pilot.

After many dinners, meetings, and the grueling hours of flight training in the retrofitted floatplanes, I feel an immense sense of happiness and relief. Our last acupuncture session yesterday with Dr. Kaz soothed my tired muscles, knotted anew from the day's punishing workout. Then came a long soak in the scalding waters of the *onsen* at the Tokyo Himemiya Hotel, complete with high-definition wall projections of the gentle mountains of Hakone, ablaze in fall colors, and the crisp air pierced occasionally by the high-pitched, staccato tweet of a recorded meadow bunting.

At least sixteen hours of blissful solo flight before me! It is a chance to quiet my unruly mind, reconsider the many thought-provoking conversations our variegated group has had, and to turn my attention to my headstrong mother. How much like my gifted mother they are, these women pilots, how they conjure up her image to me!

"Haneda, ground, Mitsubishi Spitfire floatplane *Peach 5*, southwest bay, request taxi for departure."

"Waters are calm, you are cleared for takeoff *Peach 5*," comes the crisp voice of the English translator Keiko Kobahashi has provided for us, in keeping with her demonstrated ability to nail down every last detail and possible glitch that might arise on our trans-Pacific journey.

I feel like Mistress of the Universe, the keys to my fate spread out before me on the floatplane's glowing control panel. The screen of the Garmin GPS turns from mottled gray, green and blue to completely sky blue as I head south, clear Yokosuka and head due east over the open sea.

Yokosuka is where my grandfather, Isamu Mochizuki, made his name as a fighter pilot. Whenever I fly, my grandfather is the pilot ghost who dominates my thoughts. Not the gnarled, lonely man he was at the end of his life, but the young patriot who eagerly enlisted in the Imperial Navy at age nineteen and eventually became a revered figure famous for his outstanding air combat techniques and indomitable fighting spirit. As one historian called him, "The very epitome of pilots posted to the fighter units' Mecca, the Yokosuka Air Base." Peerless as a dogfighter, he invented the half loop and roll technique (*hineri-komi giho*), and could handle the extraordinarily light-weight, highly maneuverable Mitsubishi Zero fighter plane better than anyone else. I imagine his spirit somewhere nearby, chuckling at the fact that Mitsubishi money and mechanics have put me aloft as well, but for very different reasons.

As a teenager growing up in a farming village in Saga Prefecture, Kyushu, Isamu, the son of an old samurai family, fell madly in love with a quiet, bookish girl named Shizue Ōkubo. Two people couldn't have been more different. He was athletic, intelligent, but not intellectual, someone who saw things in black and white and got things done. Captain of the judo club and a leader in both school government and the execution of practical jokes, he stood out.

A picture of my grandmother, on the other hand, could have been found in the dictionary to illustrate the meaning of the word "wallflower." Shy to the point of muteness (at least in her telling, her mischievous eyes perhaps hinting at exaggeration), she would slink around the school, head down, hoping not to be noticed. Oddly, her shyness would fall away whenever she read her poetry out loud, and she won local renown for her ethereal *haiku* and *tanka* poems, as evanescent as dreams that escape us upon waking.

At first Isamu only wanted to use her, she said. In 1922, when Isamu was sixteen, he strode up to Shizue at the end of one school day in April. "*Oi!* Pigtails! Teacher says I'm going to flunk *kokugo* (ancient Japanese literature and culture) if I don't start getting better grades. You're the best *kokugo* student in the school. Will you help me? I need to get high marks in order to have a hope of passing the Imperial Navy entrance exam." Two years younger than Isamu and too terrified to refuse, she meekly assented. Their odd courtship played out over Isamu's last two years of high school, Shizue acting as the stern taskmaster during their study sessions in the school library, which gradually increased in length, then acting as a proper young *ojōsan* afterward. She attended local festivals to watch Isamu beat the taiko drums with the drum corps, and he (still a suitor then) attended her *tanka-kai* poetry readings as her invited guest.

Devout Emperor worshipers, Isamu's family raised him to believe that the highest calling he could aspire to was to fight Japan's foreign enemies, and if necessary, die. Shizue's father Zenji, a high school principal and a peace activist, felt the relationship was doomed because of the families' stark differences. Though both sets of their parents attempted to discourage the budding romance, neither succeeded. During those early years, when democracy was in the air and Japan seemed bent on peaceful negotiations with its neighbors in the Pacific, no one could anticipate how things would change and how much those differences would matter.

In the big city, liberated young women in flapper garb flaunted their freedom and courted as they pleased, but in small-town Kyushu, the old ways prevailed. There was no chance of even a private meeting between the soon-to-be star-crossed lovers. Still, through passed notes, meaningful glances and their increasingly frequent study sessions, their romance grew, not at a hot-house pace, but more as a sapling, sheltered from the harsh elements in a crevice of a sheer mountain cliff, slowly takes root.

My grandfather graduated from high school, and thanks in part to my grandmother, breezed through the entrance exams for the naval academy. At basic training in Etajima, his goal was to emerge from a rigorous weeding out process as a fighter pilot trainee, not as someone marked for service as a navigator or an aircraft carrier-based fighter. When the time came, he was overjoyed to be picked to pilot bomber planes and wrote to Shizue, "I am one step closer to achieving my dream of bringing glory to Japan!"

Upsetting as these pronouncements were to Shizue, she kept them to herself, knowing they would alarm and infuriate her father, who was devoting more and more of his time to protesting the escalating incursions of rogue Japanese officers into Manchuria. Zenji's hopes for the emergence of a peaceful civil society wilted as he became increasingly worried by the stirrings of the nationalist and militaristic movements that threatened the fragile democracy established during the reign of Emperor Taisho.

International events lent growing influence to the extreme right-wing, including the Great Depression, trade barriers erected by the United States, and *coup d'etat* attempts by ultranationalist secret societies. The changing winds of politics directly threatened Zenji. As the leader of the local pacifist club, he first detected a shift in atmosphere at his Buddhist temple, when elders began snubbing him. Social invitations declined, then stopped. Soon, threatening glances and whispers followed the Ōkubos wherever they went.

Then on May 15, 1932, came the fateful incident that ended the Ōkubo's lives in Japan, and should have ended Shizue's relationship with Isamu. Eleven junior naval officers went on a rampage. They entered the prime minister's Tokyo residence and assassinated him, moving on to attack the home of the Lord Keeper of the Privy Seal, and then to the headquarters of the pro-government Rikken Seiyukai. They even tossed hand grenades into the headquarters of Mitsubishi Bank. If there was any question before that the military was now firmly in control of Japan, there was no longer.

The Ōkubos huddled around their warm *kotatsu* and wept over the news. They knew they were no longer safe in Saga, which had always been conservative but now was fully in the grip of the imperialist mania sweeping the country. No one mentioned Isamu, but Shizue knew what they were thinking, "It was HIS fellow Navy officers who have blood on their hands." Even though the assassins were six years Isamu's junior and part of the ultra-rightist faction that he tried to steer clear of, they shared the same determination to worship the God Emperor Hirohito and combat what they viewed as the egotism inherent in capitalism and modernity.

Numb with shock, Shizue tried to defend Isamu to her family, but her talk of his kindness and concern for her was brushed off as so much senseless noise. "Shizue-chan, you must never speak to him again," the normally soft-spoken Zenju roared at his daughter. "He is part of the military system that is tarnishing Japan's reputation throughout Asia. Our family must wash our hands of anyone who is complicit in their fanaticism!" His hands were shaking. Shizue remained silent, unwilling to assent to her father's demands.

For the sake of breaking the couple up, but even more, to save themselves from stepped-up persecution and possible imprisonment, they began behind-the-scenes talks with those who could help arrange passage out of Japan and political asylum in America. Because of the exclusion act that the U.S. government had passed in 1924, this was the only way they could enter the United States, the country that Zenji admired most for its democratic ways. It took almost a year of constant talks and negotiations on Zenji's part, but the next April, Shizue, Zenji and her mother, Satae, traveled by train to Yokohama. There they boarded the cargo ship *Nihon Maru* for their ten-day passage to San Francisco. As tears streamed down their faces, they waved their handkerchiefs at no one in particular, but to the country they loved. Not a soul was there to see them off.

Isamu was not far away, though. From the Naval base at Yokosuka, he had been busy flying sorties to China, where chaos fomented by ultra-militarists in the Japanese army had led to the Japanese takeover of Manchuria. Beneath her light wool coat, Shizue felt for the rice paper envelope holding the picture of Isamu he had sent her from Yokosuka, depicting him smiling jauntily, dressed in khaki colored flight gear and a black cap. He had been distraught at the news of her departure, but recognized that her family, now branded as pacifists unwilling to defend the Emperor, would be in danger if they stayed in Japan. "We will find each other when this is all over," he assured her confidently.

My thoughts, so free to wander in the vast blue of the sky goddess, return to the flight at hand, and I focus on the circular gray mirage formed by the Aero-Vee propeller in front of me. Despite my 454 mile-per-hour speed and the fact that I am now 26,000 feet above the Pacific Ocean, I feel the protection of *Amaterasu o-mikami*. The state-of-the-art Garmin instrumentation doesn't hurt either, making me feel omniscient and goddess-like. *Peach 5's* de-icing and heating systems are operating beautifully. I murmur my thanks to Christine Banfield and the deities of sky and sun. Only 500 miles to the first Mitsubishi fueling ship!

Five hours have passed, and I feel clearer and freer than I have in months. Thinking of my fellow pilots, I imagine us all claiming different folds of the blue sky, spiritually in tune with each other from our long training and communal dinners. So powerfully that it leaves me breathless for a few moments, I suddenly understand what Keiko intended when she conceived of The Race, the deep discussions, the sharing that went on down below, now the aloneness, the emptiness of the sky. We are at one with the essence of Buddhism, of *mu,* nothingness, pure human awareness. Away from the noise of the world and the worldly, we are free to muse on our histories, our familial conflicts and our doubts, desires and messy lives, and then to let them float away, as in one grand group sky meditation. In this state of nothingness, can we transcend our worldly lives and self-absorption and forge one of the "parallel universes" that Hamida spoke of? It is a humbling thought.

I nose *Peach 5* through a thick quilt of gray cotton ball clouds, sensing the powerful whir of the Griffon engine—muted by my headset—more through my body than my ears. Christine and the two excellent women flight instructors she recruited schooled us well in handling the unique torque of the retrofitted floatplanes. My maneuvering the stick and rudder comes as naturally as the automatic actions of a rider navigating a favorite horse through a well-rehearsed barrel race. A moment after *Peach 5* touches water, a gleaming silver ramp appears magically, connecting the cockpit door to the deck of the ship, where the smiling team of engineers is lined up, bowing their welcome. Though an hour to fill up my fuel tank seems short, I immerse myself in a luxurious fifteen-minute shower followed by a twenty-minute acupuncture session with Dr. Kaz as if it were a full day at a spa. A quick snack of rations that could politely be termed "space food" follows (although admittedly, rehydrated tofu, burdock, and lotus root are a lot better than a soggy grilled cheese sandwich!), and then it's back into the cockpit for the next leg of my flight. I look forward to seeing the greenness of O'ahu and feeling its lush, moist air.

As I ascend through the heavy cloud cover, it's as though the same spell is cast over me that made the hours of the first leg of the flight fly by. Up, up, up in the air, back, back, back in time, I am lulled into a powerful dream state by the emptiness of the sky and the hum of my Griffon.

Life for Shizue and her parents was dauntingly new and difficult in America, where the Great Depression had cast a pall over the nation. Unable to resume his profession as a school administrator, Zenji, Satae, and Shizue picked up whatever work they could find. Zenji unpacked vegetables from crates and worked on gardening crews while Satae and Shizue took in mending and alteration jobs from well-to-do white ladies. Eventually they scraped together enough money to open a small fish market near Post and Laguna Streets in San Francisco's Nihonmachi district. They were grateful for the tightly interwoven Japanese community that surrounded them, with its own newspaper, language school for children, the Japanese American Citizen's League to help immigrants with legal and immigration problems, and a new Buddhist temple about to go up just two blocks away. Throwing themselves into community events and fundraising festivals, they clung tightly to their own people in a country where they were considered fit only for work as domestics and farmhands. At night Shizue wrote *tanka* poems at the kitchen table to submit to the *Nichibei Shimbun*. Many of them, like this one, gave her an outlet in which to make veiled references to Isamu.

Every day
I look up at the changing sky
Scanning the heavens
For the smallest sign
One day it will come

Isamu, meanwhile, who had made a name for himself in the second Sino-Japanese War, was serving as an instructor for the Kasumigaura naval aviator preparatory course, which was launched to keep Japan competitive with the West in the skies as well as on land and sea. A grizzled elder already, he was demanding yet humane in his treatment of the fourteen-to-seventeen-year-old greenhorns under his tutelage. While some instructors were known to verbally humiliate and beat their charges with bats, Isamu's unquestioned flying abilities and teaching skills were held in such high regard by all that he needed only to stare down a grumbling or lackadaisical trainee for them to suddenly snap to attention.

When in December 1937 *The New York Times* broke the story of the shocking atrocities committed by the Japanese army in what became known as the Rape of

Nanking, Shizue and her parents were sickened. Almost too horrific to believe, accounts of rampant killing by bayonet, machine gun, and burning prisoners alive, as well as the rape of children and women, trickled out of China. The *Times* correspondent wrote, "By despoiling the city and population, the Japanese have driven a repressed hatred deeper into the Chinese that will smolder through tears as forms of the anti-Japanism that Tokyo professes to be fighting to eradicate from China."

Shizue wrote in her notebook:

A spider casts its vermillion shadow on
The snowy chrysanthemum
From its center, an army of hatchlings rises
I hear cries of anguish in my sleep.

She wondered what Isamu's thoughts were when he heard the news.

The landscape of war was changing so rapidly, though, that the Ōkubos could not dwell for long on the far-away tragedy. With every ruthless advance Japan made in Asia, the Ōkubos could feel the skin of Nihonmachi tighten a little more, like squeezing a tomato until it bursts. The few white customers who had patronized their store began to fall away, and the Japanese community turned inward, moving through their school and work days in a fog of anxiety and foreboding, huddling around their radios for the latest news at night.

The bombing of Pearl Harbor was like a spade tearing through the delicate flesh of Nihonmachi. Overnight, FBI agents began rounding up community leaders. Shizue's parents made her burn all her letters from Isamu, which only served to engrave them permanently in her mind where they would always be safe. A few months later, Shizue and her parents found themselves on a bus that deposited them in a concentration camp in the desolate central Utah desert. Weaker prisoners fell ill or went "funny in the head," some were carted off and never seen again. The Ōkubos survived their three-year ordeal by working—Shizue as a nurse's aide and Zenji as a calligraphy teacher to classes of prisoners, whose fierce desire to keep the culture of their home-land alive, had led to a flowering of literary and artistic creations. Satae, meanwhile, worked as a seamstress to the inmates. To create a sense of home, the family collected scraps of wood to build furniture for their barrack, Satae ordered fabric from the Montgomery Ward catalog, made and hung curtains. They collected and displayed arrowheads, petrified rocks and cacti. They tamed nature and created an oasis in this parched, god-forsaken land, where Shizue continued to write poems and submitted her poetry to the camp newspaper, *Topaz Times,* for publication.

On the other side of the world, Isamu received orders to serve as division officer in the newly formed Air Group 281 and was stationed in the northern Kuriles. From there, he was called to aid in what was becoming a desperate situation for the Japanese in the Marshall Islands and was sent to the island of Roi in the South Pacific. American forces had already invaded and occupied the territory, laying waste to Japanese garrisons and killing large numbers of Japanese soldiers and civilians through starvation. Carrier raids, meanwhile, had destroyed most of Japan's air defense. By the time fresh U.S. troops arrived on February 6, 1944, to smoke out the last remaining Japanese on Roi, there was no means of escape by land or by sea.

Although the Ōkubos had lost all contact with Isamu at the start of war, among his family in Japan and in the local Saga press, he was presumed to have died a glorious death on that day with his fellow air group members, who mounted a *gyokusai* banzai suicide attack on the enemy. In fact, as certain death loomed and his comrades rushed through the smoke, shattering sounds of artillery fire and inhumanly savage war cries, a strange thing happened to Isamu.

He heard Shizue's calm, soft voice calling him, urging him to lay down his arms and turn around. Her solemn eyes and round cheeks rose through the smoke and debris that rained down around him, and he felt a strange peacefulness and an intense longing to see Shizue again. Like many Japanese officers, he believed it was likely that he would be tortured or killed if he was taken prisoner, but he reasoned that was only just, but however, if by some miracle he survived, he might one day see Shizue again. This is how it happened that, to his everlasting shame, he ended up not in the heaven reserved for warriors who die with honor, but among the fifty-one of the original 3,500 Japanese troops on the islands of Roi-Namur to be captured.

Several days later, Isamu was shoved without ceremony into the confines of the gritty Honouliuli POW camp on West Oʻahu, which also served as a concentration camp for U.S. citizens that the FBI identified as being of Japanese descent. They called Honouliuli "Hell Canyon." Despite the interrogations, my grandfather later said that the tents and pit latrines in the POW camp were several steps above the primitive conditions he and his comrades endured on those final days on Roi. What he left unsaid was that the harsh treatment was nothing compared to the mental self-flagellation he subjected himself to every day, burning with shame and trying to escape to an imagined parallel universe where he had died with honor on Roi and was enjoying the fruits of the Plain of High Heaven. But earthly Isamu also ate cheese for the first time in his life at Honouliuli, and endured the monotony of prison life by organizing judo competitions among the prisoners and penning letters to Shizue that he was unable to send as postal privileges were reserved for U.S. citizen prisoners only.

Cut off from all news from home and the front, he still prayed fervently for a Japanese victory despite the fact that he knew that his country, its war chest depleted and people starving, was falling far short of the production they needed to stay in the war. He also knew that he and his comrades had been sent on a suicide mission to delay the advance of American troops to the Marianas, the Philippines, and Guam.

What he didn't know, however, was that the Emperor he worshipped, who himself lacked education and any sense of duty, had referred to those he ordered to fight and to die for him as "childish," and "selfish." On an oppressively humid day in August 1945, the monotony of prison camp was broken by an excited hum coming from a nearby military guard tower. From what Isamu could glean, a giant bomb had been dropped on Hiroshima. The end of the war, the American soldiers crowed, was all but assured.

As my thoughts return to Oʻahu, I see the island appear on the Garmin, a lush green oasis. My landing proceeds without incident, and when I step out of the cockpit and onto the ramp, the island's moist air wraps me in its embrace. A smiling member of the crew places a lei made of lavender and white orchids around my neck. I ask for news of the pilots who have preceded me, and the bilingual head engineer winks at me and says, "Ms. Banfield and the famous archaeologist Ryoichi-san were very happy to see each other. And Señorita del Mundo was a big hit with the crew. She reminded them of Penelope Cruz. I had to restrain a few of them from asking for autographs."

The shower, the acupuncture and the semi-palatable food already seem routine to me. And as relaxing as the pit stop is, I am surprised to find I'm eager to take flight again, almost like an avid dreamer who is awakened mid-adventure and longs to plunge back into sleep and the dream world. This dream world is not just an escape, though. Deep in my bones, I know without these hours of sustained flight, the rest of my destiny will not be able to unfold, whether it is on this earth, or in that mystical parallel world that my fellow aviators and I search for. I thank the friendly crew and try to center my thoughts as I wait for the clamp to release *Peach 5* and set me free once again.

As I rise above the clouds and see them unfurl like a vast fleece blanket below, I recall a line from Amelia, referring to the long distance of her flight "being measured in clouds, not water," as a reminder of my kinship with her and my co-competitors in The Race. It's easy to believe that up in this realm, we women are not only equal to men, but perhaps even its rightful sovereigns, the Amaterasus of our age.

News that the war ended was bittersweet for my grandfather. Isamu felt a deep sense of shame that he had survived the war. The first lesson student soldiers were taught in Japan was how to use their own rifles to kill themselves rather than be captured. Stripped of his weapons, he devised a number of ways he could commit suicide and preserve what little remained of his honor. Yet he never did, still seeing Shizue in his mind's eye, and hoping to once again feel her in his arms.

War-ravaged Japan, meanwhile, preferred that MacArthur send food before returning its POWs, Isamu discovered. Instead of being repatriated he was charged alongside his fellow POWs with the task of dismantling military operations on Hawai'i. By the end of 1946, he was still on the islands, and had re-established contact with Shizue. The Ōkubos had returned to San Francisco and were picking up the pieces of their lives. My grandmother broke down in wracking sobs when she received the letter from Isamu that had been forwarded to her by friends who had maintained the Ōkubo's apartment during the war.

It was never clear to any of us how Isamu finagled papers and made his way to San Francisco in 1947 instead of being repatriated to Japan, and it was only after my grandparents were long gone that it occurred to me to wonder about it. But my efforts to get to the bottom of the story were brushed off by my mother, making it clear this was not a subject to be discussed.

Isamu and Shizue's wedding was festive, involving a banquet at Chinatown's Jade Moon restaurant, and the recitation of many poems, songs, and speeches. Underneath the happy glow that suffuses all weddings, though, tensions were evident. Several of Shizue's camp friends who had volunteered to fight for the U.S. as members of the 442nd politely refused to attend, and she was stung again when the *Nichi Bei Times*, which before the war had gladly published her pacifist poems, responded evasively to the wedding announcement she sent in, never refusing to publish it, but never managing to get around to it either. *Issei* wedding guests, though, who secretly (and some not so secretly) harbored deep-seated patriotic feelings for their motherland, raised small cups of warm sake to each other and toasted the bridal couple.

At first my grandfather seemed to be satisfied with his role of managing the family fish store, which the Ōkubos had reopened in 1946. My mother, Sachiko, was the only child of their late marriage, born in 1948, her birth celebrated with pink sticky rice cooked with adzuki beans and a whole red snapper simmered in a fragrant bath of shoyu and ginger. As he shared in the family's joy, Isamu at the same moment felt an irretrievable loss. There was no going back to Japan, not after he had bargained away that right in order to be reunited with Shizue. Sachiko would grow up into that rude and immodest species that horrified him on a daily basis, the spoiled American girl. He would never introduce her to his parents, and he would never marry her off to the son of Air Group 281's Commander Shigehachiro Tokoro, as they had one day jokingly promised each other. He felt a sharp pain in his chest as he thought of the post-war privation his parents now stoically endured, and the glorious death his captain and his comrades had met during the banzai suicide attack on the Americans that Isamu had turned his back on.

By the time my mother was old enough to form memories, Isamu had begun drinking heavily, singing patriotic Navy songs, and then becoming belligerent.

Evenings usually ended with his being escorted home by friends. Sober, he turned bitter and caustic, and spent hours poring over a dog-eared book he had found at a second-hand Japanese bookstore about the history of the Japanese Imperial Navy.

I can't blame my grandfather. To settle amid the vanquishers of his country, cut-off from his homeland as a traitor, yet aware of the starvation and destitution his people had endured after the war, and to be reminded daily of America's role as victors in cheerful advertisements and radio programs, was all too much for him. Their child, at first so rejoiced, learned to fear his moods, and as she grew up lost herself in radio dramas, comic books, and fantasy tales of her own devising. The only things father and daughter shared was their innate bullheadedness, love for long walks—during which the "other" engaging and witty Isamu made his rare appearances—and airplanes.

For Sachiko, her aviation infatuation began during a walk with Isamu across the Golden Gate Bridge, a favorite landmark and one that often appeared in her stories. They spotted a Lockheed P2V Neptune overhead, and from that day on, it was their habit during their walks to hold hands and scan the skies for the regular Orion sorties that issued from Moffet Field Naval Air Station.

In August 1958 when Sachiko was ten, the pair, carrying *obento* lunches that Shizue had packed for them, traveled to Sunnyvale by bus to witness a blazing sunrise much like the one I marveled at in my Spitfire this morning over Tokyo Bay. Filled with admiration and awe, they watched the first flight of the P-3 Orion whose menacing stinger-like tail was designed to magnetically detect enemy submarines. The day made a deep impression on my mother. Though she was temperamentally more like her pacifist mother, the bond she felt with her father was both deeper and more tenuous, a bond based on the atavistic hunger for air, space, and freedom. She felt she loved her father more than anyone in the world. As a child, I can recall her often reminiscing about the sight of the P-3 Orion in flight as she brushed my hair and pulled it into a sleek, neat ponytail.

Many years later, I found notebooks filled with my mother's drawings of the Orion, as well as pages bursting with fierce, yet somehow fantastical-looking, Japanese naval planes drawn using Isamu's tattered history book as her guide. She had obviously studied every technical detail of the plane carefully, yet with great tenderness had imbued her drawings with strength, nobility, and an almost supernatural life force. One could tell immediately that my mother was one with the plane she had rendered so masterfully. She wrote them into her stories, and thrilled to tales of daring feats of aviation. Her favorite was that of her hero Amelia Earhart's record-setting solo flight across the Pacific from Honolulu to Oakland because it featured the neighboring town she knew well. Met by an adoring crowd of thousands of supporters, Amelia was the shining, living embodiment of flight. She preferred not to dwell on the next flight Amelia made from Oakland two years later in 1937, from which she never returned. Instead, Sachiko dreamed of becoming a champion of female aviators, just like Amelia, and setting jaw-dropping world records of her own.

This single, shared love, which connected Isamu and Sachiko across cultures and his bouts of drinking, came to an abrupt and painful end when Sachiko was sixteen. She came home one day excitedly waving a piece of paper and announcing that, with the help of the local chapter of the women's aviator group, The Ninety-Nines (which her hero Amelia had helped found), she had signed up for flying lessons at Oakland Airport's North Field. Isamu, by then two bottles of sake into the day, roared at her, "Drawing okay, looking okay. But flying, NO! You must start thinking of *omiai*, arranged marriage and family."

Their walks ended as well, and Sachiko, with no support from her mother, who had made writing poetry and keeping peace in the house her top priorities, turned away from her father in anger. Coincidentally, a young man who had been pestering her, Tad Fujikawa, a Cal senior she had met during an *obon* festival in Nihonmachi, suddenly began to seem much more interesting. Born in the Rohwer, an Arkansas concentration camp, he was four years older than she, a fiery activist who had traveled with the Freedom Riders in Mississippi and was now passionately engaged in explaining to her why the free speech movement, now underway on campus, was of vital importance to human dignity. "Don't you see?" he said earnestly. "They want teachers to sign *loyalty oaths* to stand united against us, just like the government did in camp, trying to make us denounce our loyalty to Japan!" On the one occasion that Shizue met Tad, he brought to mind the passionate young Japanese patriot she fell in love in with when she was fourteen.

I've come to think that my parents' abrupt elopement two years later was on my mother's part motivated half by love and half by stubborn anger at her father. Whatever the reason, when I was born twelve years later, my mother had not spoken with her father for just as long. In another crushing blow to Isamu, my grandmother died shortly after my mother eloped, partly from heartbreak, her friends said.

Again, the hours aloft have sped by, darkness has fallen, and I am jolted from my memories. Like a slumbering child pulled from the dream world to the earthly world, I am momentarily confused about which is real. A crackling, lightly accented voice comes through my headset. "*Peach 5*, alerting you to choppy seas and poor landing conditions. Proceed with caution, please." This cold splash of reality focuses my mind and I turn my full attention to navigating the turbulent sky and sea, more difficult at night than in daylight. The challenge is good for me and by the time I've completed the instrument landing, I'm fully in the present and realize my neck and shoulders are rigid and crying out for Dr. Kaz. I let out an unseemly yelp of joy when I see him at the top of the Mitsubishi fueling ship's ramp in his white coat, smiling. Apparently the four previous pilots also made difficult but safe landings.

I savor every moment of my stop, the warm shower, the relaxing acupuncture treatment and a much improved meal of clear soup filled with mountain vegetables, miso-marinated cod and a delicious *chawanmushi* savory egg custard studded with shrimp, lily root, chestnuts, and gingko nuts. Oddly, it was Dr. Kaz who, with instructions passed on from Keiko, coached me on how to make my final landing in San Francisco Bay. I'm to first descend to an altitude of 7,890 feet and pass through a cloud type meteorologically known as Cloud Nine, the lowest-lying type that is still too high to be called "fog," and where thunderstorms are born. I love that. This deliriously happy state we call "Cloud Nine" is, of course, born from much *Sturm und Drang,* like the beautiful baby that emerges after hours of excruciating labor pains.

Anticipating the difficulty of this final leg, I am at first loathe to buckle myself back in. Throughout the deep night, the warm shower and my full stomach are lulling, and the thick frothy matcha my server ceremoniously offered at the end of the meal begins to kick in, injecting an electric jolt into my sluggish system. Suddenly, I'm confident I can make the last leg of my flight.

I'll need every neuron and firing synapse for the leg ahead, as the rough weather continues. I have been trained so well, though, that my actions at the control panel seem to flow without my giving any thought to them. There is no separation between me and *Peach 5*, or between me and the sky and sea around me. We are all working together, part of a seamless whole. I send out a prayer to my fellow pilots for safe passage across the Pacific. Especially for Ayame, who has probably landed in San Francisco by now. Through long discussions about our different but similar backgrounds, we had bonded during training. I talked a lot about American history with her, and she talked of her family roots, which seemed so ancient compared to mine. Japanese and Japanese American women bonding over shared stories. At this moment I recall Ayame's words, "I was educated to believe that the essence of a person is carried in her genes. Why else would I develop a passion for aviation, only to find a complementary interest in my mother?" For me that genetic predisposition was passed on both from my mother, whose passion was forever thwarted, and from my grandfather.

My bibles were *Peter Pan, The Little Prince,* anything by Jules Verne, then Japanese *manga* and *anime.* I wanted to be the pilot-writer Antoine de St. Exupéry, the ever-youthful flying Peter, and Phileas Fogg in *Around the World in Eighty Days.*

As for my mother Sachiko, it was partly her unrequited love of flight, I suspect, that led her to choose to live out her years in a Buddhist monastery in Lake County, where she can devote herself to cultivating the forgiveness and compassion needed to free her mind from all of its worldly attachments.

Of course, there were other reasons. One of my earliest memories is an argument between my parents over me. "Just because you have turned your back on him, that doesn't mean Tomi should not know and respect her grandfather," my father said in a quiet but firm tone. "He has reached out and invited Tomi to visit. It's not just about getting to know him, it's about growing up with an understanding of his point of view, why he is so sad and broken, and what he was like before that happened. It's about understanding her culture."

My father had continued his social activism after Berkeley. As a tireless political organizer, he had seen and participated in every civil rights movement of his day, Black Power, Chicano Power, Native American and farm workers' rights, each movement in ways small and large were moved forward by him. When I think of him, I see him with a cigarette in one hand and a pen in the other, working the phones. He was convinced it was time to fight for redress for the Japanese Americans who had been imprisoned during World War II. He testified before the Commission on Wartime Relocation and Internment of Civilians and was absorbed in helping organize a letter-writing campaign pushing for redress. My mother was sympathetic to his work, but stubbornly preferred to express her feelings through art and poetry.

As for my grandfather, by then he had mellowed a little. He drank less and so the sadness that enveloped him, without the blurring filter of inebriation, was more palpable. Bereft of both his wife and his daughter, it was my father who reached out to Isamu, making weekly visits to bring him *senbei* and dried squid, two of his favorite snacks, and Japanese videos borrowed from the cultural center.

My visits and walks with Isamu began when I was five and he was seventy-two. When I grew older I realized that we were recreating the rituals he had loved performing with my mother—holding hands and walking across the Golden Gate Bridge, scanning the skies for passing aircraft. We never spoke of her, and at first I didn't notice that either. As our bond grew, though, I could tell that it ate away at my mother, but in a way that made her feel upset with herself. After all, just because she had rejected her father, she told herself, she had no right to impose that burden on her daughter.

My grandfather had mellowed. When I was fourteen and almost a carbon copy of my mother, I began to show an interest in flying. My grandfather was already in his mid-eighties, yet he was determined to help. We traveled by bus and BART to Oakland Airport to visit the offices of the Oakland Flyers, the flying club training facility that had opened not too long before on Earhart Road. How perfect! I felt I had come home. I didn't start lessons until several years later, though, when I was sixteen and old enough to earn my student pilot certificate. By then, my grandfather was ailing and mostly bed-ridden. I could see the joy, and the sadness, in his eyes when I showed him my certificate. My mother, also with mixed feelings, applauded my accomplishment. It was at this point that I thought they were both ripe for reconciliation. I sensed that my grandfather was ready. But the charged issue of flight, and who had a right to the skies, kept my proud, stubborn mother from accepting a truce, and although I would never call her a feminist, something about the stark inequalities, first in gender and later between generations of women, had, on a deep level, quietly infuriated her.

My thoughts are interrupted by another round of turbulence, which set my teeth knocking in my head. At the same moment, I hear a faint voice through my headset. It is ground control in San Francisco. "Come in, *Peach 5*. Rough weather will continue for the duration of the trip. At current speeds you'll be directly over the Pacific trash vortex in thirty minutes."

Some say that this decomposing soup of plastics and chemical sludge, whorled together by the waters of the North Pacific gyre, is twice the size the state of Texas, though little of it is visible on the ocean's surface. And although one of the initial attractions of The Race was the serious money and bragging rights attached to a victory, something compels me to turn the nose of *Peach 5* gently seaward and begin a gradual descent. During the course of my flight, I realize, my desire to win the race has evaporated into the misty skies surrounding me. Absorbed in the inner movie of my family's story, I have left any preoccupations I had with competition and material gain on the ground, where the atmosphere feeds them. Up here, in the thin, pure air, the mind clears, and one can take a deeper, more interior view, where rich and poor, powerful and humble, good and evil, the quick and the lame, are all one and the same. I understand with a clarity that comes of total solitude that our highest calling should be one of compassion, for ourselves, for each other, and for our home planet. So far, there are only a few stray, floating signs of the ocean trash, yet I feel its nagging presence like a stain on my conscience.

My father's death, from a sudden heart attack later that same year, was devastating to us. As it turns out, he was the linchpin that held our family together. I became the sole bearer of the silence between my mother and grandfather, and although I'm ashamed of it now, I coped by ignoring them both. The ancient Japanese poems that my mother had introduced me to when I was twelve became a new form of escape. I loved everything about them—the wistful accounts of the fleeting seasons, delicate renderings of the tedium and loneliness of court ladies, the sparkling wit and detailed entries of this perennially diary-keeping people. I loved that women were among the most revered and best-remembered writers of this period. It was natural that, when it came time to apply to college and choose a course of study, I should enter the East Asian Languages and Culture Department at Berkeley.

For her part, my mother stepped up her study of Buddhism, which gradually outpaced all other interests. A year later, my grandfather passed away quietly in his sleep, and shortly after that my mother announced that it was time for her *shukke,* to leave home life and its worldly concerns behind, and enter the monastery.

Those years passed by as in a numb haze, brightened by books and flight. I studied hard, daydreamed and crisscrossed the beautiful bay over and over, feeling totally abandoned and alone.

Although my mother is alive and well and perhaps very content at the Center, she prefers to entertain family visitors only rarely. It was a decision that left a permanent void, a little hollow scooped out of me that I finger like an old scar. After a while, I stopped caring, or told myself that I did. She had abandoned me, and I would repay the favor by pretending she no longer existed.

Up here, though, it began to seem like my family movie was now all about her. Her face, young and beautiful as she appears in her wedding photographs, seems to hover inside the invisible circle that my Aero-Vee is outlining. What would I have been like if the gift of flight, which I consider as essential to life as breath, had been denied to me?

Then something odd began to happen in my movie. The focus shifted to my mother, alone and bent over her Buddhist texts in her monk-like cell. And then back to the sky around me, which was brightening with the dawn that became a spectacular light show, a fingernail of orange rose behind me. I followed it in my rear-view mirror, gradually growing wider, like the glowing, inverted smile of a jack-o'lantern, until the clouds below were tinted a lovely pink-orange hue.

I began to see myself in a continuous line of women in our family, streaming through time like those cloudlets across the sky, women whose quietude and introspective natures masked inner steel, who sought refuge from our times and fulfillment in the pen and the book. The love of flight entered the family lineage perhaps with Isamu, or maybe even before, with a devotee of falconry in the Heian court. Though my mother and I both coveted the pilot's wings, only I was able to feel what Isamu felt the first time he took to the skies.

A piece clicks into place. This powerful cast of female fliers Keiko has assembled is the replacement part I have been missing, the organ that fits seamlessly in that little hollow my mother's *shukke* left in me. Now it is their faces I picture—one who redesigned the planes carrying us across the Pacific, four who have escaped the yoke of communism, all of us united by our yearning for flight. Our group has known both privilege and hardship. We have collectively weathered two world wars, ethnic oppression, gender bias, and misogyny. We embody the wisdom of some of the world's most ancient cultures and religions—Ancient Celtic polytheism, Native American Shamanism, Shintoism, Buddhism and Zoroastrianism, as well as Judaism and Christianity.

Our histories are intertwined like skeins of brightly colored yarn, dotted with triumphs and tragedy, acts of both deep humanity and mind-numbing atrocity. With the giddiness and euphoria that comes of inner vision and its handmaiden, hours of solo flight, I am certain now that the true purpose of our journey is not another competition, but something much bigger. My fate after The Race is not to spend the rest of my life divided among books and solo excursions in the sky, but to continue on land the journey that has begun in the air, and even before that, as the germ of an idea in the mind of Keiko Kobahashi. Then and there, I decide that I will take Keiko up on the somewhat vague offer that she whispered to me on that night of our last dinner in Tokyo. It seems so long ago now, when she touched my arm as we were leaving the restaurant and said softly, "Tomi, please consider helping me after The Race. This is only just the beginning, we have so much work to do to help heal the earth. I don't want this powerful sisterhood to break apart when it is over. Please, think about it, and come to Hawai'i to work with us."

Down below, our religious and cultural differences are at the root of conflicts that dot the globe like a measles-pocked face. Up here now, I understand Keiko deliberately assembled our group of women pilots to begin weaving a parallel world of lasting peace and love for the planet from that rich skein of our diverse backgrounds. We can see our mission clearly from up here, and we must bring that vision back with us to earth, and begin to fashion the warp and weft of our brave new world. "I'm in," I whisper to myself, and to Keiko, who is waiting on the ground to greet my sisters and me.

Just then a voice interrupted my movie. "Come in *Peach 5*. You are passing through Cloud Nine now. Prepare for landing in San Francisco Bay."

LEAH KATZENBERG

WHITE 6

It was snowing heavily and it was hard to see. A magical, muffling substance was falling from the sky and blanketing the world, peaceful fragments of neither ice nor water. The silence was all enveloping. I was reminded that each flake is known to be unique, in the same way each human and each fingerprint is unique. Every finger that has ever existed is like no other, so why was there one here now? It wasn't really bleeding, nor was it not bleeding. Draining maybe, yes draining would be the word. It was draining out onto the snow, but the snow was not melting. What a horrible shift. My pleasant dream had turned into a nightmare. I really wanted to wake up. I wanted to move too, but couldn't. I was stuck underneath something and whatever it was made it hard to breathe.

My best memories of snow are from the ski village of Gstaad in Switzerland. We lived in Bern, where I was born, and spent winter break and sometimes long weekends in a chalet close enough to a ski run that we could ski to the place without ever carrying our skis for more than a few meters because of the rough, ungraveled roadsides in the neighborhood.

My father was a diplomat who worked at the Israeli Embassy on the Alpenstrasse in Bern. It was only much later that I learned the truth about him and why we had to leave Switzerland in a hurry in early October of 1969, never to return. My father was in fact an aeronautical engineer and was implicated in the theft of the Mirage III-S plans at the Sulzer plant in Winterthur near Zürich. Sulzer built the jet engines in Switzerland under license of Dassault Aviation, France's foremost producer of aircraft at the time. They are still well known for their Falcon civilian business jet, which can be re-purposed for military deployments and also used as a small cargo plane.

At the time, Israel had ordered and made payment on fifty Mirage V planes that had been newly modified at the request of the Israeli Air Force. When French President Charles de Gaulle reneged on the deal, plans were made to steal the blueprints, and two years later my father succeeded. Since the design of the Mirage III and V was essentially identical in most other aspects, France did eventually deliver the fifty Mirage

Vs with great discretion. Still, by that time, we were building our own plane, the Nesher. There is disagreement on what Nesher means—eagle or vulture. As with so many issues, the controversy can be traced back to perspectives on history, religion, language, zoology, and more. The generally positive associations with the word eagle and the negative ones with the word vulture are historic, cultural, and emotional. It is the emotional ambiguity that I want to preserve for myself. Any weapon has a contradictory meaning depending on the direction in which it is pointed. It depends on the eye of the beholder and I don't want to forget this and think of the airplane as I do of the birds, as raptors. Thirty-nine of these Israeli-built versions of the Mirage V were sold to Argentina where they were initially referred to as "daggers" and later as "fingers."

Fingers! Of course, that's why I was thinking about fingers. I never understood why they named them that way. Clearly one had crashed and then stopped bleeding. But it looked like a finger instead of a bird of prey, living or mechanical. I still could not move and bring myself to wake from this horribly lucid dream. I knew I was dreaming, but I could not stop or escape the anxiety-riddled and surreal scenarios my brain was weaving. All of it seemed so real, the finger, the immovable weight, the snow. Maybe I saw a mirage, an actual *fata morgana*. I have always liked the sound of the Arabic word for mirage.

The snow was still not melting, nor was it cold. Not cold at all. It was rare that I could not fly in my dreams and that I was pinned down instead. The snow was still falling, but lighter and out of a blue sky. It didn't even look like snow any longer. Instead, it looked like pieces of paper. It was paper. Tiny pieces of paper, like what used to fall from buildings at a hero's welcome, at a ticker-tape parade. How could I see the tiny plane, which was no plane but an actual severed finger, and see the paper snow and sky all at the same time? It made no sense. Where there had previously been an all-pervasive silence, there were now people screaming. It was faint at first, but it was there and suddenly I felt hot and cold all at once, and I could smell it first, smell it all—the dust, the smoke, the blood, the acrid smell of the explosives. Sarah… Oh my God, where was Sarah!! My heart was in my throat and prevented me from calling out to her. Wake up I thought, please wake up now!

As I remember that terrible day, the day that convinced me with certainty that there is no God, today I am nevertheless in his domain, the heavens, darting in and out of wispy clouds, flying. Unlike in my dreams, where I can fly unhindered using only my body and concentration, now I am in an actual plane, with frost on the windshield that almost looks like snow.

I am high above the Pacific Ocean, at a current altitude of 27,500 feet and descending to refuel. My refurbished Supermarine Spitfire is in her element, purring like a contented cat, resurrected, or should I say reincarnated, thanks to the makeover at the

Mitsubishi plant in Tokyo. This state of the art avionics would have been unimaginable to the original builders of the Spitfire in Britain. It is amazing, so much technological progress among the same old hatreds, bigotry, and ignorance. After the German Luftwaffe's initially unsuccessful attack on the two main factories near Southampton, most of the production jigs and machine tools were dispersed throughout southern England and later in Birmingham by the time the Germans had leveled the two original factories.

As a retired Israeli Air Force Captain, I am in awe to fly this legend of an aircraft that played such an indispensable role in beating the Nazis in their nimble Messerschmitts. Sitting behind the wing assembly would have been useful for damage assessment in a dogfight and knowing when to bail. Using the wings as stairs to the cockpit makes sense too. No part is wasted on doing just one job.

My Swiss ski instructor used to tease me about my last name, Katzenberg. The literal translation from German into English means "Cat Mountain." Franz was his name. Whenever I did something wrong, he told me that although I might have a mountain full of cats running around in my head, I better pay attention to the only thing he could see on this mountain, namely snow, if I wanted to hold on to my feline brain. Then he would belly laugh at his own admonition, which he seemed to think of as the height of wit. I never really understood Swiss humor. It seemed absurdly simplistic in one way, yet potentially philosophically complex, if you were willing to give it the necessary consideration. Maybe that is what makes the Swiss so obsessed with measuring time. While it can be measured, unlike most things that can, it can't be bought or sold, though it can be stolen and confiscated, surely the ultimate frustration for a Swiss mind. Even worse, each of us is given a unique allotment of time but we don't know what it is.

When I fully came to, I knew that my daughter's allotment had been taken from her. I knew even before I was sure that it was her finger lying on the large shard of a broken mirror that reflected the sky and paper snow I was seeing all at once. It wasn't just her time that had been stolen on that day. It was mine too, my time with her and all that defines being a mother, maybe even a grandmother some day, too.

After my acceptance to the Mitsubishi sponsored Spitfire race across the Pacific from Japan to the U.S., I was invited to request three color choices in descending order of priority for my plane. The same was the case for the plane number, which would also determine my starting position in the staggered race. I knew that my request of the color white for my plane might cause some consternation. In parts of the world, it is the color of death and mourning. I felt bad that I had requested white in all of the three choices. Someone surely got in trouble for letting the processing software accept the same color choice more than once. Probably some of them knew, particularly

Keiko, who'd run extensive background checks on all of us. As an ex-IDF pilot, since I had lost my daughter in the terrorist attack in Tel Aviv three years prior, I was in a position to know that some of Keiko's checking well exceeded the stated parameters of our written agreements. If they knew, they didn't say. Instead, they referenced their knowledge of Judeo-Christian traditions by calling me the "bride of the sky," as if my plane were one huge extended, metallic, and fully motorized wedding dress.

One night during our training in Tokyo, and after several Kirin Ichibans, I was eventually swept up in the discussion about the urgency of a united world in need of reinventing itself collectively and cooperatively. I held forth not just on Eisenhower's famed warning about the military-industrial complex, but on all the other complexes, the medical-industrial, the energy-industrial, the food-industrial, and so on. These complexes are all-encompassing, including buying and suppressing the patents needed to turn around our impending ecological evisceration. These statements contributed to a lively debate and some disagreement on what should or could be done and most controversially, by whom? After some of my impassioned provocations, I had earned my new wings as the resident peacenik, for a while. Someone commented that my modified white warplane was really a raptor transformed into a white dove. Not everyone was that generous though. Some agreed that it was a white, privileged chicken revoking the developing world's right to pollute as much as had been done by the industrialized nations. The difference between development and adopting outdated and unsustainable technologies was not universally agreed on. In a collective sense, it was certainly true that planes of this type, particularly flying the route of the race, were previously only ever birds of war or attractions in the aerial circus we think of as air shows. On this basis alone, my color choice had been indulged in so many ways and even embraced. As an Israeli pilot I had to wonder how long this honeymoon with my new found sisters would last. Anti-Semitic and/or anti-Israeli sentiments were unlikely to be nonexistent in such a diverse group.

The regional jet that Mitsubishi started building in late 2013 also comes off the production line in white, before being further embellished with the buyers' colors, usually in the form of a stripe, or stripes, on the side and tail. I wonder whether this race is meant to appease the frustration over the considerable competition Mitsubishi is sure to be causing for Boeing and Airbus or to advertise the new jet instead? Are they saying, "We did it once and we can do it again?" The irony that the very manufacturer who had built the dreaded Japanese Zeros had now also refurbished these British Spitfires was lost on no one. Who are we, the pilots, in this bargain, and who ultimately benefits?

This is the problem with exceedingly long flights. Your mind tends to wander, to jump from place and time, as one thought triggers another. For what has seemed like a long time now, my mind can't wander anywhere comfortably or happy for long. Just to exist in such numbers as humankind does now contradicts the law of balance in nature and a sustainable future. Yet, the will to live, to have the right to it like everyone else, is perhaps strongest in those of us who have had that right taken away, or questioned for millennia.

I am no longer young and not yet old. I am orphaned, divorced, and I care about little since having buried my child. At least she won't suffer the dangers and indignities that are so plentiful in this world. Nor will she know the love and passion that can elevate existence to the point of such incomprehensible beauty and limitless wonder. Still, I keep telling myself that at least she is safe—forever safe. She is safe from this place at any rate. But where is she now? If her soul survived, what existence does it lead now? What form of existence has she assumed if everything in the universe is recycled? Is she even female any longer? I doubt that it is, but is gender part of our soul? Did something gain twenty-one grams when she joined with it? Will she greet me on the other side like my father claimed his loved ones were doing? He briefly woke up from a coma shortly before he died from lung cancer and said that they were waiting for him, inviting him to come over and join them. Like many Israelis, he had been a heavy smoker with little worry about the consequences, since the threat of death and annihilation has hung over our country since its modern birth in 1948.

Sarah was smart, sensitive, and beautiful. She was a Sabra, Israeli born, and as strong and tough and as much of a survivor as the hardy desert cactus from which the name Sabra originates. Like many Sabras with Eastern-European roots, she was dark, but with her father's piercing blue eyes, which gave her an almost startling appearance. She had a lot of her great-grandmother too, who we both only knew from photographs. My father's mother had given him to her sister, who had been issued an earlier train ticket out of Germany. They got out but his mother did not. She was murdered in Auschwitz in 1944. My father, his aunt and her husband made it to Holland and from there to London, where they waited for a visa to the United States. Before it was issued they found passage on a ship to Palestine. Getting in to Palestine was a feat due to the British blockade. For this reason alone, my great-uncle joined the Irgun. His name was Felix Katzenberg and he died before the country was officially recognized. Because he died in 1946, I used to wonder whether he had anything to do with the bombing of the King David Hotel in Jerusalem. Lately, I have been wondering whether Sarah's death was connected to the Jihadists' "divine retribution." Does it all go back to the beginning—"An eye for an eye"? When will it finally end?

Am I suffering from some strange form of Stockholm Syndrome? Am I searching for guilt to explain the motivations not of "capturers," but of "murderers?" Children of divorced parents often blame themselves, as do parents of dead children, no matter if it makes any sense or not. Am I caught up in this vicious circle? Self-reflection is surely one thing, but these thoughts are as destructive as the compression wave of the explosion itself, which lifted both of us into the air. Its payload of shrapnel, already dispersed, was made from building supplies, including nails and bolts. They tore through Sarah's heart and brain and left me with a concussion and my dead child lying on top of me. Why did it have to be her? Why couldn't it have been me? Yes, Sarah had done her duty to her country as a computer engineer in the military, but she never saw any combat and never killed anyone, unlike her mother. I refuse to make her death about me. I want to blame the idiots who drew up unrealistic and unmanageable post-colonial borders all over the world, based on dividing up resources and strategic interests, instead of honoring historical, tribal, cultural, and political ties in so many regions with ongoing conflicts today.

My own yearning for peace can't really be separated from my yearning for my country and its people. The desire to be accepted and recognized by our Semitic sisters and brothers and the rest of the world is inseparable from being Israeli. What must it feel like to be from Sweden? "Hello, I am Maja from Sweden"... no instant codification in a passionately anti- or pro- stance that has nothing to do with me as a person. Given how I look, I could perhaps pretend to be from Italy or France and see how people respond. Speaking only Hebrew, German, and English might make that a bit of a challenge though. My mind often wonders about how different the Middle East could be, if transformed in a way that would make everyone happy, at least more or less. I keep inventing different scenarios in my mind to make that work.

What if the Iraq conquest had led to a broad-based diplomatic solution for much of the Middle East? Like Yugoslavia, modern day Iraq was only possible under a dictatorship. Given the choice, Iraq's ethnically divided and opposed populations would naturally want their own sovereignty, or they would seek to rejoin the ethnic cultures from which they were severed when Iraq was established in the first place.

I often wonder where we would be today if diplomacy had achieved a peaceful surrender of Iran's nuclear ambitions in exchange for the annexation of Iraq's eastern region with its Shiite population. What if Kurdistan in the north had been recognized, including the Kurdish territories ruled over by Turkey, in return for Turkey's then-desired admission to the EU? What if Saudi Arabia had picked up the southwestern Sunni territory in an arrangement that would have demanded concessions from the Saudis on human rights and reliable rates of oil production and pricing to stabilize the world's teetering economies? And what if Palestine had been rethought as part of the same effort? Today, most people don't even remember that the territory of today's Israel, Jordan, and the Golan Heights was the geographically defined British Mandate of Palestine. In fact, it was the first and only time that the borders of Palestine had been specifically drawn.

Nor do people generally know that the Jews and Arabs living in this territory were collectively referred to as Palestinians. When the Allied Forces determined the future of the former Ottoman Empire territories after World War I, at the San Remo conference in 1920, the Mandate incorporated the provisions of the Balfour Declaration, which called for the establishment in Palestine of a national homeland for the Jewish people. This was later ratified by the League of Nations.

However, by way of an apology for being unable to protect Hashemite interests in the Arabian Peninsula, the British decided to divide the area of the Palestinian Mandate by establishing Trans-Jordan east of the Jordan River and excluding it from the Balfour declaration two years later in 1922. In 1946, Trans-Jordan gained its independence, and the tiny area of what remained of Palestine was supposed to be divided yet again instead of becoming the already disproportionally diminished Jewish homeland. By the time Israel declared itself as a nation two years later, civil war had raged within its borders and the other newly established countries surrounding it declared war from all sides against the fledgling state. After the establishment of a ceasefire, the renamed Hashemite Kingdom of Jordan annexed the territory, which is known today as the West Bank. Egypt did the same with the area known as Gaza.

It was Jordan that established the refugee camps on the West Bank, instead of integrating the Arab Palestinians who had been encouraged to join the war against Israel and sweep the Jews into the sea. Organizations like Black September, which committed the massacre of eleven Israeli athletes in 1972 at the Munich Olympics and the PLO representing the Palestinian majority in Jordan, fought both against the Hashemite monarchy and Israel. A generation of Arab Palestinians were raised and educated to hold Israel responsible for their plight instead of Jordan. Israel's famous one-eyed general, Moshe Dayan prevented an exodus of the Arab Palestinians after Israel had regained the territories of the West Bank and Gaza in 1967 during the Six-Day War. Of course, there is disagreement on how that war started. Dayan believed both peoples could live together in the same land. It was an humanistic but naïve vision, and one for which Israel arguably continues to pay the price, unlike Jordan which expelled the PLO leadership and thousands of Arab Palestinian fighters following the Jordanian Civil War four years later.

What if today's Jordan had invited its displaced brethren to join Arab Palestine, Jordan, or if not that, had ceded some of its western territory to help establish a viable independent Arab Palestinian state that left the Jewish Palestinian state, Israel, with realistically defensible borders? In turn, Jordan could have gained remaining territory from Iraq. Could something like that have worked? Surely it would have been far less controversial than any of the other post-colonial partitions, and could possibly have represented a win-win, instead of the intractable stalemates in place all over the Middle East, Africa, and Asia. I wonder about the differences from foreign meddling in both post-colonial South and Central Americas? What accounts for the comparable stability? In any event, if anyone bothers to think about those countries, history took a different turn and violence prevailed instead of any creative diplomatic solutions.

Sarah paid the price for that endless violence, and for what, World War III? From Damascus to Tehran, there is now a wasteland of refugees and poisoned water and this wasteland is internationally occupied and administrated at an absurd cost between the American, Chinese and Russian zones, all trying to squeeze out the last few drops of oil with little or no benefit going to the populations. Women and children, unprotected in camps, are being raped and starved. If Jordan fell to Syria and Iraq to Iran, the world would be on the brink of World War III. Thanks to the financial entanglements between the U.S. and China, Russia might be prevailed upon to partner in occupation rather than going to war. It's not implausible that such a scenario, or these variations, could develop in this regional tinderbox with all of the disingenuous friends who want the oil and who continue to fight their proxy wars.

Being aloft in a plane used to bring me such joy and peace. I was as mischievous as the Ichiban dragon, suspended above the earth, carried on wings and defying gravity. When I was accepted to the Air Force Academy, my father actually cried. It was the first and only time that I saw him lose control of his composure. Aloft, as I am now in my racing Spitfire, I am dragging a past behind me that I don't know how to jettison. I can't even distinguish between the personal and the collective anxieties that are clipping my wings. The Spitfire's perfectly tuned engine is pulling me at optimum capacity and yet I feel as if I am suspended in place with the clouds racing by to provide the illusion of movement. Not even the fantastic Rolls Royce engine seems able to escape the gravitational pull of loss, spiritual and worldly pollution, fanned by the new hell of corporate politics, to which I myself am contributing at this very moment by flying this kerosene-spewing relic of war, which, of course, is sponsored by a corporation. I wish I could go back, and turn down another road.

Why did Sarah and I have to go to that falafel stand? We were laughing and joking about our anticipated delight to bite into some spicy falafel balls. Sarah had been in a big fight with her boyfriend, and my now ex-husband and I had separated not long before. We were laughing at the stupid joke, not knowing that we were headed into a fire storm of symbols of masculinity and femininity, nuts and bolts, nails and ball-bearings, all carefully arranged and choreographed for a short dance of killing and maiming an arbitrary group of passersby and falafel lovers who would never get over it, if they survived.

Below the clouds now, I am visually scanning for our Mitsubishi refueling ship, and spot her at eleven o'clock, three miles north, invisibly moored to the satellite-provided coordinates. The sea looks choppy and I change course to the southeast so I can put down and approach in a northeasterly direction, perpendicular to the waves, before finding refuge in the shadow of the massive nautical structure's calmer waters, out of the wind and sun on the port side.

As the water grabs hold of my floatplane, I am again reminded of skiing, it's like skiing over moguls in a straight line without bending your knees. The floats have no shock absorbers. I'll be glad about that at takeoff. But right now, as the horizon appears and disappears to the point where I long to stick my nose in the water and forever disappear, the roller-coaster changes course and goes uphill again. I find myself instinctively bending my knees every time as if this could somehow avert this spine-jarring disaster, strapped in, as I am. At least the skiing is occurring on a flat trajectory and as the floatplane slows down it starts to act more like a small boat. I relax and even enjoy the sensation of being rocked by the sea despite the darkness of my thoughts that are matched only by the fathomless depth beneath me.

Two well-marked skiffs come to bring me all the way in, lulling me towards the protected port side of the refueling ship. I notice for the first time the discreet but persuasive security in and around the tanker. My inquiries about that are jovially rebuffed with a canned answer about the routine nature of this, along with the traditionally formal Japanese greeting that makes me want to pull myself together and express my gratitude for a moment of clarity where everyone knows what is expected of them. While I am not allowed to know my actual place in the race, the words are encouraging, as they probably are for everyone, but they nevertheless confirm the suggestion of my own favorable calculations. Flying at maximum altitude comes with the price of a prolonged climb, my strategy is based on making up for this by cruising through the thinner air resistance that the increased altitude brings. Nevertheless, we are talking about relatively narrow margins because of the three landings between Tokyo and the famous American bridge in San Francisco.

It is good to leave the cockpit, take a shower, and enjoy a traditional Japanese acupuncture treatment by Dr. Watase before changing into fresh undergarments and flight gear. I don't feel the needles penetrate my lower back, only the heat emanating from the traditional Moxa balls burning on top of the needles spread like a welcome subcutaneous liquid from the entry points. The food is disappointing. Not to make anyone sick, or stimulate her bowels, or favor one national dish over the other, the lowest common denominator ends up being some thick, tasteless mush that is undoubtedly high in protein but surely more suitable to use as mortar than nutrition. I hope the cuisine is better at the next two refueling stops.

With ten minutes to go, I touch my abdominal bullet scar for luck as I have done ever since I got it, and climb back into my temperature controlled flight suit. As I clamber off the skiff and onto the wing, I hear the reassuring purr of the RR Griffon after being told that everything on the plane is in perfect working order. I thank the ground crew, and then lower and lock my window. I can see on the countdown that the clamp won't release for another 03.37 minutes, so I take my time buckling up my five-point harness and adjusting the lumbar support of my seat. I love that the Japanese believe in constant improvement, *kaizen*, as they call it. Or at least I used to love it when I still loved and cared about things. I am very private about myself, but have an open, easy disposition, which fools a lot of people into thinking that I am a truly happy person. I briefly wonder whether Keiko suspects something, whether she's figured it out. But then she would know that it wasn't going to take place here, so why the beefed up security?

00:00 minutes—click. The clamp releases and the skiff makes off in a hurry as I set my plane against the wind in a southwesterly direction. There is timing involved in gaining lift quickly, and sucking one of the pontoons out of the chop before the other. The principle is the same as first pulling one boot out of the mud and then the second. Doing this simultaneously is nearly impossible in rough seas. Luckily, the powerful engine has plenty of redundancy and can build the ideal takeoff speed over a relatively short distance. As there is no break release on water, I have to just proverbially floor it at the right moment. I am pressed hard against my seat as the plane tears itself from the clinging water, which I imagine is biting at the heels of my pontoons as once again I race towards the heavens.

Next stop, Oʻahu. I know Sarah would be horrified at what I am contemplating, at what I have, in fact, been planning to do. After all, her father and I brought her up to be better than that. You help people in need, you root for the underdog, you stand up to the bullies, you educate whenever you can, you don't descend to their level, lest you want to become the same. No, you take the high road. These are all fragments of Sarah's early lessons in negotiating life, school, and hard-to-control emotions.

Neither Sarah nor I believed in the death penalty. Philosophically untenable, fraught with the risk of killing an innocent, and lacking in true emotional maturity, it seems impossible to justify. But I am no longer concerned with the luxury of ivory tower debates, nor am I concerned with the calm counseling of my father against my impetuousness and my never forgetting anyone's place in the big picture, and even the far bigger picture, the one beyond this lifetime or boundaries of our little planet.

I am done with all of that and worry again whether Keiko knows. I worry whether there is a governor that controls the engine should it deviate too far from the flight plan, or even whether flight control can be entirely disabled and the plane flown remotely, like a drone? Then there are the ever-expanding U.S. no-fly zones and anti-aircraft-missile batteries to consider. Would a Mayday provide adequate time to do it? Mayday—Sarah died on a May Day—the sixth. Discharging the emergency flare gun in the cockpit would require me to open the hatch to continue to see. Since we are supposed to land in Oʻahu Bay anyway, I could reach altitude and speed that would make this feasible. If I took off my parachute and fired the flare into the compacted material, it should create a lot of smoke to signal evident distress and create some confusion. Luckily, the Islamic center is not far from the coast. My chances of putting it out of business are good. With any luck, on impact I'll get some of the cowards who send their brainwashed charges to do their dirty work for them as well. Best of all, if my father was right, Sarah will be waiting for me and all of us will be together again.

Or will she? Is suicide punished instead of rewarded on the Karmic wheel? Is there a bigger picture I can't understand from the perspective of this one lifetime? My mother wanted to teach me about Kabbalah, but I was interested in slipstreams instead. Like so many secular Jews, we were not a religious family. My mother's interest in the mystical interpretations of our religion was part of a diet of other mysterious teachings, such as Ayurvedic medicine, yoga, and, surprisingly, *Star Trek*. For the last two millennia, being Jewish has not exactly been easy. Even today, the world holds Israel to far stricter and often-unrealistic standards of behavior against the relentless backdrop of suicide bomb attacks. Most are foiled but not all. Any other country in the same position would respond far less moderately. Yet, there seems to be no proportional outrage to the human rights violations committed by Arab nation states against their own people compared to the passionate criticism of Israel defending her country and people. Where does this double standard come from? Is it a type of inverted racism with less expected of Arab countries, or is it an expression of unchanged anti-Semitism?

The Kabbalistic tree consists of circles or spheres, connected by lines. The ten spheres and twenty-two paths that connect them are considered to be the oldest story in history, representing the forces of creation on all levels. In fact, *Ein Sof*, meaning "without end" in both space and time, is so transcendent that it is beyond what can be described. Therefore, it can only interact with the universe through its essence described in the ten spheres known as the *Sefirot*. As a girl, I would tell my mom that all this demonstrates is the origin of the decimal system and its metric superiority over the imperial one. As a consequence, my mother enjoyed discussing esoteric matters more with Eric von Däniken, whose daughter Cornelia attended school with me in Bern. Yet, perhaps my mother was onto some greater wisdom. Auspiciously, a crop circle representing the tree of life appeared near Barbury Castle in May of 1997, the year my mother died of breast cancer. My father died two years later. The problem with dismissing crop circles out of hand is the speed at which they appear, the perfect design, which from the ground would be near impossible to achieve, at least pre-GPS, and the fact that certain crop stems, bent to ninety degrees, should snap in half instead of allowing themselves to yield to such extreme positions as they do in these formations.

While finding the designs peripherally interesting, it has always been easier for me to ignore such things, without a good argument for doing so. I feel unease about the lack of a credible alternative explanation, and moreover the dismissal of these phenomena as hoaxes—again, given the speed, the precision, and the lack of a track of any machinery leading to the formations through the fields within which they appear. A hundred years ago anyone predicting a moon landing within fifty-six years would have been lucky to escape being committed to an asylum. A few centuries before, most were convinced that the world was flat. Not understanding and not believing, or else the opposite, fervently believing and confidently understanding what can be known at a given time, never quite correspond to reality in hindsight. Climate change is upon us, the evidence is overwhelming, and yet, large segments of the world's population comfort themselves by not believing in it as if it were not happening, as if it were some choice based on political affiliation.

Nearer to the outer edge of our atmosphere, I think again of its fragility and our collective participation in its destruction. Salk, the inventor of the polio vaccine, is often quoted as having stated that if all insects disappeared from earth, all life would cease to exist within fifty years. Alternatively, if all humans were to disappear, everything left would be thriving within fifty years. Is the need to collectively change so against our nature that we subconsciously accept that self-destruction is the easier and ultimately necessary way? Are suicide bombers just the first wave of a far more deep-rooted self-hatred within humanity, which most of us would not deliberately act upon and yet, at the same time, we do nothing that is necessary to avoid an eventual, collective, worldwide, sustainability collapse that is as good as a collective suicide?

Focus Leah! This is a mission, this is revenge, this is justice, and this is a warning that the tables can be turned. Not that this is new. The British carpet bombed civilian cities in Germany to provoke the predictable revenge of the German Luftwaffe against British civilian targets, in particular, London. This kept the enemy planes away from the British munitions factories and other strategic military targets. Nothing is new and nothing is different. Will this cause an embarrassment for Israel and Japan? Undoubtedly it will.

Yet, it will draw a contrast between what they do regularly and what we don't. We don't target civilians on purpose with murder in our minds. There is a false equivalency applied to Israel and no one else who fights terror. Is it my fault that the missile depot I was tasked to neutralize in Gaza was deliberately placed among civilian housing? Am I to live with the guilt of what we hoped to avoid by dropping leaflets before the impending raid? Well, if so, let me make it official, Israel is the worst country on the planet when it comes to its own public relations efforts.

The structure should be easy enough to see and be visible soon. The minarets, so reminiscent of contemporary missiles have silently spoken of an unknowable weapon of the future for centuries. For me they will be the lighthouses that guide me home, the beacons that will bring the relief I have been seeking since Sarah's death. They'll consume the anger that devours me like a cancer.

And there it is, sooner than I thought, the beautiful coastline of O'ahu and the impressive outlines of the mosque. I have been dropping altitude predictably and have been able to remain on course. Luckily, the bay is further up the coast than the Islamic center with its connected Mosque. It's time to act. I reduce speed as much as possible without stalling. I call in my first Mayday. I operate mechanically now. The parachute in its designated place already, I fire the flare gun into the nylon. Despite my visor, I am temporarily blinded by the brightness, but my finger is already on the disarming button of the cockpit window, which snaps off like a twig and crashes into the tail of my plane. The smoke clears instantly and I can keep focus on my final destination.

From the ground, the cabin fire must look authentic. The whining alarms inform me of the clear deviation of the flight plan I set and then they stop. The plane changes direction on its own. The fin rudder must still work. I anticipated this and turn off the engine. With the rear rudder intact, I can still steer myself to the new destination. No response, nothing. The propeller keeps turning on the command of a new master. Plan B. To override the fuel lines would only work one way. To take that control away from the pilot would be unconscionable, unforgivable, and risk their lives in a myriad of potential emergencies. I snap them off. Nothing, Bastards! And then my propeller stutters to its death.

I have never been in a glider and the image I had harbored of me sailing silently on raptor's wings was shattered by the wind-noise amplified by the missing cockpit window. Searing pain, what feels like a blowtorch held to my right calf, interrupts my next thought. The phosphorus of the flare has burned through my parachute and is headed for my bone. It hurts so much that I am crying, and so I see even less. I am not crying out of pain. Anyone shot in the gut knows pain and I didn't cry then. I cry for what I am about to do. I cry for the victims I intend to create. I cry for the pain of those who feel loss and will still take the risk to love.

I wrench at the locked controls. Please don't be on target. I didn't mean it. I don't want to kill, just die. I know I have no right to exist. It's all my fault, please let it be over, and please don't let me take anyone with me.

With that thought my left wing catches the top of a wave and cartwheels the plane with such force that first the right and then the left wing shear off. The water feels surprisingly cold. Cold like the snow didn't. Cold like my beating heart isn't yet. The phosphorus is immune to water and continues to punish me for all of my sins. I am too stunned to undo my seat belt.

"Leah."

I comfort myself by hugging myself like a mummy, slowly descending into the big blue in her white sarcophagus…

"Leah… Leah!"

I blink. "I gave you an extra ten, no time for more." "Thank you," I manage to say as I avoid the wise old eyes of Kaz, who I was always afraid could read my thoughts by just looking at me.

"Are you okay?" I blush before I answer in the affirmative. I never could lie well despite the training. Not the IDF training, but the unspoken training at home. What a fucking burden, and I only realize this now.

"Leah?"

"Yes?"

"Are you okay? You seem far away. Are you safe to fly?"

"To fly? Yes… of course! The treatment must have made me drowsy somehow."

"Really?" is the unconvinced reply. The acupuncturist says it kindly, gives me my mental privacy and signals to the aides who deferentially help me with the flight suit. Right now, I sense their downcast existence below their obsequious cheerfulness. My heart is full of love and compassion for them. Am I bi-polar? No, they checked for that during the medical exam.

"Let the ghosts go, Leah."

"What ghosts?" I'm responding a little too defiantly, looking around as if they were visible. Auschwitz, Munich, Gaza, Sarah, I asked myself?

Standing fully erect, I am a good head taller than Kaz and right now I enjoy this advantage as I resolutely find and meet his gaze.

"… all have them," is all I catch as the acupuncturist turns around with an irritatingly wise smile that lingers behind his receding figure. "Who are you?" I hear myself ask as he disappears. Kaz is on the first ship and Kaz's daughter, Dr. Sachi Watase will be waiting on Oʻahu. I let myself be led on autopilot to the cockpit, now self-conscious at my full nakedness in front of this strange man.

Kaz is usually so strict. How did he know to let me live out my revenge fantasy on his table right to the inevitable end, with the only likely outcome I had ever seriously entertained? I really must focus on more positive thinking.

"Safe flight," says another smiling face, as I prepare to actually depart the first refueling ship to start my journey to Oʻahu. Click the cockpit, click the seat belts, and click the pontoon leg. I don't even remember the flight check before accelerating and soaring off like an uncaged bird. Free, I feel free. I love the whole world and I am okay to be lonely, to exist, and even to love, at least in the abstract.

Who was that back there? What was that back there? And then it comes rushing up like a flood. The white sarcophagus shoots out of the sea and, like a heat-seeking missile deployed by the submarine of my subconsciousness, engulfs my little plane in feverish flames of recognition. The lies, the fucking lies. Always the fucking lies!

We had a beautiful watercolor by Emil Nolde of three sunflowers, saved by my father's aunt. It had hung on the fireplace mantle in Bern and I was never to talk to anyone about it. Not even to my best friend, not to anyone. Was the Gestapo going to come and confiscate it? Was it going to be stolen from a heavily guarded house in Bern's diplomatic enclave? Would it really have been vulgar to talk about a thing we all loved and were meant to cherish and pass on, instead of being the mute custodians we had become? My only relief was to auction it off one day, for no good reason at all, so that I can deeply regret it now.

What of the ski trips that never happened? Not all of them of course, but many when my father's limousine would leave for Gstaad with three pairs of skis on the roof rack. My mother and I spent the weekend indoors and alone in Bern so that the pretense would be upheld. The shared stories of two great days of skiing in school that never happened. The acupuncturist must have hit a point in my body. A reservoir of stored trauma that was so inconspicuous, that I never knew I had stored it physically. Not trauma like wearing a suicide belt past a checkpoint, mind you, just the little lie here and there. "You'll understand one day." Of course I did, a safe house. After all, who doesn't have one masquerading as a ski chalet?

The skies are clear and the clouds have vanished like the ghosts, for now at least. Ahead and all around, one of the world's largest garbage heaps becomes clearly visible. The trash vortex that has steadily accumulated from decades of dumping by the world's shipping enterprises forms itself into islands of deadly treachery. Created by so many little acts, unimaginable to be of real consequence on their own, but cumulatively they are a small set of galaxies of despair for the albatrosses that land there and gorge themselves on sustenance that will only kill them and their chicks.

On approach to O'ahu Bay, the mosque becomes visible. It is a beautiful building with the potential to be used for good or ill, as is any structure. The Inquisition, as well as the messages and acts of goodness from the new Pope, originated in the same Papal Palace. Landing on O'ahu Bay is a blur, as is the traditional Hawaiian flower-greeting, a necklace of good intentions in each dying flower petal, as transient as the wearer's will to hold on to one of them.

I've chosen to exercise my choice as an educated person to contribute to the general good, to seek out my enemies and make peace, to do this thoroughly, to live it, to act upon it, and to show up every day whether I want to or not. I have decided that it is okay for the ghosts to come too. In fact they must. The naïveté of that intention, the proverbial "small drop of water on a hot stone," was so utterly subverted by each little piece of refuse that helped to form those massive islands of trash. They are surely a testament that this can also work in reverse, for good. All small acts and gestures of good will eventually find the same gravitational vortex and will form galaxies of kindness and reason. I'll work at the secret locations where Palestinian and Israeli girls get to know each other as people rather than as enemies. If not that, then something else, but I will work to make a difference. I read about Kurt Gearheart in New Mexico, U.S.A., who started a new energy company. He has figured out how to use the world's dirtiest infrastructures, such as coal plants, for clean and sustainable energy sources. How that would change world politics! Keiko and I were talking about him and she encouraged me to contact him after The Race. For as long as I truly don't want to live, I'll live for others rather than kill them. I have a choice that comes with knowledge that so many are denied. The courageous voices from the Arab world that have started a counter-narrative to the seductive fundamentalist indoctrination are unsung heroes and need everyone's support.

I don't care whether I win this race anymore. I just feel privileged to be part of it… the human race, the airplane race, and the race towards reason rather than demise. I will take rejection with gratitude, and when I fail, I'll seek out and help empower those likeminded people who are still fighting. That good which is outside of each of us and yet deeply within is not only more important than individual success, but infinitely more rewarding. Perspective and humility aren't finite goals, they are universal values, and probably not by accident, difficult to hold onto and to truly understand.

The forecast for San Francisco is driving rain, high winds, and low visibility. Good news as far as I am concerned. I've had enough of these endlessly oppressive blue skies, or wishing for them, meteorologically and metaphorically.

Flying east means flying against time and shortening the day just as flying west prolongs it. Consequently, it will be dark when we land in San Francisco. There is another paradox for the Swiss. The experience of time can be contracted or expanded depending on the speed and direction of our own movement relative to the earth and its rotation. The circadian rhythm, when crossing multiple time zones disrupts the body's anticipated day and night patterns. Travel that exceeds the speed of our planet's rotation puts us out of synchronicity with where and when we are supposed to be. This displacement in time and space, commonly referred to as jetlag, is a word derived from the cause, the jet, and its effect, the lag. Lagging behind time is true when flying west, but lagging in front of time, or something else, isn't linguistically used to describe a position or condition. If we fly east, we find ourselves somewhere where time has not caught up with us. Time is lagging behind and we arrive in the future too early or, conversely, too late. Yet, this only happens when flying east or west. Flying north or south, in an adjusted pattern for planetary rotation, displaces us only in space but not time.

Time, what an enigmatic concept, its relativity in relation to velocity and the point of observation are all physics, but relative to experience, it becomes perceptual and psychological. When I was five, a year, even a summer, seemed endless. But then a year represented twenty percent of my total life experience. For a fifty-year-old, it represents just a small percentage of total life experience, and, accordingly, seems less or seems faster. What we measure so universally has a different meaning to each for so many reasons. If this is true, we can surely agree on other things, although experienced differently by each of us. My father used to smoke Time, the name of an Israeli cigarette brand. How much of his went up in smoke? It is the present then that I should be embracing. But whenever I try to grasp it, it too is already gone.

The food on the second refueling ship between Oʻahu and the Golden Gate Bridge is amazing. Did someone send an actual Mayday after eating the food on the first ship? Sashimi, for which I have developed a real taste, is abundant and I enjoy North Atlantic salmon that melts like cold butter on my tongue and the added sting of wasabi, suspended in soy sauce, creates a culinary collision of hot and cold, firm and liquid, sweet and savory, plus some intangible component that makes the meal feel somehow decadent, but not ostentatious.

As the clamp releases my floatplane for the last time, I still taste the ice-cold salmon. Unbidden, the taste of Radka's cold tongue after a swig from her Ichiban bottle on the way back to our rooms during training, makes an entrance on the stage of my senses. Her kiss and embrace was brief and with a wink she was gone. I remember standing there like a schoolgirl who had been brazenly kissed by one of the cool boys. My life has been devoid of physical intimacy since the dissolution of my marriage, followed so closely by the death of my daughter. For the first time since then, something stirs in me now that I didn't recognize when it happened.

Sarah regularly supported her gay friends during the annual Pride Parade, when gay Israelis ride around Tel-Aviv on bicycles in their underwear. I also think Sarah just liked riding on a bicycle in her underwear. It was a naughty thing to do and not exactly embraced by all who live in our city. The thought of Radka makes me feel similarly rebellious. I admonish myself for thinking of what Christine and Kaz would make of the matter. They have become parental figures to us all, and like all children, we are all different. Maybe those of us without parents are more vulnerable in relation to their opinion of us, which, in Kaz's case, is even more inscrutable than from the warm but reserved Brit. These parents have something in common, their countries of birth cradle Eurasia, the outermost points of the enormous landmass to the west and east, both of them are islands connected to the adjacent landmass, and yet not. Both of them are ancient warrior cultures, riding and driving on the left and facing the enemy right-handed with a sword. Both live with royalty in a democracy, and each are de facto parents of this unlikely brood of sisters.

No matter how hard I try to get Radka out of my thoughts by looking for more analogies between Britain and Japan, she keeps playing on my mind. I like her unapologetic frankness that isn't quite reckless, but feels a little dangerous. She has an edge. Behind the boisterous exterior, there is a melancholic brutality and vulnerability. I never thought of my tom-boyishness in this way. And maybe I am not really attracted to women. Maybe I just miss my daughter and imagine this would bring another kind of closeness? Or maybe she connects me with those from my Eastern European roots, those people who so readily participated in my fellow citizens' destruction. Maybe that ambivalence towards her creates this passion? Maybe I should accept that not every single feeling should or even can be rationalized. After all, it won't save me from having the feelings anyway.

So I do what I have not yet done on this journey. I take advantage of having no neighbors and turn on the state-of-the-art inflight sound system full blast. Even though I had uploaded music from Patty Smith to Sibelius, I decide on the mournful violins to start with. Only upon starting to blast *Finlandia* do I really connect its tumultuous beginning with the tumultuous weather outside. My ride is getting bumpy. Flying below the speed of sound had seemed almost quaint at times, but as instructed by Keiko, I am now headed for Cloud Nine with British and Japanese parents, an evident crush on a Czech, in a Spitfire refurbished by the Japanese to go where no Japanese Spitfire has gone before, the promised land, San Francisco, America.

Much of the weight on my shoulders has been lifted since the start of the journey, but there is one thing I cannot keep from following me, as it is already in front of me. I have more or less traveled as the crow flies. All the while the serpentine path of poison from Fukushima across the Pacific keeps flowing beneath me and I think again, "An eye for an eye" must stop, or as Gandhi famously said, "The whole world will go blind."

RADKA ZELENKOVA

BURGUNDY 7

My grandfather was a hero and my father was a traitor. I have spent my whole life trying to figure out which of these I am.

The same type of plane I fly now from Tokyo to San Francisco, my grandfather flew for the Czech Air Force in World War II. He fought the Germans in the Battle of France and was shot down over the mouth of the Somme River at the English Channel. I imagine his charred body fused to the metal of the cockpit where I sit, left hand on the control column, and right hand on the throttle. His plane was gray camo, mine, *Burgundy 7*.

I don't believe in spirits and all that shit, but if we do share our blood somehow, Děda is getting the chance to fly a Spitfire again.

A commercial jet would do this trip in one eleven-hour stretch, but the Spitfire's tiny fuel tank makes this race a puddle-jump across the Pacific via three refueling stops. I am two hours into the first stage of The Race. The way the blue and white swirls around me, I have moments when I cannot feel if I'm gaining or losing altitude or holding still.

You might wonder what I am drinking. But the answer is nothing, of course.

I can see my face reflected in the windscreen, and what I see is a middle-aged dyke with a grown-out buzz cut whose father died not six months ago and whose wife is sleeping with another woman. My life is completely falling apart, save this span of nineteen or so hours in the air, a welcome suspension that is not without its own continuous adrenaline rush.

When I signed up for this Race, my father was ill but alive. I had not yet decided if I would hop an airliner to Chicago to end our long silence. But she who hesitates is lost, and that is no longer an option. So I am dedicating this flight to my grandfather and, reluctantly, to my father.

I wonder if the fact that Lucie is leaving me proves there is some kind of order in the universe. I, who have broken relationships and hearts, am now experiencing the same from the other side.

I did have a broken heart when I was very young, but I broke it myself.

You could say I stole Lucie from her girlfriend. It was 1993, when the Czech Republic hosted the Eighth Women's European Flying Championships. Lucie's girlfriend was competing and I was her support crew. This woman was the original control freak, constantly insisting that the smallest things must be done her way. She asked me to tune up her engine with a method that violated protocol. The third time I said no, I said it with a serving of her own bitchiness. That caught Lucie's attention.

I grabbed Lucie's hand when the girlfriend wasn't looking. We snuck a kiss in the lobby of the control tower while the girlfriend was competing in the aerobatics event, where she took fourth place.

I should have known then that the same thing would eventually happen to me.

We might have survived Lucie's affair, except that her disappointment ran too deep.

"You don't really love me," she said. "You don't respect me." She was coming at me with a glass of red wine that looked like it might just keep going.

I stepped out of its trajectory. "You are being hysterical, as usual," I said. "Of course I do."

"You respect men more than women. Admit it," she shot back. "This just proves one more time that you have no idea who I really am." A few drops sloshed, fell on our carpet, which was fortunately brown.

I am still fuming about this groundless accusation. I love only women. I prefer the friendship of women. I am racing across the Pacific Ocean because I want to celebrate how far we've come as women.

But one element of what she said was true. I have always cared too much about what men thought of me, especially my father. I have hated myself for this. And it is why I broke my own heart.

When I was a child, my family lived on the fifth floor of a nineteenth-century building near the center of Prague. Mother and Father worked for the government. Mother worked mornings as a clerk in the public transportation division, when digging had just begun on a metro system that would serve the city. My younger brother, Jakub, and I did not know exactly what Father's job was, only that he was called away on emergencies at all hours of the day and night. Our neighbors would hurry into their flats when they saw him walking up the stairs, or open their doors only well after he had passed. On the rare occasions when they met him face to face, they called him "Comrade Zelenka" and proclaimed their support for this or that Party initiative.

Like the neighbors, Jakub avoided Father when he could. But Father and I had a special connection, a friendship I knew not to disturb. To me, he was the most powerful man in the world. Whatever self-worth I felt was in proportion to his attention. When he took photographs of me with his Holga or explained fantastical aspects of the universe, like black holes and neutron stars, I felt something from him like love. Still I feel that old ache in my throat to remember.

My given name was Nataša. In those days I liked the name because it was popular in Russia, and the Russians were helping our small country grow stronger. Father often held gatherings for those who were working to ensure that everyone had a job, health care, a decent flat, and a cottage in the countryside. He spoke Russian with them and unlocked the crystal cabinet and poured vodka into blue shot glasses. Father did not like vodka. But with these men, even his laughter sounded Russian.

At school I was popular. In gym class, I was one of the first kids picked for teams, and at lunch in the cafeteria, my table was always full. But I was more intrigued with the kids whom the others did not like, like Kateřina Valdová.

We were twelve in the fall when Katka first showed up at my school. She was skinny and pale, with black braided hair and dark, arching eyebrows that made her always look like she knew something the rest of us did not.

She said nothing until one day in geography class. We were playing a game of labeling a large map of Europe with the names of every country. We had to close our eyes and choose a label from a bowl, then place it on the map. The first boy correctly labeled the Socialist Republic of Romania. The second kid put her Liechtenstein label over Luxembourg and the teacher corrected her.

Katka went third. She approached the map and placed her label over the outlined shape of our country, the Czechoslovak Socialist Republic. But as she stepped away from the map, we saw that her label read "USSR."

A few giggles rose from the class. She looked at us without cracking a smile and then moved the label to the right place.

"Sit down, Comrade Valdová," the teacher ordered in a tone laced with sarcasm. "And see me after class."

After that incident, all the kids shunned Katka at recess. I felt bad for her, and one day when I saw Katka on the swings by herself, I took the swing next to hers and swung higher and faster and jumped off, the skirt of my uniform flapping up to my arms. She laughed and jumped off after me.

"What punishment did you get," I asked, "for your joke?"

"I had to write the names of all the socialist countries in the world. Ten times each."

"Did you get them right?" I asked.

"Yes, of course. I'm a good comrade," she said, the hint of a smile in her eyes.

After school we kicked a ball around in the street. Katka was wiry and fast. I could kick harder and more accurately. We played almost every afternoon that autumn. Together we could take on any pair of girls and most of the boys. I tried to bring her into my circle of friends, but they never warmed to her. Over time, I let them go.

When the snow started falling, Katka and I built snow creatures and started snowball fights. But as the days grew darker and more frigid, I asked Mother if Katka could come over to play. She deferred the question to Father, who said, "No."

"But Jakub has Michal over almost every day," I protested.

"Michal's parents are loyal to the Party," he said. "Why do you spend time with such a girl, anyway?"

I turned away.

Katka's parents took things a step further. They forbade Katka from playing with me at all. So Katka created a fictional friend, Martina, as her alibi, and we would go sledding on Petřín Hill until dusk. Even the week it was minus ten degrees Celsius, being exiled with Katka was better than being home with Mother as she cleaned our already clean flat and nursed her Becherovka and tonic, the green herbal smell of which still conjures up that time period in my memory.

Naturally, Katka and I did not call each other on the telephone. You could not know who might be listening.

In the spring I turned thirteen. A pair of falcons made their nest in the flower box outside our bathroom window, just over the bathtub. Opaque swirls on the glass rendered the birds as winged shadows to us, and our faceless, looming shapes did not frighten them away. We could get a clear view of the nest only from a window in the stairwell near the elevator, a half-flight up from our flat. Father said they were the type of falcon called "kestrels." He knew because the male had a bluish head and chestnut wings with black spots, and the female was striped brown and black. I named them "Rufus" and "Radka."

In time five eggs appeared, and Radka sat on them while Rufus hunted. On hot days, she made an umbrella of her wings to shade the eggs. Four round white babies hatched in early July. Their little spiky beaks and comically glowering eyebrows grew more fearsome as their bodies got bigger and fluffier and grayer. When Radka saw us watching, she would crane her neck scolding us to go away. Father photographed the family from the stairwell and inside the bathroom—still lifes with toothbrush, shampoo, and bird shadows, luminescent shit streaking the window.

One parent would stay with the brood while the other hunted. Radka brought back the bodies of killed pigeons, which she tore to bloody strings and dangled above the gaping mouths. Rufus preferred small rodents. I admired the birds' ruthlessness and I loved the gore.

One afternoon I brought Katka over to see the babies. We waited until 4:30 before we rode the elevator up. By that time, Mother would be into her first glass of Becher and would not leave the flat. We stayed in the stairwell.

"Oh my God, the babies," Katka said. "They are ugly and adorable, both."

"I knew you would love them."

We laughed at how the heavier Radka squawked and clawed at Rufus, who scratched and chattered back.

"Just like a real married couple," Katka said.

"Not my parents," I said. "They don't shout. They slam cupboards and doors."

Radka stood on the edge of the box and stretched her impressive wingspan. She launched forward and hovered over the courtyard between the buildings, then plunged so fast it was hard to track her. She reeled on the point of a wing and vanished behind the trees. "Father says their cousin the peregrine falcon is the fastest animal in the whole world," I said. "They can fly more than 300 kilometers per hour."

Minutes later, Radka materialized out of thin air and landed on the window box with pigeon parts grasped in her claws. As she ripped off the first bite-sized piece, Katka buried her head in my shoulder. "That's disgusting!"

I laughed and stroked the black hair around her forehead. "Don't look," I said. "It's even grosser right now." She kept her head there, even when the gross part was over. Her hair was thick and soft.

We rode the elevator down. Nobody had seen.

I wanted to be Radka. I wanted to circle the spires of Prague cathedrals, weave among the rafters of castle buildings. If an airplane was required because I was merely human, so be it. I knew my grandfather, Děda, was a pilot and that's how he died. He had escaped to France after the Nazis took over Czechoslovakia. He was shot down when Father was only five.

I imagined him doing crazy aerobatic stunts as he waited for his first victim. Then sighting a German plane, dogging it, going in for the kill. Not bothering to look behind and above him, where a German Dornier Do 17 was also waiting, ready to strike at his most vulnerable moment.

Secretly I wanted to die that way too, in a plane. Thinking now about him, I want to attempt a roll or a spin, but I can't sacrifice the time, or risk fucking it up due to the odd weight of these pontoons, a feature Děda's plane obviously did not have.

Had he survived France, Děda would have flown five weeks later in the Battle of Britain, the Allied Forces' first victory over the Germans.

Father did not often speak of Děda. But I remember an incident that happened on my birthday when I turned nine. My birthday falls on the pagan holiday of Beltane, which Czechs celebrate as *Čarodějnice,* Night of the Witches. The name day for Nataša is a few weeks after that. In those days resources were tight and parties for children rare. But that year my parents let me invite a few school friends to celebrate my birthday, name day, and *Čarodějnice,* all in one.

Jakub's friend Michal was there, a red-haired boy whose teeth went in every direction at once. I liked him, but he was a pain in the ass. At our first party game, I won the best prize, a large straw witch to burn that night in a bonfire near our cottage. Michal accused me of cheating. Other kids got on his side and the party was ruined. My face burned red.

Father waited until all the guests had left. Then he whopped me good on the *zadek* with the flat of his hand. I wailed.

"Honza, that's enough," Mother said. "It's her birthday." In fact, Mother and I had conspired in advance that if I won a game, I would get that witch. So I made sure I won the first game, and she made sure the witch was the prize I got. But I didn't tell Father her role in the conspiracy. I didn't want his anger turned on her.

He squatted down and grabbed my arms firmly. "Nataša," he began, eyes flashing as he stared me in the face. "You need to play by the rules, like everybody else."

I nodded, examining the pattern of the carpet.

"Bad things happen to people who don't play by the rules. Like your grandfather."

I stopped nodding and looked at him, not understanding. He released me.

In the kitchen they whispered like hissing cats. "What does your father have to do with this?" said Mother.

"Look where rebelling got him. At twenty-eight, he was dead. He could not provide for his wife and children."

"Those pilots got us out from under the boot of the Nazis. Or have you forgotten?"

"He couldn't see his granddaughter turn nine."

I didn't understand. I had always put Děda on the same pedestal as my father. Now Father was dragging him down to the level of some bad thing I had done. I whispered a silent apology to his ghost, still circling in a Spitfire high above us.

What I did understand was that losing Father's love was not an option. I worked harder in school to bring home good grades, and I stayed out of trouble at home.

Having a special birthday made me think I was special. Maybe being born a witch was another reason I thought I could fly. At this point in my life, though, I'm well aware that I'm not special. And this is a good thing. More women are flying these days. More women are breaking the rules.

The light on my fuel gauge shines orange, bringing me back into my body, still pinned to its chair with the five-point harness. I have no idea why I'm going over this story now, 24,500 feet in the air. I haven't let it into my head in years, though in some sense Katka has always been with me.

My GPS says only 400 miles to the first refueling stop, on the Mitsubishi ship. I start the descent, heart pounding a little because this one counts.

I signed up for this Race with the notion that I could win. I did not predict that my life would go to shit in the meantime. Now I just want to finish somewhere above last and enjoy this game in the company of international women pilots. It turns out that among these accomplished women, I am not the only dyke. Two aspirational lesbians are giving me heavy vibes—the charming but too-young Piccola and the

Israeli pilot Leah, who engaged me in conversation one night in the hallway between our rooms. She told me the terrible story of losing her daughter, and I mentioned the death of my father and my impending divorce. As we took turns saying that we were sorry, Leah kept moving just a little bit closer. I thought this was a cultural thing so I kept my feet where they were. Gradually I came to appreciate being too close to her. When we ran out of things to say and the air stayed electric, I realized why we were still standing there. I took her face in my hands and kissed her.

At one point in my life, bringing women out of the closet was my favorite hobby, my contribution to the movement. But even as Leah's lips opened into mine, I knew I did not have the stomach for more. I cannot manage anyone's coming out process right now. I can barely stay focused on the task at hand, whether piloting this aircraft or landing on the water with these godforsaken pontoons.

As I approach the water on a gentle curve, I lower the flaps and ease the nose up to slow down. My landing has too much bounce to it. Still, the ground crew claps and cheers. I unlock and raise the window. "How's my time?" I ask, climbing out of the cockpit with stiff legs.

"Four hours, five minutes," a crewmember says, offering his hand as I straddle the gap between plane and skiff. "You're doing very well."

Doing very well is good enough for now. I linger under the hot stream of the shower longer than I am supposed to. Then I lie prostrate, stuck by the needles of Dr. Watase, a peculiar character. It's quite an odd thing to have three acupuncture treatments in the middle of a race. To be forced to deeply relax when the adrenaline wants to pump.

The pasty glop they feed me is even worse than Czech dumplings. "We are not astronauts, you know," I joke with the ground crew. I wash it down with a double espresso. I climb into a fresh flight suit and then slide into the cockpit to further aggravate my already sore ass. I feel too tall and big for this tiny plane, and my feet want somewhere to rest besides the pedals.

"Good luck, Major Zelenková," the youngest crewman says with a grin and salute.

It's just seconds before the pontoon is released. Perfect.

Taking off is still magic to me, every time.

Michal never apologized for ratting on me, but I was so thoroughly shamed that I dropped it and we formed an unspoken truce. The winter before the kestrels arrived, he was failing math class. He was hopeless with fractions. I had a knack, so I often helped him with his homework. With Mother's permission, I cut up her *koláče* (pastries) into equal pieces and arranged her *chlebíčky* (mini sandwiches) in rows, searching for a key to his locked mind. Sometimes I found it.

To thank me, or maybe to calm my impatient nature, Michal would bring me flowers he had stolen from public gardens. On Easter Monday he appeared first thing in the morning just so he and Jakub could take their *pomlázky*, braided willow branches topped with colored streamers, and whip me over the backside in an old sexist Czech fertility ritual. But we girls get our revenge by throwing water on the boys, which I did with relish.

One afternoon late in July, I brought Katka again to see the falcons. "The young ones are growing so fast," she said. "They look more like Radka than Rufus."

The smell of Mother's goulash wafted up the stairwell. "Bring me a bowl of goulash," Katka joked. "I will stay here."

The elevator opened to reveal Jakub and Michal. I grabbed them each by an arm. "Don't tell," I whispered with a threat in my voice. The boys were a grade younger than me and I was a few inches taller, so I could bully them.

At the dining room table, I sat between Jakub and Michal. Father put his favorite Dvořák record on, the Symphony Number 5. "And how is our *sokol* family?" he asked as he took his place at the head. *Sokol* is Czech for "falcon."

"The babies are getting feathers," I said. "They look like Radka. I think they are all females."

"Unlikely," he said. "The juveniles are striped for the first year, regardless of their sex." Father knew so much.

"Taši," Mother asked me, "how is your friend Kateřina?"

I looked at the boys, who did not meet my eyes. "Fine," I answered, warily.

"Her father is still selling puppets?" Father asked.

"Yes. Katka said he just finished an amazing crone."

"Oh yes?" Father asked. "What other characters does he create?"

"Normal stuff." I kicked Jakub under the table. He kicked me back.

"Such as," he persisted.

I passed the dumplings to Michal. "I don't know, I have never seen them." I kept my voice light and even. "Katka says kings and queens, devils, and crones. He carves their faces out of wood and sews their costumes by hand."

Mother asked, "And he sells them at a booth on Old Town Square. Isn't that right, Taši?"

I nodded.

Finally, Michal rescued me. "I have a test tomorrow. On volumes. Taša is helping me."

"But it's summer," said Mother.

"He is taking a summer class to catch up," Jakub said, "because he has a frozen brain." He grinned at his friend.

"Volumes are even worse than fractions," Michal groaned.

"Like the volume of *pivo* in my glass?" Father held up his beer and winked at Michal. Mother clinked her Becher with Father's *pivo*, and then we all clinked glasses. *"Na zdraví,"* Father said.

"You have to look me in the eye, Taši," Michal said as our water glasses met. "Or seven years of bad sex."

I laughed. "Where did you hear that?"

Father's favorite section of the symphony was playing—strains of an old folk dance. He closed his eyes and conducted it with one hand. It occurred to me that his thick eyebrows were not unlike those of the juvenile falcons. But since giggling was not an option, I held my breath and stared into my goulash. When Father opened his eyes again, they focused on me. "What sort of music do her parents like?" he asked.

I swallowed a dry hunk of dumpling. "Whose? Katka's?"

He blinked by way of reply.

I took a deep breath. "Smetana," I said with my most charming smile. "Her dad's wild about Smetana."

After dinner I cornered Jakub and Michal in my room. "You rats," I said. "You told him."

"We didn't," they both said at once. "I swear it, Taši," Michal added.

"And I'm supposed to trust *you*?" I asked, only half kidding.

"Yes," Michal said.

Katka lived in Žižkov, down the hill from where the TV tower now stands, about a fifteen-minute walk through the park and cobblestoned streets. Her parents did not have blue shot glasses or a cottage in the countryside. But they had something much better—rock music. One evening when Katka's parents were away at a gathering, she snuck me into her flat and showed me their record collection. *Abbey Road, Exile on Main St., The Dark Side of the Moon*—I knew only that this type of music was forbidden. Katka put on something by The Plastic People of the Universe. "My dad's friends," she said. We closed the windows and doors and jumped around to the cacophony playing air guitar and drums.

When the first side finished she took me into her dad's studio and closed the door. It was completely dark and smelled of glue and sawdust. Katka pulled a string and the light of one naked bulb illuminated a row of puppets hanging from the shelf above the work desk, throwing shadows of giant noses and chins onto the wall and ceiling. Arranged on the shelf were disembodied heads, feet, and hands.

The room was haunted for sure.

The puppets were old men in uniform with grotesquely distorted features that seemed familiar. I identified one as Stalin. Then I got it—Khrushchev, Brezhnev, and our own President Husák. Katka took Husák down and placed him in my hands. His uniform was Soviet red with a yellow hammer and sickle where the military insignia should be. His leering mouth had fake foam at its corners. In spite of myself I giggled, then glanced to make sure Katka had closed the door. "He looks so nasty."

"Because he *is* nasty," Katka said. "A coward and a betrayer, Dad says."

"You really think so?" My voice sounded small. "My Father says he is helping Czech society. So there is no poverty. So we can share things equally."

"Taking over a country by force is not sharing things equally," she said, her words thick with judgment. I smiled, remembering the day in class when I first noticed her.

"What are you talking about? Husák works for the good of the people. Like Father."

"Silly. I'm talking about the Russian tanks."

I'd heard whispers about Russian tanks, but I didn't know what they meant.

"I can't believe you don't know," she said. Back in her room we sat on her bed and she told me the story of the Prague Spring. It was a period of openness for some months when we were seven. People were allowed to travel and speak more freely. But then in late summer of '68, Soviet tanks rolled across the border and took over Prague from its outskirts all the way to its central square, Václavské Náměstí. The Czech people refused the invaders' food and water and replaced the road signs with ones pointing the way back to Moscow.

"Dad showed me a photograph," Katka said. "Russian tanks on Václavák, by the horse statue. They knocked trams on their side and set cars and buildings on fire. They killed a hundred Czechs. Then we surrendered."

I was not ready to commit to believing her or not. My parents had never spoken about this. It was not in our history books or on TV.

"Now we are in the Normalization," I said. "Right?"

"That's what *they* call it. But Mom says there is nothing normal about standing in line for two hours for meat. It was not like this when she was a girl."

Suddenly, I did not know why—I burst into tears. Something about what she said made sense. But if what she said made sense, then nothing else did.

"Don't cry, Taši," she said. "I'm sorry."

And she kissed me on the lips, very quick. Startled, I stared at her.

Then I leaned over to where her face was still hovering with a concerned smile, and kissed her back.

I ran out of her flat and all the way home.

At the park that summer, Katka and I would hide in a stand of trees and practice our kissing technique so we would be ready to someday kiss boys. We even dared to do it in the stairwell a couple times while visiting the birds. We were squeamish about the tongue thing, so we didn't do that except to be gross and funny. She could only handle a few seconds before she'd pull away and whisper, "Stop. What if someone sees us? We'll be dead."

"Kači, we won't be *dead*." But our friendship was highly unusual, and anything unusual was subject to inquiry. Danger was one element that thrilled me about our kisses, made me constantly remember the last one and scheme for the next.

It was not a question of religion. Most Czechs did not believe in God then as now. It was the idea that homosexuality was caused by a decadent bourgeoisie, which is really just another creative form of homophobia. Of course, we did not consider our playing around to be even sexual, much less homosexual. That word was not in our vocabulary.

In late August my family and I took two weeks' holiday at our cottage in the countryside, and when we returned, only one juvenile falcon remained with its parents. It was stripy like Radka but smaller, with puffy breast feathers. I waited for it to take its first flight, but it just perched on the edge of the box, not moving. I wondered if it had vertigo.

By morning, though, the juvenile was gone, and so were its parents. "*Čau*, Rufus, *ahoj*, Radka," I said. "See you next year, I hope."

Fall and winter passed, and the following spring, our kestrel friends did return. Radka laid four eggs and sat on them. It was 1975 and Katka and I had both turned fourteen. Our fellow students in Russian class teased us, saying I was the husband and she was the wife. It was true that I did not really feel like a girl inside. I was tall for my age and big-boned. I refused to wear dresses or a bra, though practically speaking, I needed a bra by that time.

One day in mid-May, Katka missed two days of school. I was worried so I broke our rule and called her on the phone. Her mother answered in a hoarse voice.

"*Dobrý den, paní* Valdová," I began breathlessly. "This is Martina. I am a good friend of Katka. Is she sick? She missed school yesterday and today."

"Oh Martina," she said, her voice breaking. "I cannot talk on the telephone. Please come over." She hung up.

I ran to Žižkov, heart speeding so fast I had to stop and breathe slowly so I would not throw up. When I rang the buzzer, Katka's mom opened the door without a word. Her hair was in strings, eyes rimmed with grief and horror.

"I am Martina," I said. "Is she okay? What happened?"

"Come in. They came to get Katka's father. They questioned him for four hours. Then they beat him." She brought her hands to her face to stifle a single, terrible sob.

"Oh my God, where is he?" The news was horrifying, but I was relieved that Katka was unharmed. I took off my shoes.

"Bartolomějská." The former convent turned police station and jail.

She led me back to Katka's room.

143

I must come back into my body to make the descent to O'ahu. "Good news, Major," the head crewman says. "Keiko has relayed the message that each pilot may keep her Spitfire!"

"*Ježíš Maria*. How will I get the damn thing back to Prague?"

He laughs.

"I am not joking. Where will I refuel? And where will I land it—in the Vltava below the Castle, in a show for the one thousand Italian tourists on the Charles Bridge?"

"Good point, Major. Perhaps you can worry about that later. Would you like to shower?"

"I showered four hours ago. Why are Americans and Japanese so obsessed with hygiene?" I enter the small room where Dr. Satchi Watase is ready for me in a white lab coat. I submit to the twinge of her needles.

The crewman is right. *Burgundy 7* is an amazing, generous gift. On top of the 250,000 dollars I'll get for finishing. So unbelievable, actually, that I wonder for a second if this is all some kind of hoax. Suspicion is part of my DNA, after all.

The doctor leaves the room to let the chi flow or whatever is supposed to happen. I wish I could defect from this race to a warm O'ahu beach, drink some bright cocktail with too much sugar and ice. I imagine lying on a towel beside the baby-dyke Italian pilot, Piccola, the one who asked me when I first knew I was gay, who told me her name means "little bird."

It would certainly show Lucie, to get involved with a woman thirty years younger. But thinking about it makes me feel deeply tired. And then out of nowhere a sob chokes me and I swallow hard. This is not the time to indulge in emotions.

Back in the Spitfire, I strap on my five-point harness and take off. On the ascent I feel and hear the sickening thwack of my propeller hitting a bird, probably an albatross. I think of Rufus and Radka every time. And now I let a few tears flow, glad no one is here as witness.

I walked into Katka's bedroom with my finger to my lips. "I'm Martina," I whispered. She smiled and then her face melted.

I lay with Katka on her bed in the dark as she cried. I wanted to hold her until she did not hurt anymore. I wanted to take her pain away, whether that meant holding her for an hour or a day or a week.

"He'll be okay, Kačí," I whispered.

"They are such brutes."

"I know."

We stayed there quiet a long time, staring at the ceiling. I placed my palm on her belly, over her blouse. She did not push it away. Warmth flushed my whole body.

Then I could not fight the impulse anymore. Gently, I loosened her blouse from the elastic waistband of her skirt. Her eyes were wide and scared and her heart was beating fast like mine. I paused and just held her awhile. At the same time, I remained acutely tuned to when the right moment might be to start pulling up her blouse, so slowly she might not notice, in case I was going too far.

Her tiny breasts were stubby mounds, all nipple. She let me look, let me kiss her navel and stomach before I dared kiss each little flower once, twice, the third time letting my shy tongue taste and trace each contour.

Sometimes when I'm alone with myself I take out this memory. Just this one. Not what happened next.

She let out a moan that was pure sadness.

"Kači. What's wrong?"

She pulled her blouse back into place. I kissed away a tear that had found its way to her chin. "Mom says—."

"What, *lásko?*"

"I can't."

"Shh, it's okay."

"No. It's not. It's not."

Minutes passed before she tried again. "Your father."

I sat up. "What about my father?"

Her voice hitched on each word. "He was part of it."

At first I could not realize what she was saying, then. "No." I pulled from her embrace. "That's not true. That's not possible."

"Don't leave."

"He could not do that. He works for the good of the people." Those words bounced off the walls and fell on the carpet.

"What did you tell him about our family?"

"I told him nothing!" I shouted.

"You said nothing about Dad's puppets? Or our music?"

"Kači, nothing! *Nic!*"

Light fell on us from the opening bedroom door. We were still on the bed, our clothes disheveled. Katka's mom made a strangled noise and slammed it shut.

Katka and I both swore at once. I left the room and slunk past her mom.

"So this is why you like my daughter. Get out of my house, you dirty lesbian!" she spat as I put on my shoes. My face burned, but I could not let this insult into my head—not fully. I would take it out later as one of many things I grieved.

As I begin my descent toward the next refueling ship, it occurs to me with a sick feeling that I must be near or over the famous Pacific Trash Vortex—the gigantic mouth sucking in all the ills of our world, not swallowing what cannot be consumed. Like the garbage of my life, stirred by this flight.

I find it almost eerie that my instrument panel shows nothing out of the ordinary. The plastic is so broken down, particulate, that it is part of the water, food for seabirds. I almost wish the trash were huge and ugly, to be seen more honestly.

Back home, panting, I rapped on my parents' bedroom door. "Where were you, out so late?" Father demanded, tying his bathrobe shut.

"Katka's father is in prison," I said, mouth dry. He didn't blink. "Katka says you put him there."

"Her father is an enemy of the people," he said in his coldest voice.

Mother called from where she sat in bed, reading a book. "Your father does things in his job that you might not understand. For the benefit of our country."

"This matter does not concern you," he added. "Now go to bed."

With that order I had it up to my teeth. I screamed and beat him with my fists.

"You really are not normal, are you?" He picked me up under my shoulders and threw me into the room I shared with Jakub. "Please, stop being hysterical!"

"I am hysterical?" I sassed back. "What about you, shouting. *You* stop being hysterical."

Jakub pretended to be asleep. I cried into my pillow, and I fell and spun through dark space all night.

At school, Katka looked like a ghost, and she stared right through me as if I were one too. I sat down beside her at lunch and she picked up her tray and moved. It was the last week of school but I felt no joy in the coming summer holidays. The way things were going, summer would only mean months away from Katka.

On the last day of school I tore a scrap from my notebook and thrust a note into her hand as we walked into Russian class. "Please, *lásko,* don't hate me," it read. I watched her unfold it. At the end of class she handed it back to me. "I don't hate you," she had written. "I love you. That's why I cannot talk to you right now."

I hid the note in my pillowcase. I dreamed of her every night, visions of what we had done and what I still longed to do. But in each dream she told me why we couldn't be together, a different withdrawing and receding, new words that meant goodbye.

At the third refueling stop, the crew warns me about a storm between here and San Francisco. The pilots before me are reporting high levels of turbulence. With the amount of fuel and time I have—if I still care about placing above last—I cannot go around it. And I'm losing light.

It's hard for me to relax as I receive my last acupuncture treatment from Kaz, who has somehow materialized on this boat. This time, my limbs are restless and agitated, muscles gripping around the needles. I just want to keep going and get this last leg over with before the weather gets any worse. But I submit. Must play by the rules, as Father taught me so well.

"Close to the finish line," Kaz says, "there is a way out of the storm—Cloud Nine." I memorize the coordinates.

As I ascend, the setting sun is blindingly bright. It's a short day, since I'm traveling east as the sun travels west.

Nowhere to go but up and through.

On my last day of school, Father, who usually worked late, was waiting for me when I came home. "Who is it?" he demanded, holding the yellow scrap of paper and shaking it at me. Mother was his shadow behind him, a Becher in one hand, pulling Jakub in with the other.

My eyes darted for an escape.

"It's Michal, isn't it?" he asked.

That was such an absurd idea I bit my bottom lip.

Jakub looked at me, puzzled, before informing Father, "Michal moved to Brno."

My father, hot shit Secret Service, can search my pillows for love notes but cannot see what's under his nose.

"Tell me who it is," he said. "If you tell me, I won't punish you."

I ran out of the house and into the park.

The paved pathway through Riegrovy Sady wound its way over rolling green hills toward the beer garden. I sat on the bench at the highest point, watching a red sun sink behind Petřín like a wound opening at the bottom of the sky, lighting red the river, the Castle, the spires of Old Town Square for a few moments before flaming out. It seemed impossible that it was the same skyline I always saw, that people could be laughing behind me.

Maybe I could have pinned the blame on Michal, had Jakub not opened his fat mouth. Maybe things would have turned out differently. Michal's family had moved to Brno and was beyond my father's grasp, though his comrades were no doubt everywhere.

On the other hand, I was sick, deeply sick, of all the lying and sneaking around. Someone had to tell the truth.

I thought of an answer to the question Father had asked me. No, I was not normal, and I did not want to be. I had recently learned the words "lesbian" and "homosexual," and, recognizing the possibility of myself in the definition, had done some research. Homosexuality was legal in the Czechoslovak Socialist Republic. Maybe Father would be less mad about a girl, take it less seriously. Maybe he would not hate me if he knew who I really was, who I really loved. I would give him one more chance not to hate me.

The path still radiated warmth even at 10 p.m. when I finally walked home. I had nowhere else to go.

The turbulence starts miles before I enter the crimson-streaked storm clouds. Weather like this has swallowed many a small plane. I try to imagine the air like a road in Cambodia—bumpy in the extreme, but still solid ground, as if I'm not being tossed about like a leaf falling from a tree. I breathe, fighting to maintain the control I still have. Lightning crashes all around me. The flaps make an awful hiss. I'm losing too much time—I have to find an opening in this storm. I pull the throttle back and point the nose down to descend.

When I closed the door to our flat and took off my shoes in the hallway, the silence made me hopeful that everyone was asleep. But there was Father sitting at the dining room table, wearing his glasses, and slowly flipping through photographs. The room was dark but for one yellow light shining over him.

"Who is my daughter Nataša?" he asked, not looking at me, placing each square print upside down after examining it. "This one, she was five, I think." He was using his calm voice. The photo was one of me on a tree swing at our cottage, feet kicking forward, head thrown back. I remembered that day, how he followed me around with a camera and laughed with me.

I stood in front of Father. "She is right here."

He wrote the year on the back of the print.

"Sit down," he said, pulling out the chair closest to him. "And this boy you love." He spat out that sacred word. "His name?"

I sat. "No boy."

He looked at me over his glasses.

"No boy. It's Katka. Dad, I love Katka. I love Katka." I covered my face so he would not see it crumple. This wasn't how it was supposed to go.

"What does that mean, you love her?"

"I love her. I love a girl, okay?"

"No you don't. You don't know what you're talking about."

"Dad, I'm a homosexual." It came out in a sob.

"You're a homosexual," he said, mocking.

"It's not illegal. I checked. So you can't throw me in prison too."

"If you are a homosexual," he said, looking at the print in his hands, "you are not my daughter." He tore the picture down the middle.

I gasped.

He continued as if he had not just ripped me in half. "I won't punish Katka if you tell me about her father."

"You already know everything." But that was something I had not really thought through—what the truth could do to Katka. How could a world work this way that you have to throw away the love of one person to keep another's?

"I'll have their flat searched anyway, just in case." He gave me a twisted smile.

"No!" I jumped up and backed out of the room. "No. No. No!"

And I realized I'd lost them both.

My stomach plunges along with the plane—down fifty feet, up forty. I make a mental check for my parachute pack, as I cannot take my hands from the controls, which are vibrating terribly. *Ježíš Maria,* I swear, but I cannot even hear myself. Wind shear tries to throw me against the left door but my harness digs hard into my shoulder, keeping me in place. My artificial horizon is knocked out. My compass reading makes no sense and I am completely disoriented, spun around. But I have to believe the compass, and so I attempt to straighten out *Burgundy 7* before the next big roller-coaster dip.

I think of Děda fighting the Germans. And the fuel fire he must have lived through for a few excruciating seconds. The fuel in a Spitfire is right in the front of the plane, behind the control panel.

Do I have a death wish? I still aspire to death by airplane. But not like this. Not today. I must see Katka again before I die.

The day I told Father the truth, I understood the connection with my grandfather. Father was doing the opposite of what Děda had done. Father held parties for those who had taken over. Father had my best friend's dad beaten and jailed. As fierce as my love had been, now was my hatred of him.

That was the first day of a heat wave two weeks long, reaching temperatures in the mid-thirties. In Moravia, three senior citizens died from heatstroke. Rufus and Radka took turns shading the eggs with outstretched wings, panting. I wished we could provide them with shade or water, but we could do nothing. One brutal afternoon I saw the nest empty, eggs unprotected. Radka must have left the nest to keep herself alive.

A week later, one of the eggs was missing. Bumped from the nest. Rufus and Radka sat and sat. During those awful days, I did not speak to either of my parents and they did not speak to me. One by one, the eggs vanished, unviable. When the eggs were gone, Rufus and Radka left too. And there was no longer a reason for me to stay.

I had learned the art of keen observance from Father and I knew that he hid money in the locked liquor cabinet and where he kept the key. I packed a suitcase and a bag of food and in the middle of the night I boarded a bus for Brno. I stared out the window at the lights, my heart pounding. I would take on a new city, a new identity. I would be Radka. I wandered the streets of Brno until I found Michal's house. I waited for the sun to rise high enough that I could knock on his door.

One night during training, when a few of us were up late sharing a bottle of wine, the pilot Nanibah Jackson mentioned that the hawk is Ruth Coleman's spirit animal. "Maybe the falcon is your spirit animal." Namibah suggested to me. Now, I have no idea what a spirit animal is, but I suppose that to name yourself after a falcon is to claim a bond beyond blood and wing. I don't tell many people that detail of my life, but I did tell Ruth, privately, later.

I hear myself blurt it out loud, my voice tinny under the deafening noise, "I will not die today." With that I push the throttle past 85 percent. This speed is considered a war emergency tactic and I cannot stay here long before my engine overheats. The radiator temperature gauge blinks red and my radio buzzes with Keiko's worried voice.

"I'm okay," I say, "heading for Cloud Nine."

As I reach the coordinates where Kaz said to descend, I dip close to the ocean. Slow the propellers until they chop. My instrument panel shows a freaky virtual reality perspective on the whitecaps below. I fumble to turn it off. It's messing with my head. But I flip it back on—not a good idea to fly blind.

I pass through a clear space before I enter a lavender cirrus cloud that is much closer to the ground than typical Cloud Nine. The air is still a bit bumpy but nothing like before. The cockpit takes on the color of the cloud and even my arms and hands are violet. I laugh with giddy relief. I guess I'll live to tell this story. And my laughing goes on longer than it needs to, until my eyes stream and I know for sure this time that I have completely lost my mind.

I don't know if Father had Katka's flat searched or not. I have to assume he did.

Her dad was released from prison some months later. I heard he signed Charter '77, the famous dissident document protesting Communism and supporting human rights. Her family escaped through Austria to the United States.

I stayed with Michal's family through high school. His was the kind of family that went along with Communism because it was easier than the alternative. But they did not necessarily believe in the doctrine. This was a perfect shield for me, and for them.

Jakub told our parents where I was, but they did not contact me. Jakub would visit from time to time.

There was no point in going to university. If I were accepted, which was unlikely, I would have been forced to study Marxism and Leninism. I longed to train as a pilot, but my only chances were in the Communist military or the state-run airlines. I would have nothing to do with those. So I took a job at a teahouse in Prague and rented a flat with high school friends.

After the Velvet Revolution, everything changed. My parents split and Father exiled himself to Chicago, although he spoke not one word of English. You might think it was a stigma in Czech society to be ex-Secret Police. Not so. Their networks got them choice positions in government and corporate leadership. But two of Father's cousins lived in Chicago with their families and said they would get him a job. Mother later told me he wanted to get out of Prague, make a new start. I wondered if that meant he regretted his past.

I will never know.

I applied to the Czech Army's flight school in 1991. Father's connections could have gotten me in for sure, but I wanted nothing to do with him or them. I would rather have sucked the cock of the right man to get admitted.

And that's what I did. The admissions director's cock, to be exact. I can't say the experience made me eager to convert.

For my first mission, in Kosovo, I flew a W-3 Sokol rescue helicopter. It's silly, but those damn helicopters proved that something made sense in my life.

This will actually be my first trip to America. I might visit Chicago, just to see the famous city where Father lived. All these years of flying, I could have easily hopped a plane to visit Father in Chicago. But I did not.

I detest social media, but I admit I created a Facebook profile just to look for her. It was not so easy because she has an American surname now. But I found her—complete with husband, two daughters, a black cat, and a salt-and-pepper pageboy haircut. Her face was lined but more lovely than ever. And she still had that look in her eye of knowing something the rest of us do not. Her family lives somewhere in California—Los Angeles, I think. As I draw closer to America's west coast, she's coming into my radar.

Apparently she turned out straight after all. Though in fact, I don't believe that.

Mother stayed in Prague. A year after Father left, she invited me to lunch at the flat. The building was no longer gray. It had a fresh coat of bright yellow paint, with the Czech flag flying from a post mounted above the entrance.

The smell as I kissed her cheeks for the first time in sixteen years was even more sickly sweet than Becherovka. I recognized it from hanging around veterans. When alcohol is such a necessary part of your metabolism, you sweat it from your pores.

I declined her offer of a glass.

She asked me about flight school. I described what it was like to fly a plane.

"It's so dangerous, Taši. It's good I have no idea what you are doing out there. I would worry."

An awkward silence followed, which she broke by asking my opinion of Havel. When I turned that question back on her, she said that everything was so commercialized and expensive now. "But remember how hard it was to buy meat, Taši?" she laughed. "I'm glad certain things have changed."

"I'm Radka now, Mom."

"Oh yes—Radka. She and Rufus came back after you left, you know."

"Did they have more babies?"

"Sure. Three or four one year, two another. They stopped coming in '80, '81? Our neighbors wanted to paint the façade of the building, but your father, you know, he always pulled his strings. He made sure the project was stalled until the falcons stopped coming of their own accord."

I felt a swell of that old love—swallowing it left a bitter taste. "I am glad he used his influence to protect something worthwhile."

After I told Mother goodbye, I stood in the dark stairwell a long time, staring out at the empty window box and the courtyard below. I don't know why part of me had expected to find the birds there, even though, of course, Rufus and Radka would no longer be living.

Over the years I visited Mother often, and she grew to accept Lucie as my partner, in her own way. She died of cirrhosis five years ago.

Racing across an ocean like this makes you face something about yourself. Maybe I never fully gave my heart to Lucie. Even after twenty years.

So then, why does my heart break now?

Maybe the truth is it was broken all this time. Not a clean break—a shatter.

This trip cannot be about reconciling with Father. But maybe after this Race is over and the awards have been given—and I've gotten some sleep—I'll find Katka. See if she'll talk to me. Tell her I'm sorry.

RUTH COLEMAN

BLACK 8

The hawk is my spirit animal. It has taken all these years for me to find this out. It all makes sense now. Hawks have always appeared to me. Not just where you would expect them to, like when I worked in the fields with my parents in Texas, but overhead as I walked the hills of Colorado Springs during my Air Force Academy days. And once early in the morning at Hermosa Beach, as I stood on the sand gazing out at the ocean, one descended and hovered low over my head for a minute or two. Yes, I am sure of it. Only now, with the first meaningful friendships of my life, have I come to understand their spiritual base in me. My bonding with Nanibah and Hamidah during training awakened feelings in me that were suppressed, or that I had been denying all of my life while striving to survive in the world of competitive sports and the military.

One night during training Nanibah made this clear to me, saying, "Ruth, my friend, to Native Americans the hawk symbolizes insight. It is also viewed as a messenger and protector. Keen vision is one of its greatest gifts. Hawks see things others miss. They symbolize the ability to fly and reach the skies." And then she paused before saying, "The hawk can soar high and reach the heavens effortlessly, as you have done Ruth." Something shifted in my inner being as my friend and spiritual guide finished, "Hawks are often considered messengers who connect us with the spirit world and the unseen."

The hawk has shown up repeatedly in my life over the years and yet those worlds have remained unseen by me. Now I need to understand the messages it may carry and be receptive to my own intuition. The Race has been a catharsis for me. Being in this cockpit is so different from my military experience. This is spiritual, beautiful, and magical. Hamidah also caught on to my newfound search for a "spiritual Ruth" and gave me a whole lot to think about through the pathway to Buddhism.

A hawk appeared to me in Tokyo. I realize now that it came to me to make me aware of the reason for my being here. The hawk taught me how to fly higher than ever while still keeping me connected to the ground. As I rise both physically and psychologically, my psychic energies have awakened and now my hawk will keep these elements in balance. Her message to me is to embrace new ideas and to extend the vision of my life.

My life-long inspiration and hero has been my Aunt Bessie, who probably also had a hawk as her spirit animal. I am in the sanctuary of my Spitfire floatplane at 20,100 feet because of my Aunt Bessie. Our families were sharecroppers and like Aunt Bessie, I grew up in poverty, but with determination. The Coleman family of Atlanta, Texas had strong women to guide us. Bessie's father abandoned her family when she was nine, and her elder brothers soon left as well, leaving her mother with the four youngest of her thirteen children. And so it was with other branches of the Coleman family. Women had to be strong to raise families and survive. My father and mother both passed away at the same time after years of hard work trying to make ends meet for my two sisters and younger brother. I was sent to Los Angeles to be raised by my grandmother who lived in the Crenshaw area. Aunt Bessie, while taking care of her younger sisters, completed all eight available years of primary education, excelling in math. She enrolled at the Colored Agricultural and Normal University in Langston, Oklahoma in 1910, but a lack of funds forced her to leave after only one term. Five years later, she left the South and moved to Chicago to join two of her brothers. She worked as a beautician for several years and continued to educate herself. As an avid reader, she learned about World War I pilots from the newspaper and became intrigued with the prospect of flying.

As a black woman, she had no chance of acceptance at any American pilot school, so she moved to France in 1919 and enrolled at the École d'Aviation des Frères Caudron at Crotoy. She returned to the United States after completing advanced flying courses. She did exhibition flying and gave lectures across the country from 1922 to 1926. While flying, she refused to perform unless the audience was desegregated. Her career as the first female pilot and the first person of African American descent to hold an international pilot license inspired many, especially me.

I was the tallest girl in my Audubon Junior High School class and probably the best athlete and scholar in my graduating class. At 6 feet 2 inches, I excelled in basketball and by the time I went to Dorsey High School in the Crenshaw area, I immediately made an impact on the women's basketball team. I played on the varsity team as a freshman and in my senior year I led the team to the Los Angeles City Championships. I was the team's starting point guard and led the nation in steals. I was selected as the Gatorade Girl's Basketball Player of the Year for California. I bring all this up because it was quite an honor and it got me a full scholarship to the Air Force Academy in Colorado Springs. I gained the attention of U.S. audiences as I helped my team earn an appearance at our second championship game in the Mountain West Tournament. We couldn't beat the New Mexico Lobos in the finals, but my basketball career was still reaching new heights. I would win the Mountain West Player of the Year award and log the most steals in a single season in the history of the Air Force Academy Falcons women's basketball program. Too bad we were not the Hawks. I was drafted fifth into the WNBA, but I opted to fulfill my dream of flying like my Aunt Bessie and to become an officer and the first Black American U.S. Air Force combat fighter pilot. And anyway, it wasn't like the Atlanta Hawks wanted to draft me.

Two days after the celebratory family reunion for me, my grandmother told me she was proud of me and we talked about the Coleman family. I remember learning that another of my Coleman brothers was homeless and living on the streets in the Haight-Ashbury district of San Francisco. My grandmother asked me to find and help him. I promised I would. As the Southern California sun warmed us, we enjoyed the salmon dinner that I made for us.

We sat in her backyard after dinner enjoying our third glass of a good California Pinot Noir, when I noticed the hawk once again sitting on the telephone wires that run over the backyard. In all my years of living at my grandmother's place on Virginia Road, I never saw a hawk before, although maybe I just didn't notice. But now within a week, that hawk had visited three times.

I remember my 92-year-old grandma whispered to me, "I have had a good life, Ruth." And as she continued, I cried for the first time in over ten years, "I am so proud of you for what you have accomplished. Your parents would have been so proud of you, Ruthie. There are going to be tough times ahead for you, but through it all always remember the importance of family and the ties to your neighborhood." Grandma always quietly supported me and never spoke to me as seriously as she did that evening. I've never felt closer than I did in those moments. That night she went to sleep and never woke up. I found her in the morning with a smile on her face. She died peacefully. She was a hard-working and amazing woman. She was the pillar of my life. I helped organize the memorial and the whole Coleman clan got together and celebrated her life. It was grandmother who brought us all together once again. It was as if she were smiling even then. One week after the memorial I was ordered to go to the Middle East with my combat flight group.

I flew a Fairchild-Republic A-10 Thunderbolt II in Operation Desert Storm in Iraq. The twin-engine, straight-wing aircraft was the only United States Air Force aircraft designed for close air support of ground forces. My primary built-in weapon was the 30mm GAU-8/A Avenger Gatling-type cannon. One of the most powerful aircraft cannons ever flown, it fired large depleted uranium, armor-piercing shells. Women, including mothers, suffered serious consequences as a result of my actions. Increased rates of birth defects were caused by the chemical and radiological contaminants derived from the depleted uranium munitions used in those shells. The radiation still exists in Iraq today. Immediate measures are needed to clean up the environment and to diagnose and treat the many cases of congenital deformities that are occurring.

I could fire 4,200 rounds per minute. I found out what it was like to be a killing machine. Aided by armored vehicles, my aircraft could take out entire villages. I realized that many of my kills were in cold military terms, "casualties of war" or "collateral damage," mostly all dark-skinned women and children. I saw similarities between the treatment of Iraqis and that of second-class people like blacks and brown-skinned folks in many parts of America.

I remembered something that I read by Charles Lindbergh in *Autobiography of Values*. As an airforce pilot in World War II, he described a bombing run over the Japanese-occupied city of Rabaul in New Guinea. Lindbergh talked about releasing his high-explosive bomb and seeing a "puff of smoke so small and far way" that he could not connect with what "writhing hell" was going on. He felt he had carried out his mission and "felt little responsibility" for what he had just done.

When the joy of flying began to dissipate as my guilt increased, I resigned from the U.S. military.

"Okay Ruth, address the situation at hand!" They must have heard me talking to myself over the radio at the refueling ship because I got back instructions for the water landing and heard some laughter in the background. I could see Radka Zelenkova in *Burgandy 7* taking off. I never really bonded with Radka in training. Probably just not enough time, but I did bond with Hamidah, Raya Sol, and Nanibah. We privately called ourselves the "dark-skinned coalition."

Leah Katzenberg, Radka, and I might be the most experienced pilots in The Race, although it has been a challenge to switch from flying jets to flying four-bladed, souped-up, British Mark XIV Spitfire floatplanes. Most difficult are the landings, the hardest thing for all of us to master in training.

Hah, just as I was thinking about the difficulty of landing, especially on the ocean, my water landing was no problem. Most of us have relished the acupuncture from Dr. Watase, including me. And I had no complaints about the food provided on this first Mitsubishi refueling ship stop. I look forward to the next stop, O'ahu, Hawai'i the land of many more dark-skinned folks, the indigenous Hawaiians.

Back to my thinking of how I got here in the sky once again, but this time, I am much happier with my "mission." After resigning from the military I went back to Los Angeles with the sole intention of doing something for my people in the Crenshaw community. I stayed with my brother, who had remained in Los Angeles after my grandmother passed away. He kept her home as a vibrant household for all the Colemans who visited the West Coast. We found work and enjoyed family visits and the renewed bonds of the Coleman family. I worked at a homeless shelter and with the local Habitat for Humanity. It was hard but very rewarding work. And I must say that my height, physical condition, educational background, and certain attributes that men consider beautiful, were all assets for me in working at the shelter and for Habitat. In fact, I think being an Amazon black woman carried the day, wonder of wonders!

I still flew aircraft, but inexpensive rented planes from the small local airstrip in Santa Monica. Santa Monica Airport is wonderful to fly out of, being a bit west of Crenshaw and about two miles closer to the Pacific Ocean. I would often take a girl-friend and fly to Santa Catalina Island. The "Runway in the Sky" was built by blasting away two of the island's mountaintops and using 200,000 truckloads of rubble to fill the gap between them. To make the tricky landing on the cliffs, you have to fight powerful updrafts over the ocean, and then you have to steady the plane against sudden downdrafts the second you are over land. Tricky, indeed! Safely on ground, we would have lunch there and fly back. Often I would spot dolphins and sometimes whales in the channel off the coast of California. These were rewarding and happy times and somewhat lightened my heart about my "crimes against humanity" in the Middle East.

It was at the flight office at the Santa Monica Airport where I spotted the information and invite for The Race. I applied, and it was probably how I answered Keiko's questions about my desires for improving humanity and the planet that landed me a spot with the other fourteen female pilots. So here I am, again at 20,000 feet cruising altitude, in control, in this wonderful vast space, flying in a vintage but technically fantastic reborn Spitfire floatplane, *Black 8*, having bonded with some very interesting and talented pilots. Life is good.

There were a few periods in my life when life wasn't so good. I have managed to put them behind me, but I know that I will always be fiercely compassionate toward women who have gone through the same bullshit. Twice at the Air Force Academy I was threatened with sexual assault. My physical strength managed to keep me safe there, but the mental games continued. My commanding officer would not respond to my official complaints because an actual rape did not occur. The mental rape did not count. It was far different with my fellow pilots in Iraq. I was treated with respect and complimented on my flying skills. I left the military with respect for my fellow male pilots and their mutual respect after I explained to them why I resigned.

I say all this with angst. This whole experience, especially our training, has tempered my depression, it seems. I have never believed in God. In spite of the strong Baptist faith of my family in Texas, I never embraced any religion. It is interesting to me that for the first time in my life, I feel an affinity to a religion, but only in the way Hamidah described hers—as a philosophy of compassion and respect without the dogma that envelops so many religions, including Buddhism. It is the dogma that Hamidah strips away, and in many of the spiritual meetings during training, I sat in the back just taking in what Nanibah and Hamidah said about a way of living that respects all sentient beings. I must aim for that now in my life and let the anger and guilt subside.

All my life I have embraced the darkness of the evening. My spirit animal, the hawk, is also a creature of the evening. Even now as the sun is going down I have started to enjoy the vast space, the darkness and the stars that I am so much closer to up here. Hah, of course, they are still light years away, but everything is relative, I suppose. Buddhist philosophy has created the balance I need in my life. The brightness and the glow of this practice is a counterweight to my dark moods and existence. As a child I got to be with my parents during the nights after hard labor. It was the night basketball practices that I enjoyed and the night games at the Academy that I loved. I still embrace the darkness, it is my time to be in control.

The dark is my home, but what has been wonderful is reconnecting with enlightened thoughts rather than my athleticism, military thinking, and what I call left-brain thinking. Those old ways were necessary for me to survive in the military. But the interaction I now have had with these women has led me to reconnect with my poetry and my inner compassion. In one of our meetings Hamidah said, "To study the self is to forget the self. To forget the self is to be enlightened by a myriad of things." This adventure has been cathartic for me. My right brain is expanding. Now I need to make connections between the two sides.

One connection seems to be with quantum mechanics and physics. I took a lot of physics and math at the Academy, but quantum physics led me to strange places and made me see it as a connection between the two sides of the brain. Quantum information is like the formation of a dream. It transcends the large and small universes, reveals everything in them, and is both a source of controversy and tension about the existence of a Creator. This is thought provoking and a kind of a spiritual meditation on life. Oh man, all this flying has kept me in the mechanical part of my brain for too long. Now O'ahu is on the horizon. Glad autopilot and GPS are working well. Taking manual control now, I will land in the bay and then I will receive acupuncture and Chromotherapy from Habib. Another thing about this adventure is that it has made me willing to try anything—the great Japanese food in Tokyo, acupuncture, Chromotherapy, and new spiritual beliefs. Ah, more connections in the brain.

The therapies and food all fortified me and I am now halfway to San Francisco. I got a lot of smiles for my cool floatplane, *Black 8.* One of the crew in Hawai'i even said I was "behind the old eight ball." I cracked back at him that I didn't have any balls and didn't play pool but that I considered his remark a compliment and left it at that. Ah, there is the old competitive Ruth coming out. Got to concentrate on balance and relax a bit more. Think I will put on a spirit-lifting song by a brother, get up to cruising altitude and switch to autopilot for a while until I hit the rough weather that lies ahead, probably after the last refueling ship. Yeah, I think it is time for a little Pharrell Williams and his "Happy" song.

Okay, back to my layperson's understanding of quantum physics. Quantum information is like recalling a dream. We can't show others, and when we try to describe it, we change the memory of it. If we speculate about multiple outcomes of a situation, we also imply multiple worlds. The quantum theory of multiple worlds has been around for the last fifty years. If we buy into the many world interpretations of quantum mechanics, then everything that's possible will happen, or perhaps already has. And it might be possible to figure out how to use quantum entanglement to make parallel worlds talk to one another and exchange information.

Quantum mechanics doesn't just apply to the subatomic world as it was first believed. It applies to everything, to atoms and airplanes. The entire universe is quantum mechanical. I definitely need to reread the information about Heisenberg's Uncertainty Principle and Schrodinger's cat experiment.

These thoughts of parallel worlds and left and right brain connections all seem to coincide with my theory of the "Chameleon Effect." The dictionary defines chameleon as "a changeable or fickle person." My theory relates to the "changeable" part. This changeability has been especially notable in my life. I think it is often linked to the dichotomies of change. For instance, I was able to thrive both in the environment of poverty and the environment of a higher economic bracket. What I am trying to get at is my ability to be at home with the language and behavior in vastly different circumstances—the black community in my Crenshaw "hood," the military types at the Air Force Academy, and the upper class white folks on Wall Street or in academic circles. I am able to change my personality and language to suit my surroundings. Playing pickup basketball games in high school with all my black friends was a hoot. Occasionally it was street talk, shucking and jiving and sometimes the "N" word was used, not in a derogatory manner, but in a way that only black on black kids can get away with. It was also interesting that in Crenshaw we often called each other "Bloods" and called the Japanese American kids "Buddhaheads." Funny how now we need to be Black Americans and not Afro-Americans. Raya Sol told us not to call her Hispanic. She said she was Latina or Chicana or Mexican or Mexican American. And Nanibah said it was now preferred to be American Indian rather than Native American. We learn this fast in our barrios, ghettos, hoods, or reservations, faster than the academics of white America or the redneck racist assholes. They've got their names for us dark-skinned folks, anyway.

Personally, I think we spend too much time on the names we are called. Time ought to be spent on how we as women of color can advance ourselves and support one another, raise our children, get a good education, and in a broader sense, make this a better world. Ah, the hawk-inspired visionary thinking here.

Back in the day, there was the term "Black Power." Perhaps "Women Power" is the term for the future as we wake up and take control, but with compassion. I feel this more than ever after my interaction with my fellow pilots and Keiko.

A whole new paradigm exists before us. We need to take hold of everything possible and make things happen. I learned from Nanibah that the hawk spirit animal has several attributes and basic meanings. Now, for me in the near future, beyond the sanctuary of this cockpit, I know that I must listen, embrace, understand that the hawk is the messenger of the spirit world and I must make connections with that world to understand where my future lies. I must focus to see with clear eyes. I should step up when the need for leadership presents itself.

I am sure that my Nanibah saw that I would emerge as a leader in the whatever-might-happen-after-this-race. That is probably why she gave me this special poem, to foster love and compassion and to balance some of the more aggressive traits of the hawk. It is by Charlotte Tall Mountain, an Iroquois American Indian, who passed away in 2006 after a long struggle with cancer. The poem is tucked away in my flight manual. It is called, "Love of the World."

For the love of a tree,
she went out on a limb.

For the love of the sea,
she rocked the boat.

For the love of the earth,
she dug deeper.

For the love of community,
she mended fences.

For the love of the stars,
she let her light shine.

For the love of spirit,
she nurtured her soul.

For the love of a good time,
she sowed seeds of happiness.

For the love of God,
she drew down the moon.

For the love of nature,
she made compost.

For the love of a good meal,
she gave thanks.

For the love of family,
she reconciled differences.

For the love of creativity,
she entertained new possibilities.

For the love of her enemies,
she suspended judgment.

For the love of herself,
she acknowledged her own worth.

And the world was richer for her.

I will work hard to be "her." In the meantime, I am approaching the last refueling station. This whole flight is going by so quickly. It must be the long periods of thought and reflection, almost meditation that seems to shorten time. The ocean is a bit choppy, which will test my landing skills.

I am surprised that *Burgundy 7* is still docked. I wonder if Major Zelenkova, the Czech pilot, is okay. I had considered her one of my main competitors. Radka seemed to attract a few of the other pilots while in training. No wonder, she is outgoing, attractive and so very playful. She also demonstrated that she could adapt to flying the newly designed Spitfire floatplane better than most of us. Her military training was an obvious plus in addition to her skills. Actually, I respect her a lot but am happy that I may have surpassed her in The Race.

I am told that Radka is departing. I haven't had a chance to see her on this flight so I will wait until San Francisco. Meanwhile, after acupuncture Dr. Kaz gives me a message from Keiko. Smiling and speaking in his soft and comforting voice, Kaz tells me, "Ruth-san, there is a flight pattern that Keiko suggests you follow. As you are at a lower altitude on approach to San Francisco, there is a cloud formation called Cloud Nine that you can fly through for happiness." I am curious to find out in San Francisco if any of the other pilots flew through it and how we all felt. I hope Nanibah, who is struggling with cancer, flies through it, as she needs some magic in her life. Moments of happiness are supposed to be top of the list for helping the immune system fight the damn disease. And then there is Firoozeh. The only pilot in training I couldn't stand. She was argumentative and angry. Never had good words to say to any of us and especially antagonistic towards Ting Xu. Firoozeh seemed to have a deep-seated resentment for her. To Ting Xu's credit, she behaved graciously and even tried to help Firoozeh. Of course, Nanibah and Hamidah, in their compassionate manner, also tried to help Firoozeh. Anyway, I hope Firoozeh flies through Cloud Nine and comes to terms with her depression and anger.

I told Kaz that I will definitely fly through it for happiness, but also for the many other things about which I should be happier.

If it weren't for The Race, I would just stay on this refueling ship and sail with Kaz to San Francisco. The acupuncture and other treatments suit me just fine, as well as the great food. Alas, my hour is nearing and I must take off and fly like a bat out of hell to San Francisco. Oops, fly like a "hawk out of hell" and win this thing.

I've made the last takeoff from the refueling ship. Now for the last leg of The Race and to join the other pilots and Keiko in San Francisco.

One thing I must do after the race is to search for my youngest brother in San Francisco and fulfill the promise I made to my grandmother. I believe he is still homeless and it will be a challenge to find him. I hope he is okay psychologically and will accept my help after all these years of neglect. It is a good feeling to be free and to understand how to be compassionate towards others, especially my family.

I have come to terms with the anger over the physical abuse I endured and the guilt over my actions in Iraq. I am trying to think beyond my own self just as others, such as Jimmy Carter, have done and continue to do in their own work. In Carter's book, *A Call to Action: Women, Religion, Violence, and Power*, he documented the enslavement, degradation, and torture that women around the world have endured. He is a human rights warrior. The mindless hatred for President Carter, across the right and among a surprising number of liberals, exposed the obscenity and weakness of American political culture, where cliché overwhelms insight and bromide mutes the truth of history. Keiko asked me to read his book during training. I believe that she has further plans for us, and as I find out more, I am all in. I am happy that Keiko gave me the book and I have already read it twice.

After The Race, I want to work toward a realignment of religious and political life with equality for all females. I learned a lot from talking with the other pilots and another direction that I want to pursue is to promote new energy models separate from coal and uranium-based sources. I know this is idealistic, but I believe that idealism is needed today to move forward. I intend to win this adventure and put the money towards these world-saving causes. And my hawk will continue to guide me.

My parents and Aunt Bessie would be as proud of me as my Grandma was. I will never relinquish flying. I look forward to entering Cloud Nine as I hope for more happiness. And now I open the envelope that Nanibah gave me on our last day of training. She said, "Open this when you are approaching our end goal, San Francisco, dear friend."

It is the closing prayer from the "Navaho Way" blessing ceremony. The word "walk" has been substituted with the word "fly."

In beauty I fly
With beauty before me I fly
With beauty behind me I fly
With beauty above me I fly
With beauty around me I fly
It has become beauty again

TING XU CHAN
BLUE 9

I toss the bag aside. I suck water from my supply, and swish it around my mouth. It does little to clear my head, or the horrible scratchiness in the back of my throat. I am baffled as to where such weakness has come from. I have always prided myself on my genetically sound inner ears. However, my nausea has eased off and that in itself is a huge improvement in my ability to concentrate. I draw in breath deliberately, feeling my lungs expand and fill, and I flow through a Tai Chi sequence, moving only millimeters, but feeling the energy flow through my limbs, filling me with a sense of strength and calm. The words of Danzanravjaa echo in my mind.

> *The vigor of his white body,*
> *Vital and toned,*
> *Brings forth thoughts*
> *Of meeting with his loveliness*

Having given only cursory attention to my instruments while I regained my composure, I now turn my attention to a full audit of my instruments, leaning on the patterns drilled into us during training. Everything is as it should be. I check course, and make a few minor adjustments, but nothing is awry—a good start. I close my eyes and push my consciousness out to the aircraft, feeling myself take on its cold metal shell—its vibrations are my own.

> *Spring's gentle winds*
> *Blow softly.*
> *I take up with my friends,*
> *And we ride away.*

The wind rushes past me, flowing over my smooth hull, dragging a bit on the floats, but there is nothing to be done about that, they are as aerodynamic as such hardware can be. I sense the air swirling around me with all of my senses. As my eyes consider the information on the dials before me, my body feels every motion and vibration, and my ears judge the direction and intensity of the sounds around me. I adjust course slightly, several degrees left, right, varying my altitude, listening for the harmony of vibration that comes with the aircraft moving in concert with the atmosphere. I settle on a course adjustment that takes me on a slightly less direct trajectory. The choice is more instinct than calculation, but this has always worked the best for me.

The sky wraps around the metal skin, dipping down at the horizon in all directions to meet the vast blueness of the Pacific. I move through new physical coordinates that I have never occupied before, but the blueness is home, the *Munkh Khukh Tengri*, the Eternal Blue Sky. Below me the ocean ripples silver like grass in the wind.

When I was ten, I thought I had lost the sky forever. I have the eyes of Genghis Khan, grey-green and eagle-sharp, and I could spot a wandering sheep better than anyone else. I began riding with the herders as soon as I could walk, and I was responsible for my grandmother's herd. I had no brothers and no father, only the boys I called "cousins" who were more distant than that, but they had their own herds. But I was happy to be out under the sky, away from the old women and my mother with her long, sad silences.

There was no warning. I had not been asleep, but it was raining and the rain on the felt roof was mesmerizing, always the same, always different. The rain filled the air with its sound and softened the earth under the grass, so we did not hear the engines and the rattle of the axles. Suddenly there were voices speaking words I didn't understand and lights that blinded me and a chaos of movement all around. My mother was suddenly there, thrusting a bundle of clothes at me and putting my boots on my feet. It was eerily quiet as we were packed into the vans. Only the horses and sheep could be heard in the din of rain on metal roofs, and soon not even that.

Looking back, there were signs—the car that came in the spring, filled with men who brought gifts from the city, who we welcomed with a feast of young goat and special fermented yak milk. Then my mother's long absences—she refused to take me with her, and I know she hated going to the city. I suppose promises were made, but I had not been paying attention, oblivious out under the big sky. At first I thought my mother was responsible and I blamed her, but now I think her only fault was to bend rather than break. She chose to bargain for a better future for her family, rather than be thrown in jail again for her principles.

The radio crackles and I reach for it, trying to tune in the communication. I am still too far from the refueling station for it to be a communication about landing. There are only snippets of a human voice. I don't understand the words and there are long periods of static in between.

My mother never talked about her past or her principles when I was very young, I remember that some days, she used to be still and silent, like a statue. You could pinch her, climb on her, stare her in the eye, but it was like she was made of stone, nothing would move her. The other children would torment her until grandmother shooed them away. But not me, I could not be near her when she was like that. Her sadness would fill the house, and I would flee from the yurt until the sky was all I could see.

Later, much later, I became curious. She would not talk to me—by that time she was married to an official in the government and asking her made her more angry than I have ever seen, and very silent. She would not utter a word to me for nine months afterwards. I was a student at the time, a rising sophomore at Princeton, when I asked her on the last day of our summer vacation. Her silent fury was worse than any rage of words. I was afraid she would not let me go back to school, but disallowing it would have meant she would have to explain her anger to her husband. I carried her anger with me all year, heavy and itchy, a weight that would not be forgotten. She would not talk to me on New Year's Day, which made me cry. But when I came home for the summer, she greeted me as she always had, with no words about her silence, like it had never happened. I dared not ask.

So I asked everyone else, secretly. I had already begun, during the year of silence. There was a course at Princeton on the emergence of the modern Chinese state, taught by a professor who was Inner Mongolian. He introduced me to others on campus, other Inner Mongolians, a few from Mongolia, and a few Chinese that he had made certain were sympathetic. Their words filled some of the ache of my emptiness, my need for a story.

When I returned to Hohhot in the summer, I too pretended that everything was the same, but it was not. I quietly, carefully asked everyone I could that summer, collecting their words to fill the void, very careful not to draw attention with my questions. I announced that I was majoring in English. My stepfather would have preferred that I study a field with prestige like engineering or medicine, but my mother was relieved that my choice would not embarrass her if I failed. More importantly, it meant freedom from her quietly oppressive suspicion.

I met with everyone I could think of, gathering little pieces of information. My old friends, her old friends, friends of friends, people I had never met before. Many were dead ends—they knew nothing, or nothing they would reveal. But more people than you would have thought had little pieces of the story, and once they started talking, the words spilled out of them like the little silvery minnows that slide through your fingers when you tried to hold them.

My mother had been born in the same town where I was born, a small place that has no dot on the map. You get there by going to Bayanbulag, then following a rough track in the grass for fifty minutes, if you have a good truck and good luck. But she had not lived there for twenty-two years until the year I was born. With four brothers and two sisters, she was not missed much when she followed her beloved books to the Mongolian-Beijing high school, then on to the University of Mongolia.

All of this was easy to find, I knew it growing up, my grandmother was proud of her daughter's promise in her youth. No one in Bayanbulag knew how she managed in the city since the family had no money to send her. One explanation might be that she was so bright that her teachers took it upon themselves to look after her so that she could stay in school.

I think she caught the eye of Ulanhu, who became her benefactor. I know that sounds crazy, and perhaps even a bit egotistical—how would a girl from a poor village in the middle of nowhere even come into the presence of the Party Chair of Inner Mongolia, the most important man in the province at the time? But it seems possible and it makes some sense out of those slippery minnows I had been gathering. One of my mother's old teachers let on that her own generosity towards my mother was encouraged and that added to her paychecks. She wasn't sure who arranged it, but it was made clear to her that she was not to discuss it, and with her husband having passed on years earlier, she was more than happy for both my mother's companionship and the money. Even stranger, one of my mother's school friends had followed my mother one evening when she had declined to study together, suspecting a rival friendship. But to her surprise, my mother walked all the way across town and entered a government building. I found the site of that building, and while it is no longer there, I'm fairly certain it was where the Party offices were located. And then there is the fact that Ulanhu himself is from a very small village, not the same one my mother and I are from, but as things go on the plains, they are our neighbors. And while she lacked the elegance and fairness that the Han look for in beautiful women, among our people she was very beautiful, dark and wild with the gray eyes of Genghis Khan.

It would also explain how she ended up in prison, probably right around the same time that Ulanhu fell out of power. But it is hard to know, because so many people died. Thousands and thousands disappeared, or were sent away for "re-education." No one remembers those years. If they did not suffer themselves, someone who they knew suffered, and everything has been forgotten.

My mother's prison or "re-education camp" was Dongtucheng, in the far west. The women there were to be reeducated through work. They made clothes for soldiers and uniforms for workers. It wasn't one of those places seen on propaganda posters with smiling youths holding pitchforks—it had walls and barbed wire. Most of my mother's story came from another woman who had been in the camp with her. I found her through lots of questions and some luck, and I traveled to meet her in Wuzhen, one of the canal towns west of Shanghai. I wasn't even sure she was who I thought she was, until she saw me enter the shop. She turned as pale as yak's milk. When I realized that she thought I was my mother, I quickly spoke to assure her I was no ghost, and also that my mother was still alive. She warmed quickly then, and invited me to have tea. Jun's shop was small, hardly more than a hallway, and every surface was covered with every kind of wire, cord, rope, and string you could imagine, in bundles and spools, arranged by thickness and color and sometimes just randomly displayed. In the back behind a curtain, there was a tiny room with a single electric burner with a cord that went out the window and up to some unknown source. I had brought her gifts of tea, cigarettes, and a bottle of Moutai *baijiu*. Her eyes lit up at this, and before long we had finished our tea and had our first toast, *ganbei*, to my mother. I was steeling myself for the question everyone asked, and for which I honestly had no answer. "Why do you want to know about such sadness from the past?"

Instead, she made a statement. "You have come to hear about your father." Now it was I who had seen a ghost. Was that what I was seeking? I truly had not thought so. I had always believed what my mother had said, that my father was someone whom she met while traveling, and he had been unable to stay for long. I soon saw she was right. It was part of the silence that I needed to fill.

This was how I learned about my mother's years in prison. The women were not there by choice, they could not leave, and they lived behind high walls. They worked long hours, at least fifteen hours a day, six days a week. The seventh day they cleaned the factory and their own living quarters. The work was hard, the living situation harsh, but perhaps tolerable if you could just be one of the crowd, and not draw attention to yourself. According to Jun, silence was not a lesson my mother had learned, at least not yet. She would disappear for days at a time, several times for weeks, and when she returned, the other women begged her to remain quiet, and she would for a time. But then the anger would build in her, and she could not stand to see another woman unjustly treated. I imagine too, Genghis Khan was not only in her eyes, but also her soul—she could not adjust to captivity.

I had seen the pale scars on my mother's wrists, but now I know how she got them. To punish the prisoners, they would chain them between two beds, so they could not bend their limbs, and leave them for hours. It is hard for me to think about my mother like that, but I must. Too much has been forgotten. But the greater torture has no visible scars, the other main punishment was to be left alone in cells so small that one could not stretch out to sleep. For my mother, with the blood of Genghis Khan, to be caged must have been intolerable.

She probably would have died in that prison, but the leadership changed after 1970. The prison chief, a fellow grass-eater, took notice of her. She was assigned to work in the office. Jun apologized that she did not know more. She stayed in the factory with the other women and did not see much of my mother after that. But less than a year later my mother was released. It was not the way that other women were released, set outside with the clothes on their back, clothes they had made in the factory, to wait for the bus that came by once a month. It was at night that my mother went to Jun to thank her for her friendship, and to give her small a stash of gum and cigarettes, which was like gold in the camp. And then she left in the truck that brought deliveries from Hohhot, not as cargo, but as a passenger. Even though it was dark, Jun saw this from the tiny window in the barracks. No one left that way. Jun said she had not been sure what had happened until she saw me.

By the time she had told me as much as she knew about my mother, it was late. She got up to close the shop. I stayed in the back room. I could hear someone enter, and it soon became clear it was not a customer because her voice rose angrily. I heard her say that no, she had no guest, and I was instantly on edge. I heard the voices in the other room escalate, and caught a few words that made the heat rise in my body. I picked up my empty cup, and quietly stood and moved back towards the rear door. The argument continued. I couldn't quite make out what the male voices were saying, but I could hear her voice asserting that she was alone. I quietly unlatched the door, slipped out onto a narrow cement ledge, pulling the door closed behind me, for some reason still clutching the cup. It was dark, and there was no one in sight, just the dark water rippling four feet below. I heard them enter the room. With my heart pounding, and as quietly as I could, I crouched down on the ledge and lowered myself into the water. As I clung to the ledge with my hands, feet touching the water, I had a moment of pure terror when I knew I couldn't pull myself up—the only direction was down. I let go.

The summer night was hot and heavy and the water uncomfortably warm. I was shaking as I made my way awkwardly along the canal, moving from ledges to posts, grabbing anything I could find and cursing that I had never bothered to learn how to swim. I was sure that either my entry splash or my clumsy flailing had been heard and pursuit was close behind me. A few times I slipped on some slimy thing I had grasped and the water closed over me. I finally found a place where rungs were built into the canal wall, and I climbed out. I emerged into a park, part of the town that had been recently modernized, and a couple strolling looked at me with shock as I climbed out, sopping wet. I stood up tall and said that the fishing was very good tonight, and walked off. I immediately regretted my inability to come up with a more plausible lie, as nothing could possibly live in that polluted water. I would have left that night, but I thought that would draw more attention to me than just staying put in my rented room. I hardly slept. Sure, heard the sound of boots on the stairs and pounding on my door, and thought how ironic it was that my mother must have heard those very sounds when they had come to collect her to go to the work camp.

Sitting in my cockpit now, the memory is making me itch. I wiggle uncomfortably, trying to scratch a spot on my back that I've never been able to reach. I had itched for weeks after my escape. For all I know, the whole thing could have been just a product of my own panic—Jun might have been having a good joke on her friends, or perhaps the argument had nothing to do with me. I went back to Suzhou many years later, and the entire area where her shop had been was razed and replaced by condominiums that were designed like a Swiss villa crossed with a Venetian palazzo. No one knew of a woman named Jun who used to sell rope and string.

According to the course I am currently tracking, I should be approaching the first refueling station. I am almost disappointed. I feel like I was just getting started and I want to keep going, not come back to ground. I half consider just continuing, but that's a crazy thought certain to lead to running out of fuel somewhere in the middle of the ocean. And sure enough, when I scan the sea ahead, I can just make out a visual of what is certainly the refueling station.

I adjust my course slightly to head more directly for it, and start my descent and prepare to land. As I get closer, I can see the plane that had started ahead of me at the platform, *Black 8*, Ruth. The memory of her makes me smile, her strength and humor will be a pleasure to encounter. I land my *Blue 9* with ease. The sea is lovely and conditions are perfect, and despite my reluctance to stop, once I am out, I am glad for the break. I immediately seek out Kaz for some acupuncture. Perhaps he can do something about this nausea. I feel it gnawing at me, even with my feet firmly on deck. Ruth is emerging as I arrive, and we embrace, holding each other for a moment. Her familiarity and warmth almost makes me tearful, the stress and time alone must be getting to me.

After acupuncture, I am ravenously hungry and head for the canteen. As I enter, Firoozeh is sitting at a table, her bowl and cup empty. She must have just flown in after me and went straight for the food. She looks me up and down, and I am conscious of how disheveled and pale I must look. I haven't taken time to shower, or even brush my teeth. I run my fingers through my hair in a fruitless effort that only serves to highlight the ridiculous contraptions placed on the pressure points in my wrists. She raises an eyebrow, rises gracefully and walks past me. She passes unnecessarily close, when there is plenty of space. Startled, I fail to stand my ground and shift uneasily. I feel her breath in my ear as she passes. The word she speaks is a hiss in my ear, and I don't recognize it, but I strongly suspect it might be the Persian word for Chinese. Ironically, it sounds a little like the word "chink" but perhaps I am feeling the intent rather than the word. The door closes behind me and she is gone.

I try to brush it off, perhaps I am reading too much into it. I fill a bowl with soupy rice. I'm not fond of congee, it isn't eaten much in the north, but some Chinese pickled cucumbers would be so welcome right now. I even go back to look and see if I missed something, but there isn't anything salty or sour, just grains and gruels.

When I finish, there isn't much time left so I forego a shower and instead practice Tai Chi. As I go through the familiar movements, I can feel the energy moving within me. I am also aware of the energy around me. I can feel Firoozeh somewhere nearby, but I don't linger there.

I am back in my plane and ready to go, the engine running smoothly. Then I feel the clamp release, and the plane accelerates. The ocean is fairly smooth and the taxi and takeoff are textbook. As soon as my floats leave the ground, in the moment where I usually rejoice in my freedom, I instead feel the nausea rising. I can't take my hands off of the controls right now, and I consciously will the pressure point bands on my wrists and ankles that Kaz made for me, to work. I feel sweat gathering on my palms and forehead and trickling down the back of my neck. I concentrate on the familiar motions of guiding the plane up to altitude, and try to breathe deeply. At cruising altitude I lock in my controls and grab for the airsickness bag. Ugh. I don't know why this flight is affecting me in this way, it has to be nerves, but I hardly feel nervous. My competitive side certainly intends to put every effort towards winning, but I also feel a great camaraderie with the women with whom I am sharing the sky today. While I can't see Ruth ahead of me, or Firoozeh behind me, I know they are there. As my Tai Chi partners, our chi has flowed in unison so many times, I can almost feel them next to me. I know that Nanibah and Hamidah would welcome me leaning on their strength right now.

Raised on a reservation, Nanibah and I share much in common. We both come from cultures that are fighting for their existence and if you turn away from them, they are likely to fade into their surroundings and be assimilated. The solutions are different. I don't know if the reservations, or the "rez," as Nanibah says, are better or worse than where the Mongolians in Inner Mongolia now live. Perhaps they are better off, at least they have a nation, even if it is true that their sovereignty and autonomy are in question. And certainly the economic conditions are problematic. It is such an artificial thing to take a nomadic nation and confine it, to have it exist surrounded within a conflicting social and cultural system. The poverty, broken families, alcoholism—they are all like invasive diseases that take over in a confined and disturbed ecosystem.

There are no reservations in Inner Mongolia, just the promises of an "autonomous" region. But there is very little that could be called autonomy. When my family was moved to Hohhot, we were at least able to continue to speak Mongolian in school, and we celebrated our festivals in our new neighborhood. But now, there are so many Han in Hohhot, you have to look hard to see that it is any different from any other Han city. Our festivals are still celebrated, but they feel more like a piece of colorful theatre than something laden with tradition.

Maybe I should have stayed and taught the children what it means to be Mongolian. Instead, I learned Chinese and made my way up through the educational system. It is not that I was really given a choice. But if there had been a "rez" instead of relocation, where would I be? Maybe perfectly happy under the sky I miss so much. Or perhaps our pastures would have dried up and I would be raising fatherless children on government bread. But instead, I work for the very government that took the sky away from me, from all of my people. I take their money, and live a very comfortable life. Can one be assimilated and still resent the assimilation? Doesn't that mean that I must resent myself?

My strong and true mind
Is out of kilter with the world.
My acerbic nature
Is out of kilter with local custom.

So much had changed in the years I was away for college. Even in Hohhot, the great cement building where I had grown up was long gone, replaced by a glass and steel building with an elevator and filled with offices. My family and I had left that building when I was in high school and my mother married a businessman. We moved into a new apartment with glossy white floors and little tiny square balconies where you could fit two chairs and sit looking at the building right next to us. The people upstairs used to tie their little dog on the balcony and it would bark all night long, it was my companion as I studied for exams long into the night. I studied like a crazy person in high school and always had dark circles under my eyes. I was completely determined to escape Hohhot. I knew I needed to find the sky, and Hohhot was growing upwards and outwards and filling up with dust and pollution. It was suffocating me. Many of my friends were certain of a better life in Beijing, but I knew I had to go farther—I had my heart set on going to the United States. My new father thought that the University of Beijing was an appropriate place for me and didn't see why he should pay to send me to the U.S. for what he considered an inferior education at some small college. I only applied to three schools in the U.S. that I knew he could not refuse, and when I got my acceptance letter to Princeton, I knew I had succeeded.

It was Princeton that led me to the sky again. After years of studying, passing exams and following courses of study that were laid out for me, I was still baffled by which path to choose. I ended up studying geology, anthropology, and photography. I took them with no particular goal in mind, and they filled me with possibilities. I meandered into an English literature major, with a certificate in fine art, where I concentrated on photography. At the end of my third year, my photography professor invited me to be his assistant. I flew with him to Arizona where he was working on photographing the evidence of our human activities from the clouds above. I reveled in the horizon and the great sky, which was suddenly all around. It was almost like coming home, only the landscape was foreign, filled with spiny, bushy plants and colorful exposed rock. But the true revelation came one morning when we set out before dawn for a tiny airport hours from nowhere. We arrived just as the sky was getting light and climbed into a little C-150 with a modified window that opened fully to accommodate my professor's Hasselblad. As soon as the wheels left the ground, I could feel the air all around me. From the cockpit, with the horizon in front of me, my vision was filled with a perfect gradient from the deepest midnight blue to a glowing fire orange. As a person bound to earth, the horizon was forbidden to me, blocked by apartment buildings and office complexes in Hohhot, or trees and residences and shopping malls in Princeton, unless, of course, I was home in the grass, or in the middle of the Sonoran Desert, or climbing up a mountain or a tower in search of a bit of sky. This was better, even better than standing on a hilltop reaching toward the sky, because it was the sky. Nothing up here could get in the way because I was surrounded by air. As I rode in that plane, loading film and changing lenses, I was determined to find a way to make flying my life.

How far do they think
A loving mind can reach?
I am not deprived of my love,
It is the very center of my mind.

My rationalization is resistance, covert anti-government activity as self-love? Maybe jumping into that canal didn't just affect my skin, but it must have gotten into my blood and made me itch under my scalp. Because when I went back to Princeton that fall, I wanted to do more than take courses on the history of my people. Our small group of ethnic Mongolians and those trusted few who understood our cause began to meet. My itch was contagious, and it quickly became clear that it was an angry itch, one that was very difficult to scratch. Our cause seemed hopeless, but it would have been even more lost had we been too weak to name it.

We organized a Congress for Inner Mongolian Independence. It took over a year to set up, so between printing programs and adjusting schedules, I ducked into the library to write a few pages of my English literature thesis, titled *The Construction of Feminine Identity in Virginia Woolf and Sylvia Plath*. My heart really wasn't into it, but the successful completion of my thesis and its entirely uncontroversial subject matter were my best cover. The Congress, however, felt like a huge success. Over 50 people traveled to Princeton to join our core group, and we were all full of promise and righteous anger. I told the story of my mother's imprisonment and my relocation and others shared their experiences, many involving even greater injustices. We drafted a charter for our new organization, which we called the *Inner Mongolian People's Party*, and elected a chairperson, vice chair, and secretary. The rest of us remained anonymous.

I felt cowardly as part of that anonymous group, but the argument was that it would do little good to announce ourselves and thereby be banned from our homeland. As silent members of the Congress, we could move freely, allowing us to work from within.

But as soon as we dispersed and the energy of our collected presence began to fade, it was hard to be positive. China is such a powerful force, and we were surrounded, beaten down, our people subjected to China's whims and will.

And here I am. No, it wasn't quite that easy. But it wasn't that hard. How could they refuse the eagle eyes I inherited from Genghis Khan? Practically speaking, the commercial airline business was booming in China. New airports opened almost daily. Before I had decided on flying, I had little idea of what I was going to do after I graduated. Like many of my comrades from Asia, I had considered applying to law school, or getting an MFA in photography, in part just to stay in the U.S. However, it made sense to go back to China. Even though I was a woman and I hadn't majored in a technical field, I passed the entrance exams with ease and was accepted into a commercial pilot training program.

I am, literally, shaken back to the present by the kind of fierce turbulence that vibrates nuts and bolts loose. It felt like it was trying to shake up my very core, which, given my annoyingly capricious stomach on this flight, wasn't so hard to do. I lower my altitude slightly, seeking smoother air currents, but find even more turbulence. So instead, I gain some altitude and the shaking eases. When I realize I have been grasping the controls with a white-knuckled grip, I consciously relax, trying to breathe out my tension.

The Garbage Patch! I had almost forgotten about it. I check my position, and there is still time to adjust my course. The clouds are fairly solid below me at this altitude, so it is likely I have to lose some altitude if I want to have any chance of seeing it. Or it might be impossible to lose so much altitude and still place favorably in the race. But I had gone through the trouble of attaching my photography rig to the plane just for this purpose. It was worth a try at least.

It is not like I haven't seen my fair share of environmental destruction from an eagle's eye view. In fact, I sort of specialize in it. After I got my commercial license, the IMPP contacted me asking if I would be interested in flying some surveillance "missions" for them. I accepted dutifully, acknowledging the risks that I would be taking on behalf of our cause. In reality, I was thrilled, but didn't show it because it would have been unseemly and perhaps a bit suspect to be overly eager. I was twenty-four and longing for an excuse to fly in a prop plane over my homeland. The opportunity to do something useful for the IMPP was a huge plus.

The logistics were actually rather arduous. But in the end, I succeeded in getting a single engine private plane license. Through a private donor, the IMPP purchased a timeshare on a small single engine prop plane, lodged in a hanger at a tiny airport several hours out of Hohhot, where I made my home when I wasn't on active duty for Air China. Approximately every few months, I would take the plane out and fly over certain areas we were concerned about. I customized a camera rig to take aerial photographs that we used to document and compare sites over time.

If I were to get caught, I would be in certain danger. They would make me disappear with hardly a trace. Wouldn't that be ironic? Like mother, like daughter, only it would be unlikely that I would ever get out.

But I absolutely adored those trips. That little plane responded to every air current. I could feel the flow of energized molecules flowing over, under, and all around me. It was a clunky, beat up relic of a plane, but I kept it in good working order and I knew just how it would act in any given situation. Best of all, I loved flying in the sky that I grew up under, gliding over a sea of grass faster than any horse could carry me.

Those trips also filled me with sadness. One of the sites I returned to on a regular basis was a massive strip mine. Hundreds of miles of grass and pasture were being dug up to expose the dark black seam of coal that lay beneath the surface. On another site, fertile pasture had been converted into a huge factory complex, which had quite clearly diminished and polluted the portion of the river downstream from the plant. And every time I went out there were new homes, freshly planted orchards and fields, and more pastured cows whose restless hooves left the earth vulnerable to the passing winds... every year, there was less grass.

Every trip, I took photographs. My rig held two cameras that I could control remotely, a digital camera that was practical and a medium-format film camera that only allowed 24 exposures on a trip. My favorite images were the ones where grass filled the frame from edge to edge. Most people would find them dull, but I found them endlessly interesting. Each individual blade reflected the light, and together the thousands of blades made a subtly shifting mass of color. Most of the time, it was the most delicate green, but in the right light it was almost blue. When winter came, it turned stunning green-tinted ochre. But my favorite was when the wind bent the blades into long streaming ripples and they turned surprisingly silver. Then there were other photographs, showing the myriad ways the grass could be stripped and replaced. The pictures of the mines were horrible to look at, but the scars in the dark brooding mineral earth were intricate. If you could forget what you were looking at, you could lose yourself in the interlocking lines and shapes. The patterns created by irrigation systems and erosion control schemes were fascinating to view from above. Even the patterns of encroaching homes with their regular systems of streets, cul-de-sacs, and portioned off public and private spaces, were interesting when abstracted through the eagle's view.

The digital photographs I passed off to a contact at the IMPP, the film I developed myself. I had a friend in Hohhot who worked in a photography lab and he let me process my roll at the end of the day. I'm sure he thought I had some strange kinky tastes, but he didn't pry. I labeled, cataloged, and stashed them in a box in my closet, and never showed them to anyone.

My position indicates that I am close, but the ocean is barely visible beneath me, covered in a haze. It just looks blue beneath me. I can't make out any change in the surface of the ocean, even though I should be directly above the "Patch" now. I decide to descend a bit, in the hope that I am just flying though a misty cloud and that this haze doesn't continue indefinitely. I must have cleared the cloud because clarity returns all at once like a camera coming into focus. Below me is the vast blueness of the ocean. I check my position on the instruments and this is definitely the last known location of the Garbage Patch. I allow myself the luxury of one sweeping circle. Are those dark shapes, or shadows? I descend even further and pass right over a dozen long, dark shapes. White foam is barely visible on a few that are breaking the surface, while others are just dark blurred shapes under the surface. I activate the camera controls almost by instinct, hardly looking at the LCD, transfixed on the shapes below. They must be whales, what else would be visible at this height?

I don't know where the much-publicized Great Pacific Garbage Patch has gone. Perhaps the photographs will show more than the naked eye could see, or perhaps the mass has drifted off and I'm just photographing the vast blue ocean. I set about recalculating my course towards Oʻahu. I push up and forward and the misty clouds close around me.

The mists are massive
Over the Gobi's dark steppes:
What are the many thoughts
Of one man's dear child?

Finally, I have a visual on Oʻahu. I am thankful for the distraction. I'm sure the irony of our entry into this harbor is not lost on my colleagues in flight. In another place, in another time, it could have been one of us asked to defend our nation with a lethal payload. I cherish my Mongolian lineage, but the Old Mongolian empire was built through violence. When we founded the Inner Mongolian People's Party, we decided that violence is out of harmony with our goals.

I had already been feeling cramped, but now my whole body aches in anticipation of a greater range of motion. The fatigue is beginning to set in now, and the idea of falling into a deep sleep is tempting, but I push the thought quickly aside. This is only the halfway point and there are still hours before I can truly relax.

I guide my plane in. As I come in for my landing, I can see Ruth headed back out to her plane. *Baas*, I might have lost more time in that foray to the Garbage Patch than I thought.

Though I'm antsy and edgy, stretching out feels fantastic. I try to close my eyes for a few minutes, take a catnap, knowing they will wake me up with plenty of time to spare, but even though I'm exhausted, sleep does not come. I try to eat, thankful for the bland food, but I have no appetite. I decline massage and acupuncture because I don't really want to be touched right now, but I do consent to chromotherapy. As I lie in the light I can feel my chi awaken in response, energy meeting energy. I suit up and I am glad that there is no sight of Firoozeh yet. I am back in the cockpit ahead of time and ready to pull off as soon as the hold is released. My nervous energy has returned although I had felt the flutterings of nausea even before sitting still in my craft. The countdown, and then I am off. Too eager, I push too hard and my takeoff is clumsy, very amateur. I know better than to push the plane in this way, but I am thrilled to be back in the air. I think autopilot is necessary now, even at the expense of a competitive time.

Constantly shifting shapes surround me, moist and vaporous, remind me of the clouds that shrouded Emei Shan. I remember taking a bus from Chengdu early one morning to BaoGao, and hiking from there. It was February and BaoGao was pleasantly green, but as I climbed it became colder and snow appeared in patches and then covered the ground. The air was so moist that I could almost drink it. Lacy frost feathered out from low hanging branches and tall vegetation, having ventured impossibly far from its origins. The mist grew thicker as I climbed, and it was of an uneven density that shifted and tricked the eye. Occasionally, another hiker appeared out of the mist and then disappeared. Most visitors took the bus and tram, not that there were many visitors that season. Mostly I was alone.

Being alone had suited me then. I did not want to explain my sadness, and I was tired of telling lies about being ill to account for the dark circles under my eyes. When faced with loss, perhaps I am more like my mother than I had thought. An embarrassment really, it was for the best. As I climbed the endless stairs, I relished the burning in my thighs and calves, the cold air on the exposed skin of my face. My breathing was a reassuring rhythm, labored but regular. I could not see much farther than the stair step right in front of me. Everything was white. The air was milky with mist, the ground muffled in snow, the trees feathered with thick hoarfrost.

And then the steps ended on a large, flat pavilion. The light was different here, still shrouded in mist but also brighter, lighter. It was easier to breathe—gravity had less of a hold here. Another flight of stairs, wider, stretched out beyond what I could see. I could hear bells somewhere nearby, and caught a waft of incense. I was on a broad expanse of stone, walled in mist. There was a sense of space outward and below and I felt that I could still smell the tops of the trees I had passed down below, but there was nothing to be seen but bright swirling moisture. I sat on the stone, facing the emptiness, and let the emptiness fill me. It settled in my fingertips and crept into my core and my empty, aching uterus. I can't say how long I sat there, but when I finally stirred, the light had changed and it was a rich, glowing blue that bathed everything in its cool light. My fingers and toes numb from the cold, I rose stiffly. The light was fading fast now, and I was suddenly afraid and unsure what I would do. I hadn't meant to stay there so long. My plan had been to continue on and find lodging at a monastery further down the trail. But to continue in the misty darkness would be madness, I didn't even have a flashlight. I hurried down the steps and followed the pavement. I saw a few other figures hurrying along, but no one stopped to talk to me. I walked through the small town in just a few paces, and came upon the place where the path continued. There was a woman there with a pack, examining a map with a flashlight. Nothing in the town had been very inviting, but I went back to one place that advertised lodging where I could see a light in the back. I knocked once, then again, and someone stirred and answered the door. Yes, he had a room, 200 yuan. Then he laughed a great toothless laugh, and said for me, twenty yuan. I said that would be fine, I would take the room, but would he please wait a minute. I ran out to the trailhead, where the woman with her flashlight was. I asked her if she would like to share a room with me, in Chinese, then English. She looked dubious, so I reverted to the universal symbol for sleeping and gestured for her to follow me.

I introduced her as my girlfriend, and the proprietor raised his eyebrows but made no further comment. The first floor was set up as a restaurant so I asked if he could give us a meal, and he found us some noodles and hot water. The room was just a room with a big double bed. It was unheated, but there was an electric blanket and a table with a bowl of water on it. The toilet was in the hall, lined with a plastic bag.

I learned that my new roommate was from Syria. I don't think I have ever met anyone with whom I shared fewer words in common. Usually English was a good bet for at least introductions, but we had to communicate totally in mime. I figured out that she was twenty-two and her birthday was the fourth day of the first month, assuming we were talking about the same calendar, and that she had four brothers and no sisters. It was a mystery to me why she was so far from home and all alone in a place that was so far off the beaten track. Otherwise, though, not having to talk suited me. Once we turned out the light, our only communication was our shared island of warmth on an otherwise frozen mountaintop.

I woke early the next morning. The water was frozen in the bowl. My roommate was sound asleep. I crept out of bed and pulled on my frozen boots. I paid the proprietor for the room and dinner, and gave him a little extra to give her a bowl of noodles for breakfast.

I spent the next day climbing the endless stairs, up and down and around Emei Shan. The fog had lifted, and after descending several hundred stairs down from the peak, I could see that the paths were green again and lined with bamboo and vegetation. I passed quiet monasteries, staying long enough for my incense to burn before traveling onward. There were a few other pilgrims on the mountain, as well as vendors selling carved sticks and bottled water. I ate lunch in a little restaurant set up under a canvas awning in a hollow where they served bowls of hot soup with vegetables. That night I paid ten yuan to sleep in a monastery. They brought me to the kitchen and sat me at a table with a bowl of plain rice and boiled squash, and it was one of the best meals I think I have ever eaten. That evening, I lay in my bed and listened to the sound of drums and bells and soft chanting that seemed to permeate the damp stonewalls. The dormitory was unheated, but the beds had electric warmers that made them steam as the settled moisture rose from inside them.

The following day I hiked mostly down, following the curve of the mountain. The air grew warmer, the vegetation greener and more tropical. Watching me from above and behind the trees, I had seen monkeys the size of school children but much more robust and with long hairy arms and inscrutable faces. Now I saw more of them moving together in groups. As they watched me, it made the hair rise up on the back of my neck. I wondered if it would have been better or worse to buy the peanuts that vendors sold to feed them. It seemed like a bad idea to me. What would they do when they had eaten that little bag? Would I be next? I longed for a big stick, and scanned the edges of the path for any likely candidates. There was nothing to do but to move forward.

A large monkey stepped out onto the path ten feet in front of me. I stopped, unsure what to do. Suddenly my backpack tripled in weight and hairy arms wrapped around me. I don't know if I screamed or not as I frantically tried to throw off my assailant. I tripped, and tried to protect my face. I heard the yelling of a human, and the weight on my back disappeared. A hand reached down and helped me to my feet, speaking quickly in a dialect I didn't recognize but the intent was clear. I was unhurt, but I was shaking from adrenaline as I rose. The speaker was a short, wiry old man wielding a solid looking stick. The monkeys had backed off and were watching us from fifteen feet away, peering from behind trees and vegetation. There were at least six of them, three large ones and three smaller ones, females or younger males. The man with the stick started walking and I followed, intent on not losing him. But he was quick on his feet, and I was soon falling behind despite my efforts. I picked up a big rock and carried it in my hand as I walked.

But the monkeys did not come back for me, and the path led into a nature preserve with raised paths that crisscrossed a shallow ravine. Uniformed park rangers stood with big sticks as tourists came and threw peanuts at small packs of monkeys. I hurried by. I had had my fill of monkeys.

My trip to Emei Shan had been just a long weekend rest period between flights in Chengdu, but it felt like I had been to another world and back again. I was eager to get back home to Hohhot, where my sweetheart, Du Yi, was waiting for me. We could try again, and this time, we would be ready.

Suddenly, there he was, nestled between the altitude dial and the barometer. Or, rather, there were those eyes, looking at me the way he used to. He was dressed for our wedding in traditional Mongol embroidered silks. He makes for a passable Mongol, even though he isn't Mongolian at all. But he tried his best. He proposed to me with gifts of salt and honey, and we said our vows hours from nowhere, on top of a sacred Mongol mountain, overlooking valleys dotted with *gers* and goats. It was a small wedding party, his two adult children, his mother and his best friend from Beijing, my stepfather and my mother's brothers and their children. We rented stout horses and had a litter for his mother. At the top of the mountain, we stood on a granite boulder and said our vows in the snow. It was beautiful.

My mother chose not to come. Her absence was a statement. She had sent her good wishes.

Last summer Du and I went to visit her. I thought my mother would be overjoyed as she had hinted with an increasing lack of subtlety at my single status. She and my stepfather lived a little over an hour outside of Hohhot. He was an official at Mengniu, a very successful dairy company. The executives lived in company housing near the company's flagship dairy. The houses were arranged around cul-de-sacs and all built according to what looked like four variations of the same house. The houses were "ranch" style with large picture windows in their living rooms and two-car garages. Every house had a white-picket fenced yard and a plastic mailbox with a red flag on it. It looked like someone had transported a New Jersey suburb to the grasslands of Inner Mongolia.

My stepfather gave Du the grand tour. The milk plant was filled with spotlessly shiny stainless steel and busy workers were dressed from head to toe in spotless white uniforms, all visible from a raised walkway with giant glass windows so that you could look down on every step of the process. Then he took us around the little town and picturesque suburban settlement. My mother followed along, playing the proud wife with obvious relish. She had always been lovely, and even though she was no longer young, she was an elegant figure in her Chanel-style jacket and matching skirt. Her hair was pulled back into an elegant chignon and she clutched a stylish handbag.

But there was still something wild in her grey eyes, a spark from that youth who had traveled from the plains to the city and back again. This new elegant incarnation of my mother was another example of her resilience. It made me uneasy, though. It was so far from the grass, from our roots. It felt like a movie set where the whole town was made up of elaborate façades.

My mother initially was in fine spirits, joining all of the conversations and cooking us a superb Mongolian feast. The next morning though, she was cold toward us. After breakfast, Du went and talked with her in her study. We left soon afterwards. It was clear we were no longer welcome. My stepfather begged us to stay, saying she would get over it.

Before, her critical silences had made me sad and curious. Now, they made me angry. It was true Du was twelve years older than I, had been previously married, and had two children who were in their twenties. He wasn't a Mongol. But I was no young woman who needed counsel. I was thirty-seven and I had met someone who was sweet, gentle, and intelligent. We could be in two separate cities, and we would order the same dish at the same time, and would call each other and laugh about it. He was the one for whom I had been waiting for the last twenty years.

I have spent far too much time pointlessly mulling over the patterns in her silences towards me. Perhaps she was afraid to lose me, so she felt the need to push me away first. It is sort of a self-centered theory—who is to say that she truly loved me that much? Alternately, if she had loved my father, perhaps I was a reminder of what she could never have, and what she had lost.

I must have fallen asleep! My mileage gauge and GPS tell me that I am only a few miles from the last refueling ship. So glad that Keiko agreed to put autopilots in our floatplanes. I hadn't realized how tired I was. The nausea is hitting again, and that concerns me. I have my hunches, but don't want to deal with them.

This time my sea landing is superb. Tired and all, I think I have mastered this aircraft. The Mongol gods are watching over me. I just needed to be in touch with my roots.

Again, with the nausea, I hesitate to eat, but gratefully stand in the hot shower for as long as possible. As the warm water relaxes my muscles, I stroke my body and wish Du was here in the shower with me. We have had a wonderful marriage and our lovemaking has grown in satisfaction through the years. I try to quell the desire for my husband as I lay naked under the sheets for Dr. Watase's acupuncture treatment. I am pleased that Kaz comments on the strength and beauty of my body. I can't figure out why in this acupuncture session he is smiling so broadly as if he knows something I don't.

Once again, acupuncture has invigorated me, and after putting on a clean flight suit, I give Kaz a hug and thank him for the many sessions of healing acupuncture. Before I run to get back into my floatplane, Kaz gives me a weather report that suggests the possibility of isolated storms forming over the Pacific off the coast of California. And some apparently unrelated instructions for the landing, a particular target altitude and instructions to fly through a particular cloudbank. Sounds impractical, but apparently the message has come from Keiko, so it is not easily dismissed.

My takeoff is excellent again even in the choppy waters, now only four-plus hours to the Golden Gate Bridge. The sky is not quite as clear as it looked from the refueling ship. Above, still far off, there is a bit of darkness. It looks like it may not be totally on our flight course though. I have grown fond of the sanctuary of this wonderful flying machine. So many past memories and issues I have had a chance to think about in the long hours of solitude. The best aspect of this whole adventure has been the time that I am in control, a time to deal on my own terms with destiny and yet to be in the moment. I will always thank Keiko for this opportunity. I look forward to spending time in San Francisco with Keiko and the pilots who choose to stay for a while. Du will be there to meet me as well.

I wonder where the other pilots are, and how they are faring. Ruth was gone by the time I got out of my plane at the last refueling ship, and I was sort of glad not to encounter Firoozeh again. I am surprised because I'm apparently a bit behind the mark, or Ruth is ahead, so Firoozeh must be even farther behind, or she has somehow gotten ahead of us all. Not likely though, as she really is the novice pilot of our group.

Firoozeh has always been a little cold towards me. She constantly takes what I say and reinterprets it to fit her black or white stereotypes. She seems to blame me for being Chinese. If blame is to be passed around, I blame myself too. I don't like to think of myself as Chinese, but what else am I if not Chinese. It is what my passport says. I can assert my heritage as much as I like, but when people meet me, they see China. How can I blame them? I speak Chinese, fluently, Mandarin and even passable Cantonese. There are Inner Mongolians who don't, and they don't have the same choices in life that I have had. I could renounce the Chinese side of myself and move back to some remote village, but then I would be powerless when the government came to relocate that village, or the mining company came to move us all to new lands. It is ironic, to have any chance at preserving our culture, at fighting for our culture, it is necessary to live this double life, to be Chinese and not Chinese.

Could I ever leave China? What if I were forced to leave? If the Chinese government ever found out about my involvement with the Inner Mongolian People's Party, I might have to flee. I could hasten that choice—it has occurred to me that I could publish my archive of aerial photographs of environmental destruction, for example. If I did that, it would certainly end my ability to continue to make those photographs, to monitor those sites. Maybe I could do it anonymously, and still continue my work? Would I be more valuable in Inner Mongolia, or outside of it? Could I make that choice—the choice to possibly never be allowed to return to the country I love because I want to serve the country I love? And then there are my thoughts about America. How could I serve the country I love from America?

I suddenly become aware that the sky is filled with color. It is all around me, in the cockpit, and glowing on my skin. I reach out and try to ride with the winds. They are now shifting, affected by the darkness that is large now, rearing up on my left, swallowing the light. But the light from behind me is deep magenta, almost red, slanting across the sky.

It makes me think of fire, staring into a flame. I'm staring into flames and the tears are flowing. It was a mistake, but I had been certain it was meant to be. I was going to have a boy filled with the spirit of my ancestors. I think even then I knew something wasn't right, I was never sick the way women were, and I was so very tired, like the life was sucked out of me. Then the cramps came, and I knew he was lost. It was so humiliating, sitting doubled over on a toilet, filled with mourning and pain that came in waves. I was alone. I had been sharing a room with a female flight attendant, but she had gone out with the other attendants. A wave of pain hit me, and I instinctively reached down and he was born into my hand. He was tiny, only a few millimeters long but perfect to my eyes, nestled in a sack of fluid the size of a golf ball. The next morning I put on my uniform and flew back to Hohhot with my crew, thankful at least that it was the end of a cycle and I could be home, without having to explain myself further. Du and I took a trip that weekend to the Xilamuren Grassland, which was as far as we could get into the grasslands on a weekend trip. We would have rented horses but I wasn't up to it, so we rented a motorcycle and rode until there was just grass in all directions. We built a pyre in the middle of the grasslands, and sent our son's spirit up to the sky gods.

A flash of light brings me back to present. I hope desperately that I have not charted a course that will take me through the worst of this storm. I can't see the other side of it, which worries me. A crosscurrent tosses the plane. I hear the propellers straining. A gust like that would have ripped apart the little plane I flew over the Mongolian plains. Fear threatens to take over, and I'm nauseous again. I reach out, trying to feel my way through the currents, but I can't get beyond myself. I grip the controls uselessly, my head pounds. Maybe I should fly low, or try a sea landing, but that would be giving up one danger for another, perhaps a worse one. The waves would toss the plane around like a toy.

My mind is racing with unproductive thoughts. I reach inward, for the flow of life, the flow I tap into when moving through my Tai Chi. I feel the tips of my fingers, my toes, the roots of my hair. Everything is connected, even the storm's power to destroy or create. Grounded within myself, I breathe. I feel my breath stronger, more solid than the storm around me. I reach out, I see myself from outside of myself, looking down on myself and then focusing outwards. For a moment, the storm is chaos around me, darkness, I can't see anything and it makes no sense. But no, there is a pattern. I feel it. I follow a current up, higher, climbing up. Glancing at the altimeter,

I realize I'm right around 23,456 feet. Below the chaos is swirling. Here, the currents are swift, but there are patterns. I shift from one current to another, abruptly, and the plane protests, the engine strains, and for a moment it almost feels as if the currents will drag the nose up and flip me, but I just manage to hold on.

> My utterly perfect lama,
> Through the blessing of emptiness,
> Let us be joyful, fading away
> Into cosmic openness

There is only darkness ahead, but somehow the darkness does not feel so dense. Then, the storm is behind me. At this altitude the atmosphere is almost still. It is suddenly so clear above that there are stars. There are some clouds ahead, and my rapidly descending course to 7,890 feet takes me through the uppermost stratum. I am following Kaz and Keiko's strange instructions. Oddly, I feel no fatigue, just a sense of quiet. I can still feel every nerve in my body, and I have become aware that I'm not alone. There is another presence, in my womb. This one is a girl. She is strong, this one, fighting for her independence, differentiating herself from me even now.

Ahead, there are lights clinging to the dark rim of the Pacific.

FIROOZEH IRANI

TURQUOISE 10

I, Firoozeh, am in my cockpit. I adjust my eyeglasses and wonder what I am doing here. Here I am, a two-time cancer survivor taking such a risk on this long flight. But since I am so close to death, I don't mind taking this risk. I adjust the oxygen that has been retrofitted on these old Spitfires that Madam Kobahashi has resurrected. The oxygen is vital to bringing down the CA 125 cancer antigen. It fluctuates from ninety to thirteen. As I get angry, it goes up and as I calm down and breathe, it goes down. Keiko Kobahashi has provided us with strategies and training and an acupuncturist, but it is Dr. Lad's ancient Indian Ayurvedic practice of *pranayama* that helps me most. Ah, but my mind wanders as I relive my story—why I am in The Race, where I have come from, and what my intent is. I am not as simple a being as some of the other pilots. I do not have just a single ethnicity and spirituality or religion. I am a mongrel. That's what they used to call me in school when I was little. A Zoroastrian Parsi, from Persia, from a race thrown out by the Muslim invaders, we came to India. We came almost "Indianized," went back to Iran, got thrown out by Muslim fundamentalists again, returned to India to become more Indian than the Indians, and then moved to the great land of the freedom of religion, the U.S. of A.

Yes, I am Firoozeh Irani, named after the stone of my birth, turquoise from Iran. By the good graces of Ahura Mazda, I was saved and transported to worlds across the vast Pacific to join this race. But now I have come from the middle of the ocean, from Oʻahu, where I had finally landed, brought by a mother and husband who attempted to make the islands of Madam Pele home. My wanderings have been far and wide like those of my people, diasporic, from the land where the lizard and the lion keep Jamshid's court. I have come from Iran and my people are from Iran. My religion is from Iran. I am Zarathushti. That is the original religion of Iran before the Muslim invaders came and drove us from our homelands, not once but more than twice, originally in the eleventh century CE, and then again after the Shah was overthrown by the Americans. Then we made India our home for the second time.

When the first wave of Zoroastrians immigrated to India to escape the Muslim persecution in 1100 AD, they arrived on the west coast of India and asked the Rajah to allow them to stay. Unable to speak the language, they stirred sugar into a bowl of milk in the presence of the Rajah to show that they will mix with the local people like sugar mixes with milk. They adopted the local customs and language and asked only to be allowed to follow their religious practices in peace. This is what I, Firoozeh, was seeking again, many hundred years later.

A seaworthy people, having made the rough voyage from Persia to India, my people had established nautical routes of trade primarily with China and came to be called Chinai. I come from the family called Chinai, because we were traders with China. We took spices and mahogany woods to be carved and, silently, I say this to you, even elephant tusks. Chinese carved them into those great bridges of stories, like willow pattern plates, like storyteller bracelets. These hung in my home in south India, until from there, too, we were driven out and sent back to what we thought was a hospitable Shah, a Shah celebrating the twenty-fifth-century anniversary of Cyrus the Great! The Shah, who, despite claims that he tortured his enemies, at least brought a modicum of Westernization and freedom to women, until the Americans intervened in the name of protecting human rights and brought the long, dark shadow of the Ayatollahs to our glorious land of turquoise, of Shiraz's rose gardens, of ancient white pillars engraved with the figures of "Asho-farohars," divine angels.

It is on the backs of women that many of the successful migrations and movements of our peoples were accomplished. Several of my fellow women pilots have asked me, "What is the role of your women? Is it true that women from Iran and India have been subjugated, put down, and have quietly acquiesced?" I answered, "No, this is not true, and even as I go through my trials and tribulations, I have been strong and survived cancer and divorce." At the center there is a Chinese woman with whom I have to work out my karma. See how we have picked up Indian concepts? I talk of karma, a Hindu notion that has penetrated our consciousness.

When I was growing up in Iran, where my family lived in the late 1960s and 1970s to reassert their Persian roots, I saw many smart Air Force officers who would circle the Empress Farha Diba. I would often think, "What fun to be smartly dressed in all that blue and gold and to be bowing and scraping and be admired and also in possession of the great power to fly those jets and soar in the vast blue!" That is also partly what brought me to this race! Yes, that is what I thought. But in those days as I was only in my twenties, I thought that the only way to wear one of those uniforms was to marry an Air Force officer. But now look, I have done it on my own. Not in a uniform, but through the graciousness of Allah and lots of money to easily corruptible money-hungry Air Force pilots, I was able to learn to fly in secret for three years. I am not sure why Keiko chose me for this race. I may not win this race because I am a novice pilot, and because of the bones I pick with my competitors who do not understand me and keep asking Keiko to reject me. But I will at least have worked out my karma! Yes, I want to be a strong woman, like my ancestors.

We had more freedom then as women than we have now, as Iran has changed so much. Muslim Iran is putting us women down unnecessarily. There is nothing even in their *hadith* (A report on something the prophet Muhammad did, or one of his sayings.) that justifies putting women behind veils and shrouds. Genetically, we are not women who can be covered up under the *purdah* or *burqa*. From the daughter of Zarathustra, Pouruchista, and Pantea Arteshbod, the great commander of Persian armies, we've always had women fighters and pilots. Islam has brought submission to women, even though the most honorable Khadija was the one who provided the prophet his opportunities of advancement from her own funds and monies and he respected her greatly.

Looking at it from the Muslim perspective for now, the Prophet, blessed be his name, was married to Khadija, a woman older than he, who was the key to his success. Without the support of Khadija and her brothers, the prophet would not have been able to build his empires, either that of business or religion. And his youngest wife, Ayesha, he protected by *hadiths* that said adultery and rape must be proven by witnesses! It was for protection! The prophet was no misogynist. Do not put that at his door.

And in ancient Iran, there were many, many women goddesses and angels. In my Zoroastrian religion, there is Avan, the goddess of water, Maha Boktar, the moon, and Khurshid Amshaspand, the Sun, all female deities. And these I look to and call upon, as I fly this vast Pacific. Avan goddess of water, protect me from drowning, and Mah Boktar the moon, keep me company. But ah look! As my mind has been wandering over aeons, and telling my familial history, I am beginning to see that I am coming to the first refueling ship. How time flies when you are dreaming of the past, and living it, as though it is the present!

Now the training in Tokyo has paid off. I land perfectly on the water and even see crew members on the ship clapping. Are they aware of my difficulties? Throughout training I kept to myself only to have animated and sometimes frustrating conversations mostly with Hamidah, the Tibetan, and Ting Xu, the distant Chinese woman. Ting Xu, flying in *Blue 9* seems to be here. I have much to resolve with her, but this is not the place. Lousy food, but I am hungry and go to the canteen to nourish myself as best as I can. I intend on bypassing Dr. Watase's acupuncture for a longer stay in the shower under hot water. Ting Xu comes into the canteen on her way to her floatplane. We are obviously not on good terms, but I still pass by her and whisper good luck.

And now I am off to the dreaded Oʻahu to refuel and once again deal with negative memories.

"Oh island in the sun, willed to me by mother's hand." Apologies to Harry Belafonte! It is my island. My mother made it her home for 20 years, and there are many Persians and Iranians on this island, even the founder of eBay, Pierre Omidyar. Didn't I tell you we were a diaspora people? From Iran to India, India to Iran, back to India and from our not belonging there, like so many others, we sought refuge in the land of the Lady of Liberty. This is also the story of my mother and me. My mother grew up in poverty in India, but she managed to put herself through school. With her education, she became a powerful university administrator. She had the opportunity to host the Shah and his wife, the Empress, who at that time came to India to offer that Parsis could return to their land to practice their religion in freedom. She took the opportunity and moved as an administrator to the university in Isfahan, to be near the ancient sites of Zoroastrianism. Alas, a well-meaning, but naïve President Carter sought to replace the Shah with what he thought would've been the benign religious reign of the Ayatollah, but he ended up bringing in a fundamentalist Islam that would expel us again. So we were back to India, where I gained my education and began my flight training, thanks once again to money that bought me time in the air. But India too became hostile to us under Mrs. Gandhi. Although married to a Parsi, Firoze Gandhi, no relative of Mahatma Gandhi, her "Emergency" imposed un-democratic measures upon all Indians, causing us all to move in great waves to the U.S.

And that is how I, Firoozeh, and my mother ended up in the U.S again. It is hard for my co-pilots to understand, that even though I look weak and seem perpetually to be confused with technology and understanding meanings, my mother and I have been strong women, pioneers who have built and rebuilt our lives over and over again, from one historical and personal moment to another, shedding the scabs of origin wounds. We do not live in nostalgia for lost origins. During World War II, when British Tommies were all over an already British colonized India, Meheroo, my mother, made herself fluent in English, joined the Poetry Society, befriended British families and made every ethical effort to become educated and to educate. It is out of this strength that I was born from her arranged marriage with my father, an engineer to whom she was married for twenty-five years before he dropped dead of a heart attack over forty years ago.

In 2007, I moved to Honolulu, of all places, to care for my aging mother. She moved there in 1973 after Mrs. Ghandi expelled all the non-Marxists academics. But just as I was recovering from my chemo fog, I suddenly found that my husband of thirty years was leaving me. Mother was indignant at my suicidal mentality. "What? Why would you do that for a man?" she would say. But I get ahead of myself. Here is what happened and this is why I have to talk more with Ting Xu and Hamidah Gyamtso as soon as we can meet again. Christine Banfield and others don't understand. Besides, the lives they have led, they are white women with white privilege!

In 2007, I contracted a second cancer. Breast cancer is endemic to the Semitic peoples, and we Zoroastrians from Iran are somehow considered Semitic medically, but by census data, Caucasian. Mother had said, "Come to Honolulu, we can take care of each other." I had now been married to the white man for thirty years. But Mother got him a job there because she wanted the whole family together on what she called "her island," her adopted home. A Farsi-Hindi-English-Gujerati speaker, she had begun to think of Hawai'i as her 'āina.

My mother bought my husband and me a house on a rise behind her tall condominium. It was a new Asian-style multifamily house with two separate flats, one upstairs and one downstairs. She knew I liked to have my study area separate. While the view from the point was spectacular, looking to Waikiki to the west and Kahala to the east, next door was an old termite-eaten omen of bad love luck.

Next to my house in Honolulu, which is probably not my house anymore, but next to what was my house, there was a delicate, beautiful Japanese house that had been built by a wonderful gentleman called Endo for his Japanese bride. Not a single nail held together the various red and Burmese woods, and even koa wood, which he had cut with his own hands to make the slats that fit together with a joiner's craftsmanship, like that of Shakespearean joiners. He had delicately constructed this house with its tilting roof, a perfect *feng shui* roof, where the four sides turn upwards towards heaven to ward off all evil. The shoji screens, too, were built without a single nail. You know, that house is now being eaten by Hawaiian termites. It's a great metaphor. He brought his bride there and unfortunately there came upon them disaster after disaster, disharmony and bad luck. Somehow with the movement and migrations of peoples, we see that perhaps we are meant to stay in one place and not to move, because as we move, we find more disaster, disharmony and bad luck. This poor Mr. Endo's family was totally decimated. He brought a beautiful bride and her son from a previous marriage, but the son was somehow affected by chemical fallout from the '45 mushroom cloud that the Americans unleashed over Japan. He later died of muscular dystrophy, leaving his mother so brokenhearted that she just sat on the *lānai* with her grief. I don't know that we can call it a *lānai*, it was a Japanese balcony, and she looked out through her shoji screens across the water at Japan, and sighed and wept and sighed and wept. And unlike Madame Butterfly, she had no *sakura* to comfort her (too hot in Hawai'i for them), and so she sat with her pain without the delicate cherry blossoms that she loved.

Somehow this new house of mine that was built next door to Mr. Endo's plot of land seemed to have absorbed all that sighing and weeping, and somehow, that cancer ate away at me and at my white American husband, like termites eating into that house, that new house that had been built on one of Madame Pele's rocks, the rocks they say not to build upon because they embody bad luck.

As I lay dying next to this crumbling house, while I was taking treatment there in Honolulu with a Japanese doctor who is skilled at treating cancers, my family fell apart. Though I had gone with the advice from mainland doctors, this doctor disagreed with that counsel from the mainland doctors, and gave me very strong chemo, not dependent upon my height or weight. And so at that point I was completely wiped out. It was also a very strong form of chemo that is not FDA approved. It was brought from Japan by some of the Japanese doctors who are able to practice in Honolulu, a very strong combination of Carboplatin and Oxyliplatin. My mainland doctors had objected to the decision, afraid of the drugs' side effects. My Indian oncologist, who is a friend of my mother's, had also advised against the medications, saying to my mother, "She will not die from the cancer but from the treatment."

But as I found out during that eleventh month in Honolulu, a dragon had come soft-footed into my home. I was in a total chemo fog, completely wiped out, unable to do anything. I had to try to do things for myself since there was no one to help me. I had been trying to cook my own food and I also tried to drive because my aged mother had to be taken care of. I was angry all the time at Mother for having brought us to Honolulu, because I felt the doctor was not listening to me and was just filling me with chemo regardless of what happened to my platelets, the part of the blood that helps it clot. My platelet count went down, down, down, and would not come up. But the doctor also introduced me to a practice called EFT, which stands for Emotional Frequency Therapy, and involves tapping on the sides of my palms while I sit and visualize my blood platelets going up, up, up. Eventually the doctor said, "Aha, didn't I tell you!"

While I was focusing on these treatments, my husband totally went astray, and he is now involved with a Chinese woman who is much more central Asian in looks. She is bigger, square boned, not the typical petite, subservient Chinese woman, but of the central Asian highlands. She's a big woman. She is dark skinned, even though she tries to embody the charms of the lighter-skinned, smaller-type Chinese women. Her name is Shie Xie, or Water Dragon.

When I woke up and realized that the cancer was being healed and the doctor proclaimed me cancer-free, I tried to pick up my strength and begin to move about. As I was doing this, Shie Xie called the house to tell me that she had been having an affair with my husband.

As I emerged from my chemo fog, I discovered that Shie Xie had taken control of my husband's mind and heart. When she saw me getting better and getting stronger, she started to call the house to tell me, "You cannot get well, you are supposed to die. Your doctor on the mainland has given you a terminal diagnosis and a period of six months to live. Your bone marrow is gone. Your blood is totally washed out. Since you will not be able to live very long, I have asked your husband to divorce you—he has already proposed to me. He was expecting you to die in six months. You must die in six months. Why didn't you die in six months? You cannot come about and reclaim your marriage—your husband has proposed to me."

Much later I woke up and got more messages. She sent me texts. Shie Xie did not mind forwarding to me dirty texts, sexual texts, texts that have begun to be called "sexts," that had been sent to her by my former husband, her husband now, the white American man. Shie Xie took him for long dinners at the Korean restaurant Kim Chee, fed him Kirin beer to which she added Chinese drugs, and ginseng, gingko, and damiana, to evoke passion. He would drink Kirin, and in his sour state write her these strange sexual sexts. Can you blame me for having an angry attitude toward women and life in general?

O'ahu or a garbage patch? Yes, yes, it is the driftwood and the dead wood from the Fukushima disaster that has been washing up by Kane'hoe Bay. I see the outline of the island, and my mother's building, Kahala Towers, standing tall and pink along the west coast of the island, where she has made her home since she left India. There is too much air pollution. Madame Pele has been spewing sulfur dioxide in the air again! Ah, as I come low over Waikiki on the east side of Diamond Head, what are those outlines in the shallow water, whales… or surfers? They say the whales are coming close to shore, as are the sharks. The Hawaiians say the *aumākua*, the ancient ones, are restless.

My hands are shaking as I begin to realize I am coming into O'ahu… the trauma and the anger coming up again.

Uh-oh! Over the radio transmission, "Come into water landing, *Turquoise 10,* at Pearl Harbor, O'ahu."

"Oh my, I do not want to land on O'ahu," I think. But that was part of our route and our trip. We had agreed with Madame Kobahashi that we would do that. I had planned to ask Ting Xu some things, though she will probably not be there to have that talk. She and Hamidah were the only ones I talked to in training and it was not always nice to talk with them. I remember some of the conversations and the tension of our Tokyo talks.

"Tell me, Ting-Xu," I asked, "what is the Achilles heel of the Chinese women so I can defeat this woman who stole my husband? How can I show that she is all about greed?"

And as I remember, Ting-Xu said, "Yes, you have to think about how China has changed these days. China has changed into this large, capitalist, money-hungering monster. And that is the reason why the women who are coming out of China are beginning to embody more and more both an inferiority complex and a sense of helplessness, that through men, and men alone they can become powerful. This is the reason why Shie Xie has latched on to your husband, because she thinks that through a white man, and through a white man alone, she can come into her power. That sense of power has been passed down to all of us through the example of Madame Mao and how she came into power."

"Oh, no, no," I argued with Ting-Xu. "Madame Mao didn't just come into power by marrying Mao, she also helped make him. She was a strong woman. She was a very strong woman. She worked herself up through all the physical exercises—Tai Chi, the martial arts—she worked through all of that. She was not just a weak woman who married a rich man. Yes, like Evita, she too got seduced by power, and I see that that power, that desire for power is there in Shie Xie, too."

Hamidah had joined us and she interjected her tiresome Tibetan Buddhist perspective, "But, Firoozeh, you have to accept this. You have to…" I interrupted, "Pah, why do you have a Muslim name and husband?" I said this to her out of disrespect and confrontation. Angry Firoozeh on the attack again, I was not one to ever keep quiet.

"Oh, no, no, no, I am not going to accept, I'm not going to forgive. I am making up my mind that I am going to fight. I'm going to be vindictive. I'm going to bring these people down. It is this strength that I have admired in the Persian pilots. It is this that I admired in the Shah's army and in the Shah's Air Force. Yes, this is the reason why I wanted to fly and prove myself able to be a successful race pilot. No, Ting-Xu, you and Hamidah cannot try to tell me to be subservient, to embody all these senses of femaleness and forgiveness and so on and so forth. Why is it that we women are asked to forgive and men are not asked to forgive? Why is it that we are supposed to accept what comes to us as our lot, whether it is through men and husbands, or through whatever mean things they do to us? Why is it that we should accept these things?"

"Besides, I am Persian by ancestry and ethnicity, but also Indian by virtue of having literally grown up there. Remember, I am the mongrel, and Hinduism like Buddhism has no sutra on forgiveness. In the Ramayana and the Mahabharata, there is war, there are gods and goddesses, Narasimha and Durga and Kali, who fight and are victorious."

I once asked Sri Sri Ravi Shankar about forgiveness and he said "No, no forgiveness in our Vedas—compassion, yes, but no forgiveness. Gautama, the Buddha, took the notion of compassion, not forgiveness, hence we have karma. We cannot just get release by forgiveness. We have to work our karmas out, on the wheel of fortune, turning and turning. It is not like being Catholic, go to confession, get forgiveness and go out and sin some more. It is sin no more, so that you do not have karma, Firoozeh, in all your moving and migration, you have acquired heavy karma."

After my outburst, Hamidah sighed and said, "It is unsubstantiated anger."

"Unsubstantiated?" I flared, "What do you mean? I am totally justified! What are you supposed to do when someone comes like a soft-footed thief in the night when you are in your chemo fog to steal your husband?"

"But the eightfold path is a way for you to heal yourself, Firoozeh."

"Ah, Hamidah, you preach to me too much. Why are you telling me about Buddhism? I too have my prayer wheel with *Om mani padme hum* inscribed in it. I too worship the lotus feet of the goddess."

As the three of us went to eat in old *shitamachi* neighborhood of Tokyo, we continued to argue. "Oh women," I thought to myself, "always at each other's throats!"

Oʻahu was not being good to me again. I was getting worked up and worrying that my cancer antigen marker would go up. I eagerly looked forward to the refueling and resting to be over so I could fly on to San Francisco. "San Francisco, open your golden gates!" I thought. The next and last refueling ship is more than four hours away, along with flying through some rough weather. I think I have been lucky so far in my water landings but the next one will be a challenge for Firoozeh!

Now, nine hours into this adventure, I am ready for any challenge, but, most of all, I am starting to understand the aloneness and meditative quality of being in control in this little sanctuary of a cockpit. Better to call it the 'pilot enclosure' as I don't want to associate it with "cock" or "pit" in any way. There I go again, the anger and unhappiness. At least I am becoming aware of it and accepting it. These days I wonder if that is my true personality.

Winding my way through and around the big weather clouds, I think about how I, Firoozeh Irani, wound my way around the questions that Madame Kobahashi asked me while choosing the fifteen pilots during the interview process. The anger in me may have only been noticed later in training. Or, maybe she knew my background all along and wanted some diversity or balance or challenge in the group. After this race, most of them will work for a worthy cause of some sort with Madame Kobahashi or with their own people or tribes. Not me. I have to address my karma and come to terms and settlement with personal issues. Hamidah called it self-centered and narcissistic. I asked her, wasn't that what enlightenment was all about? Anyway, I can't do anything for anyone else unless I am at ease with, and understand, myself.

After dwelling on these thoughts for the last three hours, the last refueling ship is in sight. I am the only floatplane docking at this time. The ocean is much too choppy and landing is very difficult. I manage to land but I scrape my airplane against the mooring dock, so they will have to repair a bit of the left float. The technicians have said they can do it during the hour I am here. Finally, some food that satisfies my taste buds. I need spice. I hate bland. I hate raw fish. A hot shower and a clean flight suit will do after I eat. No acupuncture for me although Dr. Watase, who does not seem disappointed, catches up with me, "Firoozeh, you are the angriest woman in this grand adventure. Your health and survival will depend on how you relinquish the anger. Listen to Hamidah. And it might be important for you to fly through Cloud Nine as you approach San Francisco. You must know that your pilot sisters all care for you. And I do as well." Dr. Watase gave me the coordinates for Cloud Nine and then gave me a hug.

I am told that there is some dark weather from here to San Francisco. This might have scared me in the past, but for some reason I am up for the challenge and I might even fly through Cloud Nine. I have dealt with worse situations. The feeling of "freedom" is good. I have felt free in the sky. I owe nothing to anybody, except perhaps, to Madame Kobahashi for choosing me to be a part of this adventure. I haven't had the time or the inclination to think about my negative past and my life until now, while flying through the heavens for this long period of time. I have Madame Kobahashi to thank and I will someday find a way to repay her. And, I am sure I have my female deities to thank as well.

Okay, my floatplane is repaired and I will master this last takeoff for San Francisco.

Back in the plane, I say to myself, "Yes, I, Firoozeh, am a strong character. *A survivor!* I am a character who fights against the injustices and the whips and blows of fortune and time that come against me. And this race and my time in the air have allowed me to realize my strength! Yes, I can be strong and I can go back to my original young aspirations that formed when I saw those pilots in the Shah's Air Force in their blue uniforms. I thought, yes, I would like to be strong like them and I will fly. But, no, I cannot be dependent upon just a man and a marriage and a family. This is my story. This is the way my story has developed. Only now, maybe I do need to finally deal with my anger, and find happiness in my life. It won't be easy.

I did come from lands far away and far between, but I now am coming into my own land, which is in my heart. It is my strength, it is my story, this is where I belong, this is my identity. But my identity is not in my land, or any land. I am not Persian. I am not Indian. I am not Buddhist. I am not Zoroastrian. I am me. I am Firoozeh, who has the strengths and the embodiment of all these different cultures. I, who pray in many different languages, and who has the strength and the embodiment of the karma of different religions and the karma of different cultures. But, no, I don't need to believe in karma. No karma is going to knock me down. I am going to think deeply here as I strengthen my mind. And as I strengthen my mind, I realize that I don't have to be competitive. I don't have to look out of my cockpit to see whether the orange plane is flying past me or the green is flying past me, and whether I am able to come out stronger or faster. I am trying to come into my own self, and that is what is important.

I, who have survived cancer twice, rebellious military movements, uprooting from my motherland, uprooting from places where I had made my home, uprooting and coming into the long stretches of sandy beaches in Honolulu to start a new life. And there I am just myself, just another grain of sand among the many grains of sand that are around me, and yet one that won't be blown way, that won't become just a non-entity.

We all received a written message from Ayame while in training. It had the first lines from Yosano Akiko's long poem *Sozorogoto*, translated as *Rambling Thoughts*. The poem was published in the inaugural issue of the feminist magazine *Seito* or *Bluestocking* in September 1911.

The day the mountains move has come.
Or so I say, though no one will believe me.
The mountains were merely asleep for a while.
But in ages past, they had moved, as if they were on fire.
If you don't believe me, that's fine with me.
All I ask is that you believe this and only this,
That at this very moment, women are awakening from their deep slumber.

I, Firoozeh Irani! The poem is symbolic of what I did not appreciate during training as shown by my little interactions with some of the other pilots. The poem did not mean a lot to me then. I now have to thank Ayame for the poem, as it totally represents my waking up from a slumber of anger, jealousy, physical pain, and psychological pain, much of it self-induced, but at times for good reason, I think. I must talk with Ting Xu and apologize for all the meanness and for misinterpreting her words to fit my polarized, angry position. Perhaps, just maybe, Ting Xu and I might be friends someday. I still need to deal with my anger and work things out with Hamidah. I think she meant well and spoke with compassion. Compassion is something I must practice along with finding happiness.

It won't be easy for me, that is for sure. I have been angry for much too long for change to happen quickly.

I am guiding my *Turquoise 10* toward Cloud Nine, and then to my landing in San Francisco where I will face the other pilots and Madame Kobahashi. I shall see how this Cloud Nine works! And although Hamidah always told me to live in the now, for the first time I am looking forward to the future. I know I have to work on my identity, "the self," but not in a self-centered way. As I fly onward, I, Firoozeh Irani, am prepared to move forward as well.

LUDMILLA LITVYCK

RED 11

I'm at 7,620 meters above the great Pacific Ocean. There is much silence in this cockpit. It is during this time that I reflect on what needs to change in me and what will happen when this race is over.

Solitude is a luxury that I'm not used to. I have lived at least half my life, but this is the first time I don't have to think about Russia when I'm flying. Mother Russia is a place I will never go back to. Ekaterinburg, where I was raised, is where the last tsar and his family were brought to their violent deaths. When I learned to read English, I read stories that the tsar and his family were not dead, that they had not been killed, and that the time and place where they died was also a myth. For all of us who lived in Ekaterinburg, we knew not only that it had happened there, but exactly where—in the woods behind the church was the spot where their bones were buried. It was to us a grand joke that when the government came to search for the long-buried bodies, they didn't ask us, the locals, who knew. That's how it went in my neck of the woods. And like many ordinary Russians, living in a depressed state and nurturing a love/hate relationship with my country is my heritage.

Despite all the modernization, my *Red 11* floatplane, which I named Lily, is a surprisingly difficult aircraft to fly. The floats create an aerodynamically unbalanced racer while the wings obscure a view of the water on takeoffs and landings. The added pontoons act like pendulums that could compromise the effectiveness of the ailerons at the ends of the wings and over-correcting with the controls could create oscillation, rocking Lily from side to side and initiating a spiral dive. Despite hours of test flights and years of experience flying conventional aircraft, my reconstructed Spitfire does not handle like the nimble fighter that the British used to win the Battle of Britain in World War II, or even Aunt Lydia's Yak 1 fighter, which was patterned after the Spitfire.

Ah, my Aunt Lydia… by leaning to my left, to port, the top of the white lily painted on the front of the fuselage is just visible. This emblem symbolizes my Aunt, Lydia Litvyck, a World War II fighter pilot who flew a Yakovlev Yak I with a white lily on its nose. The Soviet press called her the "White Lily of Stalingrad," but most people simply called her Lily. Lydia Litvyck was the most decorated female fighter pilot in the Soviet Air Force during World War II. I had never heard of her until my father wrote to me about her in his revelatory letter. So I call my red floatplane, *The White Lily,* to honor the aunt I never knew.

Lily was difficult to handle at the start of the race. Multiple tests demonstrated that she rode the waves poorly, at first bucking up and down at low speed and then rocking side to side from pontoon to pontoon before breaking free of the water. The engineers at Supermarine LTD had discovered this problem in 1943 when they experimentally fitted three Mark 9-B Spitfires with pontoons. The westerlies blowing from Tokyo out over the bay caused a further complication. The floatplanes had to take off into the wind, and this meant flying toward the mainland before making a low-level turn to the right in order to aim toward the United States. So the barge that served as our base was almost half a mile from shore.

My test hops reminded me of newsreels from 1927 as Charles Lindbergh tried to lift off from a muddy Roosevelt Field in Garden City, Long Island. Overloaded with fuel, the *Spirit of St. Louis* bounced down the runway and then barely cleared the telephone wires at the end of the 1,524-meter runway.

At takeoff, it was essential to control my emotions so I didn't make a mistake by opening the throttle too quickly, causing Lily to veer to the left and into the dock. And, raising the pitch of the propeller at the wrong speed could dip the port wing into a wave and topple us. My eyes flitted back and forth between the instruments and the bay, reassuring myself that the oil pressure and temperature were all gauging properly, and that my Aunt Lydia would be proud to ride with me.

A voice through my scratchy headset said that my start was approaching and I acknowledged that Lily was sufficiently warmed and ready for flight. Slowly I pushed the throttle forward, and the deafening roar of the Rolls-Royce Griffon increased accordingly. The slow acceleration allowed me to control the plane's torque reaction, and besides, a careful start wouldn't make much difference in flight time over thousands of nautical miles.

Predictably, Lily began veering to the left as she moved forward. My gentle application of right rudder corrected the problem as the nose of the racer bobbed up and down through the light chop. After more than one hundred-twenty meters my speed was great enough that the pontoons began cutting through the shallow waves and the ride smoothed out. Every so often the pontoons hit a larger wave and the vibration from the impact traveled through the struts into the fuselage and concentrated in the Spitfire's original aluminum seat.

With the weight of the extra fuel and the drag of the pontoons cutting though the water, it took twice as long a run to achieve flight speed than it would have taken an original Spitfire rolling down a runway on properly inflated tires. Once at flight speed, Lily bounced along the waves until she finally broke free from the bay.

At 91.4 meters, I began pushing the stick to the right, causing the ailerons to initiate a shallow right turn. When it felt like Lily was falling off to starboard, a little nudge on the right rudder peddle raised her nose and she continued on the shallow turn while still gaining altitude. My strategy was to fly neither too high, nor too low—only high enough to allow a good speed, and a controlled descent if the engine cut out. However in the event of a devastating failure, there would not be sufficient time to restart the engine, or regain my composure, before I plunged to my death in the ocean. After what seemed like only a few moments, Lily reached 1,068 meters. Flying due east in about two minutes, I throttled back a bit to prevent wasting fuel. My tank held 313 imperial liters of fuel, good for 700 nautical kilometers, running at a cruising speed of 520 kilometers an hour. My advanced radar kept the previous racer in sight, but not for long as the Griffon engine used up the fuel load in just over an hour. When I reached my cruising altitude of 7,600 meters and double-checked that all was well, my compass setting, throttle, oil temperature, fuel, altitude and GPS location, my mind finally began to settle down.

I am now at 5,486 meters, having descended from 7,620 meters, which is where I feel most comfortable for now. Although looking off into the horizon, I see clouds forming that might bring with them conditions too rough for my little plane, forcing me to work a little harder than I wish. Better to be out of their path. Comfortable enough to relax a little, I am thinking now about my more distant past, and why my family was allowed to live. Neither Cossack nor Jew, we were both. And I think now, more than ever, it was because we could crawl inside a small machine and give it buoyancy and show other people how to do the same. As a teenager, in the early 1980s, my country was so poor that my family was more concerned that the family's flying days would end than they were about what kind of person I was. When I was given a scholarship to the Bauman Higher Technical School (MHTS), part of the Central Aerodynamics and Higher Dynamics Institute in Moscow, all doubts were put to rest. The flying legacy of my family would carry forward. It was good to be away from my family and my time at the technical school was meaningful. In my second year, I was taught to fly, and by the time I graduated I had a full Russian pilot's license. I had discovered my passion for flying, but the best thing about being away was discovering my sexual life.

My first flight instructor, Valery, instructed me in more than just flying. I knew that he preyed upon many of us young women, yet when he invited me to dinner, and later to his room, I let him do whatever he wanted. He wasn't dismayed that I was a virgin. He was tender and careful with me at the beginning. Our sexual relationship carried on for a year until he found another young woman, probably with more experience than I had. I learned a lot from him about flying in the sky, and sex. I connected with my body and experienced what sex was all about. I had forgotten much of this until now, but I have never forgotten is Natalya. Six months later, after my affair with Valery ended, as I was leaving my aerodynamics class, Natalya tapped me on the shoulder.

"We have been in classes together for the last year and we never have formally met." I was amazed that the smartest and most attractive woman in our class would want to talk with me.

I nervously responded, "I have noticed you in classes, and it would be nice to chat with you. But, talking about advanced aerodynamic design would be boring." We both laughed and our friendship began.

Natalya was a city girl, born and raised in Moscow. One nice thing about her was that she was totally unaware of how beautiful she was. She was outgoing and compassionate. We thought and talked about what compassion was, and it made me realize how lucky I was to have met Natalya in my early years. We spent a great deal of time together. After three weeks of sharing dinners and long talks, we were at her apartment having dinner one night when she shyly asked me, "Have you ever had sex with a woman?" I had begun to have feelings of more than friendship for her, "No, I have had a relationship with only one person and it was with a man."

We were both silent for quite a while, and I remember my heart pounding as she came around the table and kissed me. I can still taste the vodka on her tongue. I told her how excited her kisses made me, something I had not ever really experienced with Valery. We made love through the night. We fell in love and the rest of that year was totally remarkable because of her. We knew that we would have to part after graduation. With Russians, parting seems to be a way of life. Of course, this was my first love, and what seems to have been my only love, and it was terribly hard to part from her. For Natalya as well—she had a job waiting for her in Moscow, of course, government sponsored. We did what we had to do.

I returned to Ekaterinburg to fly and teach. My heart grew cold as my mind grew large. Matters of the head were easy to resolve. Matters of any meaningful relationship meant time and attention, attention that took away focus from the design of a wing or the fastest way to achieve lift, or even the optimal altitude for forgetting what it is that pains one's heart. Trapped in Ekaterinburg with limited options, I grew weary and depressed. This was my first feeling of a slow death, depression and thoughts of death, not a great combination. I also started to feel that I knew nothing of the world and other people. I slipped into darkness.

"*Red 11*, clear to approach refueling ship. Choppy waters, land with care." The experience of landing on water is one that most pilots never have. A water landing for most aircraft is death, and here again I look to death as a way to explain the life that awaits me. A floatplane is neither. Once the craft is in water, really, it is a boat, and one must be a captain of an entirely different kind. As an experienced pilot, this kind of landing takes great care, even though it looks to the spectator to be soft and easy. This particular landing is not soft and easy. As the waves wash across my windshield, I begin to think about how one must give up something in order to get something better. "This is all part of it." I say to myself.

I knew very little of good food, massage, acupuncture, Buddhist philosophy, and essentially other cultures besides that of America, before this adventure. My experience training in Tokyo was eye opening. I absorbed so much more than I had learned while I was in New Mexico or leading a sheltered life in Russia.

After landing successfully, the first thing I go for is a hot shower and acupuncture, followed by sumptuous Japanese cuisine that I grew so fond of in Tokyo. I am sure that some of the other pilots have chosen other kinds of food, probably a big mistake in my opinion.

As my heart rate slows with the first refueling experience behind me, I begin thinking about the convoluted tale of my parents' and grandparents' lives. It was my good fortune to leave the Soviet Union for a year to study at the University of New Mexico, and now to be invited to participate in this race. My mind keeps returning to the letter from my father, sent when he lived in Moscow and before they moved to Ekaterinburg. I had almost memorized it after reading it for what seemed like hundreds of times.

My Dear Ludmilla,

You are old enough to understand what I am about to tell you, and I hope you will also understand why I have withheld these family secrets for such a long time. It has not been easy.

Your grandparents Vladimir Litvyck and Anna Vasil'yevna Kunavin came from a farm eight kilometers north of Moscow where they worked as tenant farmers on land belonging to a wealthy kulak. They decided to seek a better life and walked to Moscow, where they found work in a factory. Most of the men had been drafted or joined the tsar's armed forces, which created a great demand for wage laborers. Your grandfather quickly discovered that conditions in the factories were just as debilitating as being a tenant farmer. And, subsequently, both Vladimir and Anna became socialists, members of the Russian Social Democratic Party.

They married in 1918 just as the civil war was beginning and survived the famine caused by that conflict. In 1922, they had a daughter named Lydia, but most people called her Lilia. She was an adventuresome girl known for her

independent spirit, wild clothes, and wicked sense of humor. I was born a
year later.

Now you know the secret... we are Litvycks... Jewish people from Latvia.
But our last name is also a derogatory term for an Ashkenazi Jew from Eastern
Europe. So, my father's family was originally from the large region that stretches
from Latvia to the north through what is now eastern Poland and encompasses
part of western Ukraine. My family was ethnically Jewish, but both my parents
abandoned the synagogue when they became Marxists and joined Lenin's Bolshevik
wing of the social democrats. And while I was aware of our Jewish roots, your
mother and I brought you up as a good, sensitive atheist.

My father was a bright, loyal member of the Communist Party and held
important positions within the local organization. He worked for the transportation
department in Moscow as a railroad worker during the 1920s and became a
deputy commissar in the early 1930s. He was then posted to Eastern Russia when
I was quite young. Lily and I grew up in a single-family apartment that our
parents, through their political and occupational connections, were allowed to use.

All went well until 1936 when Stalin accused some central leaders of the
Communist Party of treason. These leaders had played critical roles in the Bolshevik
revolution of 1917. Suddenly they were on the outs, suspected of supporting Leon
Trotsky. Trotsky had led the government's military defense against the counterrevo-
lution, but now, he was suddenly considered a counterrevolutionary? These were
clearly trumped-up, political charges. I remember father sitting at the dinner
table and exclaiming how shocking he found Stalin's accusations. He wondered
how the central leadership of the revolution could have turned against what they
created. In the end the accused were found guilty along with dozens of others
and executed.

Things got even worse the next year when the Great Purge expanded and
cleansed the party of anyone who asked questions or challenged authority. The
accusations of treason spread like wildfire and produced incredible distrust and
paranoia among the Russian people. Children misunderstood comments their
parents made at home and then reported them to the authorities. They disappeared
just as targeted Jews did in fascist Germany and Italy. Whole offices were closed
for political reasons. We were very frightened, but we had nowhere to go. My
father was one of those accused as the witch hunt exploded. He was in the east
when the Purge hit the transportation department and the management of the
railroads. He was not lucky enough to have been sent to Siberia for retraining
and punishment. Stalin's men simply executed him. And that was that.

He had done nothing wrong. He had been a loyal Bolshevik, but I suspect that
he stood up for his Marxist beliefs and his right to express them at work. After all,

that is what the revolution was about. The party had been based on Lenin's insistence on the importance of internal democracy and debate. But he was NOT a counter-revolutionary. If that made him a Trotskyist, so be it.

I always suspected that our name Litvyck was partially to blame, maybe mostly to blame. A wave of anti-Semitism spread through the Soviet Union as part of the Great Purge of the late 1930s. It was like a repeat of the pogroms under the tsar during the 1880s, or like the waves of mounted Cossacks that Stalin sent to slaughter Jewish peasants on tenant farms during the nationalization of agriculture at the end of the 1920s.

When people learned what happened to my Papa, they looked at the rest of us, not as victims, but as if we were traitors. It was a terrible time to have had a Jewish last name. Mama began re-using her maiden name, Kunavin, for political protection, and I did the same even though I was only a teenager. Lydia kept the name Litvyck because she was well known in the communist youth group, the Young Pioneers. She had been learning to fly airplanes as part of the Osoaviakhim flying club.

After the German fascists invaded the motherland, your aunt Lydia tried to join the air force as a pilot. At first she was rejected, but after recording a few hundred extra hours of flight time in her logbook, she was accepted as a pilot in 1941, at only nineteen years of age. She immediately started training in a Yakovlev Yak I, a lightweight fighter built with wooden wings covered with fabric. Even though the Soviet officers were skeptical of female pilots, they were so desperate for anyone with flying skills that they took her in spite of their un-Marxist prejudice against women with skills normally associated with men.

You must be wondering why your aunt would join the Soviet air force as a fighter pilot after your grandfather had been falsely accused of treason and executed. First, we hated the German Nazis and were petrified at the thought that Hitler might win and gain control of the Soviet Union. But secondly, this was Lydia's way of proving Stalin wrong, that the Litvycks are not traitors, but patriots of the highest order.

And Lydia did just that. In a two-year period she flew sixty-six combat missions, was shot down twice, wounded once, was solely responsible for eleven kills, and jointly responsible for three others. She was the most decorated female pilot in World War II and was awarded the Order of Lenin, the Order of the Red Banner, the Order of the Red Star and the Order of the Patriotic War. This is something to be proud of! And, what was so amazing about Lydia's combat skills is that she was able to fly planes constructed with antiquated materials and destroy the most sophisticated all-metal Nazi aircraft.

However, on August 1, 1943, a few days before her twenty-second birthday, Lydia did not return from her fourth sortie of the day. She had already shot down two Messerschmitt 109s that day before she was killed over Ukraine.

Curiously, Stalin did not bestow upon Lydia the most important honor, Hero of the Soviet Union. This award was not granted to any soldier who went "missing in action," because there was the implication that without a body, the person could have been a deserter rather than a hero. This was an injustice in the light of Lilia's flying record and of her ultimate sacrifice—and another insult against the patriotism of the Litvyck family. Long after World War II, one of Lydia's squadron mates found your aunt's grave and the remains of her Yak 1 fighter. Locals took the searchers to many known crash sites before they discovered her crashed Yak and remains in a nearby grave.

When I read about the discovery, it was clear that you should know the truth about the family. I am embarrassed that I was so fearful after my father's execution that I hid, and I hid my wonderful sister and her exploits from you for all these years, and that I also hid my father's belief in justice and equality for all workers, a conviction that led to his execution.

You remind me so much of my sister, Lydia. Will you accept my apology for not revealing her to you sooner? I am so sorry.
All my love,
Your Papa

Spitfire Lily is still at 6,096 meters and cruising exactly at 515 kilometers an hour. I recheck all of my instruments and continue on with the race. But my mind wanders again to my experiences in New Mexico, and how I became a better pilot there and was fortunate enough to be invited to participate in this challenging event.

It was during my stint in Ekaterinburg that I saw a notice advertising grants for Russians, who spoke English, to study in the United States. I applied to the foundation for the exchange grant, but was stumped when the application requested a desired city and region. My suspicion was that most applicants would choose major cities that were the peers of Moscow such as Chicago or New York City, but the competition for these slots would be intense. One of the English language magazines circulated in my classroom was *National Geographic* with its clear writing and beautiful reproductions of photographs from around the world. I remembered an article about New Mexico and decided to choose the Southwest. I structured my essay around the multiple ethnicities of the people who lived in that region, and pointed out their similarity to the diverse ethnic peoples and nationalities that were combined within the Soviet Union. To my great surprise, I was selected to study at the University of New Mexico in Albuquerque.

I was becoming accustomed to the dry climate and hot burritos when Papa's letter arrived. Two weeks later, the campus newspaper, *The Daily Lobo,* published an illustrated story about a photography exhibition at the University Art Museum. One image reproduced in the review was a self-portrait by Anne Noggle. She depicted herself as a pilot, her head pulled back as she began to pull up into a loop. The text commented that Noggle was not just a pilot, but had been an American military pilot during World War II, who had ferried bombers from the United States to Europe. I felt that his woman was a sister to my previously unknown aunt. Noggle was teaching a studio course in photography, and I ventured over to the art department to see if she was in her office.

Professor Noggle was holding office hours when I arrived, so I knocked on the open door. She looked up, and although she did not recognize me as one of her students, she simply said, "Come in, please." After explaining that I was an exchange student studying in the English department, it was clear that she was confused by my visit. That was until adding that I was related to Lydia Litvyck. Her eyes opened fully and she exclaimed, "Really?"

"Yes, really!"

My explanation included bits and pieces of the story from Papa's letter. Noggle had known of my aunt, and told me about her experiences delivering bombers to Europe. Sitting in that small office in the new art department building, it was impossible to imagine this photography professor piloting a massive, four-engine B-24 bomber over the Atlantic. As we parted, Noggle invited me back, "so we can talk again."

Noggle called and asked me out for lunch and I readily accepted. While we were eating, she reacted visibly when I called her "Professor Noggle" in my most formal Russian way. Clearly she was very informal and lightly scolded me saying simply, "Please, just call me 'Anne,' not 'professor.'"

As our friendship developed over several weeks, she invited me to meet other friends outside of the university community. Soon she was clearly treating me like a daughter, providing me with an insider's view of American culture. One day Anne called and asked if I would like to accompany her and a photographer friend, Judith Golden, to the National Atomic Museum at Kirtland Air Force Base on the east edge of Albuquerque.

The next day was hilarious. As we drove up to security I worried about whether they would allow me on the government Air Force base. As I showed my Russian passport, I kept thinking about how in Russia they would probably strip search an American woman trying to enter a military complex. No strip search happened, maybe because of Anne, her reputation, and credentials. So our trio of women walked through the museum and the grounds filled with aging examples of fighters, bombers, and missiles. We must have been quite a sight. I was wearing a formal, out-of-fashion dress from Russia while Anne was in blue jeans and a shirt, and Judith wore a party dress with pointy, turquoise cowboy boots. All of a sudden Anne said, "Wait," and pulled out her camera. She posed Judith in front of a red Bomarc missile, bent down, and photographed her friend. After a couple of hours of hanging out with the two artists, Anne dropped me off at my dorm. Ten days later she called and said, "Stop by my office," saying that she had something for me. The present turned out to be *Vertical Stance*, a surprising color photograph of Judith, but posed to make a joking comparison between military weapons and male anatomy.

Later in the spring when the March winds were howling through town, Anne asked if I wanted to fly before returning to the Soviet Union. It was her way of connecting me to my Aunt Lydia. It was an incredibly generous and psychologically powerful gift. Over the next weeks, I soloed in a Cessna 172. Anne paid for the flights. I developed my flying skills further, while my love for flying deepened. Private aviation simply did not exist in the Soviet Union, and virtually all pilots were connected to the Air Force in one way or another. It just wasn't possible to go to an airport and rent a Zlin for a couple hours of sport flying.

Suddenly, awake from my reverie, I realize that time has elapsed and I have almost missed my Oʻahu refueling stop, which could have been fatal. I check my fuel level, oil pressure, and GPS while pushing the stick forward and pointing the nose down. Pearl Harbor is barely visible six or seven miles ahead. At 1,067 meters I slow Lily down and check in with the station to learn of the local conditions. The wind is blowing from the west at sixteen knots, which is high for landing a seaplane even in the protected bay. The plan is to fly past the sea landing area in the harbor at 305 meters, make another slow right turn while continuing to descend, and then line up with my nose aimed directly into the wind. Lily has descended to 152 meters after the slow turn, and now down to less than 322 kilometers an hour. I keep easing back on the throttle and pull back on the stick raising the nose, which also increases my descent.

Leaning to the left I see the water and am alarmed that the chop in the middle of the harbor is much rougher than it was in Tokyo Bay. Fear sets in and I quickly radio, "Lily of Russia, going around one more time." Immediately I push the throttle forward and the plane's nose lifts as its speed increases. After going around that second time, I line up the Spitfire for landing. Pulling back on the stick, I raise the nose so that the rear of the pontoons will hit the top of the waves first. Lily slows to 201 kilometers an hour and drops me toward the sea. I can see the water rising toward me thirty meters, then twenty-three, and then fifteen meters above the ocean. Fortunately, the waves turn out not to be so bad and I have safely made it to the halfway point of my adventure.

As a child in Russia, I was given a doll that was supposed to be a Hawaiian woman. I remember she was longhaired and thick-waisted and wore a skirt that I was told was made of grass with a coconut shell top. Until now, that was my only experience of Hawaiʻi. Perhaps the women here do look like that doll, but I saw no one other than the ground crew. I was told that spectators had gathered on the shoreline to admire the aircraft, but I hadn't seen them. After that arduous landing, I could do nothing but close my eyes for the entire hour between landing and take-off. I even missed acupuncture from Kaz's daughter, Sachi.

The weather has turned and the storm I am fighting has made me adjust my altitude again. I worry about my oxygen intake, wondering if my judgment is somehow impaired as I have gone up and down 3,048 meters in the last hour. My focus is on the instruments in front of me. The energy that I need to keep up my spirits is gone, replaced by random, melancholy thoughts of my past and the country that I will never return to. My papa's letter meant a lot to me. Understanding my family and my history means that I can carry them with me, and my memories and stories can survive, apart from Russia.

During training, I became very close to two of the other pilots, Hamidah and Ayame, for very different reasons. Hamidah, the Tibetan pilot with her frank understanding of my depression, offered possible ways to deal with depression in a spiritual manner. And Ayame Kobahashi seemed to bond with all of us, yet our personal bond was more than respect and friendship. She told me about the portal at the 33rd Parallel and 7,149 meters above sea level.

A tailwind is pushing me toward the last refueling stop more quickly than I had anticipated. I concentrate on dropping at an appropriate airspeed so my air pressure does not become an issue and my thoughts don't become hallucinations. I think that might have happened earlier in the flight. I am not prone to dreams or belief in magic, so I will never tell anyone about my hallucination.

Time had seemed to stop at that moment and the sound of my floatplane motor and the wind and the radio had all become quiet. Everything got brighter, and suddenly I was seated with my Aunt Lydia in a twin-seater Russian Yak.

I remained silent as Aunt Lydia welcomed me to the 33rd degree latitude. She pointed out that this is the latitude of Baghdad (Babylon), the cradle of Western civilization and also of Xi'an, the cradle of Chinese or Eastern civilization. The 33rd Parallel also marks Trinity Site, where the first atom bomb was detonated in New Mexico, U.S.A., as well as Nagasaki, the city devastated by the second atom bomb that the U.S. dropped on Japan in 1945. Odd places like the Bermuda Triangle and the Lost City of Atlantis also exist on the 33rd Parallel. Looking out of the Yak window I could see all of these sites. I get the chills just thinking about it now. It must have been my fatigue that led to this hallucination.

As we flew further into the portal, Aunt Lydia explained that all these sites were related and that speaking with Hamidah would help me understand the inter-relatedness of all things. Aunt Lydia also encouraged me to speak with the Japanese pilot Ayame, daughter of Keiko. Ayame knew of the 33rd Parallel, having been introduced to it by her college friend, Barbara Grothus. Grothus had been to many of the sites along the Parallel and developed a theory about what the sites signified. Ayame, in turn, had had the funds to support the trips Grothus made around the world.

Grothus gathered and developed "pollen" to represent things like gunpowder, the Buddha, atomic weapons, empire, and other aspects of the sites. What I mean by "pollen" is that, with the idea that landscape has memory, she gathered rocks and soil from the various 33rd Parallel landscapes and ground them into a pollen-like dust. She mixed this pollen to symbolize the cross-pollination of cultures, and the important role that women play in this mixture. It was the "women" part that had interested Aunt Lydia, and now she was passing that interest on to me.

I woke up from my hallucination and no time had passed according to my floatplane's time gauge. But eight hours had passed on my wristwatch. I reset my wristwatch and will follow up on this with Ayame at the end of this race. In the meantime, I don't want to mention this to anyone—it all may be an illusion anyway. And this Russian deals with facts and reality not with illusions. Or so it was before this adventure.

The last refueling ship is within sight.

"*Red 11*, you are clear for landing." I must not have lost any time and I must have hallucinated because *Turquoise 10* is just taking off. I'm glad because I don't want to deal with the Iranian pilot.

"*Red 11*, White Lily coming in."

Even with the uneven weather, my landing and docking is perfect. The crew even compliments me. This time I won't miss the good meal and acupuncture. It dawns on me that for some time now I have been treated with a respect and compassion that I had never found in Russia. As I receive acupuncture to bring my energy levels up, Dr. Kaz reveals to me, "Madam Keiko has asked me to let you know that the weather may be a bit rough after refueling, but soon it will be clear flying into San Francisco. As you descend into San Francisco, you will have the opportunity to fly into what we call Cloud Nine. There is no wind disturbance in this cloud, only a feeling of happiness."

I can't believe what I am hearing. Better yet, I am now in total acceptance of what this, depressed pragmatic Russian woman might have dismissed as nonsense back in Tokyo, and most certainly would have done so in my daily life—Cloud Nine?

I totally accept what Kaz has just told me. This must be the catharsis that I was destined for.

My departure from the refueling ship for San Francisco is full of smiles and happiness. My flight plan calls for a slightly higher altitude in this leg of the journey. My concern was the rate of fuel consumption, but again, the tailwind is with me and unless the wind shifts, I am not worried. With clear air and the wind pushing me along, it is like floating on the sea. There is an occasional rise and fall, but the thrust is always forward. When the wind is against you in a small plane, it is like riding a horse that doesn't want to accept the saddle or the weight of a person on its back. Not entirely unpleasant, but challenging to the nerves and a reminder that in most of life, one's instincts are superior to most forms of knowledge.

I awaken from a brief nap and take back the controls from autopilot. I dreamt of vodka! It is true. Russians have it in their veins, as sure as blood and without regard to religion or class standing. The most pleasant thought when I awoke is that my next stop will be San Francisco. I am clear now, as I thought I was before, but these hours alone have given me the chance to think about the person who I once was. Never did I think about how difficult it was to be who I was and what I wanted in my country. Maybe it was harder for my aunt and for my mama to do what they wanted to do, but that was not my legacy. Everything is relative though, and hallucination or not, the idea that we are all tied together or cross-pollinated, delights me.

The legacy that *was* left to me was the love of flying. I have never learned any other kind of love. I fly now for the love of flying. I fly toward Cloud Nine already without melancholy. I look forward to talking with Ayame and Hamidah. I look forward to the future and still cherish the moment. I have hope and I am eager for more happiness. The love of flying is what brought me here, and it will be here with me when I land. This is where it all begins. The end is the beginning.

CLAUDIA SCHUMANN

GREEN 12

I can't believe I am actually flying this plane, just free as a bird. A middle-aged and overweight bird, mind you, but still, free at last.

My grandfather would have a fit if he saw me now. His own granddaughter in the mother ship of the enemy, a *Spitfire!* After all, the Spitfires were the ones that fought the German ME-109s in the Battle of Britain. Maybe he wouldn't have a fit, maybe he would find it amusing. I never met him, so I have no idea if he had a sense of humor or not. All I ever knew of him was the picture my grandma had placed on the grand piano in her living room. It showed a young man with short hair that seemed to be glued to his head, wearing a white shirt with a stiff collar, his face frozen in time with that weird, solemn expression they considered fitting for photos back in those days. No selfies, pulled out tongues or duck faces back then, I guess. Photos were a serious matter, and chances were folks didn't get that many taken in their lifetime.

Another photo of my grandfather existed, but it was kept in a drawer for obvious reasons. In it, he was wearing his Luftwaffe uniform, and that wasn't something we could joyfully display on a piano in East Germany in the 1970s. He looked even stiffer and more uncomfortable in this one than in the photo taken before the war, more vulnerable too. Maybe the fact that Germany was losing the war and Hitler was a complete dick had already dawned on him. Maybe my granddad had even sensed that his life was to end very soon. Who knows? Grandma wouldn't really talk about him or the war. She concentrated more on the post-war period in Germany when women collectively turned into hunters and gatherers, waiting for husbands who would never return, selling and swapping stuff at the black market and cursing the times they were born in. "We would even eat raw sorrel," Grandma informed me occasionally when memories overwhelmed her. "Or nibble on horseradish roots that we had dug out of the ground."

I shivered at the pure thought of eating such ghastly food, but even worse was the idea of wearing knitted underpants, something Grandma also liked to elaborate on. "They were itchy. So itchy, you have no idea. And sometimes you would have to share them with your siblings. Things were only washed every two weeks back then, not like today, when people wear a shirt for a day and then throw it in the wash."

"You must have all been quite smelly," I said.

"No, we weren't," she'd snap. "Women took much more care with their appearance back then. Not like today, where they have all their private parts hanging out and their hair in a spiky mess." She pretended to be disgusted, and then she'd form her hair into a spiky mess and giggle. That was why I loved her so much.

As I glide through a sky that is the color of my husband's graying hair (what's left of it, anyway), I think of the grandfather who never knew his own granddaughter, much less that she has followed in his footsteps. Flying that is, not fighting a lost cause for a mad killer with a stamp-sized mustache, whose voice could drill scars into eardrums.

Would my granddad be proud of me? I hope so. I even managed to land the plane safely on water at the first Mitsubishi refueling ship. I can't believe I actually managed a water landing on the open ocean. Being so out of practice, I thought I would be the laughing stock of the race, attempting again and again to land the bloody thing on water, all to the amusement of the giggling Mitsubishi workers watching me. But far from it, I landed it just as brilliantly as the Russian pilot, Ludmilla, who started the race ahead of me. I guess all that excessive training helped after all. Or was it maybe the acupuncture we all had to have? I did not like that at first, and I couldn't for the world of me understand why everyone else seemed to be so keen on being turned into a human hedgehog by Dr. Kaz. Acupuncture, I thought, come on! What's next? Tarot readings, Aura Therapy, Ouija Boards? In fact, I thought *Mumbo Jumbo*. But I have to admit I did feel good afterwards, the way you feel after a long nap or after a refreshing walk on a spring day or when you have fallen in love, although these days the latter is just a distant memory.

Three more hours to the next refueling stop. Oʻahu lies behind me now, I wish I could have stayed there. I could have wandered off the plane, rented a car, and driven myself to the next beach, where I could be lying right now, palm tree swaying above, and straw-spiked coconut drink in my hand, instead of fretting about the race, my ability to finish it, and my next water landing. I shouldn't fret. I am perfectly capable of it. I really should quit my annoying habit of worrying about things that haven't happened yet. What was it grandma used to say? "Future problems can worry the future, Claudia, not the present."

I lean back and start relaxing. The wind is good, the clouds have now morphed into a layer of creamy white frosting, and the navigation system on board tells me everything is going smoothly. It is amazing how well they refurbished these old planes at the Mitsubishi plant in Tokyo and that I am sitting in one of them, and that I am actually flying again since flying is something I had buried in my past and vowed that

I would never again revisit. The most amazing thing, however, is the fact that I can keep this gem of a plane, should I ever make it back down to earth. I had to really control myself not to shriek like a teenager when Keiko announced that. In fact, at first I wasn't really sure I understood her. I thought something had gotten lost in translation and she meant a little model of the plane—something crappy and plastic and made in China to take home as a souvenir and to show your grandkids, if you ever had any. Thinking of that sort of thing, but to keep the real, actual plane? Who has that kind of money? Who has that kind of money to *give away?* It is like telling Tom Hanks, "Hey, keep the Apollo 13 as a token of our affection for bringing it down safely!" Actually, better not think about Apollo 13 right now, that makes me nervous. But it just goes to show, never say never.

It *is* kind of surprising they picked me to fly in this race though. I mean I have never been picked for or won anything, not in school and not at college. I didn't even win any of the stupid medals in the annual school Olympics way back in East Germany, where absolutely *everyone* won something however poorly they performed. They practically forced you to take home one of their rubbery medals dangling on a red ribbon, imprinted with the inbred-looking face of a joyful East German Youth.

I slipped through the net though, remaining medal-less throughout my life, much to the relief of my grandma, who hated the East German regime as much as I did. She was the only one who really understood how *much* I hated it because grandma was a free spirit, too, unlike my mother, who didn't care about politics as long as they would let her pursue her favorite pastime, being an excellent German housewife. She mopped, scrubbed, dusted, made her own sauerkraut in a large barrel, cleaned the windows every week, arranged curtains with military precision, and generally safeguarded her surroundings to prevent them from being dirtied in any way by visitors or by her own daughter. I'd like to say it was just a desperate attempt to find a new man in her life, to lure a member of the male species into her spotless gingerbread house, and then to lock him into a cage of sauerkraut, pork sausages, and dainty curtains, but, unfortunately, I think part of the cleaning frenzy was for her own pleasure. With all that excessive cleaning, she had no time to care about the government. Anyone could see that.

I, however, hated the pointless political discussions in school that weren't really discussions because the teachers were always right. I hated the propaganda and the absurd old men from the government celebrating themselves and their comb-overs. I hated the fact that we couldn't travel anywhere, that we couldn't buy the nice things my cousin Evi could buy simply because she lived on the other side of the Berlin Wall. But life is not fair, and so we just got on with what we are given, I suppose.

And what life gave me were the hand-me-downs from Evi, real Levi's jeans that effortlessly catapulted me to the front lines of East Germany's fashion avant-garde.

In hindsight, I should have thanked Evi for never getting fatter or skinnier than I and for making my teenage years bearable with clothes that smelled so damn good of non-Communist washing powder, clothes that had been to Rome, London, and Paris and therefore made me, the lucky wearer, almost feel as if I had been there too.

Needless to say, I never made it to Rome or London before the Wall came down. I did, however, make it to Prague and Budapest, and in the eventful summer of 1982, my mother informed me that I would even make it to summer camp in Russia. She had finally met a new man, and I guess she wanted me out of the way a bit over the summer.

"I am not going to labor camp in Russia. No way. You have got to be kidding."

"Summer camp," my mother corrected gently. "You'll have lots of fun and sports and new friends."

"I am nearly eighteen. You can't make me. I want to spend the summer hitchhiking and camping with my friends. You know that. I am not going to Siberia."

My mother pulled out her ace card. "But it isn't Siberia, silly. It is Batumi, a beautiful town on the shores of the Black Sea. Sun, sandy beaches, salt water, a tropical place. This is the chance of a lifetime."

With that casual remark, she hit my weakest spot. The word *tropical* made any young East German practically collapse into a heap of ecstasy. *Tropical* meant not Communist, not grey, not falling to pieces, and not run by power hungry ogres.

This, of course, wasn't true as I realized the minute I arrived in the town of Batumi. It was run down, much more run down than East Germany, and they worshipped Stalin, the most power hungry ogre of all over there. He apparently grew up in the nearby town of Gory, and the locals had his picture displayed in all of the empty food shops.

The summer camp was disappointing, too. There were my fellow East Germans, complete and utter nerds, because who else in their right mind would go on such a trip? There were even more pointless political discussions, this time with "our Russian brothers in arms," a bunch of sorry-looking youngsters with ill-fitting clothes, made even more complicated by the fact that every boring statement was clumsily trans-lated by an interpreter with a heavy drinking problem.

Then there was Igor.

I noticed him only after three insanely dull days and only because he was flying dangerously low above our heads in an Antonov An-2, one of those Russian agricul-tural aircrafts, real chunky workhorses. He wasn't spraying anything, but he was about to take our heads off.

"Who is that moron?" I asked our counselor.

"I think it is Igor," she said, glancing nervously up to the sky.

Igor. Did he only have a single name, like a planet or something? Was I supposed to know him? "Who is he? He is going to crash any minute, you know."

"He is the son of the camp director. I think he is practicing his flying. He wants to become a pilot."

"He is *practicing?* How old is he?"

"Your age, I think," she said quietly trying not to let her nervousness show.

"Is that allowed?" I was stunned. They had a teenager *practicing* his flying right above our heads, for God's sake!

"Well," she shrugged her shoulders. "I know technically we are in the Soviet Union right now, but this is Georgia. They kind of do what they want, I suppose."

Envy raged through my veins like poison. This Igor brat was allowed to fly! He was actually, physically sitting in a plane that could take him out of this miserable place, off to nearby Turkey, to the West, to freedom, and what did this rambling idiot do? He just kept circling around like a retired eagle, one lame round after another. I hated him instantly, and when Igor approached me that night at the "cultural event with our brothers in arms" (drinking, an army choir thundering on about Mother Russia, and more drinking), I ignored him.

"I like your jeans," he repeated a bit louder, probably assuming I was deaf or something. "Very nice jeans. You sell me?"

"Piss off," I replied, which he didn't understand. Apparently what he heard was, "Yes, I would absolutely love to sell you my only priceless possession, my very own Levi's jeans."

"You sell me? What you want? I give what you want. You sell me?"

"There is nothing that I could possibly want from you," I hissed, eyeing up his hideous outfit. Trousers made from some weird shiny fabric, a gray T-Shirt with a Cyrillic slogan on it, and brown work boots even my dad would have refused to wear. A key dangled on a leather string around his neck. A key... Then a thought hit me. I suddenly knew what he could give me, which is, of course, why Igor ended up being my "first time."

Not *that* first time, that had already happened in the most unromantic manner with a guy whose name I could barely remember. All I recall is that he had asthma and that I thought the entire time he would die on top of me because his breathing was getting heavier and heavier. He didn't, but he got a nosebleed when he finished, which was also vaguely disturbing. No, Igor was the one who helped me fly a plane for the first time in my life.

Because Igor really, really desperately wanted those Levi's, and I really, really desperately wanted to know how to fly, we made a deal. I will never forget that first flight with Igor. He smelled suspiciously of some alcoholic beverage, but he acted completely in control. God knows how we actually communicated with each other, him with his pigeon German and me with my rudimentary Russian, for all I had learned in school were useless phrases like "Long live the leader of the communist party!" or "Excuse me sir, where is the museum of the Great Russian Revolution?" None of it any help when you are 3,000 feet up in the air next to a semi-drunk Russian, but somehow we managed, and on the very last day of what had surprisingly turned out to be the best summer camp of my life, he let me fly his plane, causing an adrenaline rush like I had never experienced before. I was hooked on flying like a crack whore. I had to get my next fix, but that was impossible in East Germany. I would have had to join the army or the Secret Service and spy on my friends as a price. But sometimes miracles do happen, and in my case, it was the miracle of the Berlin Wall that came down in 1989. Suddenly we were all so free, but the freedom was overwhelming. Some people couldn't cope with it. They lost their jobs, their money, and their dignity while others became savvy investors almost overnight. My mother found excellent new cleaning products and was delighted. Surprisingly, she also found the love of her life in the guy she spent that summer with when I was sent to Batumi.

Me, I just wanted to fly planes, so with the help of pretty much all of my grandma's savings, I joined a private aviation college, got my pilot's license a few years later, and started to live the best years of my life. My grandma was so proud of me. She had been such a strong woman all her life, down to earth with a great sense of humor. She always wore this strange necklace—a simple silver chain with a pendant she had made out of the first Deutschmark she had ever earned herself.

"It is important to have your own money," she explained to me, "and not depend on anyone else, especially not a man. Nothing good ever comes out of being dependent. Remember that."

"Of course," I replied, shaking my head at the absurd suggestion that I could ever be so foolish. I *had* my own money. I earned a good salary, and I had a dream job.

I choke, suddenly overcome with the memory of her smile, the faint smell of her soap, and the way we sat in her kitchen and made dumplings and giggled about the women outside in the street, an army of apron-clad gossipers going about their daily business of backbiting the absentees. I stroked her necklace, which is now mine, although I don't deserve it because I had made a mess of my life. I had disregarded her advice and become dependent on a man faster than you could crash a plane.

I somehow thought Grandma would live forever. I somehow thought this fabulous life would also go on forever, especially after I met David—gorgeous, funny David with his messy hair, leather jacket, electrifying smile, and jokes. He had a way with women that made them melt every time he entered a room. I had never laughed so much with a man or felt so carefree, so wanted, or so beautiful in my life. I flew all over the world and would come home to have him nearly tear off my uniform. In the early hours of dawn, I often touched his warm skin when he was fast asleep. For two years, I was as madly in love as a person could be, and I thought everything was perfect, at least until the day when he said that awful thing to me.

"Jesus, Claudia, I don't want to have a kid! I thought you were on the pill? How could this happen?"

"I forgot. I thought… I thought you would be happy, I mean…"

"Well, I am not. I don't want that kind of responsibility. I want to travel and live abroad and see things. In fact, I have just been offered a job at a hospital in Bern."

"When you say you don't want that kind of responsibility, do you mean now or…" My voice was a hoarse croak.

"I mean never." He actually had tears in his eyes, just like me, although obviously for a different reason. Then he left, but not before ripping my heart out, tearing it into pieces, and then trampling on those pieces, leaving me dumbstruck and in shock. Alone and distraught, I would have no one to turn to for help and comfort. As it turned out, Grandma died the same day I miscarried.

The GPS shows me the next refueling stop is ahead, although I can't see much because the clouds have thickened. I feel a rush of excitement as I descend. God, I have missed flying so much. Most of all, I missed the silence of it, which isn't really silence, just the absence of any human-produced noise. No kids quarreling, no cars honking, no music, and no TV, just the wind rattling, the humming of the engine, and my own breathing. I suppose the sky is the only place where a person can be completely alone these days. You can't even be alone in the bathroom, for someone is guaranteed to knock on the door sooner or later and shout, "Are you done? I need to go!" You can't be alone in your house because the world intrudes via phone calls, e-mails, doorbells, barking dogs, and voices shouted in the neighborhood. You can't even be alone in the forest, for some idiot in neon colored hiking gear is bound to be trekking through the woods the minute you start to admire the peaceful scenery.

I can see the docking area now and land smoothly on the water again. There. My confidence roars, and I wink at one of the workers at the station as I get out of the plane. He winks back, and for a moment I feel I am not just a menopausal woman with a disappearing waistline and unwanted advice from doctors for "women of my age," who also seems to inhabit a cloak of invisibility these days as far as men are concerned. No, for a moment, I am Claudia, goddess of the skies and water-landing superwoman with a swing in her step, who just nailed the damn plane perfectly on the water and is, therefore, entitled to a wink or two from the cute young worker.

On the ramp to the ship, I ran into Ludmilla. "What are you up to, comrade?" I ask and give her a mock salute. We grin at each other and hug like long-lost relatives. Coming from the same kind of background means we understand each other without words. I almost contemplated asking her during training if she knew Igor, although chances were pretty much zero with the collapse of the Soviet Union and everything. He could be an alcoholic now, dragging his belongings in bags with him through the streets of Batumi. Or maybe he sobered up and joined the Russian army or the police, and has the face of Putin tattooed on his chest. Maybe he moved away and now lives in Afghanistan. Maybe he is long dead.

"Got to go, got a race to win," Ludmilla replies.

"You mean the one I am winning?" I tap on my watch. My flight time so far has been much better than I expected.

"Touché!" she snorts with laughter and walks on. I like her. At first I didn't. I thought she was way too perfect, way too goody two-shoes for me, but it turned out she isn't. She has a dark sense of humor and the honesty of a child about her. There is no falseness in her. I know that—I can almost smell it. In fact, it was she who helped me practice landing on water. None of my male pilot colleagues back in Germany would have done that. They all just waited for me to fail, lingering in my shadow like bloodhounds, ready to tear me apart at the slightest mistake. I shake off those memories. I shower on the ship and eat without counting calories and without resigning myself instinctively to the healthiest and, therefore, the most boring dish on the menu. I eat what I want—starch, fat, meat, you name it. I am a grown up woman, and I need fuel, because, just like I told Ludmilla, I have a race to win.

Back in the plane an hour later, I start the engine, and I am on my way again. Four or more hours to the Golden Gate Bridge in San Francisco, and then I am done. "Let's see what you can do, my little plane," I murmur. There are some dark clouds ahead, ganging up on me like angry bullies, but I decide not to worry. I have dealt with the likes of them before, twenty-two years ago when I was at the peak of my career. *But you are not the same woman you were back then*, a mean little voice whispers in my head. *You are much weaker now, just a shell of your former self.*

The voice is right, of course. Because the baby, the one David didn't want me to have, and nature didn't want me to have either, the baby that was never meant to live, changed everything inside me. I couldn't think of anything else. I cried for days, for weeks. I cried so much I threw up. I had dreams of Grandma, David, and my baby, whose face I could never quite make out, and every time I woke up, none of them were there anymore. Flying and my career as a pilot should have saved me, but it didn't. It became irrelevant. The only thing that mattered was the baby.

That is why I married Thomas, one of my colleagues, only six months later. His long-time girlfriend also had dumped him, quite suddenly. He was just glad someone else took over, and he didn't have to do his own laundry and cooking. I liked Thomas simply because he was available and because he liked me enough to put up with my endless crying and the ever-increasing stack of baby clothes I hoarded in my wardrobe. Thomas was a cheap carbon copy of David, a B-version. He wasn't the love of my life, but he had broad shoulders and a deep, comforting voice. He would do, I told myself. It was a marriage of convenience that would have made Jane Austen turn over in her grave. The thing is, Thomas was happy to have a child with me, and he even expressed some joy when it turned out we wouldn't just have one baby but two.

When the twins were born, nothing in the world prepared me for the tornado of shock, fear, love, and panic that motherhood brought with it. I loved Maja and Rosi more than anything in the world, but they drove me insane with their crying, their neediness, and the way one screamed the minute the other had finally gone to sleep. I felt completely overwhelmed by looking after two colicky babies and running a household, yet I couldn't bring myself to let anyone else look after them, least of all Thomas. He was so clumsy and he didn't seem to have a clue what to do with them. He watched sports and didn't even look away from the TV when he put a bottle into their mouths. And, there was the undeniable boredom of being alone with little children all day long, but other women didn't seem to mind.

"I am just glad I don't have to go back to that god awful office," one of my new mommy friends confided in me. "I hated that job. You are lucky you got two kids in one go, you know. I am going to have another one as soon as I can and stay home forever. He can earn the money, and I'll make the nest."

Shaking my head, I told Thomas that night what my friend had said, hoping he would find her just as laughable as I did. He didn't.

"Can't see what's wrong with that," he said. "I have a good job. You don't need to go to work. You can stay home and look after the kids. Isn't that what you wanted?"

"Well, yes, but I also want to go back to my job. I am a pilot, just like you, remember? I am not going to waste my days making applesauce and cleaning baby puke off the high chair."

He just shrugged. His ignorance pissed me off so much that I went back to work when the twins were only six months old, although I could have stayed home for a year, according to the German laws for new mothers. I went back to flying to show everyone I could do both, be a mom and a pilot. I should have known better. Jokes from my male colleagues about taking a breast pump on board were the least of my worries. I was unbelievably, monstrously tired. I lived on caffeine, and stronger stuff sometimes. Thank God, one of my friends was a doctor and gave me prescriptions without asking too many questions. But while I just about managed to pull myself together in the cockpit, things fell apart the minute I got home. Maja was cranky, and Rosi was clingy. I went through three nannies in four months. I felt guilty every day, when I left the twins with yet another temporary nanny from the agency, and also when I stayed at home with them and told the office to take me off the schedule for a week. Most of all, I was angry at Thomas, who announced out of the blue that he was taking on more intercontinental flights.

"Are you now?" I commented in the most sarcastic voice I could muster up. "Good for you. But unlike you, I can't do that. I am stuck here in Babyville."

"What do you want me to do?"

"I want you to stay home with them for a change as well, for God's sake."

"Why me? I already look after them when you are not around."

"The nanny looks after them when I am not around."

"I spent all last Saturday with the twins when you flew off to Madrid. I have a right to some time off too!"

That moment was when I realized it. We were arguing about who had the right to spend the *least* amount of time with our beautiful, precious daughters, the babies I had wanted more than anything in the world. How utterly perverted was that?

I gave in. I quit flying and stayed at home. When people asked me when I would return to work, I kept my answers vague and superficial. Deep down I knew I wouldn't be able to compete anymore in that male dominated world of flying, so I acted like it was my choice to be a stay-at-home mom. What an awful euphemism. I mean, where else would a mom stay, in a bar, in a roadside motel?

So we slipped into this routine called marriage, working together like a military operation, exchanging short commands in the mornings—"parent night," "drop off at school," "dry cleaner," and in the evening "in the oven," "back Wednesday," "call Jeff and Sue and cancel that thing." Thomas advanced his career and earned the money that my life now depended upon (sorry, Grandma) while I grew older and fatter. Now and again when I found myself cleaning toilets, searching for Barbie's cocktail handbag under the piano, cleaning cat puke off the floor, cooking a dinner no one will eat because the twins are fussy, and Thomas is abroad, and stuffing the wash into the dryer only to find it dirty and on the floor again the next day, I wondered if I had become my mother. I realized I hadn't because despite her cleaning madness, at least my mother found a man who loved her and whom she loved. I also realized that marriage is hard enough when you really love the person you were married to, but it becomes almost impossible when you don't.

I almost left Thomas when the kids were about seven years old, but he never found out about it. He never knew how close he came to being kicked out of this suburban farce and how close I came to running away with Matt. He was my children's guitar teacher at the time, always dressed in some graffiti T-Shirt, torn jeans, some leather jacket, all of which he was a little too old for, even though he was five years younger than I. He lived in a different universe where dreams accompanied by cool music were still possible, where a whole afternoon could be spent strumming the guitar in the sun on the balcony, where people didn't get up before noon and where they ate bad food and still remained slim. We met in his apartment, had sex under a poster of Led Zeppelin and I was almost as happy as I had been with David, but then the twins got mono and were sick for weeks and I realized I couldn't just run away or move into Matt's one-bedroom apartment.

I broke it off and told him I would never be so happy with anyone else again. It sounded a bit too grand, a bit too dramatic, but I meant it and I cried all the way home afterwards. Two weeks later the girls announced they hated playing the guitar anyway, and soon after, Matt was gone.

The first time I saw her, I wondered if Keiko had kids. She does, of course, I later found out. She didn't look like a stay-at-home mom to me, nor did most of the other female pilots. There must have been a fair number of moms among them though, I thought, but probably more of the "stay-in-the-cockpit kind of moms." And then I saw that Ari had a picture of her kids in her wallet. I saw the way she looked at them when she thought no one would see her. It was a mix of sadness, longing and relief. *I love my wonderful children, but, thank God, they are not here to bother me.* I instantly knew I had found a soul mate. We bonded over wine and coffee and realized we shared a similar background. How on earth had the others done it, we wondered? How had they managed to not lose themselves in the years of motherhood like we did? How had they stayed so goddamn strong? None of them looked as disillusioned and disheveled as we did. And I bet not even Ari depended on a man as much I did.

I slow the plane down because there is a storm ahead. The plane almost jumps in the air as I try to avoid turbulence. Bloody fantastic, I need a higher altitude or to catch a strong tailwind if I want to keep my good time. I want to finish this race so badly, not just for the money and to keep my plane, but more just to prove to myself that I am still capable of great things. That was the real reason I applied to take part in this race, and I guess Keiko sensed this. She is clever that way. Nobody from my family knows. I was too embarrassed to tell them—too afraid they would laugh. My former piloting career is something that is talked about in the manner you talk about the deceased, in a hushed voice and with mild nostalgia. A few years ago, when the girls were teenagers, and I mentioned going back to work, Rosi nodded and agreed. "Totally, Mom, you could like work part-time in the flower shop at the corner. I think they are looking for someone."

"Or like even in the office at the airport or something," Maja contributed. "They would be crazy not to take you. You know so much about planes and stuff." Indeed, I did know a lot about planes and stuff. I just wouldn't let anybody know that.

Right now my husband and daughters think I am spending time hiking with an old friend in the Alps. So while they are imagining their mother sitting next to some Edelweiss on a mountain meadow, breaking into a yodel, and admiring the view of the mountains, I am actually battling a storm up in the sky.

But here is the saddest thing... they probably don't even think of me at all because the precious babies, the ones I gave up Matt and everything else for, moved out two years ago and call once a month if I am lucky, and my husband has been seeing one of the stewardesses on his route. I am scared he will leave me, because what will become of me then?

I stretch out my arms, starting to feel uncomfortable because the seats on these planes were not made for size eighteen women like me. They were made for skinny male pilots who never had a dent in their career. I can feel anger rising up in my throat and stare at my reflection in the black screen of the GPS—my hair, which I cut short and dyed red recently in an attempt to look younger, with my puffy face, smudged eyeliner, and my… wait a minute. I freeze. The reason I can see my reflection so clearly is because my GPS has turned black. It has stopped working, and because of the thick clouds outside, I can't see a thing. I have no idea where I am going, and the storm is snapping at me like an angry dragon, tossing my little plane around like a toy.

"Shit, shit, shit," I murmur. I try to reach ground control, but there is only static noise and a silence that is no longer comforting, but eerie. I panic.

A lump grows in my throat. I try to remember instructions from training a few weeks ago, even from my training years back, but it all blurs together. I just can't focus. It serves me right for thinking I could take part in a race like this. The black screen of the GPS is the abyss into which I will fall any second now.

I blink, rub my eyes trying to see better, which is pointless, since the clouds are even thicker than they were a few seconds ago. It is denser, getting even darker in the middle when a shape with sharp contours suddenly materializes. Oh my God, that is no cloud, that is something else and it is heading straight into me! My heart stops for a second, I scream, I swerve the plane to the right and in one seemingly endless moment of horror, I wait for the screeching sound that will come from the left, when the other plane (because that *is* what the shape turns out to be) will shred my little Spitfire into pieces.

The sound never comes. There is a flash of light—I see a horrified, frozen face in the other cockpit for a split second. I can't even recognize if it is male or female, and then it is gone. Just like that. The clouds are closing up again, making me feel like I am sitting in my own personal horror show complete with liquid ice puffing up around me.

Sweat collects around my neck and collarbone. As I try and wipe it off, my fingers get hold of something. It's my necklace. Grandma's necklace, the first Deutsche mark she ever earned. My lovely, funny, strong grandma, she wouldn't have sat here, sobbing. Grandma would have either done something about it or pulled herself together and faced death with dignity, like she did when the doctor's told her she only had a few weeks left to live.

"I am not done yet," she said and then simply refused to die for a good seven more months, time enough to sort out all her affairs, visit old friends, and prepare herself for her death. In the end, she died in her garden looking out at the fields of spring flowers in bloom, not tied to a machine or a bed, like she should have been, according to the doctors.

I clutch the necklace firmly. I too have things to do still, and I am not going to die. The little voice in my head mocks, *what things?* But this time I silence it. I too want to live. I want to show my girls what I am capable of and that I am not just Mom who picks up clothes off the floor and who could get a job in the local flower shop. I want to be a pilot again, be independent so I can finally look Grandma in the eyes if I ever meet her again. I never believed in God or an afterlife, but now, faced with my looming end, I am not so sure anymore. If I were to live, I think, I would change. I would leave Thomas, who, after all never did anything wrong to me. I was beaten by motherhood and just gave up, so he assumed I was fine with my life.

It dawns on me that I am not even jealous of his girlfriend. Maybe it's true love, who knows? Why shouldn't Thomas find true love in his life? Everybody should. I thought mine was David, but how could it have been if he didn't want to be with me? Maybe my true love is Matt and if I survive this race and if he still wants me, I can find happiness with him even if it is late in life. I made a promise to Grandma who had faced much greater adversaries in her time, and I want to land this goddamn plane safely so I didn't give up my precious Levi's for nothing all those years back. "I just want to fucking see something!" I swear loudly and almost as if prompted, the GPS flickers and comes back on. The sky in front of me is empty, no more ghost planes coming my way.

"Jesus!" I laugh hysterically and cry at the same time, suddenly grasping that the GPS was out only for a few seconds. Or was it? Did I just imagine all this out of fear, lack of confidence, and some form of cockpit cabin fever? For the remaining time of the flight I sit like a statue, watch the GPS like a hawk and manage not to close my eyes even when I sneeze.

San Francisco finally pops up at the very edge of the screen. As I descend, I steer, and take deep breaths until I can finally see the Golden Gate Bridge.

"I am not done yet," I whisper as I land and wonder if San Francisco would be a nice place to start a new life. After all, even though I probably didn't win, I will still get $250,000 for taking part in the race and get to keep my plane.

I stumble out of the plane like a drunk, suddenly overcome by tiredness and joy and an overwhelming feeling of gratefulness. To Keiko, for letting me be part of this and to whomever was watching over me up there today. And to myself, for pulling this one off and for letting Claudia, goddess of the sky, emerge from the cocoon of a frumpy housewife.

In the terminal I wave to the other pilots who have gathered behind a glass wall and signal me to hurry over, but as I said—I am not done yet. I pull out my phone and dial home.

"Hello?" Thomas answers after the third ring.

"It's me," I reply.

"Yes. How's the hike?" he asks without any enthusiasm, his mouth full of something.

"I wasn't hiking. I am not even in Switzerland. I am in the United States."

"What?" He stops chewing. "What do you mean?"

"I just flew a Spitfire from Japan to the United States. I almost died, but I get to keep the plane."

"What?"

For an educated man he has a very limited vocabulary. "Look," I reply, "It is a long story and I will tell you one day, if you want me to. But for now let me just say that I am staying in San Francisco, at least for a while. But even if I do come back, I won't be coming back to you."

Silence. Then a muffled noise his voice, sharp and impatient. "Claudia, are you all right? Have you been drinking?"

"You heard me right. I am leaving."

"Claudia, don't be ridiculous, you and I…"

"… should never have gotten married. It was a mistake. But it is not your fault and not mine. It's just life. And now we will go on in different directions and you can stay with Hannah. That is her name, isn't it? The stewardess you've been seeing?"

"Claudia, I… yes it is." His voice is barely a whisper now.

"And do you love her?"

There is an even longer silence and I am almost about to hang up when I hear it. "Yes."

"Then you should be with her. Don't waste any more time. I will call you again in a while."

I finally hang up and wave back to Ludmilla who has popped open a bottle of champagne behind the glass wall. I should go and join them. But then I scroll down the contacts on my phone, because after all those years, Matt is still in there. We are friends on Facebook, too. He never married and he still looks the same… or almost—crazy T-Shirt, leather jacket and all, just less hair. I could call him and he would probably be here tomorrow. It is tempting, especially when I think of his easy ways and picture him singing a love song for me. But I decide not to. I need to do this alone.

Grandma was right. We women should never depend on anyone other than ourselves. I certainly will not—never again.

I walk over to join the others in that room, which has a perfect view of the San Francisco Skyline.

It is as beautiful as a new beginning can be.

I guess I just need to find a flower for my hair.

NANIBAH JACKSON

YELLOW 13

All this water! I've been away from my homeland in the American Southwest for too long. I miss my people and the dry desert landscape. I miss the old traditions that my Laguna mother taught me and the stories that the elder women would share with us over campfires throughout the night. I miss the Navajo land that is home to our people, where my family is and where I come from. And I feel that they must miss me as I have tried to be a conduit between the Laguna and Navajo nations and beliefs.

Flying at twenty thousand feet over the Pacific has put me in a trance for the first five hours in the air. I call it a spirit quest of sorts. I am in awe of being here in the clouds in heaven, isolated in this cockpit for hours upon hours. It has also taken my mind off the medical issues that have emerged for me, as well as the the cultural and environmental issues of the Navajo and the Laguna pueblos, at least for a while.

Three hours before I land and refuel on O'ahu. The only times on this flight that I have been nervous are the refueling stages, even though the first ocean water landing and refueling went without a hitch. The sailors got a kick out of my *Yellow 13* floatplane. I suppose the choice of color for me and the lucky number were good omens for me in this adventure. The best part of the refueling stop was to have a twenty-minute session of acupuncture with Dr. Watase, whom I grew so fond of during our Tokyo training days.

I think of my father who, with my mother's consent, gave me a traditional Navajo name. It isn't heard very often except on Navajo land. Many names end in "bah," because "bah" can mean a type of warrior or person of war. I like that, but it's not me. Navajo is a descriptive language, and "Nanibah" describes a happiness one might feel after something one thought was lost and gone forever is regained. I not only wish this for myself, but also for my people, who today seem so lost. Some elders feel that even after four centuries of oppression, the pueblo religious beliefs and dignity are still strong and vibrant, our pueblo languages are still spoken, and the sacred kivas are still intact. Perhaps there is some truth to what some of the elders believe, but there is still a great deal of abuse and misuse of Indian ceremonies. Vine Deloria Jr.

said it best in *The World We Used to Live In: Remembering the Powers of the Medicine Man*. He believes that throughout the reservations in this country, the loss of the old ways is so prevalent that many Indian Americans are willing to cast aside traditional ceremonies that have survived for hundreds of years while the mainstream consumer society squanders everything in the culture at large. The majority of Indian people today have little understanding or remembrance of the powers once possessed by the spiritual leaders of their communities.

I am concerned for future generations. For me, losing traditions and spiritual ways came after years of traditional education. I was the first in my family to get a university degree. Although I majored in Cultural Anthropology at the University of New Mexico, I too have embraced consumer mentality, and although I have learned a great deal, I have also lost a great deal in the process. and I know that there are many challenges ahead for me.

The big challenge in my life thus far has been to survive and recover from colorectal cancer, with the help of western medicine. Through all of this, I thought I had achieved a balance in the life that was returned to me. Now, I am not sure of any balance, and am depressed by what I have to deal with physically and with the spiritual state of my people. I am battling cancer once again and I am too young to be messed up this way.

Only a few years ago, after a long flight in a Cessna I rented outside of Albuquerque, I started hemorrhaging blood. I never had a colonoscopy even though my mother had had many polyps removed from her colon. Heck, I was only twenty-three years old. I accompanied several family friends when they had colonoscopies and knew the procedure. Their post-colonoscopy ritual was to rest for an hour and let the anesthesia wear off, get dressed and eat something, and that was it. They usually got test results back a few days later. None of them ever had negative results. Good for them. After my colonoscopy, I knew I was in for trouble when the nurses avoided eye contact with me and led me to a private waiting room. That was when my five-second theory of life took hold. The good western doctor who did my exam took five seconds to show me the pictures and without hesitation or biopsy reports knew it was a cancerous tumor in my rectum.

My family had me see the medicine men on the Navajo rez whose Diné healing powers are immensely complicated. I looked forward to this traditional treatment. As an Indian, I am fortunate that the medicine men saw me and also worked with the white medicine docs. I laugh to myself at this moment because I am now getting treatment from white, red, and yellow skinned docs.

Back then, I learned that the Navajo medicine men use a two-step process of diagnosis and healing that is just as sophisticated as western methods. The medicine man or diagnostician is to discover not only the cause of the illness but also to recommend the treatment to be used. Sometimes he recommends actual therapeutic measures, although usually he simply says what kind of chant should be performed over the patient and recommends a particular practitioner who can apply the therapeutic treatment.

There are three kinds of diagnosticians used by the Diné. They are the *Hand Trembler*, the *Star Gazer,* and the *Listener*. My father explained to me how each one did his thing. When a stubborn ailment seemed to be the problem or when it is a desire to learn if a past event has cast a bad influence over a person, the Shaking Hand ceremony is generally used. If an important decision is to be made that will affect the whole family, such as whether a part of the family should undertake a long journey, the Star Gazing or the Sun-Gazing rite is often used to influence the decision and also to determine the proper time to start. The Listening Rite is effective in locating children or lost animals and in obtaining information concerning distant relatives. This ceremony is also used if the Navajo has been having very bad luck and thinks that someone is casting an evil spell over him.

At that time, I saw a *Hand Trembler* and a *Star Gazer*. It was nine years ago but the rituals are still so clear in my memory. It seems that the aloneness of this flight has recalled in me deep memories. I liked the *Star Gazer*. It might just be due to my relationship as a pilot to the stars and light. The *Star Gazer* used a crystal and my little brother to assist in this ritual. They went outside and I stayed in the family house. He prayed the star-prayer to the star-spirit asking the star to show him the cause of the sickness and the treatment. He then began to sing star-songs and while singing he fixed his gaze directly at a star or at the light of a star reflected in the "glass rock," or quartz crystal, which he held in his hand. As if in a trance, the singing continued and the star began to throw out a string of light, and at the end of this, the *Star Gazer* saw the cause of the sickness in me, like a motion picture. If the strings of light are white or yellow, I would recover. If red, the illness is serious and dangerous. If the white light falls on the house and makes it bright as day, I would get well. I am happy to say that our house lit up white. I received chanting from the *Hand Trembler* and then went the route of western medicine.

In Albuquerque, after CT scans and consulting a gastrointestinal surgeon and oncologist, I had my first surgery to remove the rectal tumor which was verified as cancer, but without any clear information about how deep the tumor had penetrated my rectum. In any cancer, there is what is called staging, usually from one to four with four being the worst. They couldn't stage me given the lack of total information. I knew it was not bad from my rituals with the *Star Gazer*. Nevertheless, it was still cancer.

I wanted whatever cancer I had to be removed, so in discussion with my surgeon and oncologist, I opted for another surgery. I was told that there was a chance to "reconnect" my colon to whatever rectum was left, or I might end up with a colostomy. A colostomy closes up the anus and reroutes the colon to an opening in your abdomen. The protruding colon, called a stoma, is where the body's waste is eliminated into what I call my "shit" bag.

Well, I woke up in the hospital, and thanks to morphine, didn't feel a thing after having been cut open both in the front and the back of my abdomen. Of course, they had to remove my rectum and also took out my appendix as a freebie. I remember lying there without a care in the world. It was the first time that I wasn't making lists of things to do or worrying about anything. Today, all I can remember is constantly chatting with my roommate who had just lost a kidney. We talked about food— green chile cheeseburgers and lobsters, whatever came to mind as we absorbed our intravenous fluids for three days. On the fourth day, my surgeon visited me with the pathology report. The five-second life-altering announcement this time was that they found no further cancer and it was all gone. There would be no chemotherapy or radiation treatments. On the fifth day, I was wheeled out into the glorious sunshine and driven home. I learned what not to eat and how to clean out my medical bag, and how to deal with the big economic bureaucracy of the medical supply business. I have learned to cope but have not forgotten my roots. I once had a rectum. Now I have a beautiful stoma that I call Siddhartha, Sid for short. Of course, Sid was once Sid Vicious. I haven't thought about this in a long time.

Two weeks later I was in my rented Cessna, flying out of Double Eagle airport, outside of Albuquerque, and in the clouds, smiling.

Funny how another recent five-second announcement and this long flight have rekindled thoughts about my body and my survival. I am not a vain woman, but the fear of how men will respond to my colostomy and medical bag does seem like a turnoff. My man of the future must have understanding and compassion. When I have bouts of low self-esteem, pity, and depression, I try to counter that with an appreciation of the moment, and my enjoyment of a productive life, with or without a male companion. Being a pilot has given me those moments plus a sense of power and control so I believe I can deal with anything. Heck, I am closer to my maker up here as well. Do I want to win this race? Naw, just being involved with my sister pilots, who also have issues, both in their lives and in their cultures, that are far greater than mine, has given me some relative sense of peace. Another five-second announcement was reminding me of impermanence. Things are what they are and will come to be. So be it.

The next five-second announcement came two days after we began training. I had lower back pain that I thought was due to prolonged sitting in the cockpit. We all had to have physicals and along with my blood tests, I always ask for a CEA test for cancer. Since my initial surgery eight years ago, my yearly CEA test readings were low, meaning no cancer. This time my numbers were surprisingly elevated. and it only took five seconds for the doc to say, "You had better get a CT scan because your cancer has probably come back." Heck, I had been feeling just fine until finding this out. I realized I needed to work on my psychological response. and that has been a very tough thing for me to do.

Between early flight training in the floatplane, I got two MRIs, a CT scan, a PET scan, and finally a biopsy to a trouble area in my lower back and abdomen. The Japanese oncologist that Keiko brought in was great. I got first class treatment that allowed me to continue to train in Tokyo. Keiko took care of the bills and I was grateful for her compassion in letting me continue in The Race as long as I felt physically able to perform after my radiation and chemotherapy started.

The diagnosis was not good. I have a recurrence of the colorectal cancer, and although there were no tumors in major organs, the cancer was in my system and could metastasize anywhere. I was stage four, which is the worst. The cancer is not in my colon, but the cancer cells from my previous colorectal cancer have probably migrated to my lymph nodes and lumbar area, leading to cancer in the abdomen, lower back and blood stream.

My first cancer treatment was two weeks of radiation on the L-3 region of my spine. Cancer lesions had formed there and were compressing the nerves. Shrinking this cancer should help reduce the swelling on my right leg and lessen my abdominal and lower back pain. The radiation caused fatigue and I tried to get plenty of rest when I could and not let it affect my training.

For chemo treatments I had to have a "port placement" surgically implanted. Today's chemo drugs for colon cancer vary, along with their side effects. I received and continue to receive a cocktail of three drugs, and was told that it is a good thing the recurrence happened more than one or two years after my initial surgery. Nevertheless, the chemo-treatments can improve my survival rate giving me an average of two to six more years to live. It seems in my case, it is not curable. Ten years ago, a person with my diagnosis was given nine to ten months to live. I began chemo four weeks into training. Every two to three weeks I will become toxic with chemo. The applications will stop if my white blood count gets too low or if I get really sick. Many of the initial chemotherapy drugs are to combat its side effects.

In the early mornings before training began, I started chemotherapy—first, a blood test through my chest port and then a saline application to clean out the port. A round of chemotherapy took four hours, which gave me a chance to sleep a bit. I left the facility with a pump in me that slowly released the heavy-duty 5FU drug, the one that causes all the side effects. Two days of that and the pump was removed. I had acupuncture like the other pilots, but Dr. Kaz did special things to help me deal with the Chemo side effects—nausea and sensitivity to cold. After the session and before we left Tokyo, I was given an injection to help prevent complications from bone metastases in my spine.

I'm concerned about nerve problems in my fingers caused by one of the chemo drugs, so I'm taking vitamins to counter this. I don't it want to affect my flying. I also had to customize the straps on the five-point cockpit harness so that it doesn't rub on the port area. Nausea is at a minimum, but sores in my mouth and nerves affected in my teeth, make it difficult to eat without a lot of pain. I've got a concoction called Magic Mouthwash that essentially comes from HIV research and that has helped a lot. And then there are my fingers and toes, which have turned brown. I am dark skinned, but this extra brown tone in my fingers makes me think that my hands are dirty and need to be washed. These are my major complaints, but I am doing well for now.

Predictably, all my thoughts up here are about this cancer stuff, both past and present. But I do know I have so much more to live for and I still have contributions to make to my people, but I don't feel as emotionally stable as I would like. Several times in training, and on this flight, I have turned off my headphones and just screamed. Therapeutic stuff, I think.

O'ahu looms ahead. The Hawaiian Islands have always interested me, and in my cultural anthropology studies I wrote a couple of papers on Hawai'i. Hawaiian indigenous history is similar to the story of the American Indian. In the Hawaiian story, it is about early New England missionaries coming out to give the happy people of Hawai'i good ol' Christian religion and get them to relinquish their pagan ways. When it became economically viable, the whites claimed land ownership and began to raise crops for profit, undermining Queen Lili'uokalani. The Hawaiian Islands were recognized as important for naval control of the Pacific Ocean, so the United States annexed the islands and took control. Today, many Hawaiians are trying to reestablish the roots of their culture, language, and spirituality. Former U.S. Senator Daniel Akaka introduced legislation to extend federal recognition to those of Native Hawaiian ancestry as a sovereign group similar to Native American tribes. I hope this happens.

It was a one-hour cathartic stopover in Hawai'i. The landing went smoothly and I received three medical treatments in the short time I had for refueling. I began with some acupressure on my wrists for my nausea with Sachi Watase. Then the oncology nurse drew blood to check my CEA level. I will get the results when I refuel again halfway between San Francisco from O'ahu. The combined meditation and Chromo-therapy session with Habib, was wonderful. I thank Hamidah for teaching me how to meditate and for introducing me to the healing powers of Chromotherapy. I will continue these practices and I will teach both of them on the rez. The sense of self-realization and compassion that has awakened in me is critical. I think my participation in this adventure with the other pilots has helped me cope with my cancer recurrence. The evening discussions on impermanence, uncertainty, and Buddhist philosophy with Hamidah have also been helpful and have coincided with my reading about American Indian spirituality and beliefs.

I have found my place in all of this. My goal is to finish The Race at the Golden Gate Bridge in San Francisco, donate the $250,000 to American Indian causes, especially the suicide prevention programs run by the women of my pueblo. And Keiko is gifting each of us the Spitfire floatplanes that we flew. I will contact the Spitfire museum in England about their purchasing my airplane, and then I will get myself a small Cessna. I will donate the rest of the money to Navajo language education and to organized cultural programs at Laguna pueblo.

The preservation of the Keres native language of Laguna, Acoma, Santa Ana, Zia, Cochiti, Kewa, and San Felipe pueblos is vital. Each of the seven varieties of Keres is generally intelligible by speakers in each pueblo, but the number of people fluent in the unwritten language continues to decline. Over the past thirty years, attempts to revitalize the use of Keres have included language classes, development of a Keres dictionary, and a variety of grant-funded programs, all financed by state and federal governments, which unfortunately have been problematic because of ever-changing funding policies and a dependency on government money. I hope to counter that with my donated funds. No strings attached.

Traditional ways of teaching a language don't always work with languages like Keres, in part because it's not a written language. Keres is not currently taught in Laguna schools because no successful structure for teaching it has been developed. And, there are not enough teachers certified to teach Keres. These problems need to be addressed and money will help, but it is the community and good intentioned Indians who will create a structure that works.

Of course, I have more chemotherapy sessions left to do every three weeks because I am metastatic. I completed one before leaving Tokyo and will do another session with the Japanese docs in San Francisco before I decide when to go back home. I realize that I need to get back home and receive traditional healing treatments from the Navajo medicine men. I think chanting sessions might not be enough. I have lost sight of my important past traditions these past few years, but this flight has returned them to me. I and future generations need to help maintain the world we used to live in. American Indian philosopher, Vine Deloria Jr., who has had a big influence on me, said it best, "There are many powers available through the ceremonies and rituals of American Indian tribes, and these can be applied to our daily lives to enrich our well-being and enhance our understanding of life in the physical world."

Besides the chemotherapy in Albuquerque, I also need to find a good acupuncturist. I must remind myself to ask Dr. Kaz if he can recommend someone. With my growing "chemo brain," there is too much here to contemplate. The chemotherapy dulls the memory and the sharpness of my thinking. Multitasking is getting harder. Better focus on flying to the next refueling ship.

I've been thinking of checking out the Great Pacific Garbage Patch, but my race time seems to be pretty good and since I have a chance to win this thing, I will stay at the higher altitude and hope to catch a tailwind. And even though this plastic waste area is a major environmental issue, I am focusing on the issues Ryoichi brought up regarding nuclear waste and our planet's future. For me, it is specific to the tailing deposits that are still radioactive on my mother's Laguna Pueblo—the Jackpile-Paguate Uranium mine and the tailing deposits on the Navajo rez around Gallup from the United Nuclear Corporation. The Jackpile-Paguate mine is in an area of canyons and arroyos, and includes more than four square miles of disturbed soil with three open pits, thirty-two nuclear waste dumps and more than thirty stockpiles. The area was mined from 1953 until 1982. During that time about 400 million tons of rocks were moved within the mine area and about twenty-five million tons of uranium ore were transported from the mine to a mill about forty miles away. The U.S. Environmental Protection Agency has made the site a national priority Superfund cleanup site after more than a quarter of a century of contamination from uranium tailing deposits. Things always seem to move slowly when it comes to dealing with the U.S. government. Now they want to build more contemporary uranium mining developments on the Apache rez in southeastern New Mexico. "Good for the economy," they say. Personally, I like the casinos we have across New Mexico on Indian land. Now that's good for our economy!

Things are moving fast now with my desire to undertake western cancer treatment and to embrace the treatment by the medicine men. Hopefully, these treatments will give me a longer life and more time to fulfill my destiny. This journey has been both an outer and inner one. The women on this journey have become a community and I want to figure out how to join them and Keiko on the pathways that we discussed in training. The goal of total, closed-loop recycling is a start for community-based alternatives. Christine theorized that, "As communities, we will be better equipped to respond to massive economic, social, and climate changes. And we must be flexible and agile in our thinking and processes." This is also needed for the American Indians—to band together in family and in community, to shun white man's consumerism, to eat better with more natural organic food grown on the rez, to embrace our natural environment, to dream, and to see geology become genealogy. The sacred site of Shiprock on Navajo land in New Mexico will become Winged Rock, which is much more than a remnant from a volcano. It is of the utmost importance to embrace the spiritual morphology of plants, animals, rocks, and rivers because it forms and contributes to the cosmology of the people who inhabit a place.

It is time for the witches to re-emerge. In most cultures, the voice of the "feminine" is emerging. That voice for the Diné emerges from the land itself. In our desert, for the Diné, she appears as Changing Woman. I learned as a young girl about the ritual of *Kinaalda* where each young Navajo girl is initiated into womanhood. It is Changing Woman who is honored in the ceremony of first blood. I was taught about the magic of *Kochininako*, or Yellow Woman. When my mother took me to the old storytellers on the Laguna rez, the stories of Kochininako were always told. She belongs to the wind and travels the whole world swiftly with dust and with windstorms. She is another reason why I fly the *Yellow 13* floatplane.

For the Navajo, Changing Woman can shift shapes like the wind and cut through stone with a voice like water. When she approaches us, carrying offerings of white shells found in our arid country, she reminds us that there was a time when ancient seas covered the desert. The irony here is that I come from this dry land and now fly with the wind over this huge sea of water. This was meant to be.

Changing Woman gathers seeds and plants them as dreams in the sand and then calls forth rain. She is the one who embodies the Moon, honoring the cyclic nature of life. I now believe that our community of pilots constitutes the rise of the voice of the witches of the past. We begin again like the Moon. We can no longer deny the destiny that is ours by being women who wait. Waiting to love, waiting to speak, waiting to act—this is not patience, but pathology. We are sensual, sexual beings, intrinsically bound to both Heaven and Earth.

Damn, just when my chemo brain was really getting heated up, the weather has shifted a bit for the worse and the last refueling ship looms ahead. Now I must make another secure landing. So glad that Kaz made it to this last refueling ship to give us all acupuncture. I have become dependent on his healing procedure.

I am getting to be a pro with these water landings. I am very glad that the twelve pilots before me all made it to this refueling ship. Now some of them have probably finished and are waiting for the last three of us to join them. Everything went smoothly despite the rough sea, and now it's on to San Francisco with this iffy weather. It's going to mean looking for clear skies and avoiding dense weather clouds as well as following the interesting suggestion from Kaz and Keiko to descend into San Francisco at 7,890 feet and fly through what they call "Cloud Nine." I must concentrate on flying, but I continuously have other thoughts, especially after getting my CEA results at the refueling ship. With chemotherapy and radiation, I have suffered, but moved from a CEA reading of 40.7 to 5.8. All kinds of my cells are dying, but most importantly, many of those dying are the cancer cells! Although cancer will be with me for the rest of my life, it is time to be happy! If Cloud Nine is what I think it is, maybe I don't need it! I can't explain the happiness that I am feeling at the moment. All this thinking about my cancer woes, the spiritual nature of my culture, and my hopes of returning to those teachings and beliefs, along with my "chemo emo," has brought me to tears of happiness. I am in the moment. I am flying in the clouds, alone in the sanctuary of my cockpit and in this vast space. Darting in and out of cloud formations, finding clearings and open sky, I am in control, and I want to be no other place than in this moment.

In my euphoria, I have been banking the aircraft back and forth. I will never tell Christine or Keiko about my happiness antics, but how many times in my life will I be able to gaze down over the vast Pacific, dart among the clouds, cry and smile, roll my airplane back and forth, rising to 20,000 feet and still soaring up in altitude. I am in the moment. My future and life expectancy can wait until I am with the other pilots, women, or maybe goddesses.

I am seeing more albatrosses at this altitude, which is strange. I am at 23,456 feet and am freaking out! During one of my happiness aircraft rolls, my engine seemed to cut out. The comforting sound of the roaring engine just disappeared. I think, "I have had it, my engine is dead!" All sound just seemed to disappear. Then, everything in the sky seems to brighten, like opening the aperture on my camera two stops.... It only happened for a moment as I banked away and down and stopped the happiness rolling. Now, I am freaking out, wondering about my chemo brain and hallucinations, but my floatplane is operating fine. I suppose I won't report this to anyone as well.

The strange moment brings me back to me something my mother told me before I left for Tokyo which now feels like a lifetime ago. She told me that *space* is so important to the Indian perceptions of the world, and that *space* can be created by the medicine people and in the past by the witches. The energies and information in these *spaces* can be transported from the larger cosmos to the particular location where humans need help and sustenance. And she told me about the Mayan bird god, *Kukulkan,* also called Quetzalcoatl by the Aztecs and Toltecs, I will go to the Temple of the Sun in Chichen Itza and clap my hands. The voice of *Kukulkan* calls back to you if you are worthy. It is more than an ordinary echo as the Mayans always built architecture of magic and spiritual belief. It is said that the presence of the sacred bird god has always been there and knows to withhold its voice until summoned by the right goddess. Maybe that is me or one of my other sister pilots. Thank you, Mother. This is calming to think about.

Time seems to have passed very quickly, maybe because of the effort of dodging in and out of clouds for stability and safety, and now the instruments show my approach to San Francisco. Maybe twenty minutes more of flying. I descend to 7,890 feet and enter Cloud Nine. I hope I can keep this happiness with me even with so much to work on. Open skies loom ahead. Should be no problem to transmit my arrival and receive permission to fly under the Golden Gate to finish this race. I guess I made it! I can't wait to meet with my fellow pilots and eat and dance and decide what we will do in our lives. My newfound friends or "dark-skinned sisters" have all finished their flights by now and most likely are waiting for me. Hamidah, Raya Sol, Ruth and I have agreed to work together for all women of color. Of course, I think Keiko will help us make those decisions. I am thinking about something that Terry Tempest Williams wrote because now it resonates in my brain in these circumstances. "I am a woman with wings dancing with other women with wings." And so am I.

PICCOLA UCCELLO

CHARTREUSE 14

I am thunder. My cockpit, during take off, is in the heart of a deep storm. Through my shaking seat, I can feel each one of those twenty-one hundred horses in this papa Griffon—bareback—as the air whines outside. It screams when I split it. God, I love the feeling of adrenaline coursing through my fingertips straight into the yoke. It's a wild ride and I'm in total control.

Airspeed and altitude good, we are climbing steadily. Nice smooth ascent, pitch and roll, balanced. GPS locked on, all systems going strong, everybody's having fun. *E certo!* Just like that, I'm flying again. What do you know? *Mamma*, you can open your eyes down there, "She's at it again," she's saying. But don't I make it look good? God scooped me up with a finger and flung me up here. Flying, if I come close enough to heaven, I could probably lick His nose if I tried. Someday, in outer space, I'll touch a star. It'll be just like touching His fingertip.

The sound of screaming air has melted into the back of my brain. Now I can relax. *Olio d'Oliva* handles like a dream, a real spitfire! She's such a smooth ride, smooth like olive oil, the perfect color for me. I wonder, if I ask them really nice, maybe the *Agenzia Spaziale Italiana* will paint my rocket ship this color green when they finally decide to send me into space. Or maybe I'll do it myself with spray paint the night before launch.

Mamma would cry for days if I shot into space. She nearly fainted when I told her about this race. Mamma's not built of very strong mortar. She's not sturdy like *Papa* and me. Mamma's made of lace and cotton, a real lady with red ribbons in her veins instead of blood. I don't know what she'll do without me. She'll have to start pestering Gionni like she pesters me. "Be sweet and meek," the little girl she always wanted instead of the daughter who turned out like a boy. *Scusa, Mamma,* you tried as hard as you could, but I'm just going to keep doing crazy stuff—*pazza*—I know. I can't help it. If I were in a knitting contest instead of a flight race, I would bring home last place for sure. I swear I would drop every single stitch. But up here in my cockpit, this is where I can do anything. This is where God put my brain and you, Mamma, were the one who taught me that we can not question God's will. Only be grateful for the encouragement it gives us.

That was one thing Mamma could never understand about me. I know God's will in my life. It's a clear message—I must fly. It is so natural, so fulfilling, so meaningful to fly. And so close to God, too! But she has a different interpretation of His will. I guess that's where the violence of religion comes from—everyone sees God's truth in a different way. A lot of smart people think that there is only one peak at the top of the mountain of truth and that the most direct way to get there is science. Professor Bianti always taught that way. Science is a direct translation of the language of the universe. But I don't know about that. Reverend Manetti also taught that way—same but opposite. He and Mamma always said the cleanest passage to the peak of wisdom is through God and that close examination of His word held answers to every question. I think they're both right. The real truth has to be somewhere in the middle. Science and God do not have to be mutually exclusive. I think the Reverend would agree that God is a brilliant mathematician and I think Bianti would support my hypothesis that a lot of science is shrouded in the mystery of God's will. That's where the thrill of discovering answers comes from, uncovering truth from the bosom of the greatest mystery.

The reason I'm flying right now is mostly science with a little bit of miracle. But if I win this race, it will be mostly miracle with a little bit of science. *Caro Dio*, please let me win! This victory could change my life. It would mean the difference between getting that internship at the A.S.I., and having my résumé passed over *again* for "lack of experience." But if I win, there's no way the recruitment officers could ignore me with a victory in the trans-Pacific Spitfire race under my belt.

Here comes the coast... and there it goes. *Bellezza!* How the world opens up beyond the shoreline! Everything solid drops out, and then only the endless continuum of wide open ocean. It is a vastness that I find thrilling. Mountains, oceans, sky, or space, the magnitude of vast places always gives me chills. All that energy swirling around makes me want to jump straight in and be swallowed whole.

Ooh—chills.

From the ocean's depth, and the power of all the hidden life below its surface, I can feel its gravity pull on *Olio d'Oliva* like a great hand. But my gauges are set. I'm a third of the way to my first stop. I had a good start. Let's climb. I want to see what's going on with the Cirrostratus and see if I can outreach the fingers of this great ocean. It is a smooth ascent, I feel the pull of it on my skin.

I want to pull some loops and eight's right now! I'm itching for one. All this space... I've been throwing some loops with *Olio* for the last couple weeks. I know how she likes to do it. and I'm making good time, but do I really want to spend sixty precious seconds on some goofing off? Maybe a barrel roll instead. That way I won't be losing any forward motion. Here we go! Invigorating!

If the A.S.I. recruiters took me on a test flight, they'd already know I'm the best pilot around. I got star reviews from both my flight instructors *and* my test results for aeronautics, physics, mechanics, and astromathematics are all perfect. All my instructors as well as the Dean have recommended me. I have years of flying experience. I even sent them pictures and schematics of the remote-controlled astro-surfer that I designed and built in my last year of *scuola secondaria di secondo grado*. So I'm a few years under the required age limit, so that should be further incentive for them to accept me. I'm ahead of my peers. I'm qualified in every way for an initial evaluation and possible internship. Why is it taking them so long to acknowledge my application?

I bet the only reason they haven't accepted me into the program yet is because I'm a woman. Unfortunately, the administration takes a patriarchal stance on the issue of groundbreaking scientific endeavors. But one of the administrative heads is about to retire. Maybe he'll be replaced by someone more innovative. I don't see why there is still so much hesitation to include women in problem-solving positions. It's clearly a more efficient way to think about problems—from multiple perspectives, duh. There's no doubt women's brains work differently than men's. Why would any committee aimed at furthering human exploration go about doing it with the power of only half the human race?

It must be for political reasons, or financial ones. Most scientists I've known have had the sensibility to approve of having women in the field. Their hearts are in the passion of learning, not what may or may not look like a stable enterprise to investors. Politics and money bastardize everything with real heart, and all because of the bottom line. Anyone with a passion knows you're ready to give all you have and be broke and in debt if that's what your passion calls for. And with a passion like space travel, a piggy bank doesn't go very far. So scientists have to appeal to businessmen for money and that's where the whole house of cards falls down, because a businessman's passion is the bottom line. It doesn't really include the nationalistic or even humanistic drive to add to the legacy of knowledge and space travel. Ironically, it's the comparative and symbolic pairings of passions that compel people to work together, form societies, grow a base of knowledge together... yet where passions differ, a wedge is stuck between our partnerships.

Women are much better equipped to reconcile those differences constructively than men whose impulses so often lead to fighting. Maybe I should try dating a girl. *Merda!* I'm thinking about it again! It won't go away, it makes too much sense. Francesca is one of the smartest *ragazze* I've ever known. Part of the reason I admire her so much.

Well, it was only a matter of time before she popped back into my head. I haven't stopped thinking about her since I left San Benedetto del Tronto for training. I wonder if she's still mad at me. I miss her so much, but I'm terrified to talk to her again. Eventually, she's going to change my mind. I don't know how much longer I can resist a sin this logical.

But dating a girl is an unspeakable breach of the Church's sacred laws, not to mention Mamma's sacred laws. If Mamma ever found out that Francesca and I had kissed, she would turn away from me. But in many ways, my friendship with Francesca *is* a relationship. We've been very close for so many years. We depend on each other. She was there through everything—my crash and surgery three years ago, and when Papa was sick for so long. She helped me study all through secondary. We spent almost every night together during her spring and summer breaks from school. And I know she loves me. And Mamma loves her. Mamma always tells me I should spend more time with Franchi. She thinks she's a good female influence on me. She thinks if I hang out with her enough, I'll start to wear dresses and let my hair down the way she does. The difference is Franchi is beautiful. She has delicate features and skin like glass and smooth, perfect hair. If I put on the same outfit as Franchi and we stood side by side, it would look like a before and after picture of a girl who turned into a troll.

I guess I broke her heart the last time we were together. When she... kissed me that way I... I don't know what I could have done instead. That feeling was such a rush of everything, the way her kiss made my body feel, it was the same feeling I had had when my Cessna went down. The way my stomach fell straight through the bottom of me, and my head so hot and my hands so cold. My heart was beating so hard I could feel it in my throat, panic, couldn't think. My only impulse was for escape. So I pulled away. I left her standing there without even looking back. The worst timing, too—the day before I left for training, I wasn't even able to explain myself in person! It's so awkward just texting all the time and she knows I'm no good at talking on the phone.

I wonder if she's mad at me. Her texts have been so distant and cool lately. Maybe she's just busy, but what if she's getting used to my not being around? It's been almost two months since I left San Benedetto and I miss her so much. But if I see her again, will she try to kiss me again? I hope so. No! I don't hope so. It would be too easy to fall for that devil's trap. Franchi is no devil's trap! She's an angel... mostly. She's so tender and soft. Not like kissing a boy at all. I already know the way her body fits into mine. We've shared a bed so many times. I even know how slowly she likes to kiss. The way she pauses to look in my eyes before she kisses my cheek with every *ciao e arrivederci*. I always liked the way she keeps her lips on my cheek for three full seconds. It makes me calm. And she always smells like sandalwood.

Maybe she has always loved me? I mean, of course she has always loved me, but it's a different sort of love now. How long has she felt that way? Do my feelings match hers? I want another chance to kiss her. I wonder if I tried to kiss her, would she accept it, or push me away the way I did to her? I have to call her when the race is over. If I win, she'll be so happy for me, maybe she'll forget the way I abandoned her. Then she'll hug me again and I could put my nose in her hair, *ma no!* Piccola, you are thinking only of what you want, not what makes sense. You are falling into a day-dream, like flying into a cloud, beautiful and bright with sun, but blinding and so temporary. I wonder when I'll see her again. It's a funny thing—the hole made by her absence feels heavy in me.

Love is only an animal impulse. It must be controlled to evolve the higher order human. Society is not set up to accept the silly girlish desires of your perverted fantasy. But is it only a fantasy when it feels so real? There is no doubt Francesca and I need each other. I haven't stopped thinking about her since it happened. But we can't fall in love. Why can't we just be best friends the way we were before? Can we go back to that place? Maybe that would be best. When I see her, I'll tell her I need her to be my best friend, not my lover. It wouldn't be allowed any other way.

GPS says only a few more miles to the refueling station. I think I can see it beneath the clouds. Good. The challenge of landing on this pinhead will give me something else to rest my mind on! Landings and take-offs are the biggest time factors in a race like this. I have to make a perfect landing the first time. I'm coming in a little too high, decelerating. Concentrate, Piccola.

"Angelo di Dio, mio caro tutore,"

I keep getting closer and closer but the fuel ship doesn't seem to get very much bigger. It really is a pinhead.

"Al quale il suo amore mi ha affidato qui, mai questo giorno,"

Decelerating, keep her balanced. I see the flagger, I see the part of the ocean that I need to land on. It's a runt area.

"Mai questo giorno essere al mio fianco per illuminare,"

Decelerating! I'm coming in too fast. *Caro Dio* protect me—please stop my plane safely on the ocean and not in the ocean!

"Custodisci, reggi e governa. Amen!"

Floatation gear is solid. Decelerating, almost there, you can do it!

"It's too fast!"

Whoa! *Selvaggio!*

Okay, I made it. I made it! Let me swallow my heart again. They are smiling at me and waving, I did it. Don't be too proud of yourself, Little Bird. Everyone has to make that landing. I hope they have food here. I'm starving.

"The Bible shows the way to go to heaven, not the way the heavens go."
—Galileo Galilei

Olio d'Oliva, I'm back! *Caro*, did you miss me? Come on, let's blow this pinhead. We've got a race to win. Giddy up, *Olio!* Systems on, grab me and let's go. I hope all your 2,000 horses are awake and wild because they're gonna sling shoot us off into the ocean and beyond.

"Here we—Whoa! *Dio mio!* What a ride!"

Just like a roller coaster. Well, my senses are peaked now, that's for sure. Every nerve tingles. I'm so awake. I still feel the adrenaline tickling me from the inside. That thrill in my pelvis from rapid acceleration always turns me on. GPS locked onto Oʻahu. Let's go.

Oʻahu—I never thought I would see Hawaiʻi. *Nonno* Uccello told me learning to fly was the best way to see the world. He always said, "If you want to get somewhere, Little Bird, you have to fly there yourself." *Nonno* would be so proud of me now. I bet he never thought I'd be a racer. I probably wouldn't even be a pilot if it weren't for him. He taught me everything, took me under his wing. I love you, *Nonno*. He and Mamma were always bickering about my lessons. Every time I would hear Nonno's voice get gravelly, and he'd start into "*Mamma, Piccola Uccello deve imparare a volare!*" I always knew I was getting a ride in the mail plane, because he always won those arguments.

A fair day, blue sky piled on blue coast. I'd sit in the hard little molded plastic seat and put on the five-point harness. Then he would babble at me, talking about seaplanes and seabirds and sailors and he'd holler out those loud, dissonant *Marina Militare* songs to me while initiating take-off. A little bit of his dusty magic and then the old sea bird would lurch a couple times over the rollers and then lift up, like some big hand came and picked us up off the water. And I couldn't think of anything else but the earsplitting roar.

When I was old enough to start working in the garage, he showed me the underbelly of that old seaplane and gave me my first ratchet set. That man's hands never were still. He was always building something, writing something, painting, mending, and tinkering. "*Mani mai inattivo,*" he would tell me, but he was always working with a smile on his face and a song on his lips. Couldn't sing worth a damn and he didn't care. He sang loud!

"Ha ha! Oh, *Nonno, mi manchi tanto.*"

He had a way of teaching without meaning to. Just by spending time together, I learned how an engine worked and all about aerodynamics. He taught me the basic physics of flight although he never called it that. In my young summers when we'd ramble along the coast in the mail plane, he would give me my lessons in stories. Stories from his life and adventures, although now, thinking back on it, there are some things he never talked about. *Nonna*, of course, we never talked about her. He talked about when he was a young man, flying the mail plane in the middle of national restructuring. But he never really told me anything about the war. We talked mostly about birds, and flying. He taught me how to sort the mail, but I always thought it was a stupid, tedious job. And even though Mamma would swat at him every time with a dish towel, I'm glad he argued with her on my behalf to give me those early lessons. Nonno shaped my life, and this is the shape he gave it… aerodynamic.

I remember a story Mamma once told me about Nonno e Nonna, when they first started dating. He was such a romantic. He would pack a lunch and bring Nonna to the Sibillini Mountains. They'd go flying all day when they were in love. Nonna must have told her that story.

I wonder if Nonna was a woman like Mamma, so pretty and delicate, so soft and quiet. Or, if she was a woman more like Nonno, loud and boisterous, like me. I bet Nonno preferred a woman who could keep up with him. Although he was always so proud of Mamma's fine virtues, he taught me how to appreciate them without idolizing them. He was a man whose attitudes and thoughts were all his own. It is my noble mission to emulate him.

I loved him then because he was always smiling and singing, because he always had some project to show me. But I love him even more now because he always encouraged me to play with the scrap engine and break apart machinery kept in the barn from before the war. He alone was the savior of dirt! Everyone else, even Papa and Gionni, would holler at me to wipe the grease off my face and put on clean pants, but Nonno never made me do that. Mostly, he wanted to make sure I was learning something. And he was ferocious about my being true to myself.

I'll never tell Mamma the things he whispered in my ear after she laid into him about making me into an undesirable girl. She would say, "You're roughening her up. What boy will want burlap instead of cotton?" And Nonno would whisper in my ear, "Cotton fades and tears. When I go up into the clouds," and he'd wink and grip his age-old flight sack, "I only take what won't blow away."

When I get back to San Benedetto, I'm going to pack a lunch and fly Francesca out over the Sibillini Mountains and we'll talk it all through, there, in the clearing where I took her two summers ago after Nonno died. That place has answers. In a clear sky, middle of spring, after the engines have cooled and the propellers are resting, the movement in the breeze has more to say than any other type of silence. God bless Franchi, she knew when to stay quiet and listen to the valley. Sometimes, silence is the best advice.

I need some advice right now. I feel that I'm losing my grip on who I am. Who do I want to be? All these years, I've been so defiant against Mamma, would never stay still in the dresses she put me in, couldn't keep myself from eating and laughing with my mouth open, and I was forever breaking and building things. She wouldn't even be happy with the perfect math and science grades I'd bring home because I refused to take home economics and failed literature. But I wonder if there was a reason for all her efforts in shaping me. She must have known all along that something was wrong with me. She must have seen the sin growing in me the whole time. Maybe that's why she always pushed me to be more delicate and feminine. She was trying to save me from myself and I resisted. Now I am so confused.

Radka is a lesbian. It's amazing how much she looks like Leola whom I worked with at the garage. Brilliant mechanic, anything from a toaster to a Ferrari, Leola could fix it. She had huge hands, and the same haircut as Radka. I remember when I found out Leola was a lesbian. What a burden that secret was! But Leola wasn't crazy. She was brilliant. And Radka's not crazy. She's wonderful. She's happy and she's intelligent. I don't know her very well, but her life doesn't seem sinful or unbalanced. Maybe she's hiding demons. I suppose we all are.

I remember when Leola told me that coming out as a lesbian helped her find her greater self. We only talked about it one time, but I remember a lot about that conversation. I was so unsure of what to say. I felt awkward, but Leola talks about everything as if it were just plain fact. She told me coming out was like throwing up, terrible in the process, but so much better afterwards. I should go by the garage when I get home and see how she's doing. Maybe she can tell me if I'm a lesbian. The thought makes me shudder. It's so wrong. Wrong? Or disallowed? The connection between morals and rules is tentative at best.

I could use a little help finding my greater self. I'm used to these thoughts floating through my head by now. They've been there for so long. It's getting harder to ignore them, but I don't know what to do about them. Every relationship I've had with a man over the past few years has fallen short. But I don't want to quit men. I like men. Falling in love with a man is fun! It's like making a new best friend who can also give me an orgasm. I've always been a boy's girl. Because I act like a boy, I think like them. I don't create the drama and stupid emotional shit and play games like so many girls. I don't need them to take care of me. Boys like it that I'm strong—and I love sex too! If I become a lesbian I would have to give up sex! That must be terrible! No, I guess I can't be a lesbian. Dating a girl would just be a big tease. What more can you do but kiss and make out?

Although, boys give girls oral and I guess girls could give girls oral. And, I guess I know how to make myself cum. Maybe that's what they do? Piccola! This thinking has to stop. Enough already! You are conversing with the devil. Just stop. Please. Maybe Radka could tell me. I can't ask her that! Think of something else, think of something else! Think of something else! It is easier to talk to women about sex than men. Men get too distracted by their bodies to actually put thought into the topic. Women are more able to focus their thoughts and think objectively. Am I thinking objectively? If I forget for a moment about all the mixed bag of nuts that my feelings are, what are really the points of the topic? Papa would tell me to make a pro/con list. That's how he makes decisions.

Pro: women share my perspective. Con: in problem solving, it is better to have multiple perspectives. Pro: women are more able to talk through emotional disagreements. Con: women tend to induce more emotional disagreements. Pro: dating a woman would be new and exciting. I might discover something that helps me to mature like Leola said. Con: if Mamma found out, she would be so hurt and ashamed of me. Pro: I am attracted to women. Con: I am also attracted to men. Pro: lesbianism is progressive, enlightens society to women's rights and choices. Con: The Church is not progressive. I wonder if God were on the A.S.I. board of directors, would he hire female astronauts? Everything I know about The Church suggests not, but God knows my heart. He instilled it with this passion for flight. He gave me the mind and drive to satisfy my passion. Why would he construct a mind and life for me leading up to a clear goal unless he intended me to follow it? But why try to draw comparisons anyway? Space travel is not as unnatural as lesbianism... is it?

Olio d'Oliva, you are my closest confidant now. Only you know the poison in my brain. These thoughts are sick ones, greedy for pleasure. Just because I love someone doesn't mean I should be their partner. And just because I love space doesn't mean I should go there.

Merda! I wish I could take that thought back. It will never be un-thought now and I will forever be guilty for answering questions of passion with logic and ignoring the advice of God. Is this my moment of epiphany? Has God just enlightened me with this inconvenient answer? I can hear Mamma's voice, "He doesn't always say what you want to hear, but you do have to listen." Maybe God has just told me through my own logic that I have been wrong this whole time, all the effort throughout school, all the daydreams and goals. All the fulfillment from learning to fly, and after stubbornly—stupidly—telling my family and friends beyond any doubt that I knew this was the direction of my life, now I have to take it all back. God doesn't want me to be an astronaut. He has given me this problem with women to see through to a different trajectory of thought about what is really most appropriate for my life. And it's not women. And it's not space travel.

"*Cazzo!* What the hell is it then?"

Always when the hardest questions scrape the air, silence is the most cold-hearted. What kind of sad and terrible revelation is this? Isn't God's word supposed to be most definite and have the vibrancy of truth? Aren't revelations supposed to provide a sense of unquestioning purpose and vehement drive? But I don't feel that way at all. My heart feels as cold and unresponsive as these sheet metal wings. If passion and space and Francesca are not my life, what on God's Earth is it then? There's nothing I want more, I guess. God would say it's not about what I want. Is this what it feels like to be called into the service of God?

"This sucks! *Ah! Cosa? Olio*, why are you yelling at me?"

Altitude monitor is off balance. I'm too high! And GPS has me almost 2,000 feet off trajectory. I'm losing focus. Thank you for snapping me back to reality, *Olio*. I'm so glad I have you as a friend now. Let's fix these problems and get back on course. I can't believe Keiko is letting me keep you forever! It's the best gift anyone has ever given me—and she doesn't even really know me! I've heard of this Japanese generosity before. They have a very hospitable culture, but an actual Spitfire to keep! I could hardly believe my ears when she told us. You and I are going to have many, many journeys together. I'll learn everything there is to know about the Spitfire so another mechanic will never lay hands on you. When you feel sick, I will fix everything. I promise. And you, you promise to take me wherever I want to go.

I wonder what Reverend Manetti would say about my little break down just now. I think I know what Papa would say. That is why Mamma always stopped me from talking through these types of discussions with Papa. Papa's not as active in religion as Mamma. They've fought over that so many times. But, which one was trying to protect me from the worse truth? Mamma by telling me God should be my only passion and that all other decisions would fall into place? Or Papa by telling me that passion for greatness and happiness will be looked upon with gladness by God, but not society? That I should fight for the things that make me happy. Why must happiness be such a struggle? If this is enlightenment, I'd rather be dumb. I've never felt so sure that I know nothing. Even as I cling to the integrity and intensity of the goals I've set for myself, they feel as dirty and useless as spent motor oil in my heart.

Well, *merda*. Here I am flying. If I'm not going to become an astronaut then why am I here? I might as well quit the race. Hell, if I decided that all that I am and all that I've worked toward is wrong and against God, then I might as well land my plane right here in the middle of this ocean. Now there's a dark thought.

That thought is the most offensive of all to God. The biggest *vaffanculo* to the creator of the entire world and all things beautiful in it is to refuse to appreciate any of it. Suicide is to take the most glorious and the most immense gift ever given, life and all it implies, and throw it down to the mud, smash and destroy, cut the red ribbons from the package, spit on the love He spent, and drop it into the cesspool of my own blood, dirty with ingratitude.

After Carimen killed herself, Mamma never spoke to that side of the family again. She still won't. One act tainted the family's bond so badly that the blood ties have rotted forever. At least for Mamma. I barely knew Carimen, but I know Mamma's other cousins. They are good people. Was Carimen really so evil? She must have been evil to commit such a deed, but why? Why would anyone? I can certainly understand moments of hopelessness and bleak frustration and purposelessness and loneliness, terrible uncertainty leaking into the corners of thoughts and imaginings. I can feel the fingers of desperation scratch my brain even now. But what possession could move such a thought to deed? The answer can only be the mystery behind the Devil's tongue.

Dio forgive me, I did not really mean to debase my life with such ugly intention to destroy it. But why throw me into such a fit of doubt now? Mamma says all the answers are in God's Word, but the older I get, the more questions I have that are unanswered. If I keep trying to repress the God-given impulses of my heart, am I not suppressing the purity of what God created in me? Do I deign to improve upon God's creation? Of course, people try to improve themselves all the time by trying to become closer to his image. *Non so!* I just don't know. The truth seems so far away, and as mysterious and terrible as the Devil's tongue.

I can't do this anymore. Thinking about this is making me exhausted and sad. I have to concentrate. Check my levels. How is everything going down there *Olio d'Oliva*? Air speed… good, velocity… maintained, pitch and roll… balanced. Gas level…

"Whoa! *Dio mio!*"

Where am I?

"Is that…?"

It is! I almost flew straight past Hawai'i. GPS says O'ahu is impending. You got a little lost for a minute there, Piccola. You have a state of the art GPS in front of your face, but nothing can save you from being lost in your own head. *Olio d'Oliva* is hungry. We made it here right on time. I guess I'm hungry, too. Nothing distracts from the appetite like mental anguish.

At least O'ahu has calm seas and Pearl Harbor is so beautiful. This should be a quick and easy landing.

"We cannot teach people anything; we can only help them discover it within themselves."
—Galileo Galilei

"Alright *Olio*, back at it."

Deep breath, O'ahu was just what I needed. I was getting a little cabin fever on the last jaunt. This race isn't over yet and I could still win, but not with all those heavy thoughts weighing me down. Maybe once I get to *San Francesca*—I mean! San Francisco.

Merda.

Once I get there, maybe I should just… not land. Maybe I should just keep flying. I'll find some small town airstrip and refuel. Then I'll just take off again and fly straight ahead. I'll just fly and fly for the rest of my life. That way I don't have to go home and deal with stupid love problems. I can just love the sky and my plane. Maybe I could finally enact that vision I've had since childhood, ever since my first flight with Nonno in the CANT Z.509, that old slumdog mail ship, I miss it so much! Such memories of great afternoons in that plane, and that airship was the first place I ever got the vision, the one where I just fly on and on forever.

My journey would never have to stop. I would pass over all the city skylines of the world. Pass above every monument, brick wall, and wooden house that humans ever built. I could swoop down low over the fields and plains and forests and lakes and follow the course of rivers until it got too messy with towers and trees and power lines, then I would just pull up and head back into the clouds, my highway in the sky. It could be the most epic road trip in history—road not included. I could spiral longitudinally up to the North Pole and fly straight through the *aurora borealis*. Then, double back and spiral all the way down. The circumference of the globe is only 25,000 miles at the equator. All I need is *Olio d'Oliva* and a few sandwiches, and all she needs is me. We would stop for gas and food and that's the only time I would have to talk to anyone else. The rest would just be my thoughts and me. Maybe if I flew forever, eventually, I could figure some things out.

I remember the story Francesca told me about the millionaire who lived in his personal jet plane and followed the sun continuously so he could live in perpetual daytime. If I flew over the world in the opposite direction of its rotation, then it's like I'm flying at double speed, my velocity plus the velocity of the turning Earth below me. If *Olio d'Oliva* could fly as fast as the Concorde, I could stay in the sun forever. Then again, if I flew high enough at a leisurely pace straight east while the earth rotated east beneath me, it would be like I wasn't moving at all. I could be a satellite. Someday I will be. Someday I'll blast into space. Then love won't be able to bother me. It will be a distant thought, a world away. The sweet analytical relief of thinking rationally is so blissful and relaxing for the mind. Emotions are exhausting. I wish I could just remove myself from life on earth and exchange it for life in the air. I wonder how quickly I would go crazy if I tried that. A few hours a day makes my mind feel relaxed. It's like meditating to stare into the sky ahead of me, always changing in its subtle ways, yet always so much the same. But, I confess, if I only looked at the sky for days and days, I think I would go mad. There's nothing to focus on except the inconstant shifting clouds.

Clouds can be very misleading. They are to pilots what waves must be to sailors. I've come to know their personalities and the ones to beware of, like the cumulous towers, big challengers of the little plane. They rise far up against me on both sides. I have to fly straight into their belly. The only way out is through. There are spirits inside cumulus. I see them pass by my windshield every time I go through. Maybe they're angels. Or maybe they are the souls of Earth's dead. Perhaps the cumulonimbus puffs everyone thinks are so beautiful are actually purgatory, holding the remnants of our souls until Heaven and Hell open up. When it rains, we are drenched with the fallen, on their way down. Just gave myself chills.

Cirrus is my favorite. I like these wisps, like smudges. They remind me of paintbrush strokes, they are so artful. They have such variety of shape that they seem to arrange themselves with disregard for any natural order. Like those over there, crazy snakes zigzagging through the sky. Non-threatening, they don't interfere much with my vision, they are just decoration. When they are bright with sun and the sky is blue, the colors against each other make me so happy. In high wind currents, their motion reflects the wind-blown surface of water. I love the way nature often repeats itself in design. Like how a stretch of cirrocumulus clouds looks just like rows of cotton, or a field of Hydrangeas. And the tops of stratus clouds at dawn echo the leafy heads of woodland trees. The design of nature is so perfect and intelligent. God certainly has an eye for beauty and chaos.

I bet rain clouds never feel guilty for ruining a picnic on a sunny day. They are just themselves, even when it's inconvenient for others. Don't I deserve the same freedom of self as the cloud? But it is cheating logic to anthropomorphize inanimate things and compare their moot imaginary feelings to my own.

Feelings—what a problem they are. That's one frustrating thing about Franchi. She feels so much. We've had so many fights over little comments I made that she took too personally. She could use her energy more effectively if she could resist reacting to her emotions. She needs to spend more time thinking objectively about the situation and making more rational choices instead of speaking as soon as she feels. Mamma does the same thing and it always drives Papa and me *pazzo*. It's not that hard to just remain inactive when there's tension, speak minimally until you've thought about the situation objectively. Too much emotion is why women have a bad rep in serious professions like space exploration and politics. Under high stress, a lot of women succumb to their frustrations and say and do things that are irrational. It's hard to work with someone like that when everything is on the line, so I do understand where a stereotype interferes with real life. That was my problem last time I saw Franchi, too. I reacted to her kiss without thinking. It felt just like falling, scary. I didn't know what to say to her and I just couldn't have her looking at me with her questioning eyes anymore. But if I had planted my feet and been more objective, maybe we could have talked about it together and figured out each other. It's my fault that it's awkward now. I should have trusted her to help me think it through. She is worth the effort it would have taken for me to stand with her and to admit I have no idea where my heart is.

I don't think I want to take what I have with Franchi—our years of trusted friendship—and turn it into something romantic, because if I've learned anything about romance, it's that you can't count on it for shit. People's hearts are so fickle when it comes to romantic love. One day you're in love, the next, you can't stand each other. One fight can finish a relationship you thought was steady. That happened with Michael and me. And it happened with Dominic, too. With Michael, it was his fault. He decided to break our-year-and-a-half relationship for that Roman chick that moved into his building and then she dumped him three weeks later. He should have known better. And luckily, that break-up ended up being the best thing for both of us, even though it took me a couple weeks to realize it. But with Dominic, I have to take most of the blame. I can't explain it. One day everything was fine and then I just woke up realizing I didn't love him, didn't even really care for him, like my heart just changed its mind for no reason. I assessed that relationship for days, trying to figure out why my feelings had changed like that but I still don't really know why. But it's a lie to stay in a relationship I'm not genuine about, so I had to break it off. I feel bad for him but if I don't understand my emotions, I can't fix them, so it's better to just let them go—clear the mind and clear the heart. I know I hurt him, though. I still regret not being able to give him a better explanation of what happened. Just goes to show, even with the best of intentions, and even if both people are honest with each other, it seems inevitable that things fall apart, and usually bitterly. A solid female friendship is much sturdier, less chance of jealousy and destruction. If we change our relationship into a romantic one, I'll have to worry about her breaking up with me and losing everything we have. Maybe I should try a practice run, like date a girl for a while just to see how it feels. Then again, who better to try out something new with than someone I know for sure loves me?

At least gay people help with overpopulation. More people should be conscious of overpopulation anyway. Gay couples take in adopted kids, which is much better for everyone than making more babies. The planet can barely sustain the amount of people we have as it is.

We even had a discussion about this during training, when Ryoichi brought up the Pacific Garbage Patch, which should, come to think of it, be right around here some-where. The thought disgusts me, a huge floating island of people's crap that collects in the ocean and stays there, trapped by water currents. I've always had limited respect for people who liter. It's so shortsighted, selfish, dirty, and disrespectful. But even people who throw their trash in a can are only sending it somewhere they don't have to see it anymore. It still exists, decaying over decades, taking up space, leaving chemicals in the ground.

There's another progressive idea—recycling! I wish everyone knew how important it was. That's one thing I can't stand about my family. They don't recycle. Even after I put the separate container in the kitchen next to the trash, they still don't. Ridiculous! The amount of times I've fought with Gionni about rinsing out his soda cans and putting them in the recycling, you'd think he would get it by now. But he doesn't. Not even Mamma—clean, orderly, precise Mamma, who loves animals and plants. I keep catching her throwing her plastic away. And, Papa's the worst. He gets all those daily papers in the mail, barely looks at them, and then he puts them in the trash. It pisses me off! I've tried to explain to them why it's important, but they don't listen. At least Nonno used to keep a compost heap in his backyard. But I'm pretty sure the family who bought the house after he died got rid of it—fools.

There are so many things my family doesn't understand about me, and about what's important to me. It's like they don't take me seriously. Papa tells me to get a "real" job when I've told him a million times about my applications to A.S.I. "Something steady in the meantime," he says. As if school and flight school aren't enough to keep me busy. They think flying is a hobby to me even though I tell everybody flying is my life. When I win this race, maybe they'll see how serious I am. And when I get home, I'm going to show them all pictures of the Garbage Patch and tell them that's where their plastic is ending up. I wonder what it will take for people to finally realize their own impact on the Earth.

God filled the Earth from the center out to the crust with everything we need to cultivate and grow. The world really is Eden, an endless garden of resources, with healing plants, delicious fruit, and clear water. I guess innovation is one of those ouroboros human qualities, of which we have many—the silly serpent that eats itself. He satisfies his hunger, but to what end? Human ingenuity keeps building and destroying, building and destroying in the process—so shortsighted. It's childish, the impulse to keep going in one direction because it's good now, but with no thought for the future. Why isn't littering a sin?

The Commandments need an overhaul. I see where they're well intentioned to guide morality, but after a certain amount of time, doesn't any piece of advice become outdated? Life was different when Moses was alive. They couldn't even imagine a society like ours, just as I can't imagine a society 2,000 years after this. My guess is, either there won't be one—I want to be off of Earth when it finally explodes—or, they will have evolved in ways that bring us even further from the original Word. And why is it that societies seem to naturally move away from holy advice? Even the most faithful people I know admit that it's hard to keep the faith all the time. I know sin is a challenge God places in our souls to determine the pureness of the heart. I understand that free will is a blessing and a curse. But I wonder, if the love of God is so compelling, why even good people stray? Is it because evil is easier and people are lazy? Is it because evil feels more satisfying than goodness? Is it because human nature is truly closer to a state of evil than to a state of good? Or is it because our unit of measurement for goodness hasn't been updated in 2,000 years and maybe it's possible to still have a pure heart even outside the strict guidelines of the Bible. Are these thoughts blasphemy? My man, Galileo, said, "I do not feel obliged to believe that the same God who has endowed us with sense, reason, and intellect has intended us to forego their use." It's almost as if we're set up to fail. Simply by thinking and wondering, I find myself breaking the rules. And even though I use the Bible as a basis for my moral decisions, I still feel like my life and choices can be made well outside of religion. Exploration—mental, scientific, and worldly—is a pure progression.

Talk about progression. This leg of my journey is closing. I see the refueling ship. My body is aching. So is my mind. I need to break this silence. I am a difficult conversation partner for myself.

"Passion is the genesis of genius." —*Galileo Galiliei*

Salve, Olio. I am back again for you. My new partner and dear friend, let us share a deep breath of fresh air in my cockpit, good food in my body, and something new to think about. It's the last leg of our first journey together. What shall we find in the air and ocean this time? I'm so glad I tried the acupuncture on the refueling ship! I've never been keen on trying it before. Those needles look like something out of a horror movie. I never thought pin-pricks would be something I'd volunteer for, but I feel amazing. Probably what helped more than the needles was talking to Dr. Kaz. What a special person he is, very wise. He suits my vision of an Eastern medicine man, aging gracefully, with calm hands and ancient wisdom. Everything he says leads to non-sectarian spirituality. I can't get it out of my mind, what he told me after he asked me about God. I said, "I can't be frustrated with God because I trust there's a purpose for everything he's sending me, but I do get frustrated with religion for all my unanswered questions. It leaves me so unsatisfied sometimes. Sometimes, when I pray, I feel unheard." It spilled out of my mouth like a mess. I didn't even know I was going to say it until it was said. Then, as I lay there feeling guilty, I realized it was actually true. He told me, "Religion is not for you alone. Religion is for you, along with others. Religion is a common ground where many meet to journey together. It is not where the answers are—the answers are already in you and in your spirit. The answers will be easy to find when you understand spirit. In English, it is called Spirituality. Don't ask God to tell you the answers. When God flows through you, the answers will be found." No one had everever put it that way to me before. It's true, isn't it? Religion is for the masses. It's what people gather around. But the private part of religion feels different. When there's no pomp and circumstance of church tradition or dressing up, or holding hands, when it's just God and I alone together in my mind, it feels different. It feels more potent, more intimate and more spiritual. And it's usually when I ask God a question in silent prayer that I receive a satisfying response, as opposed to asking Reverend Manetti or the Bible. It makes sense. It's logical. The truest answer to satisfy my soul would come from within my soul. I only need to turn on the searchlight of my spirituality inside me, and invite God to speak inside my thoughts and memories. That's when I feel closest to God, when we are alone. Not when I am singing hymns next to *Mamma e Papa*, and certainly not when I'm searching verse after verse for a solution.

"Where God flows through me, the answers will be found." I like that. It kind of takes the pressure off trying to figure out these questions I've been churning over. Dr. Kaz said, "The more you know, the less you understand." That is what it feels like when I try to apply the knowledge of doctrine that I have learned to my questions—the more I think about it, the further I am from understanding it.

There are storm clouds brewing ahead and more clouds blowing my way from the north. Is this a sign? Is it some sort of metaphor? Or is it just unfortunate weather patterns? Deep breath, *Olio,* I've flown through worse storms, although none over the insatiable mouth of an ocean. I'm a good pilot and *Olio* is a remarkable plane. This storm is becoming ugly, but I don't believe it is here to kill me, so the only way out is through. Batten down the hatches, *Olio.* We're going in.

Raindrops like firecrackers on my windshield. I can hear the hail against her body like enemy fire. I'm sorry, *Olio,* my beautiful prize. It can be buffed. To fly through a storm well, you can't bully your way through in a straight line. You have to feel the motion of the air currents and let them guide you without losing control. Use the storm's own force to keep you moving through it. Wind and water have their own rhythm. If we follow the flow of the natural current, we will stay synced with the storm instead of being completely at odds with it.

When I fly, I feel a synchronicity with the sky. I am more certain of everything in a cockpit than in any other place. My cockpit, just big enough for me, with all the tools I need within an arm's length. Once I get the flight sequence started, I don't have to do anything else. I know all the procedures by heart. When I encounter a problem in the air, *Io so,* I know just how to fix it because I *feel* the solution. Planes have become second nature to me. I don't have to think too hard about them any-more. This ease makes me feel freer than anything else in the world.

This storm is beginning to scare me a little bit. It is vicious outside. and it is getting harder to hear myself think with all that howling and rattling. But there is no need for panic because I know what to do. If it's possible to fly through this storm, I know I will. I am a good pilot. It is because I'm not entirely certain it is possible to fly through this storm that I'm afraid. Even the best pilot in the world might be blown down by the fury of nature through no fault of her own. My course is set. If I deviate at all, I could be thrown off course by hundreds of miles, especially with such low visibility. I could easily get lost over this ocean, and I only have enough fuel to make it to America.

America. I've heard so much about it. It sounds like a carnival of dreams and nightmares, a place where anything can happen—the best and the worst. It is a grin that bares sharp teeth, a country of the richest, happiest, freest idiots in the world. Do they even deserve what they have? Do I? Or, has everything that I thought I earned, simply been given to me?

Well, I suppose the only thing I've truly earned is what I've made of myself. I have earned every bit of my character. And I like who I am when I'm flying, and I like who I am when I'm fixing things. And I love myself most when I'm with Francesca.

There it is. The answer God has left for me. What I have most to be proud of in the world is my integrity as a person, my trustworthiness as a friend, and my natural ability to fly. It is good to be who I am, a well-oiled machine. I can fix myself continuously and make that my truest mission, because that's what I have control over. And because my mind is the temple that I offer up to God, I will make it the most splendid place it can be.

I feel invincible. The cracking hail and furious rain are shaking me up like a toy. This gray monster could easily swallow up this plane. I could crash out here and die before anyone knew what had happened. But I'm not worried about dying. I know I won't, especially not right now, after rethinking all these answers, I am ripe with possibility, I've never felt more alive. I will ride out this storm like a roller coaster. I am on a trapeze without a net, inside the gigantic maw of this endless ocean, which is hungry enough to swallow me whole. I dance on the edge of mortality, but finally I am sure-footed. I cannot slip because I dance with God in me.

I was meant to fly. I was meant to find this storm in the sky, and for it to shake and destroy all the order in my thoughts. But the maelstrom has left me clean. I am crying. I am crying as furiously as this storm. I am finally one with the sky as I've tried to be all along—such vastness, such open freedom, the everywhere of the wind, and the life-giving breath of air. Of course, it is in me, I am a pilot. I move through it as it moves the same through me. Endless as it is, it is all and nothing. The sky is a wonder because of its emptiness and its fullness. Sweat dampens my clothes. Tears pool beneath my chin. My heart aches and I am ravaged by the violent uncertainty of all the things in life that fall down on top of me. The rain and hail of questions, pressure—Mamma, Reverend Manetti, A.S.I., school, love, and loss, doesn't matter. I am Piccola Uccello, "Little Bird." I have always been a child of the air. When everything is falling down, I fly. Up and up. The sky will grab and hold me, like God. I only needed to be certain. And now I am. My revelation has been hiding behind these storm clouds the whole time.

"Dio! Dio mio. Tutta la bellezza!"

Just look, Little Bird. Look what the world has left for you, a gift beyond all imagining! The storm has spit you out into Heaven. Never has blue been this blue. Never have the clouds looked so golden. This air is smooth as silk—do you feel that, *Olio,* this sky, like candy, so kind, so welcoming. The sun has dried my tears and all the violence and black-green tumult is suddenly behind us. We are picking up speed again. I can practically feel the storm opening my heart and freeing my spirit. This must be it—the Cloud Nine Nonno always told me about, a childhood story brought to life! Flying has always been my greatest blessing. *Olio d'Oliva,* my closest friend and confidant, you promise to take me anywhere in the world? I think I'm ready to go home. I have something to tell Francesca, and something to give her.

But, one last stop before all that! I see San Francisco Bay waving me in. I will have to remember to bow deeply to Keiko for inviting me on this journey! I wonder if I won the race.

ARIANNE MAYA PARKER

OCHRE 15

Looking down and outward over the light-washed wing of my plane, my eyes drink in an endless expanse of blue water and sky, a canvas of cerulean deepening first to ultra-marine, then to indigo where the surface of the ocean appears deepest and darkest. Whitecaps fleck the water, just barely visible from this altitude. Tails of white cirrus clouds streak the horizon like wisps of cream, creating shadows that hover and slip across the water's surface, belying the depths below.

This is what I love about flying—the sky in the afternoon expanding, an infinite page of light and dark. Soaring high above it all, strapped into my snug cockpit, the day is filled with promise, and a heady sense of limitless potential.

My "family" sits mounted atop the cockpit dashboard directly in my sight line, keeping me company. Most pilots have a good luck charm, a small mascot to keep them steady and on course, but I have my own little pantheon: Durga, goddess mother of the Hindus; Totoro, one of my kids' favorite Miyazaki movie characters; and a tiny white-painted clay bird, no more than an inch tall, that I call No Name, perched on a miniature carved hillock of grass, twisting cautiously around to look ahead to the front of the plane.

You might think that it's powerful Durga who helps me the most—she is the Hindu mother goddess, responsible for the victory of good over evil, and I am partly of Indian descent, so she is important to me. Totoro is my nature-spirit, and he reminds me of my kids, Max and Mia. But it's No Name who is my favorite. He reminds me not to judge a book by its cover, things are not always as they appear on the surface, perhaps anyone, no matter how small, can take hold of their fear and fly.

Maybe it was a good start today. I am happy, really, to be last in line in this proces-sion of Amazons. As always while flying, the conscious half of my mind feels perfectly clear. I know I'm here simply to finish this race, not win it, preferably all in one piece. I have the route memorized and have rehearsed in my head for every emergency and contingency I can think of, though Keiko seems to have thought of everything down to the smallest detail. I hope I have no cause for worry.

But the part of my mind that is not so clear, my emotional state, my unconscious, that part of me remains a blur. I'm amazed just to be included in such a *macha* group of women, and maybe a little intimidated. Keiko must have had a reason for selecting me. I've turned the issue over and over in my mind, and still can't figure out why she included me, other than maybe my mixed ethnicity had something to do with it. My birth mother was Indian, reportedly from a high-caste family, from Hyderabad, and my birth father, a first-generation immigrant to the U.S. from Hungary.

But in such an exotic, internationally mixed group of accomplished women, that in and of itself couldn't be reason enough to pick a housewife from the Pacific Northwest to compete in this race. There is nothing about me or my quiet suburban lifestyle that seems even remotely akin to the lives of the rest of the pilots in this group. I've got two kids, a husband, house and dog, along with two pet birds named Niko and Charlie. I only started flying again three months ago after years away from the tarmac. What was Keiko thinking? I am grateful to be up here, if a bit bemused as well.

Sometimes I think I've been a chameleon all my life, blending my color to match my surroundings. I've always done what was required of me out of an innate sense of duty and maybe a need for praise and recognition. Immature of me, maybe, but who hasn't longed for a pat on the back? Still, all my life, I feel as though I have required validation from the outside, like the moon requiring light from the sun to allow it to shine. That's not what I want to be. It's as if I feel the need to apologize for existing. Somehow my own light isn't good enough. How wimpy is that?

I cut that thought short by making a quick check of the plane console. Altitude… check, winds… check, everything A-okay. And then I am again engulfed by my uncertain thoughts, surrounded by infinite blue. I turn the music in my headset up a notch and try my best not to think too much.

Time is strangely, alternately expanded and compressed here in the cockpit of my Spitfire. My brain humming, U2 melodies pouring via my ear canals directly into my head, mere minutes of sky and sea turn into hours, and suddenly time seems to sputter and stop at the point of my first refueling landing. All goes according to plan. And thanks to my uncle's floatplane training for the umpteenth millionth time, my landing is pretty much painless.

Dr. Kaz is there, my favorite part of the refueling ritual. I could never admit this to Matt, but I find his compassionate eyes beautiful. The directness of his gaze is disconcerting. He never seems to miss a beat. As usual, I stuff my emotions down into their own compartment deep below. He seems to sense my discomfort, as well as everything else I am feeling, all the more disquieting for me.

"Flight going well so far?" he inquires kindly. "How are you holding up, Ari?"

"Fine, just fine," I reply. "Everything is hunky-dory so far." Discomfort be damned, I grasp about for words, wanting to be honest with him. "Though I've got to tell you it's comforting to see you all the way out here. I've flown floatplanes for decades now but never this far, out in the middle of nowhere like this."

"Well, it certainly can be unnerving. Up on the table with you," he says softly. He pokes and prods, gently and deftly. I feel expanded, refreshed, taller, and somehow lighter when he is through with me. My eyes seem to open a bit wider, and I know I am sitting up slightly straighter, thanks to his ministrations.

"Don't worry, Ari," he continues after treating me for almost fifteen minutes in nearly complete silence. "We've got you covered. Keiko…"

"I know," I interrupt. "Keiko clearly has thought of everything. And I trust her, to a point. It's just that… I don't know…" I fumble, not knowing what it was I meant to say to him, my thoughts and feelings as usual a jumble, feeling slightly embarrassed. "To tell you the truth, I just don't know what I'm really doing here. Other than to finish, I suppose." I glance up into his face nervously then just as quickly catch myself, hating my lack of self-confidence, and look away.

He considers this for a moment before speaking. "Being alone in the cockpit has a way of bringing you back to yourself," he continues. "For better or worse, you're alone with your thoughts way up high in the sky, and things can get intense." He paused. "Just make sure you're open. Open for anything. Don't fret. You'll be ready."

He leads me out of the small, bare treatment room, his hand resting gently on my shoulder. I hesitate briefly before turning about to give him a quick, lopsided hug. For just a split second I manage to look into his kind eyes before jumping back up into my plane and latching myself in with as much optimism as I can muster. I wave to his small, disappearing figure as I take control of the throttle, automatically switching back into pilot mode as my mind focuses on getting the Spitfire back up into the sky.

After several bumpy minutes I am above 20,000 feet again, back into the blue, soaring into what looks like some less than perfect weather. "Here goes," I think, and plow straight ahead, U2 tunes blaring, my thoughts still muddled. I decide to let them unravel. Just set them free and see where they lead me. What do I have to lose?

First, I think of my father and his predicament. Though rarely talked about in my family, I was adopted at the age of eight months. My birth father was an educated man from Hungary, about five feet nine and-a-half inches, a Catholic, with auburn hair. He came to Seattle in order to become a doctor. To this day, he doesn't know that I exist. Whatever the reason, my birth mother chose not to tell him. That is where the known facts surrounding him end and my own personal fiction begins.

Once in his residency at the University of Washington, one misty Seattle morning he spied a beautiful Indian grad student working in the lab upstairs from his shared office. Her hair was long, dark and glossy, her eyelashes thick, her skin golden. She was a member of a high-caste Brahman family from Hyderabad, studying at the UW for the length of her two-year fellowship. Their eyes met on the staircase when he rushed up to his office early one morning.

These two souls fell instantly in love. And kissed…

Two hundred and seventy-seven days after the culmination of that love, I was born. My given name at birth was Baby Girl Stevens. (Not *Gupra*, *Chama*, or *Chopra*: Stevens, another mystery.) I was small for a full-term baby, a mere six pounds. I refused to take normal infant formula. I suppose I was longing for time at my mother's breast, like any newborn, only my mother's breast was not permitted to be there. She had left the scene, *exit stage left*. It wasn't until the nurses tried a meat-based formula that I finally started eating, and everyone breathed a sigh of relief.

Two hundred and forty-two days after my birth, I was legally adopted by a young, well-meaning Jewish couple who were just getting over the sadness of a stillborn child, their first. They were unsure of whether they would ever be able to have children. I guess I conveniently filled in that gap for them. It was kind of like getting a new puppy after the death of a beloved pet. They were careful to tell me how I was special because I was "chosen," and for the most part, I have always believed them.

They re-named me Arianne, after the first initial of my paternal grandfather, Aaron. And they gave me my middle name, Maya, in a nod to my Indian mother. A small nod, but a nod nonetheless.

In spite of the odds, my mother did manage two more births by C-section, resulting in my sister and brother, Sarah and Michael. I was born relatively light-skinned, so I blend in pretty well with my mom's dark, olive-skinned features, while my sister and brother took after my dad, fair and lanky. My Jewish siblings were completely different from me both physically and emotionally. I grew up feeling like a square peg pushed into a round hole, needing to make myself conform in order to feel loved and have a sense of belonging.

The small, local hospital of my birth, once situated downtown near South Lake Union, no longer exists. It was bulldozed when I was in my late teens. An office building stands there now—a vaguely contemporary structure of glass, steel, and concrete, completely generic in shape, form, and purpose—a "commercial space for lease" sign perennially planted in front, which, come to think of it, is a pretty good metaphor for how I feel much of the time.

When I am flying, I have a set purpose and goal. Any lack of a sense of cosmic purpose that plagues me in other areas of my life is replaced by simple mechanical certainty, and that enables my mind, ironically enough, to roam free. Though it has been a long time since I've flown regularly, my body and spirit seem to settle right back into the ways of a pilot—the long hours spent sitting in a cramped cockpit, alone, the icy winds above a certain altitude, the stiff muscles, and forced attention to technical detail. All of it comes back to me surprisingly quickly.

Even at the height of my flying days, I never felt like I was all that good at it. Just the prospect of having to talk to air traffic control scared the living daylights out of me. I practiced the military alphabet by posting it on my bathroom mirror, and rehearsed air traffic control lingo incessantly in front of my uncle and any other acquaintance unfortunate enough to cross my path. I made my brother (he was more willing than my stuck-up, argumentative sister) take the part of the tower, reading out what ATC would say, and then I would answer appropriately.

"Cessna seven seven bravo runway two-six clear to land," Mike recited, to which I would reply, "Runway two-six clear to land, seven seven bravo," and so on, until I had lost the better part of my monthly allowance to Mike, whose patience would nonetheless run thin after a while.

"I don't know why you bother with this stuff, Ari," my brother would say. "Why don't you try mountain biking with me sometime? It's far out!"

I was bothered because I *had* to fly and I was deathly afraid the guys in the tower would laugh at me.

"One thing's for absolute certain, Ari," shouted my uncle over the din of his float-plane's engine on one of our summer afternoons up in the air. "ATF has no time *whatsoever* for shrinking violets. They don't want to waste a precious second repeating anything, *anything*."

Got it, no repetition, righty-o, Uncle Art.

Despite my paranoia, I enjoyed flying more than just about anything. It felt like a drug, the most extreme endorphin rush, better than training on my bike, better than any drugs I tried in college, even better than dancing. True, when I heard about this race through an old aviation friend, I had to get my act into gear and get myself down to Boeing Field again. The kids are old enough now to stay on their own for an afternoon here and there. Matt was supportive, at least on the surface. His parents agreed to come out for an extended visit from Spokane.

So Max, sixteen, and Mia seventeen, are at home spending time with their grandparents and their dad. Not such a bad thing at all, really. But now that I am here relishing it, yes, but still, I wonder what's next. What the heck am I really doing here?

My pragmatic side goes a little crazy with skepticism thinking over Keiko's entire proposition. Keiko is awarding each of us our plane, an incredibly generous gift, especially considering the lavish generosity of this entire project, from start to finish. Can Matt and I even afford to take care of this plane from here on out? How much will it cost to house it and keep it properly tuned up? My mind just goes into overload and shuts down.

Automatically, I turn to check the cockpit controls, just as my uncle showed me, annoyed somewhat with the many computerized features on the refurbished Spitfire console. It's all digitized compared to my uncle's DHC-2 Beaver. I loved that plane, supposedly one of Harrison Ford's favorite planes out of his private aircraft fleet, a vintage 1960s model, updated locally by Kenmore Air to have a few extra bells and whistles, but nothing like what Mitsubishi money has done with these Spitfires!

Various signals, lights, bleeps go off at regular intervals, reminding me to check altitude and winds aloft.

I scowl, irritated, but am also grateful for all of Christine's technical advice back in Tokyo during our weeks in training. And I smile again quickly enough. I am here, now, in my plane, in complete control of my destiny, traveling from point A to point B. It is the loveliest feeling. A feeling I almost never have on land.

Throughout my life, and I am no longer young, a forty-something who will turn fifty soon enough, more often than not I have felt stuck, mashed somewhere in the middle, neither Indian enough nor European enough to feel a cultural pull one way or the other. For the most part, my parents were faithful left-wing liberals, bringing us up to appreciate all different faiths, colors, and religions. I never lacked for attention, although I rarely felt the least bit understood either. I stood apart, utterly unlike my siblings, Mike and Sarah, who always seemed to feel secure, understood by my parents and entitled to whatever was given them. I was day-dreamy and hesitant, always doubtful of myself, fascinated by dreams and the subconscious. I made up fantasy friends and characters, spinning stories about them and drawing their pictures in colored pencil in my sketchbooks.

Matt is kind enough to call me his swan. He says I am a swan in the midst of a family of ugly ducklings, and that it is a shame I just don't seem to get the fact that I am truly who I am in my heart.

To which I reply, hogwash. Isn't there a whole lineage of kids who convince themselves that they are really the progeny of parents other than their own? Sitcoms are stuffed full of characters like that. I don't see the point of worrying about it. If my birth mother or father wanted to find me, they could and would. But they don't seem to want to find me, so I continue onward from that point.

My paralyzing timidity as a kid drove my robotically practical parents to order up a visit with Uncle Arthur and Aunt Bea the summer I turned thirteen. "It will be good for you, Ari," said my mother in her bossy manner. "You're way too sensitive. No one can tell you anything." Meaning she felt I didn't take her criticism well. Silently rolling my eyes behind my mother's back, I stubbornly stuck my chin out and went anyway, completely unaware of how life changing this event would be.

From then on, summers were my salvation, my ticket away from the tensions at home. For years, every July and August I joined my uncle and aunt at their home in Everett, making the bumpy drive in my uncle's pickup down to the airfield every sunny afternoon he could get away.

"Ari, let's go!" he'd bellow as I scrambled to grab sneakers and a jacket. Art let me ride in the open bed of his dusty white Bronco, bouncing along the roads leading south to Boeing Field. On less sunny days I would sit next to him in the cab, listening to him reminisce. "One day years ago," he once recalled, "your aunt and I headed out over the pass to Spokane just to see the falls. No other reason." He laughed. "Crazy Palouse crop dusters had the nerve to call themselves pilots, they were crazy, yes sirree." He chuckled again. "They'd do wild things, loop-de-loops and sudden death vertical drops from fifteen thousand feet. Always assumed they were high on some of the pesticides they used to dust the crops. So one day Bea and I went out, same as usual. I left her in the middle of a grassy field with our picnic while I took care of some business at the airstrip. Next thing she knew, she looked up and there it was, a giant heart painted across the sky followed by, 'Bea will you marry me?' spelled out in white smoke. I paid one of those loony crop dusters to go up with me and write it out. And that was that, your aunt and I've been together ever since."

My uncle and I spent our afternoons soaring across the Sound in his little floatplane, swooping down to catch close-up views of orca pods leaping through the glittering water, eagles and great blue herons fishing for their lunch, flying low in the sky above the lakes and sloughs. It didn't take much to be in love with flying over our green-carpeted, wet water world, especially when the soggy Seattle cloud cover parted for those few treasured weeks and every wet surface glimmered in the sunlight.

We didn't talk much since the engines were far too loud for anything but cursory conversation. But wordlessly, Uncle Art and I shared so much on those afternoons—the magic of being aloft, and the sense of freedom it granted us. He and his pilot friends were a motley bunch, alike in no single trait other than their love of flying. I sat and had coffee and eggs with them at the diner next to the airfield on weekend mornings. They talked and I listened, absorbing all that I could, quietly determined to know everything I needed to know to become a pilot. I found that the less I talked, the more I listened. The more I listened, the more I learned. Not once was I put down for being dreamy and hesitant. Little by little, I lost some of my self-loathing and became surer of myself. In the sky, my self-consciousness peeled away like the skin of a tangerine and my mind opened up, segment by segment. For the first time in my controlled, highly regulated life, I truly felt limitless, weightless, my spirit full. I finally became comfortable in my own skin, at least while suspended in the air.

"Ari, my dear," Art once told me, "always remember this…" He paused for effect, his fork magically suspended in that moment in time, hovering over his plate of hash browns and sunny-side-up eggs. "You can't judge a book by its cover." My face sank slightly, deflated. He continued, his normally booming voice brought down to almost a whisper. "You are not like them," he said, gesturing vaguely in the direction of the rest of the restaurant. "You may not realize this yet, but you are your own woman, unique from the rest. You don't have to pretend to be like them. I want you to remember that."

I thought about that long and hard afterward. But that was a tough nut for me to crack. In fact, I don't think I've quite cracked it still. Maybe that's why I am here, flying this crazy retrofitted floatplane in the first place.

Once I made the transition from high school to college, any remaining insecurities seemed to matter little to everyone else. I found the anonymity of being a little fish in a big school refreshing. I learned to play up my mixed heritage occasionally by streaking my hair blonde and ignoring any sense of modesty my sensible mother had tried to instill in me, going to clubs and dressing in high heels when I felt especially like flouting my family's unspoken yet strict rules.

I met Matt on a blind date arranged by friends. For our third date, I took him up in my uncle's floatplane and showed him the San Juans. Matt followed my directions to the letter, strapping himself in behind me, obedient as a Chihuahua, and equally as terrified of heights as those dogs are. It was midsummer, when the light in the Northwest lasts and lasts. By nine p.m. we were still soaring high above Orcas Island when I finally turned the plane around and headed south for home. Back on the ground, Matt was exhilarated but shaky. He swore he'd never go up in a floatplane again. And he hasn't. But somehow I grew to love him anyway.

We married straight after we both graduated UW. Within a year, I applied to grad schools and was offered a spot in the creative writing program at Yale. Matt and I talked about it, Matt even hastily applied to Yale himself, in applied engineering, but didn't get in, and I couldn't see how to make our relationship work long distance. I felt like a master's degree in creative writing might not do me much good anyway, who really needed it? So I turned Yale's enrollment offer down, thinking there would always be other chances to prove myself. Matt found a job with a downtown Seattle biogenetics firm and I found work as a technical writer at Microsoft and ultimately became a pretty good computer whiz. We settled down into a comfortable routine, with well-cushioned corporate salaries, health benefits and the amenities of suburbia.

The summer days of flying with my uncle became less and less frequent, and he grew older and older, until those days stopped altogether before I even had time to become aware of the fact. Several years ago, Art passed away, and I felt a small part of myself wither, even as I continued looking busy and successful to everyone around me.

O'ahu. A close call on landing, my visibility limited by cloud cover moving in rapidly. It looks like a storm is ahead. But I am intact! I had Habib beam me with some purple light. I first learned about Chromotherapy in Tokyo, during our late-night post-training sessions when we would sit up half the night and just talk about whatever was on our minds. I like Habib. He is certainly unusual, such a combination of opposites. Hamidah is a cipher to me. She is all too quiet and calm, at least on the surface. I'm not sure of her authenticity. I thought the whole Chromotherapy thing might just be a sham, but was willing to give it a try. Maybe it's my imagination, but I feel light, expanded, relaxed. I wanted to follow it up with a full round of qigong, but didn't dare do more than a few minutes' worth for fear of making the slowest time of any of my fellow Amazons. I imagine them in a row, breastplates and helmets gleaming. Or maybe they are warriors of the forest, in leather gauntlets, armor woven from tree bark.

My body feels re-harmonized, loose, light, and ready, perhaps ready enough anyway, to climb into the cockpit again. Two legs left on the journey, the refueling stop beyond O'ahu, and San Francisco beyond that. Something tickles at the back of my mind, like an itch that needs to be scratched. But like any good pilot, I put that feeling away in its own compartment and concentrate on the leg of the journey ahead. Word has it the weather is not cooperating, but I'm used to storms, I tell myself. They are one of many things the Pacific Northwest is excellent at providing, along with coffee and planked salmon. And landing on water is second nature to me, having landed countless times in my uncle's floatplane on Lake Sammamish, Lake Union, and Lake Washington, under all kinds of conditions.

Eventually, Matt and I decided to have a child. I had never been more than marginally interested in having children, but curious about the actual biological process of child-birth and what it would feel like to have a life welling up inside of me over a period of nine months. I wasn't disappointed by the experience. Pregnancy really was an amazing, albeit an out-of-body, and at times alien, experience.

My first pregnancy miscarried. My disappointed father, so eager to be a grandparent, took me shopping the afternoon following my D&C to buy me a pair of pajamas at his favorite department store. He meant it kindly, but it felt like being awarded a kind of consolation prize. I still have the unworn pajamas in a dresser drawer. Of course I couldn't tell him the truth. I was secretly relieved.

Barely twelve months after my initial miscarriage, there was Mia, born on Christmas day. Matt and I, in our complete parenting naïveté, questioned whether or not doctors would really work on Christmas morning. My water broke at 7 a.m. exactly, and soon enough, there she was, my terrifyingly unpredictable Christmas present, complete with tiny red and green pointed elf-hat, hand-knit by some thoughtful hospital volunteer. Would she cry or would she coo with delight? Would she be a calm baby, or make us howl with frustration and lack of sleep? Would l have enough breast milk for her? And on and on.... Max followed her seventeen months later. Because our children came so close together, we were awash in diapers, changing tables, car seats, bouncy chairs and strollers for several years in a row without a break. That meant exhaustion on my part. My body, my libido, my imagination, all wilted like so much spinach salad set out on the table on a hot afternoon. Any thought of a creative life for me disappeared, any professional designs related to my graduate studies went down the kitchen sink along with quantities of pumped breast milk, applesauce, and spoiled baby food.

I took up Tai Chi Chuan again. I used Tai Chi to ward off my fear—fear of being empty inside, of realizing I hadn't yet fulfilled my creative desires. I became a workshop junkie, juggling Tai Chi and qigong studies with my kids' lives. And I was happy enough, at least for a while, but creatively frustrated. I didn't have Uncle Art anymore to get me back into the sky. At some point, I finally figured that I'd have to do it myself.

I got back to the airfield little by little, once a month to start. Each time made me feel deliciously guilty, like I was stealing a treasure from my family. Some women spend their down time in spas, I thought, and here I am, in the canteen at Boeing airfield with a bunch of air jocks, breathing in the diesel fumes, and feeling ecstatically happy to be there!

I had an hour to kill waiting out the early morning cloud cover, so I took a stool at the counter and read someone's discarded copy of the Times. Pilots surrounded me, chatting of this and that. But my body froze at the mention of "a race." I glanced over from my cup of coffee and asked them exactly what they were talking about. The moment I heard those guys out, I just knew this was my chance to do something, to reignite? Set the world on fire? I'm just not sure what I'm really doing here, now, at this moment in time, suspended over the infinite blue ocean and mulling over my past. But, I knew without question I had to do this. Uncertain and hesitant Arianne, but absolutely sure of myself. Or at least I was...

So here I am again, back to myself, like an echo.

A random thought keeps tickling at the back of my brain. Why on earth did I make that comment at the evening gathering during one of our late-night talks? I just blurted it out, the bit about women being the key to the future of the world. Do I truly believe that?

Women, motherhood, an issue I still fight with. I lost several friends after leaving the corporate comfort of Microsoft. The thing about having people write you off is that there is no heroic scene where you get to defend yourself and your ideals. There is just a gradual quiet coming at you from all directions. Several women wouldn't return my emails. One acquaintance apparently forgot who she was talking to when she commented on how "I would just get so bored doing nothing but taking care of Sofia. I don't know how these women do it. How do they keep their brains engaged in the real world?" I murmured agreement, feeling too uncertain about myself to either argue or point out my position in all of this. Of course I should have. My hesitancy makes me into such a coward. Maybe I'm only realizing that now.

Things seem momentarily fuzzy. Is it me, or is it the sky? Sky full of angled light, the weather clouding up, birds in the distance. At home I love birds, but out here they are a nuisance, and should be avoided. The sun is getting lower in the sky. Darn. My brain feels like a chalkboard that has been erased and rewritten on too many times.

What was it I was trying to accomplish at this height? What was it that was lacking? Oh, right, altimeter needs attention and with the cold setting in up this high, I must concentrate fully on the plane, but still...

I realize with a dull thud in my stomach that I am lost. I feel as though I've forgotten my name. My children and my husband know me, but for the rest of the world, I don't exist. I am nobody, with a heart and soul that has been chiseled away until I don't know what's left. Worst of all, I am completely numb. I recognize my good fortune and appreciate my home, family and possessions. But I've been hollowed out, rotted from the inside as if by a fungus. My soul is weeping, weeping and I don't know how to console it.

I am lost, even though I can pinpoint with scientific accuracy my exact coordinates and position in the sky. Utterly and completely at sea within myself and surrounded by infinite blue.

I am lost within and have no idea where to begin again, or even if beginning again is required.

I cut the music off from my headset and allow myself to cry. It is surprisingly easy to sob and fly simultaneously, a thought that makes me smile wanly through my tears. I cry for all the lost time—the mornings spent driving my kids to school, or the afternoons spent driving to and from daycare, play dates, dentists, or teacher meetings, when I could have been writing or pursuing some kind of meaningful career other than computer technology. I squirm with self-loathing, speechless and so entirely full of rage I want to scream.

So what the heck? I'm in a cockpit, it's not as if anyone can hear me. I scream loudly, self-consciously at first, gaining volume and power as I curse, then letting go and pounding my fists against the dashboard, close to little No Name and the Pantheon. It doesn't last long, but it feels good. When I am through, it is quiet, save for the endless droning engine and the wind.

Suddenly I freeze, strapped inside the little cockpit, listening intently. My entire psyche feels poised as if at the edge of a precipice—my ears sense rather than hear a change in sound. There is as always the ceaseless, roaring whir of the Spitfire's propeller, the constant air current rushing against the little plane as it hurtles through space more than 20,000 feet above sea level. But there is another layer of sound—I can just hear it, a frequency, almost like bells. Chimes, wind chimes, maybe? Am I nuts? I listen harder, focusing as acutely as I can. I am sure I hear the sound of chimes in the wind, as if brushed by an invisible arm. Gradually, the sound increases until it fills my eardrums in a sonic wave. Intuitively, I take the plane up and down ever so slightly, trying to tune in to the frequency of the sound with the altitude of the plane.

When the plane hits 23,456 feet exactly, the sound intensifies. Colors around me brighten. Just outside, storm clouds blow about, the wind currents rip around the plane. As I turn my head, tiny rainbows erupt from my peripheral vision. The engine suddenly goes silent, causing my heart to complete a 360-degree somersault within my chest. Without warning, as if from outside the plane, someone has pulled a giant cord. There is nothing but undulating rainbows and silence, clear and complete.

I should be terrified but I'm calm, as if some part of me had been waiting for this to happen, the whiteness of the light, the sacred silence. Time slows and the wind around me makes not a sound, as the late sunlight refracts into rainbows and prisms of light.

Looking out over the wing of the plane to the northeast, I see a grey smudge in the sky, rapidly moving toward me. What on earth? Gradually the dark mass comes into focus, and I realize with a start it is birds, a vast flock of them, hundreds of winged creatures. Stranger still is that they are not of consistent size and shape This is not a typical flock of birds. There are large ones and small ones, bent-necked herons and white-headed eagles, sparrows and finches and gulls and geese and maybe a crane or two, more species than I know how to label and count.

Fallout! Yes, of course, caused by the storm. Migrating birds suddenly confronted with storms over large bodies of water are forced to descend and seek the first land available!

They come closer toward my flight path and I have no idea what to do or how to avoid colliding with them. I am panic stricken—it looks like they are headed straight for the Spitfire.

Before I can maneuver to avoid them, they organize by size and form a tight ring around my plane, leaving just a few feet of space between them and the plane. Making up the inner ring are the smallest birds, the starlings, finches, and sparrows. Concentric rings expand outward. Next are the medium-sized birds—gulls, hawks of various kinds, geese, and ducks. In the outermost ring are the kingly birds of sky and sea—albatrosses, eagles, cranes, and even a great snowy owl and a pair of great blue herons. They are held in perfect formation as if by an invisible force.

The birds are clearly in control of my plane's trajectory. Far, far below the plane appears a patchy texture on the surface of the dark sea. The plane, controlled by its full bird escort, slowly circles downward toward it. As we get closer I can make out piles of trash, a multicolor striped lawn chair splayed open at a strange angle, a limp basketball, and pile after pile of floating white plastic bags. Oh, I thought, they want to show this to me. This is of concern to them. But what am I supposed to do about it?

Then, just ahead of the plane and its ring of birds, maybe 500 yards southeast above the horizon line, appears a wondrous sight that makes my jaw drop—a massive vertical hole punched through the clouds, lit by the setting sun in front and looking through to a framed backdrop of indigo night sky scattered with diamonds of starlight. I glimpse the constellation of the Seven Sisters outlined by the undulating frame, shimmering and winking. Wisps of cloud edging the giant hole circle in slow motion, majestically rotating like the arms of an upright spiral galaxy. I stare, breathless, speechless with amazement as I fly my tiny plane, encircled by birds, directly into what can only be a magical portal.

I blink. Two, three, four blinks.

Late afternoon sunbeams softly light up the insides of my eyelids to a reddish glow. Slowly, I open my eyes. I seem to be inside a tree house, within a giant kitchen. Cupboards line the walls all around me, carved with intricate woodwork patterns. Mounted on the wall in front of me directly at eye level is a *hamsa*, a hand palm carved of wood, meant to ward off evil spirits. To my right, a huge hearth burns with glowing embers. Birds of every shape and size are chiselled into the slabs of stone surrounding it. To my left, the wall is covered with masks of all different types. They seem to be made of every imaginable material—wood, clay, paper mâché, ceramic, and even plastic. I recognize styles from all around the globe such as round sun masks from the American Southwest, a horned devil from México, various faces from Africa, Bali, Polynesia, even from the *commedia dell'arte* of Italy. One of the African masks looks at me with long, slanting eyes as I stare at it, its face narrow and pointed. "Nice day to fly," it says, its full lips barely moving.

In response I just sit there, wide-eyed and mouth agape, staring at the talking face while feeling strangely weightless. Words refuse to form on my surprised lips. Blinking again I look down at my feet and sure enough, they aren't quite touching the ground but hover an inch or two above it.

I look up and see a woman looking my way, a mixture of mild concern and amusement plays across her face. She appears to be middle-aged, dressed in green and grey, the top section of her thick auburn hair tied back in a thick ponytail held with double hairbands, the remainder of it flowing down around her shoulders. Emblazoned in charcoal and scarlet across her shirt is an abstract image of a pair of eyes. I've seen something like it printed on the lids of gift boxes sold at the drugstore back home. Somehow it strikes me as familiar, though I can't quite place it. Next to the woman hovers a small deer, no more than fifteen inches tall. As I peer at it, it lopes away soundlessly, straight through one of the enormous windows, into the sunset.

The bottom edge of the sky turns a vivid shade of burnt orange as I hover, watching its color slowly change from orange to red, red to violet. We seem to be ensconced in the branches of a giant evergreen tree. Hemlock or cedar, maybe, I could easily be 150 feet up in the air. Small, shiny silver pails line the branches of the tree at regular intervals. What on earth could those be for? Stranger still, whenever I tilt or turn my head, small rainbow prisms sparkle and refract in the light, distracting, but kind of pretty, too. They begin to fade as the light deepens.

"Arianne, welcome. My name is Inanna." She speaks with an unexpectedly thick accent, Slavic, maybe? I manage to shut my open mouth. "I imagine you might be thirsty?"

"Ummm, well yes, I suppose I am."

She gestures to a cup of tea, which appears to have been sitting on the kitchen table all along. I don't remember seeing it there a moment ago. Yet it is steaming, and like me, hovers a short distance above the surface of the wooden table. The table is carved as if for a family of giants, made from thick slabs of cedar, with carved ball and claw feet capping off each of its sturdy legs. I notice a pair of rustic bronze sconces on the wall with the masks bearing the same ball and claw motif. They, too, suddenly seem to be lit. The sky outside the huge tree deepens to periwinkle edged in orange, red, and gold. It dazzles my eyes. I walk lightly over to the table to sit, trying to remember to breathe.

The tea tastes real enough, and is hot. It warms my hands. "What on earth am I doing here?" I ask, and feel as though I am talking to myself, from within my own head. No sound emanates from my mouth, yet I can hear myself speak clearly.

"We've brought you here to talk," she says in her thick accent. "Relax... All is well. This is just the best way we could dream up to hold a meaningful conversation with you."

"Oh," I manage. "You want to talk?" The voice inside my head hesitantly trails off.

"Yes, directly to you." Her response is firm. "Look, I'll be brief. You've got to trust Keiko. As far as people go, she is definitely one of the better ones." She laughs gently, a tinkling sound. "She has some good ideas about what the future could hold, and we trust her. Right, Turtledove?"

For the first time I notice a small brown bird perched on top of the ladder-back chair closest to me. The dove's beak doesn't move, yet she gazes directly at me as she speaks. "Keiko definitely has some interesting ideas," she says, "but we believe you hold some key thoughts as well."

What can I say? I half hover there in silence, still somewhat dazed by the craziness of it all. I have to be dreaming. There is no other explanation. And if I am dreaming, who is flying the plane? The thought only worries me more.

"Look, here's what we want you to do," Inanna continues, as if to cut that line of thinking off. "Just hear us out. Give Keiko's idea a listen. Keiko ultimately wants you and your family to join her. With your inherent spiritual being and your technical computer savvy, you can be the mainstay of the new group with international communication. Stay open minded. It will give both you and the planet a fighting chance."

I swallow, my throat slightly dry despite the tea. What on earth is she talking about? Wait, she isn't really talking. This is my imagination putting words into her mouth. Only it all seems so real, hyper-real somehow. "Okay," I thought. "Speak slowly. I'll hear her out, if she really wants to talk to me, that is."

"Oh, yes," answers Inanna. "She will want to speak with you before too long." She pauses and takes a breath, her bronze hair rising and falling in waves around her shoulders as she breathes in and out. "I have one or two other things I'd like to say," she adds after a long moment. "To put it simply, you must trust yourself. No one's perfect, right? Decisions don't need to be made based on perfection. They just need to be made. Use your gut," she spoke, touching her stomach first then pointing to mine. "And might I respectfully suggest," she added, "that your family is not the set of personalized demons you sometimes make them out to be. They are your rock, your strength. And you are theirs. You are lucky to have them. You've made your choices, and now you must follow them through. No use crying over spilt milk. Go home to them. Love them and be with them."

I close my eyes to blink. When I open them, I am where I last remember being, strapped into the Spitfire cockpit, deep indigo sky surrounding the plane, the wind currents still irregular and swirling about me, storm clouds moving off in the distance. I have to be off course, but God only knows how many kilometers. No radio signal. Damn. Keiko and the folks at control will be worried.

Birds appear in the distance, flocks of them. I can see their strange, mixed silhouettes by starlight, sparrows and eagles, cranes, and owls, an aerial Audubon's encyclopedia of winged species.

As the ringing in my ears dies down, I hear nothing but white noise coming from the control panel. The graphics are still, a blank screen. I try rebooting the console computer. No go. The Spitfire has dropped altitude. It seems to be propelled on a carpet of magic. Without working instruments, I can only guess at my elevation, maybe 10,000, 12,000 feet. The storm has passed. Wisps of clouds trail behind the plane in the dark sky. Pinpoints of starlight and constellations—the Pleiades, "Subaru" to the Japanese, or the Seven Sisters, filter through the storm's remnants. Strange, I have always driven a Subaru. My mind feels loose, but lucid. It is as if the stars are a giant connect-the-dots puzzle, and I draw lines to bring them together. My ears ring slightly with the sound of chimes. I have no idea what just happened to me, but I feel strangely unconcerned, calm.

The console reboots on the third try, though the radio stays silent. I'll just have to communicate back to home base whenever I can.

I fly onward by sheer instinct. The floatplane seems to still be carried by magic. My insides feel entirely changed, as if shaken by an earthquake and now completely settled into a new tectonic formation. I feel quiet, grounded, certain. Flying up there in the middle of the night, high in the sky above the silver-edged sea, I feel rather than see connections, though I have trouble putting them into words. I just know they are there, and that is enough.

And there it is, the moon rising on my left, full and brilliant.

The way I see it now, right at this moment, it would be just as easy to base my choices on dreams as it would be to base them on waking reality. Only just now, of the two parallel worlds, dreams seem to be the more real and convincing of the two.

I have missed the second refueling ship and yet I have a full fuel tank. I must have been in the portal for hours, carried forward by a magic spell.

Following the moon, I set a course northwest, back home. Forget San Francisco and the Golden Gate. The finishing money does not matter. When the others ultimately figure out my whereabouts, I feel they will respect my judgments. Keiko will have to understand, they all will have to. I need to see my family, plant myself next to them and begin again. I have a plethora of choices to make about what to do next. I will have resources, love, and support surrounding me. What I need to do next is focus, using the same persistence and stubbornness that got me piloting a plane in the first place.

I might look like a feckless housewife from Issaquah at first glance but that's okay. I have a depth the others know nothing about but hopefully will soon realize. I am stronger than I look. Books cannot be judged by their covers. Keiko must have known this all along. I know that I will be involved with Keiko in the future.

Arianne made it back safely to her family and let Keiko know what she had decided to do so as not to worry the other pilots who have already mourned her disappearance. Arianne bonds with her family, showing compassion and love as they hear her story of the flight. They understand her needs. Keiko extends an invitation to Arianne to come to San Francisco.

As she and Matt stepped off the elevator, Keiko's spacious top floor office spreads out before them. The decor struck Arianne as impressive, yet calming. White carpeting reflected back the light shining in through a bank of large, expansive windows lining one wall. Their view centered above a courtyard lined in lacy red and gold Japanese maple trees. Opposite the windows was a wall full of pictures including a small group of Japanese woodcuts, mostly pictures of Keiko, mementos of her rise to the top of the Mitsubishi ladder. There was Keiko, standing in the middle of group after group, grinning with her cohorts surrounding her. Keiko shaking hands, Keiko smiling for the camera. Arianne had never met someone simultaneously so politically savvy and yet genuinely concerned for the welfare of those around her. She turned to face this slightly mysterious woman, more curious than ever about her.

"Arianne," Keiko began. "I have brought you here to make you an offer. I would like you and Matt to teach and handle the technology we need at our compound, *Shinatobe*, on Kaua'i." said Keiko, briefly and somewhat abruptly.

"Teach," repeated Arianne, as if testing the taste of the word on her tongue.

"Yes, teach," continued Keiko. "I am certain that you are not the only woman to ever be in the position of wanting to help others and yet feeling helpless to do so. Teaching, in my opinion, represents the height of giving back to others, honoring those who have helped bring you to this point in your life, and to honor all of those you can help in the future." Out of the corner of her eye, Arianne discerned the black figure of a crow standing on the corner of the window casing closest to her. It cocked its head, turning its sharp eye to meet Arianne's.

"We'll do it," she said simply as Matt smiled, squeezed her hand and nodded his head. The words sunk in after she spoke them, moving deep into her chest and gut. She felt rock solid, a good feeling, a feeling of power. "And thank you for everything, Keiko." she added. "Just everything. I'm sure I'm not the only one of this group who is incredibly grateful to you for all that you have done for us."

"It has been a true pleasure," replied Keiko, a small, serene smile played across her lips.

EPILOGUE

We are all gathered to celebrate finishing The Race. As fellow pilots, we are aware how privileged we are to have lived among the clouds for precious moments. We savor our new understanding of each other's unique concerns and personal histories.

The winner, Ruth Coleman just finished reciting John Magee's poem in honor of Arianne Maya Parker, who did not finish in San Francisco. As we conclude the dinner, the mood is festive. We are happy to see Ayame and her mother together. Ayame leaves momentarily but returns with a message from the airport control tower. Ayame shares the message with Keiko and immediately asks for our attention.

"I have great news. A message from Arianne just came in. Somehow she flew to her family's town in Washington. She apologized for not finishing the race and being with us." As Keiko smiles, Ayame continues, "Some of you can guess as to what my mother will present to you now, which involves a new adventure."

We all stopped chatting and eating and waited for Keiko to begin speaking as she rose to address us.

"I am so happy that all of you did finish and that Arianne is safe and sound. Many of you realize now, or will soon realize, that The Race was not about the competition but about the collective journey. It was about the inner travels in each of you—the catharsis, the epiphanies, the self-forgiveness."

Pausing for a moment, Keiko continues, "I have resigned my post as the head of Mitsubishi and I have taken the wealth I made at Mitsubishi to start what is no longer a fantasy for me but a new reality. I have purchased land on the Hawaiian Island of Kaua'i and built luxurious living quarters. They are arranged similarly to the way that Spanish haciendas in the United States Southwest were during the nineteenth century. Following this design, there is an open structure in the center of the living quarters for group dining and private or group gatherings. There is also a large learning center with state-of-the-art technology for teaching the techniques of organic farming, energy independence, and other community needs. An organic farming center, including barns, fields, bee-hives, and all necessary tools and equipment, simulates the Konohana Family complex in Shizuoka, Japan. The technical facility for the site is cutting edge and our digital capacity is capable of reaching all corners of the world. Our power grid is composed of wind turbines and solar panels. And we are looking to develop more concepts to help preserve the environment and care for all sentient beings, so with that in mind, we have included a healing center. Above all, we want to empower women. I have named the complex *Shinatobe*, the Japanese Goddess of the Wind, and I am asking you to join me, to express your own desires for *Shinatobe* and to contribute your individual expertise."

"I can talk with each of you after dinner tonight and I will be here in San Francisco for the next two months. I will fly any of you here after you have made your decision as to whether or not you will join this important adventure." Keiko thanked all of us for participating in The Race and told us how much she looked forward to working with us.

Many of us contemplated what Keiko had just said.

Christine Banfield and Ryoichi, who already knew of Keiko's plans, immediately travelled to Kaua'i to work on finishing construction at the site. Knowing that all the pilots were given their floatplanes after The Race, and that some would fly them to Kaua'i, Christine and Ryoichi also supervised the construction of a sea landing base close to the complex. Women techs were brought in for maintenance and upkeep.

Ayame Kobahashi went with Christine and Ryoichi to get the organic farming community up and running. Her educational background and experience at the Konohana Family organic farming community provided the expertise she needed to get the season started and crops planted in the perfect weather and soil conditions at *Shinatobe*.

Hamidah Gyamtso and Raya Sol del Mundo met with Keiko immediately after dinner. Raya held back and listened to the conversation. Keiko asked Hamidah if she and Habib would bring their Chromotherapy practice to the healing center at *Shinatobe*. Knowing that this is just what she and Habib wanted, Hamidah wholeheartedly agreed. She had one request that Annie, her retired service dog, would have to clear Hawaiian immigration regulations and accompany them. Keiko had no problem with that. Hamidah and Habib would also join Arianne at the learning center and conduct meditation classes as well as work with other guest religious leaders. The first seminar would focus on spiritual leaders moving away from politics to take a global lead in promoting non-violence, and mutual respect for all religious faiths and beliefs. Hamidah and Habib sold their home in France and settled at *Shinatobe*. Dr. Watase and Sachi along with other healers, nutritionists, herbalists, and yes, western medical doctors, became part of the well-equipped healing center. The main emphasis for the staff was to provide affordable, proactive cancer treatment to patients from all walks of life, from anywhere in the world. Except for Habib and Kaz, the healing staff con-sisted entirely of women.

Raya spoke to Keiko. "I want to contribute to *Shinatobe* and work with my comrades, Hamidah, Nanibah, and Ruth. I am not sure what I can do but for starters, perhaps I can work in the healing and learning centers."

Keiko responded, "Raya, with your history and background you will surely contribute to the learning center. But for the time being, work in the healing center and assist the staff in any possible way. I know that your energy will be greatly appreciated."

"If Nanibah comes to the healing center, I need to be there and help Nanibah with her cancer treatments." Raya whispered softly.

Keiko understood and told Raya that Nanibah would probably go back to her reservation and establish such cultural services as an Athabaskan language center as well as continue her chemotherapy and Navajo healing work. Keiko finished with a hopeful thought, "Nanibah is getting another chemotherapy treatment here in San Francisco with my doctors and then I am flying her back to New Mexico. We hope she can come to *Shinatobe* and receive broader clinical treatment for her cancer as well as work with Hamidah and Habib in the learning center. We will know more as time passes."

After Keiko's whispered plea that last night before The Race began in Tokyo, Janet "Tomi" Mochizuki knew there would be an epilogue to their trans-Pacific flight. She was pleased to find that she assumed correctly, that Keiko would continue to weave the tapestry the pilots had begun in the sky. It would be a tapestry for both the next and future generations, fashioned from the interwoven strands of technology, ancient agricultural techniques, energy efficiency, and shamanic wisdom and embellished by the labor of the pilots and many others. The misunderstandings and minor feuds would continue, no doubt, but she prayed that the clarity of solitude and flight would stand their group in good stead as they turned their energies to healing a planet in distress. And she congratulated herself on guessing correctly, too, that the real purpose of assembling this extraordinary circle of women was not to mimic male competition, but to serve as a kind of cleansing, or purifying act, to give each pilot her time alone in the sky to exorcise demons, clarify goals, and to feel a part of a new world order.

She had already decided she was in, so Tomi saw no reason to delay plunging right in to her work at the learning center. The day after landing back home, she drove to the center to visit her mother. Their conversation, stilted at first, gave way to mutual surprise and delight. It was as though the painful sharp edges surrounding the death of her father, Tad, and her grandfather Isamu, had aged and mellowed, worn smooth by the speed and velocity of *Peach 5's* great journey. Mother and daughter hugged goodbye, and Tomi, after stopping off at her apartment for a night of rest, headed back into the city to meet Keiko, and to begin weaving the next chapter of her story.

She wanted to learn more about the sustainable farming practices of the Konohana Family, and place her hand in the rich, healing soil of *Shinatobe*. Tomi decided she would dedicate herself to assisting Ayame, Christine, and Ryoichi during the days, and lead tanka poetry workshops for the cancer patients in the evenings. She desperately hoped that if Nanibah was well enough, she would join the rest of the pilots at *Shinatobe* to help her lead poetry workshops.

Leah Katzenberg waited until Keiko had spoken with Radka Zelenkova. Keiko took Radka aside and said she'd be honored if Radka would join her at *Shinatobe* on Kaua'i. Radka joked that she liked the "women's" part of this plan, and the ecological part, but she'd be no good at the community part. "We'll keep working on you," said Keiko.

Privately, Radka thought the whole thing sounded too woo-woo. But she was torn, as she had begun to feel a certain kinship with the other pilots. Leah urged Radka to come to Kaua'i, but she resisted.

Leah was disappointed that Radka hadn't accepted Keiko's offer, but she had already made up her mind to go to Kaua'i and work with the other women. After her long depression, Leah was eager to re-engage emotionally and physically, and to contribute and make a difference in the world. She asked Keiko if she could work with young adults in the organic fields. Keiko understood that this could help Leah heal from the loss of her child, and she gratefully accepted the offer.

Leah had not been deep-sea diving for a long time. She smiled to herself at the thought of being able to do that again at *Shinatobe*, once again to feel four atmospheres of pressure on every square centimeter of her body at forty meters underwater.

Before she left San Francisco, Radka spent an evening alone with a bottle of sake and a computer, trying to track down Katka online. But her Facebook profile had been deleted, and Radka could not remember Katka's new surname. Google searches yielded nothing. Perhaps now was not the time, Radka concluded.

Radka returned to Prague feeling sadness and relief, but also with a deep sense of emptiness. She spent a week at her cottage in the countryside, pulling weeds and harvesting her fruit trees. She missed her new friends. Something had happened to her during all those hours over the Pacific Ocean. She couldn't imagine returning to the military, and the idea of working for Czech Airlines no longer seemed right. She needed a total break from flying. Images of Keiko's ecological complex infiltrated her dreams, and she woke up in the wee hours of every morning wondering if she was making a mistake. Hawai'i could be a chance to do something completely different for a while, process her recent losses, and gain strength and energy from a stronger relationship with the earth.

Once Radka resolved to join Keiko and the other pilots, it took her just a few weeks to close up her life in Czechia and fly to Hawai'i. She was grateful not to be in the cockpit of a Spitfire this time.

At first, she worked with Ayame as a gardener growing food, taking instructions from others. That's what she wanted, so she wouldn't need to make decisions. Her mind and heart needed a long break. She resolved not to get involved with anyone, despite being surrounded by beautiful middle-aged women in their beach clothes. But soon she had to abandon that resolve, because something began happening with Leah. Their connection had a lightness to it that felt restorative, not oppressive.

One day, Leah brought Radka an injured barn owl that she had found hopping along the side of the road. Radka took the owl in for several weeks and nursed her back to health, using information from YouTube videos. This experience gave Radka the idea to start a wildlife rescue center and sanctuary on the land, where injured creatures of four legs or two wings could be rehabilitated, and rare creatures would be safe from hunters and poachers. Keiko and the other pilots loved the idea. Radka founded the center and brought in two of Hawai'i's top wildlife biologists as her staff. Leah joined Radka and worked with her. She kept her hand in every aspect, learning how to feed and care for the animals. She didn't miss flying because she was helping her winged brothers and sisters fly again.

Ruth Coleman didn't wait to meet with Keiko. Instead, she left a message for her, "Keiko, I need to fulfill a promise I made to my grandmother and find my homeless Coleman brother somewhere in Haight-Ashbury where he was last reported. Let me see how this works out and I will hopefully meet with you later as I want to devote my life, along with my fellow pilots, and you, to working at *Shinatobe*."

During the next two weeks, Ruth discovered that the homeless shelter situation in San Francisco was pathetic. In Haight-Ashbury, The Homeless Youth Alliance closed in 2013. At the end of two weeks, she found one last shelter still open, the Safe House of San Francisco. This was a long shot at finding her brother. The Safe House executive director brought her global experience to bear in advocating for women, by protecting them against sex trafficking and developing programs for survivors of domestic violence. In addition to her work at Safe House, she worked to strengthen resources for women in the Bay Area. She had already set up temporary housing for more than 300 homeless women, rescuing them from the violent street life of prostitution, addiction, trauma, and abuse. Upon learning all of this, Ruth almost felt like volunteering at the Safe House and staying in San Francisco. As though she was in a synchronistic dream, Ruth found her brother working at the Safe House as a paid staff member. He had found the noble job of caring for others and had been off the streets for several years. After spending a week with her brother working at the Safe House, with a heavy heart, Ruth said goodbye. She was very happy however, to find her brother in such good shape. Before leaving to see Keiko, she donated a sizeable amount of money to the Safe House and also gave her brother some money. Her winnings from The Race were already being put to good use both for women and for family.

Keiko was elated that Ruth had fulfilled her promise to her grandmother and was ready to work at *Shinatobe*. Keiko asked Ruth to be the director of the whole project. Keiko recognized Ruth's leadership skills and how much the other women respected her. Not only did Ruth travel to *Shinatobe* and work as the director, but she got Keiko's permission to build a sports facility on the complex. The facility had an aerobics center, weight room, basketball court (of course), and track. The entire staff at *Shinatobe* used the facility as well as patients and guests. Healing the body and the mind, eating well, and interacting with individuals from all over the world was a good beginning for global harmony.

Ting Xu Chan waited her turn to meet with Keiko. Keiko knew that she would have to return to China and meet Du. Keiko hoped Ting Xu would return with him and have her baby at *Shinatobe*. Ting Xu's contribution would be decided if they returned. Keiko flew Ting Xu back to China and kept her fingers crossed as she knew that Ting Xu and Du could contribute either to the healing or learning centers.

Three weeks later, all "three" of them arrived at *Shinatobe*. Ting Xu immediately fell in love with her new environment and being with her sister pilots once again.

In her personal diary, Ting Xu wrote:

> *I think it is only the distinct strangeness of Hawai'i that has helped me keep my composure so far. The colors are a riot of hues and assault my vision from all directions, so unlike the long contemplative bands of textured monotones of the steppes of Inner Mongolia. The air is rich with moisture and heavy fragrances, so unlike the dry, lightly seasoned wind that runs across the grasslands.*
>
> *Keiko has been an attentive host. She came herself to meet and take us to the complex, and has given us a tour with great enthusiasm and humility. We have just climbed the spiral staircase up and around the tower that she calls the "tree-top" meetinghouse. I am more than a little out of breath, because lately my lungs seem to compete for space with my growing womb. I declined all offers of assistance so that when I arrived at the top, Keiko and Du were already enjoying the view, which is spectacular. The beautifully arranged gardens, facility, and farm stretch out before us on one side, and on the other we can see out across the fins of velvet green volcanic cliffs to the deep aqua water. The sun is just setting, and the sky is filled with impossibly rich mauve and orange tones that vibrate against the cool blues and greens of the landscape. In this utterly unreal beauty the reality of Shinatobe comes rushing in and tears flow down my face.*
>
> *I cannot in this moment tell you whether they are tears of joy or sadness. Keiko's invitation to join her and work with my sister pilots could not be more perfect, especially when my beloved Du has agreed to join me. He took a sabbatical from his professorship at the university, and I was able to secure medical leave from my job with China Air. But we both know that it is unlikely that we will ever be allowed to return. During our layover in Japan, I mailed the final draft of my manuscript to my German publisher. My book documents the environmental destruction wrought on my beloved homeland and is filled with the highly detailed aerial photographs that I have taken illicitly for years.*
>
> *I am also filled with an immense sense of loss, because with the publication of this book and the cessation of years of secret work for the Inner Mongolian People's Party, I am acknowledging that my homeland is lost. Our people have been overwhelmed by the onslaught of Chinese assimilation. Yes, there are pockets where the*

old language and the nomadic way of life are still practiced, but those people are like tamed wild animals, happily kept on a leash for the amusement of the civilized.

I look forward to what I will contribute to Keiko's effort. It is difficult to see beyond everything that I have ever known. Even my body is changing in ways that are impossible to describe as Du and I prepare to welcome a new baby girl into our lives. At this point in my joy, I hope it is possible to cultivate respect and tolerance in those who will be the future leaders of our world. I shall work towards that here.

During dinner, Firoozeh Irani sat with Hamidah and Nanibah. Firoozeh engaged in a little small talk and even attempted to apologize in her own way, but mostly she kept to herself. Firoozeh wanted to leave, but patiently waited to talk with Keiko and thank her for the opportunity to be in The Race and for the time to think and come to terms with some of the personal anger and blame that has so oppressed her. Firoozeh realizes she has a long way to go to overcome her problems and to become capable of embracing uncertainty and the joy of any moment.

When Firoozeh did meet with Keiko, she expressed her desire to come to *Shinatobe* to help herself heal. But first, she told Keiko, she must see family and work things out. Keiko hoped Firoozeh would eventually join her—a Middle Eastern voice was needed at the learning center.

While imbibing too much vodka and champagne, Ludmilla Litvyck and Claudia Schumann laughed and chatted throughout dinner. Their shared cultural background and upbringing, along with their mutual bonding during The Race, created a friendship. They chuckled over stories of their relatives flying in World War II against one another but on different fronts. Claudia expressed her respect and amazement for Ludmilla's aunt Lydia. Both Ludmilla and Claudia hardly noticed the long wait to talk with Keiko. Ludmilla hoped Claudia would come to *Shinatobe* and join her.

Ludmilla and Claudia went up together to meet Keiko. Keiko asked the ongoing question, first to Ludmilla, "Will you join us at *Shinatobe*?"

Ludmilla had thought all this out already. "Keiko, I will join you at *Shinatobe* and contribute as best as I can. I want to start with Christine at the sea landing facility because of my technical knowledge and I want to keep flying whenever I can. I would like to bring my *Lily* and also work the organic fields with Ayame. The soil and the sky seem so fulfilling. But first I need to fly to New Mexico and visit my friend Anne Noggle and go to the Navajo reservation to see how Nanibah is doing. I hope we will all fly together there in the southwestern sky."

Keiko smiled and happily agreed, then she asked Claudia, "What about you Claudia? Will you join us and your friend Ludmilla at *Shinatobe*?"

Claudia had also thought out her future but was not as clear as her friend. "I am not sure, Keiko. Thank you for including me in The Race. Being here is the start of a new beginning for me. My whole life has been involved in my relationships, and my motherhood. I do want to think outside of my current relationship box and work with you and the other women at *Shinatobe*, but first I want to stay in San Francisco, start these new beginnings and be independent for a while."

Keiko nodded and suggested, "While you are here in San Francisco, I would be happy to have you run my San Francisco office on a part-time basis. Essentially, I would be happy for you to come to *Shinatobe* when you are ready and work with Ruth to help run the place." Claudia agreed and was happy to continue contact with the other pilots, but for now, from a distance.

Nanibah Jackson enjoyed being with Hamidah over dinner but she didn't eat much because of the side effects from chemotherapy, a constant, predictable condition that she tolerated. She drank lots of water though. Nanibah had no trouble waiting to speak to Keiko and enjoyed the moment. Nanibah knew she would have to go in for more chemo from Keiko's oncologist the next day and probably start a new routine of drugs. She had learned from her most recent blood tests, that her CEA marker had risen.

Without hesitation Nanibah explained to Keiko that she had to head back to her family and the rez in New Mexico. She needed to continue her chemotherapy treatment in Albuquerque as well as work with the Navajo healing men. She intended to get the cultural learning center and Navajo language school funded and launched. She also wanted to find an acupuncturist.

It took a while for Nanibah to accomplish these goals but both the cultural learning center and the language school got established due to her funding and guidance. She continued to fly and even had flying time with Ludmilla and her friend Anne Noggle. Seeing Ludmilla and her continued contact with Hamidah made her miss the other women from The Race. So, one day she said her goodbyes and flew to *Shinatobe* to work at the healing center where she continued her chemotherapy treatment. She received acupuncture from Kaz and Chromotherapy from Habib. Keiko promised to fly in some of the American Indian healers to work on Nanibah.

Piccola was truly surprised and honored at Keiko's invitation. She thanked Keiko after the meal and discussion had concluded, telling her, "This adventure has changed my life already, although I'm not sure yet how. I love the idea of joining you and the others at *Shinatobe* and beginning a different type of life there. It invigorates me, the thought of what you are doing by bringing such powerful women together." And Keiko could see the truth of it in her eyes. "But, Keiko, I hesitate because one of the very ways this experience has effected me so deeply is by reasserting my drive and determination to pursue my dreams of space flight! I cannot decide here, after a lavish meal and surrounded by the buoyant energy of these amazing women. It would be too rash. I must return home. I need to see my family and my best friend. Then, in a private place, with a sober mind, I will determine my answer."

Keiko smiled, "I am impressed with you, Piccola. So young, yet already displaying such wisdom. I respect your answer and will welcome you to *Shinatobe* any time, whether as a long-term resident, or occasional visitor."

Returning home to San Benedetto del Tronto after nearly two months away, Piccola found many family members, friends, and professors waiting for her with high praise, adoration, and congratulations. Her best friend, Francesca was, apart from her mother, the most ecstatic of the group to welcome her home. Late that night they shared a kiss that established a stronger relationship, both old to them, and new.

Piccola shared with Francesca every detail of Keiko's spectacular visionary society of ecologically responsible women. They both felt a deep pull toward the cause. After all, they shared Keiko's fierce belief in the capacity of women to shape a better world. Yet Francesca agreed that Piccola should take her time making a choice. This decision would determine the direction of her energy in the next few years, a foundational time in her life.

Piccola submitted an updated application to the A.S.I. and, a week and a half later, received a call from one of the board members of A.S.I., a woman newly elected to the position. They spoke for an hour about Piccola's future goals in space exploration. While the board member assured Piccola that she was an impressive candidate for the position, she noted that there was more to being an astronaut than academic brilliance and mechanical skill. Astronauts were also chosen for their well roundedness, their worldly wisdom, and astute problem solving. She advised Piccola to take the opportunity of her youth to experience the world before trying to escape it.

The next day, Piccola sent word to Keiko that she and Francesca would both be honored to be members of her community.

Indeed, the two women proved to be invaluable assets to the community. Francesca worked mostly in the gardens, growing food and other useful herbs, and in the kitchen, offering her innate Italian sense of savory cooking. She also brought a loom with her and was quickly designated as the mistress seamstress of the group. Piccola, naturally, was in charge of maintaining and fixing all the community's mechanical tools, from the toaster to garden machines.

One perfect Hawaiian night, Leah took in the half moon illuminating the cove and pristine beach like a cliché from a romantic novel, thinking about the strange turn her feelings had taken toward Radka.

Radka and I were both laughing at the situation. We had spent quite a bit of time together, having found that once we started talking, we didn't seem to run out of things to say to each other. We enjoyed being ourselves in each other's company.

Tonight had been just one of several nighttime swims we had had over the last couple of weeks. Skinny-dipping became a proxy for the intimacy between us that was more than platonic, a sensuous thing that ebbed and flowed between us like the waves. We shared a pulse, something acknowledged by being naked together, openly looking at each other, each waiting for the other to make the first move.

The tension was exquisite—the waiting and waiting for the big wave that would sweep us into each other's embrace and then what? Would it all dissipate? Radka shared her opinion of me as an aspiring lesbian as part of her ongoing curiosity. Unlike in Tokyo, she never made a move though. If this was going to happen, I would have to own it and I felt out of my depth.

Radka had always known that she was gay. It was part of her identity and as natural to her as proposing a sex change operation to the men who dared to hit on her. She did this with a smile on her face, the way you explain to a lost stranger that they had come to the wrong address. Rarely was anyone offended.

Wondering what it would be like to sleep with a woman was similar to contemplating a journey into space. I never felt opposed to it, but nor did it ever come up as a real possibility. I felt I lacked the qualifications, and as it dawned on me that I might be qualified after all, I realized that my copilot was vastly experienced and I, not at all.

The wave came that night in the form of an uncomfortably cool breeze. We got too cold lying next to each other on the towels and covered ourselves with additional ones to keep the wind at bay. Between the crashing waves and whistling air, we had to move closer to keep hearing what the other was saying. As the wind gusts attempted to whip off our towels, we secured their ends under our bodies, and as we did our hands eventually found each other.

Slowly, very slowly, we got closer like two moths wriggling around in their cocoons. We were like that for a long time just playing with each other's hands. When we eventually spread our wings and our hands and mouths found each other, there was just flight, suspension, and the shuddering into nothingness where we found everything.

Rather than dissipating, the sex between us was so good, that neither wanted to do anything else. It filled us and then it fueled us. After the long barrenness I had come to think of as a fact of my life, my surrender to her brought great happiness and joy. Our passion also brought good energy to others. In particular, I was transformed. One night, around a campfire, I even danced. I danced and danced with others and by myself, until I collapsed on a blanket, in a sweaty heap. Radka greeted me with an ice cold Ichiban.

"You looked as if you were in a shamanic trance," she said. And then we laughed uncontrollably. In that instant we knew that she had succeeded. Keiko had resurrected not just old airplanes—she had reawakened the witches after their millennial sleep.

CODA

Someone who dreams of drinking wine at a cheerful banquet may wake up crying the next morning. Someone who dreams of crying may go off the next morning to enjoy the sport of the hunt. When we are in the midst of a dream, we do not know it is a dream. Sometimes we may even try to interpret our dreams while we are dreaming, but then we awake and realize it was a dream. Only after one is greatly awakened does one realize that it was all a great dream, while the fool thinks that he is awake and presumptuously aware.

Chuang Tzu (Zhuang Zi) c.370 B.C.E. – c.287 B.C.E.
Wandering on the Way: Early Taoist Tales and Parables of Chuang Tzu
Translated by Victor H. Mair

CONTRIBUTORS

Note to reader: Listed in italics at the end of each contributor's name is the title of the chapter or chapters each author wrote, or in the case of chapters with multiple authors, made a significant contribution.

Patrick Ryoichi Nagatani *(Prologue, Training, Christine Banfield—Silver 1, Ayame Kobahashi—Champagne 2, Hamidah Gyamtos—Orange 3, Ruth Coleman—Black 8, Ludmilla Litvyck—Red 11, Nanibah Jackson—Yellow 13, Epilogue)* lives and works in Albuquerque, New Mexico. He retired in 2007 from the University of New Mexico where he was Professor of Photography in the Department of Art and Art History, a position he held for twenty years. Nagatani earned an MFA from UCLA in 1980 where he studied with Robert Heinecken. Early in his career he taught for twelve years at Hamilton High School in Los Angeles and for six years at Loyola Marymount University. He also briefly taught at The School of the Art Institute of Chicago. In addition to his many public lectures, seminars, and workshops, his work has been widely exhibited on a national and international level.

Nagatani has always been interested in studio set-ups and staged photographs beginning with his landmark Polaroid 20 x 24 work to his later *Chromotherapy* images. As a "tapist," he has made large-scale works using masking tape, many of which depict Buddhist deities. He documented the Japanese American relocation/concentration camps of World War II as they existed in the 1990s. These images and the accompanying book, *Nuclear Enchantment*, explore a narrative about the historical and contemporary marriage of nuclear culture to his present home in New Mexico. In 2008, he was recognized with a retrospective exhibition at the University of New Mexico Art Museum and monograph, *Desire for Magic*, presenting thirty years of his *œuvre*. Michele M. Penhall organized the project and Christopher Kaltenbach designed the book.

Nagatani continues to be an active member of the Atomic Photographer's Guild. Some of his many awards and honors include The Aaron Siskind Foundation Individual Photographer's Fellowship, The Kraszna-Krausz Award for *Nuclear Enchantment*, the Leopold Godowsky Jr. Color Photography Award, the Eliot Porter Award from the New Mexico Council on Photography, two individual artist fellowships in 1984 and 1992, from the National Endowment for the Arts, and the California Distinguished Artist Award from the National Art Education Association and the National Endowment for the Arts. He is an honored recipient of the New Mexico Governor's Award for Excellence in the Arts, and in 2008 he received the Honored Educator Award from the Society of Photographic Education.

Nagatani recalls this personal anecdote: So I recently went to a 7-11 store and met an elder American Indian man. I asked him what tribe he was from. He enthusiastically replied "Navajo." Then wonder of wonders, he asked me, "What tribe are you from?" I happily said, "Japanese American." We both laughed and I asked him if he was kidding me by asking what tribe I was from. He quietly said, "No, we look alike and are brothers." I smiled and retain this moment of happiness! Namaste!

Marie Acosta *(Raya Sol Del Mundo—Copper 4)* has been the Artistic/Executive Director of the, La Raza Galería Posada at the Latino Center of Art and Culture in Sacramento, California since 2008. Previously, she was an actress with the San Francisco Mime Troupe, the Executive Director of San Francisco's Mexican Museum, the Executive Director of the Latino Arts Network of California and she served as the Director of Cultural Arts and Tourism for Henderson, Nevada. The California State Assembly named her Woman of the Year. She received the Directors Award from the California Arts Council and is a recipient of a Gerbode Fellowship. Acosta is the curator of "El Pantéon de Sacramento/Día de los Muertos," an annual open-air installation of *altares* and *ofrendas* in Midtown Sacramento. She was the co-author and co-director of "La Pastorela de Sacramento" in 2013 and was a member of the acting ensemble of "FSM/Free Speech Movement" by Joan Holden at the 2013 San Francisco Playwrights Festival.

Kristin Barendsen *(Radka Zelenkova—Burgundy 7)* is an award-winning writer based in Santa Fe, New Mexico. She co-authored *Photography: New Mexico*, and has published over 100 stories in international magazines and newspapers. She is a former contributing editor and writer for *Yoga International* and *Yoga Journal* magazines. Her essays have appeared in *The Sun* and *The Best Women's Travel Writing* 2008, and her poetry has appeared in *Sequoia* and *American Poet*. Her awards include: the Academy of American Poets Prize, the Michael Jasper Gioia Poetry Prize, two Southwest Writers awards, and a Solas Award for travel writing. *Photography: New Mexico*, published in 2008, was a finalist for a New Mexico Book Award. Barendsen studied creative writing and studio art at Stanford University where she graduated with distinction. She has lived in Thailand and the Czech Republic and has traveled to thirty-two countries on five continents. She is currently collaborating on a nonfiction book that is slated for publication by Flatiron Books/Macmillan in 2018.

Felissia Cappelletti *(Piccola Uccello—Chartreuse 14)* is a freelance writer, editor, artist, botanist, and herbalist living and working in Denver, Colorado. Her poetry is included in the 50th volume of the *Journal of Experimental Fiction*.

Christine Chin *(Ting Xu Chan—Blue 9)* lives in Ithaca, New York. She is an Associate Professor of Photography and New Media in the Department of Art and Architecture at Hobart and William Smith Colleges in Geneva, New York. She was introduced to photography by Emmet Gowin at Princeton University, where she received her BA in 1997, and she studied with Patrick Nagatani and Jim Stone at the University of New Mexico, where she received her MFA in 2008. She most frequently builds ephemeral sculptural objects in the studio that are incorporated into her photographic storytelling. Recent projects have addressed genetically modified food, alternative energy, artificial intelligence, and biotechnology in medicine. These projects have been shown nationally and internationally at venues that include the New York Hall of Science, Canon Communication Space in Beijing, and the New Mexico Museum of

Art. In 2006 she received a Fulbright Fellowship for her Alternative Alternative Energy project in China and spent ten months traveling and working throughout the country.

Randi Ganulin (*Arianne Maya Parker—Ochre 15*) lives just outside of Seattle with her family. She is an Associate Professor in the Department of Fine Art at DigiPen Institute of Technology in Redmond, WA. Ganulin grew up in Los Angeles where she took her first photography class while in high school from Patrick Nagatani. She worked as a designer and illustrator before pursuing her graduate studies in photo-based media. In 1994 she received the Javits Fellowship in the Visual Arts, and in 1996 her MFA from Otis College of Art and Design. Her work has been shown in numerous venues across the United States and is included in several public collections, including the New Mexico Museum of Art in Santa Fe and the Center for Fine Art Photography in Ft. Collins, Colorado. Details of Ganulin's personal biography form the basis for Arianne's story in *The Race*.

Feroza Jussawalla (*Firoozeh Irani—Turquoise 10*) is Professor of English at the University of New Mexico in Albuquerque. A native of India from a Parsi background, she attended the University of Utah as an exchange student in 1973 and stayed on to do her M.A. and Ph.D (1980). She taught at the University of Texas at El Paso and moved to UNM in 2011. She is a scholar of Postcolonial Literatures and the author of several books and articles including, *Interviews with Writers of the Postcolonial World*, and *Conversations with V.S. Naipaul*, both published by the University Press of Mississippi. She is also the author of a collection of poetry, entitled, *Chiffon Saris*. In 2014, she received the Alumni Teaching Award from the University of New Mexico Alumni Association.

Nancy Matsumoto (*Janet Tomiko Mochizuki—Peach 5*) lives in New York City and Toronto, and is a freelance writer and editor specializing in the areas of sustainable agriculture, food, arts, culture and health. She has been a contributor to *The Wall Street Journal*, *Time*, *Newsweek*, *People* and *The Los Angeles Times*, among other publications. She is a contributor to the online *Densho Encyclopedia of Japanese American Incarceration* and co-author of *The Parent's Guide to Eating Disorders*. She is currently working on an English-language translation of her grandparent's tanka poetry collection, ミシガン湖畔/*By the Shore of Lake Michigan*.

Dolores Richardone (*Ayame Kobahashi—Champagne 2*) lives in Los Angeles and has worked in the entertainment industry for thirty-seven years. As a Film and Television World Wide Publicity Executive she created, implemented, and supervised the publicity campaigns for major motion picture studios and entertainment companies including The Jim Henson Company, Morgan Creek Productions, Chasen & Company, E! Entertainment, International Documentary Association, Weintraub Entertainment, Lorimar Entertainment, and George Schlatter Productions. Intrinsic to her work is writing creative and collateral materials including press releases and feature stories for motion pictures, television, talent company executives, and corporate offices. Richardone has known Patrick Nagatani for forty-eight years.

Andre Ruesch *(Leah Katzenberg—White 6)* lives in Massachusetts, where he is a Professor at the Lesley University College of Art and Design. He was born in 1961 in Zürich, Switzerland and grew up in an alpine region known as the Saanenland. He began to pursue photography in the early 1980s, while working for a volunteer organization in Asia. Upon returning to Europe, he earned a BA in photographic studies at Edinburgh Napier University, Scotland. Subsequently, he moved to Albuquerque, New Mexico, where he received an MA and MFA in photography at the University of New Mexico. During his graduate work he studied with Patrick Nagatani, Betty Hahn, and Eugenia Parry. Ruesch's work has been shown in museums and galleries internationally and published in the *British Journal of Photography*, *Art in America*, and *Asian Art News*.

Ulrike Rylance *(Claudia Schumann—Green 12)* lives in the Seattle Eastside with her family. She is a German author of Children's Literature, Teenage Fiction, and humorous novels for adults. She also writes under the pen names Ulrike Herwig and Caro Martini and has published over fifteen books with German publishers. In 2013 her children's book, *Emma in Buttonland*, was translated into English and published by Sky Pony Press, New York. Rylance has won numerous prizes for her books and she has just signed film options for two of her women's novels. Her current projects include a detective series for children and a Chick-Lit novel with a magic twist.

Julie Shigekuni *(Ayame Kobahashi—Champagne 2)* lives in Brooklyn, New York, and Corrales, New Mexico. She is Professor in the creative writing program at the University of New Mexico and is the author of four novels, a collection of short stories, and a recently completed young adult novel. Her work on *The Race* is an extension of her devotion to Patrick Nagatani who has been a mentor and friend through years of wonderful and life altering experiences.